And there appeared another wonder in heaven;
and behold a great red dragon . . .

And there was war in heaven. . . .

—Revelation 12:3, 7

The Dragon

Other books by Alfred Coppel

Night of Fire and Snow

Dark December

A Certainty of Love

The Gate of Hell

Order of Battle

A Little Time for Laughter

Between the Thunder and the Sun

The Landlocked Man

Thirty-four East

ALFRED COPPEL

The Dragon

Harcourt Brace Jovanovich

New York and London

Printed in the United States of America

The lines from "The Second Coming" on pages 378–79
are reprinted with permission of Macmillan Publishing
Co., Inc. from *Collected Poems* by William Butler Yeats,
copyright 1924 by Macmillan Publishing Co., Inc.,
renewed 1952 by Bertha Georgie Yeats.

Library of Congress Cataloging in Publication Data

Coppel, Alfred.
    The dragon.

    I. Title.
PZ4.C785Dr   [PS3553.064]   813'.5'4   76-54584
ISBN 0-15-126500-3

First edition

B C D E

For Julian Muller and Robert Lescher

—my shipmates on the *Argo*

Boyar (bo͵YĀ·r) . . . A member of a peculiar order of the old Russian aristocracy, next in rank to a *knyaz* or 'prince,' who enjoyed many exclusive privileges, and held all the highest military and civil offices: the order was abolished by Peter the Great, and the word is in Russia only a historical term. . . .

—*The Oxford English Dictionary*

PART ONE

1

The wind that blew across the Talimupendi Plain came from the Altai Mountains and it had the frightening cold of those ancient lonely peaks in it. The sky was a threatening gray darkness; there would be snow by nightfall. But Choy Balsan was not concerned about that. He was certain that both he and his captive would be dead before the last light of this bitter day faded.

Colonel Balsan was a thick, stocky man, with the broad, brown face of the Mongol. There were ice crystals on his sparse beard and drooping mustache and on the shaggy fur of his hat and parka. His felt vest and half boots were stiff with the cold, and his face ached at each cut of the cruel wind.

The captive, a petty officer of the Chinese People's Liberation Army, had stopped struggling and now produced only an occasional moan. Balsan carried him trussed like a deer across the bow of his fur saddle, and the man involuntarily twitched with each step the shaggy pony took across the rocky plateau.

Balsan drew from his parka the map showing the minefields. He hoped it was reasonably accurate. It was a miracle that the KGB had been able to produce a usable map at all. He was traversing a part of the most heavily guarded military reservations in northern China. At the moment, there was nothing to be seen but the empty expanse of the frigid Talimupendi: a high plateau of rocky desert, lichen-covered outcrops, and dry salt pans. It was a Martian vista that seemed both vast and unpopulated, but that was an illusion. The true nature of the region could be seen in the occasional tangle of rusting barbed wire, the places (obvious to Balsan's eyes) where the earth had been disturbed to place a mine, a heat or pressure sensor, or even a television spy.

He did his best, with the help of the map and the information he had coldly tortured from his prisoner, to avoid these secret traps. But he knew with absolute certainty that he was pursued, that soon there would be aircraft and mounted soldiers, and that he would be cornered and killed or captured. He did not plan to let the Chinese take him alive. He knew their methods of interrogation too well for that, and there would be special treatments devised for an officer of the Glavnoye Razvedyvatelnoye Upravleniye, the Intelligence Directorate of the General Staff of the Soviet Army.

The Chinese soldier stirred, and Balsan pressed a fist against the small of his back and spoke in Mandarin. "Be still, Comrade. Your pain will not last much longer."

Balsan was sorry that the single survivor of the three-man patrol he had ambushed had turned out to be only a noncommissioned officer. It would have been too much to expect that he might have snared one of the scientists or engineers the GRU believed were working down in the marshy sink of the Turfan Depression, but a commissioned officer, at least, would have been more useful. Still, it was remarkable that he had been able to penetrate this desolate fortress, make his observations, and—thus far—survive. The man he carried across his pony's withers like a hunter's kill was a bonus. His captive had already talked, under persuasion, about the security patrols. Under more severe inducements he might yield a few words about the installation he and ten thousand other soldiers were guarding in the Turfan.

Balsan turned in the saddle to look to the northeast. The dull light made distances deceptive, but the wind had swept away the bitter dust and he could see the dark loom of the snow-laden hills beyond the Turfan. Of the Depression itself, he could see nothing now. It dropped from the high plateau like a vast oblong bowl. Fifty meters below the surrounding land, the sluggish Algoy River fed a network of marshy streams in the sink, the ground soft in what passed for summer in these latitudes, and frozen into a salty, alkaline waste in winter. A hellish place to have built a scientific installation. The labor involved, Balsan thought, must have been immense. But the very harshness of the terrain was a defense of sorts against discovery, and the Siberian storms that swept down from the northeast made satellite observations extremely difficult.

There had been speculation in Moscow that the Americans, with their more advanced space-spy technology, were watching the developments in the Turfan. But if they were, they were not sharing their information with the Russians.

The pony stumbled on an outcrop of rock, and the Chinese uttered a stifled scream of pain. Balsan caught him by the hair and twisted his head so that he might look into the pallid, frozen face. The man's eyes were glazed and bloodshot, his mouth hung half open, and a bloated tongue showed between the broken teeth. The chances of obtaining more information from this human wreckage grew slimmer with each step the shaggy pony took, Balsan realized. He accepted it with a stoic fatalism his ancestors—men who rode with Ogotai and Chepe Noyon—would have approved.

Ahead, invisible in the fast-fading daylight, lay the low hills where Balsan had set up his camp. There, among the rock upthrusts and badlands, he had left his yurt and ring of fire stones. It appeared to be the camp of a wandering solitary nomad, one of the outlaw horsemen who were still to be found in the emptiness of High Asia, a man cast out of his tribe for transgressions of ancient Mongol law.

In such a guise, Balsan had crossed Sinkiang from the borders of Soviet Kazakhstan, a Mongol warrior mounted on a long-haired pony, armed with short lance, double-reflex horn bow—a figure belonging as much to the twelfth century as to the twentieth. Time had a way of becoming meaningless in these desolate lands where the caravans still traveled trails invisible to all but the Mongols and Uigurs and Kazaks, those who lived out their lives on horse and camel, pulling their solid-wheeled carts and felt yurts across vast distances in the manner of their ancestors since time immemorial. On this mission, Colonel Balsan, of the Soviet Army, became Choy Balsan, a nomad of the Yakka Mongols, a hard little man with bright, intelligent black eyes, a weathered face, and the bowed legs of the lifelong horseman.

At the settlement of Turfan, north of the Turfan Depression, he had questioned the Uigur villagers. The men of Turfan, their women hidden from the stranger in the old way, spoke to him of a new dragon spirit in the marsh. These men had seen the white sky flashes of the atmospheric nuclear tests at Lop Nor many times. They were accustomed to them. The thing in the marsh, they said, was different. The thing in the Turfan was new, a spirit that spoke to the sky with thin bright beams of a terrible red light. Balsan thanked them and turned south, into the high desert plateau.

It had taken him three weeks to traverse the final fifty kilometers to his destination, threading his way through the defenses, avoiding the patrols of the People's Liberation Army, skirting the minefields and electronic devices. And then, twenty-four hours ago, he had stood on the rim of the Turfan Depression, photographing, taping, recording, and encoding with the sophisticated equipment he had carried a quarter of the way across Asia in his horseskin saddlebags.

He had only just finished his work when the patrol happened by. They had come carelessly, in the way of southern-bred Chinese, talking and joking, and he had killed all but one with his silenced machine pistol.

But his assault on them meant discovery. He realized that and knew he would die for it. But, he was determined, not before the precious tapes in his saddlebags were transmitted.

He rode now with a curiously satisfied half-smile on his lips. He had enjoyed this assignment. A lifetime as a Soviet soldier— half of it spent as an agent of the GRU—had failed to give him the sense of completion he had derived from this mission. The weeks alone on the trail, the quiet slippage of time that had permitted him to live as his ancestors had lived were splendid gifts; the trials were worthy of his race and honor. Die he most probably would, but it would be as a Mongol horseman. Few of his blood would know such a glorious ending in this benighted age of machines.

The Chinese made a gasping sound, and Balsan looked at him once more, holding the lolling head by the hair. A trickle of blood had escaped from the prisoner's mouth and had, since he hung head down across the saddle, run up into an eye, outlining it with a grotesque, crusted red ring.

Balsan voiced a silent curse. The man was too badly injured to survive. He was, in fact, visibly dying—the eyes, half open, sightless. The quick, shallow breathing had degenerated to a helpless, windy sucking. More blood, sluggish and sticky in the freezing evening air, came from his nose and mouth.

At the same moment Balsan heard the first distant whack-whacking sound of a low-flying helicopter.

"You have disappointed me, Comrade," he said. "We have come to a parting, you and I." He leaned to the side, enough to permit his hand to slip behind the captive's neck and cup the chin. Then his arm tensed and abruptly, swiftly rose. The soft snap seemed too insignificant to signal the breaking of a spine and the ending of a life. He let the soldier slip to the ground and kicked the pony into a gallop without a backward glance.

It was beginning to grow dark when he reached his campsite among the rock outcrops. He dismounted, removed the saddlebags, and let the reins drag so that the horse would stand. There was much to do, but he took the time to put a few handfuls of grain into a depression scooped in the cold earth for the pony to eat. Then he unpacked the tapes and the radiosonde, and inserted the cassette into the transmitting case.

This done, he paused to listen to the sounds the wind brought him. The helicopter was still five to six kilometers distant, he judged. But it had been joined by others.

He took a gas cylinder from his saddlebag and checked the pressure on the gauge. The tank was full. He broke the seal and adjusted the valve and nozzle. He unfolded the balloon from the kit taken from the bag. The material was something the Americans had developed. It was called Mylar, and it was so thin and transparent he could scarcely believe that it would not tear in his hands. It seemed almost weightless. Next he assembled the twenty-meter trailing line and the radiosonde harness. He assembled the transmitting module and connected it to the trailing line.

He paused again to face the wind. It blew steadily from the northeast, as the meteorologist in Moscow had assured him that it would.

The helicopters were getting nearer. He caught sight of the first, approaching slowly out of the north. He suppressed a wry smile. Even at a distance, he recognized the Russian Yak, old now, but quite serviceable. He had flown such a machine himself many times. Since it was a troop carrier, there would be at least a section of fifteen soldiers aboard. Three helicopters—forty-five men. The odds were unfortunate.

He crawled into the felt yurt and emerged with a length of plastic tubing affixed to a stock, reel, and sending unit. A second trip produced three RPG wire-guided rockets. The odds would improve soon, he thought. He assembled the weapon, placed it aside with its two reloads, and began inflating the Mylar balloon from the gas cylinder.

The light was fading fast now and Balsan allowed himself to consider the possibility of a respite, perhaps even a chance to escape. Then he heard in the distance the noise made by a light-armored tracked vehicle. More troops. They would not do this to trap or kill a desert wanderer. They must have surmised what his purpose was, who had sent him.

The wind was growing colder, and an occasional flurry of snow materialized in the dry, freezing air. The pony had finished eating and was turning, making a nest in the earth where he might lie down and shelter from the wind. Balsan looked at the animal with love and admiration. It had a short, broad head, thick legs skirted with long hair, a broad furry back, and a short, sparse tail. But to Balsan the animal was handsome. On such animals his people had once ridden to the gates of Vienna, and the Great Wall had not sufficed to keep them from the porcelain pavements of the Forbidden City. "Warm yourself, companion," he said softly to the pony. "The night will be cold."

He watched the Mylar balloon rising in wind-shivered bubbles as the gas filled it. He secured the holding line to a jutting spur of rock and went back into the yurt. When he emerged again he had four magazines of nine-millimeter bullets for the machine pistol. He placed these with the rockets. The helicopters were very near; he could see them circling to the south. The pilots must be using infrared sighting gear, he thought, to see so well in this half-light. North of his position, an armored personnel carrier crested a rise in the ground six hundred meters away. Each time the engine accelerated, he could see blue fire through the inefficient flame-arrestors on the exhaust. The engine sounded as though it was laboring and detonating. The refineries the Americans had helped the Chinese build to exploit the great new oil finds in the south were still incapable of producing military-grade diesel fuel.

But the lumbering machine came on, and Balsan reached for the rocket launcher.

The helicopters were landing somewhere behind the rise against which he had erected his yurt.

The balloon, half filled now, was rising from the ground like a quivering, translucent ghost. Much of the gasbag still trailed on the ground, but he knew that he must not fill it more lest increased internal pressure at high altitude burst the Mylar before its work was done.

With something like a smile on his lips, Balsan walked to where the pony had nested. The animal whickered softly at his approach but did not rise. He caressed a coarse-haired ear and loosened the surcingle holding the furry saddle. Then he removed his horn bow and quiver of arrows and carried them over to the place where his other weapons waited.

The balloon was clear of the ground and tugging at the holding line. Even half filled, the Mylar globe towered eight meters above him, slanting to the southwest, bobbing and shuddering to be free with each gust of the wind.

It was nearly dark now. Balsan considered the fate that had caused him to be found one half hour too early to allow him any hope of escape.

He set the pressure switch on the radiosonde so that the device would begin to transmit at two thousand meters. He would have preferred to wait until it had reached at least ten thousand. That way he would be sure that the listening stations in the Kazakh Soviet Socialist Republic would get the first transmission. But with his pursuers so near, he dared not delay.

In the gloom it was difficult to judge ranges accurately, but he estimated the armored vehicle was now within range of the RPGs. A file of soldiers had deployed around it and advanced at a walking pace.

Balsan looked carefully at the balloon and slashed the line. For a dozen meters the balloon dragged the sending unit along the ground, tumbling and crashing into the rock outcrops. He held his breath and hoped that the device was strong enough to take the abuse. Between one puff of wind and another the balloon rose enough to clear the ground, but it seemed to gain height with agonizing slowness.

He heard a shout behind him and the sudden clatter of a helicopter taking off. One of his pursuers, more quick-witted than the rest, had realized what it was that was rising into the darkening sky.

Balsan glanced at the approaching armored vehicle and then

at the balloon, which now scudded southwestward, driven, but held down, by the wind, the black shape of a helicopter moving to overtake it. He did not hesitate. He loaded an RPG into the shoulder launcher and fired at the helicopter. The rocket, trailing glowing exhaust gases and a thread of wire, arced upward. He tried to hold the sight on the target, but the wind affected his aim and the rocket missed. He saw it explode with a flash of yellow and white far to the southwest.

He reloaded and fired again, knowing that the helicopter could easily destroy the Mylar balloon. Another miss, and another useless explosion downrange.

He glanced for only a moment at the approaching armor. If he used the last RPG on the helicopter, there would be nothing to use against the steel-skinned vehicle coming toward him.

He turned away and fired again at the helicopter, now at extreme range. He held the sight on the point of fire made by the Yak's exhaust pipes as the rocket, spilling wire, flew into the night.

The helicopter seemed to dissolve in a bubble of fire. It fell, raining fragments. The balloon was out of sight.

Balsan dropped the empty launcher and picked up his machine pistol. He removed the silencer and began to shoot at the advancing Chinese soldiers. He heard a shout, a scream of pain, and a rattle of return fire. The armored vehicle rumbled closer.

He discarded an empty magazine, reloaded, and turned to fire at the soldiers approaching from the opposite direction. Frightened by the noise, the pony rose to his feet and bolted. He had not gone a dozen meters before he was cut down by a fusillade of automatic fire from the approaching Chinese.

Curiously, the death of the pony affected Balsan more strongly than his own rapidly deteriorating position. He howled obscenities and curses at them in his native dialect and sprayed the advancing armored car with machine-pistol fire. Bullets whined and ricocheted in the now nearly full dark.

Snow was whirling in the air and dancing in the sudden glare of a searchlight. Balsan threw down his empty machine pistol and stood empty-handed in the light. The Chinese, shouting, bolted toward him. It was then that he knelt, drew the double-reflex horn bow of his ancestors.

Five young soldiers of the People's Liberation Army fell with Mongol arrows in them, dying an archaic death as the armored vehicle, spitting machine-gun fire like some mythic Asian monster, rolled over Choy Balsan.

2

The rain, battering the tall, draped windows, made a rattling sound. Harry Grant, with an airman's instinctive sensitivity to the weather, noted that the wind was from the northwest and would drive the storm past Washington by morning. There would be sunshine, of a sort, for the President's departure.

He lay naked in the bed, his hands behind his head, staring at the dark ceiling. A thin shaft of light from the Georgetown street penetrated the narrow gap between the drapes, and a branch, swayed by the wind, interrupted the beam of light with each movement, sending a black needle across the illumination.

He was a thin man. His bare chest was badly scarred by burns that had seared his flesh. His injuries had come from an F-4 crash into a flaming, oily sea. He called them his legacy from Ho Chi Minh.

The woman beside Grant slept quietly, with deep regular breathing. He wondered again how she, so spring-tight and aggressive in her waking moments, could sleep so peacefully. Perhaps, he thought sardonically, it was the peace of convinced righteousness. No one in Washington was more certain than Jane McNary that she stood on the side of the angels.

Grant stole a glance at his wrist watch on the nightstand. The luminous hands of the complicated steel chronograph (a belligerent gift from Jane—she had presented it with a speech about "steel for the Iron Colonel") showed twenty minutes after five. By seven he was due at Andrews to inspect Air Force One and talk to Ortiz and the flight crew about accommodations for the

President's guests. And by afternoon, the aerial caravan of President, politicians ("statesmen" would be a kinder word), and news people would be over the Atlantic on the way to England. With the President's Senior Air Force Aide, General Tillotson, nursing an ulcer at the Bethesda hospital, the travel arrangements had fallen to Colonel Grant. Serving as an aide to the President was not an appointment to Grant's liking, but Cleveland Scott Lambert, President of the United States, need not inquire about the personal preferences of officers on the Colonels List of the Air Force.

Jane stirred and put a hand on Grant's chest. He suppressed an instinctive urge to pull away. Even after so many years, he was still conscious of the ugliness of his own mutilated flesh. The treatment he had received from the North Vietnamese medics had been primitive and, understandably, not gentle.

The woman beside him was slender, almost to emaciation, not at all like Bethany. Not in any way. His wife (he still thought of Bethany as his wife) had been soft to the touch, voluptuous. And she had lived with a cloying dependence that had held him in a kind of bondage until the unexpected day she told him that she no longer wished to live as a service wife. She had the honesty to add that she had found a man more suited to her tastes. There had been a hard core under the smooth skin and the sweet manner.

With McNary the metal was on the surface. She was thin, intense, consumed with self-righteousness and pugnacity. She had served her time in what she still called "the Women's Movement"—like that, with an upper-case emphasis. She had served her time in other movements, too, though she imagined, naïvely or wishfully, that few, including Grant, knew about her youthful fling with Marxism.

Tyler Davis, one of the sentinels of the National Security Council charged with reviewing the personal lives of the men who stood near the President, had presented McNary's dossier to Grant long ago, insisting that he read it through. The implication was quite plain. It was unsuitable for one of the President's White House staff to be conducting a liaison (Davis had actually called it that) with an unfriendly member of the press corps whose political past was suspect.

To his credit, the President had never broached the subject to Grant. Nor had he ever suggested what would have been worse—that Grant use his friendship with the radical Ms. McNary to soften her attacks on the administration.

Davis had taken the trouble to catalogue all of McNary's affairs, and they were many. She slept with writers, politicians, bureaucrats, and, on occasion, with men she picked up in the street. It was Davis's considered opinion—and the opinion, Grant assumed, of the National Security Agency computer—that Jane McNary, syndicated columnist, politically unreliable, was a flaming nymphomaniac.

The investigation had outraged Grant and he had told Tyler so. Tyler had responded with an appeal to a nonexistent friendship, asking how one so dedicatedly apolitical as Colonel Harry Simpson Grant could indulge himself emotionally with a militant fire stick like McNary.

What Tyler did not know, and what McNary understood with great clarity, was that Grant was not emotionally involved, that he had not been involved emotionally with any human being since his return from three years as a prisoner of the North Vietnamese. He had seen life reduced to bare minimums. He had lived in circumstances where emotional ties to other human beings could be manipulated by torturers and used to obliterate personality, human dignity, and honor. And Grant was a man who lived by such unfashionable notions as honor and dignity.

He disagreed with most of what McNary believed. He disliked her politics, her cynicism, her stridency. But he respected her quickness and intelligence, could not fault her sincerity and the strength of her convictions. And he was a man. McNary, as dozens, and possibly hundreds, of men in Washington had cause to know, was a rare experience in bed.

She opened her eyes now and said, "He never tires, he never sleeps. The Iron Colonel."

Grant suppressed a rueful smile. She had used him hard and often, and, despite the fact that he was in good shape, he was nearing fifty and felt it. He said, "It's near time for me to leave."

"Screw and run, you sexist." Her eyes seemed to glow in the darkness; her fine-boned face was like a carved mask.

"I am due at Andrews soon."

McNary sat up in the bed. Her breasts were hard and flat, but feminine for all that, with small dark nipples. She said, "Do I get to ride with the first team or am I stuck with the workers?"

At the suggestion of her Washington editors, she had been included in the press contingent traveling to the Sissinghurst conference with the Presidential party. Paul Lyman, the White House Press Secretary, had done his best to have her stricken from the list, quoting from her last phillipic against the administration's "reactionary stand" on nuclear disarmament, which was the purpose of the meeting in Britain between NATO and Warsaw Pact countries. But the President was certain that he could charm even the militant Ms. McNary, given time and the gracious surrounding of Sissinghurst Castle's rose gardens. Grant was less sure of this than his President, but Grant was a soldier and such decisions were not within his purview—for which he was grateful.

"You ride the Number-One Bird," he said. "The President's orders."

"I suppose I'm expected to be impressed."

"Just reasonably polite," Grant said, with a touch of asperity. McNary could be a trial after love-making. It didn't make her mellow; quite the reverse. It was as though she resented the force of her own considerable appetites.

"Cleveland Lambert is a dinosaur. He is about to become extinct. People aren't polite to presidents any more, Colonel Harry."

Grant sat on the edge of the bed and lit a cigarette. "Count me as a dinosaur, too. I think they should be."

She took the cigarette from him and stubbed it in an ashtray. She pressed herself against his naked back and set her teeth lightly on his neck. "All right. I'll behave. For you."

He ran an almost affectionate hand through her frizzy hair. It was reddish and had the texture of fine wire. "Forgive me, McNary, but that's bullshit."

She lay back in the bed and laughed. "You're the only man I know who still apologizes when he uses a vulgar expression to a woman."

Grant began to dress. He said, "Take me as I am."

"I do. Oh, I do." She regarded him speculatively, weighing the moment. There were rumors in town and she suspected that Grant might just know whether there was any truth in them. "The word is around that there has been quite a lot of hot-line traffic lately. True?"

Grant, buttoning his shirt, said nothing. He had been expecting her to ask about the messages that had been flying between Washington and Moscow. Somehow no secret was ever secure in Washington. There always seemed to be some bureaucrat or politician who was willing to curry favor with the press by leaking classified information. The long-past, almost-forgotten case of the Pentagon Papers had set a style that still persisted.

McNary said, "I've heard that Kirov is suffering a case of Peking jitters."

Who could have put her onto that, Grant wondered. Not Margaret Kendrick or her people. Since her appointment as Secretary of State, Mrs. Kendrick had rigidly tightened State Department security. Senator Prior? The old man was bitter against the administration and had old scores to settle with the President. But Grant was reasonably certain that the Senate Foreign Relations Committee had not yet been told about First Secretary Kirov's appeal to the President.

"The Iron Colonel's lips are sealed," McNary said caustically. "That's why Lambert the Dinosaur lets him come play at my house."

Grant controlled the familiar surge of irritation at her manner. This was the McNary touch. She never stopped trying to use the people she knew, even those with whom she shared her bed.

"I'm not one of your White House sources," he said.

"I don't have any White House sources, Colonel. I don't need them."

"Good, then," he said, and took his raincoat from a chair.

"But there have been messages from Moscow," McNary said. "You can tell me that."

"Good night, Jane. Or good morning," he said.

"I'll get the story, Harry."

"There is no story."

"Fuck you, Colonel. Button up. It's raining outside."

He closed the door to her apartment and walked down the silent, too-warm hallway toward the fanlighted door to the street. Sutton, he thought—DeWitt "Horse's Ass" Sutton, Senator from California. It had to be Sutton who was feeding her the story. Sutton, who got morality in the post-Watergate tempests, was a member of the Senate Overwatch Committee on Intelligence. The committee had sources—"informers," Grant would call them—inside the National Security Agency. And the NSA monitored all government communications, even those between White House and Kremlin.

The streets were wet, cold, and quiet at this hour. From his car, Grant called the duty officer at the White House. Commander Davenport, a smooth Navy Regular, was officer of the day in the Military and Naval Aides' Office.

"I'm on my way to Andrews, Silas," he said.

"Roger, Colonel." A pause, and then, with a touch of salacious malice in his voice, "Good night?"

"Fair, Silas." Guess? Rumor? Observation? It was a pity, but no one could move in this town, Grant thought, without the

Word spreading. No matter. "Is there anything on General Tillotson?"

"Routine medical bulletin at 2400 hours. He's doing as well as can be expected."

Tillotson's ulcers would keep him in the hospital for at least another week. There was no chance that Grant could miss this trip to Sissinghurst. He had hoped for a week of work at Luke Air Force Base, where he was overdue for an air-to-air-gunnery refresher course. That would have to wait now until his return from England.

He reached Andrews early, at 0630 hours. The rain had diminished to a drizzle and there were breaks in the clouds to the northwest. A pale star showed through a gap in the overcast.

Colonel Carlos Ortiz, the President's pilot, had Air Force One on the ramp before the VIP terminal. One was a giant C-9, converted to the President's needs. The follow-up aircraft, a wide-bodied Lockheed, stood behind One, dwarfed by the white-and-silver monster. The flight attendants were mustered; the airplanes were stocked with food, drink, and fuel. Now, typically, there was nothing for the crews to do but wait.

Ortiz, a dapper American of Mexican descent, greeted Grant warmly. The two pilots had served together in Vietnam and had high regard for one another. With Ortiz at his side, Grant inspected the aircraft. Carlos Ortiz knew his job too well to need close supervision, so the inspection was a formality.

Back in the Operations Room, the two men drank coffee and watched the weather sequences as they appeared on the Weather Service computer. Grant was preparing to return to his quarters at Fort Myer to shave and change uniform when Ortiz said, "We had a strange one this morning, Harry. A call came from State asking that we dispatch the stand-by Presidential 767 to Hurn. That's near Bournemouth—miles from Sissinghurst. You hear anything about this?"

"Nothing. You say the request came from State?"

Ortiz sipped at the tasteless brew in the Styrofoam cup and nodded. "From State with a capital S. The Secretary made the request. Herself. In person. I sent George Barrow out with a stand-by crew on the 767. They cleared Washington Flight Control at 0540."

Ortiz waited for him to comment, but Grant remained thoughtfully silent. It was strange indeed that an old aircraft be added without prior planning to the President's flight, that it should be dispatched to a minor British airport this way, and stranger still that the request should have been made by Secretary of State Kendrick in person and at such an early hour.

Presently, Grant asked, "Any special instructions to Major Barrow and his crew?"

Ortiz nodded, his dark eyes alert and curious. "He is to land at Hurn and stand by there until he receives further orders. Oh, yes. The aircraft is to be parked away from the main operations area and there will be RAF security troops on hand to guard it. What do you make of that?"

Grant felt a premonitory tightness in his belly. It was a feeling familiar from his days of combat. The before-a-mission sense of alertness.

Ortiz said, "Do you really not know anything about this, Harry? Or should I just mind my own goddamn business?"

Grant shook his head. "I know only what you've told me, Carlos."

Ortiz smiled. "Maybe *el Jefe* will enlighten you and then you can enlighten me, *amigo*. Anyway, Barrow is on the way and Madame Secretary should be content." Ortiz, who assumed the Latin tradition of machismo, vaguely disapproved of a woman secretary of State, even though Margaret Kendrick, a sixty-year-old foreign-policy genius, was as strong as any secretary in memory. "Is everything else running on schedule?" Ortiz asked.

"As far as I know. You'll be notified about an exact ETD as soon as I get back to the White House."

"Well, I'll be here. Barrow's ETA at Hurn is about 1500 hours, their time."

As Grant drove through Dillon Park an occasional fitful drizzle caused him to turn on the windshield wipers, and the surface of Pennsylvania Avenue Extension gleamed with the dampness of the rainy night. But the overcast was definitely breaking, and he could see blue dawnlight in the sky beyond the clouds.

The morning Washington commuter rush had begun, and his progress toward the river was slow. As far ahead as he could see, a Christmas tree of automobile taillights glittered and winked as the lines of traffic inched along the broad roadway. There had been yet another fuel shortage earlier in the autumn, but somehow Margaret Kendrick had soothed the manic dispositions of enough Arab sheiks to assure the American motorist his three hundred liters of high-test gasoline for another year. The Congress was debating still, as it had been for more years than Grant cared to remember, some politically safe policy on domestic energy. The gentlemen of Capitol Hill were no nearer a solution now than they had been in the days of the Nixon-Ford administration, when the "Sheikdom Shakedown" first provoked the idea of U.S. energy independence.

He was opposite Anacostia when the light began to flash on his car telephone. It was Silas Davenport from the Military and Naval Aides' Office.

"Where are you now, Colonel?"

Grant instantly detected a note of excitement in the naval officer's voice, though it was standard procedure to be extremely guarded in radiotelephone communications. "Anacostia," he said. "I'm on my way to Fort Myer."

"You'll have to cancel that, Colonel. You are to come right in."

Grant had worked for the President long enough to expect the unexpected. But Cleveland Lambert was not one of those politicians who made a practice of starting the working day before eight in the morning. Something was up.

"Right," Grant said into the handset. "I'll be there directly."

"Directly" in Washington's morning traffic meant another half hour on the road. He considered turning into Anacostia Naval Air Station and demanding transport by helicopter, but decided against it. The time saved would be negligible, and the act would be—in Grant's opinion—overly dramatic. He preferred the low-key approach in his work and scorned the customary Washington VIP behavior.

He arrived at the Aides' Office shortly after eight and signed in. Davenport was still on the OD's desk. "The Man wants to see you right away. I'll tell Miss O'Donnell you're on the way."

As Grant walked swiftly in the direction of the Oval Office, he was aware of tension in the air of the Executive Mansion. Entering the office of the President's secretary, he caught sight of General Clinton Devore, the Chairman of the Joint Chiefs of Staff, and Admiral Jay Muller, the Chief of Naval Operations, hurrying out to a waiting staff car. Devore, a sleekly handsome Air Force officer, newly appointed chairman, looked angry. Muller, a less temperamental sort, accustomed to serving the Navy in the Washington jungles, looked concerned. The two men were the most dynamic officers of the Joint Chiefs, and neither was given to dramatics.

Ivy O'Donnell, the sixtyish spinster who commanded the President's corps of secretaries, looked up as Grant came into the room.

"You're late, Colonel," she said severely. "You'll have to wait."

Grant, accustomed to Miss O'Donnell's brusqueness, acknowledged his cold reception with a nod and, prepared for a long wait, took a seat next to a warrant officer, one of the specially selected custodians of the nuclear codes who waited always within voice call of the President, the grim black briefcase chained to his wrist.

The door of the Oval Office opened, and Grant received the first of the many mild shocks that were to continue throughout this day. The two men who hurried by without a glance were Mikhail Baturin, the Soviet Ambassador to the U.S., and Reuben Ritter Richards, the Secretary of Defense. Grant could imagine no stranger companions. Richards was a draftee from the inner bastions of Wall Street, a man so given to lecturing the nation on the threat of Communism that he was known to the liberal Washington press corps as "Three R Richards," for Rapid Rearmed Reaction. He had also been dubbed "the Last of the Cold Warriors." Richards accepted both tags without protest. To find him in close company with Baturin, the latest silky-smooth Soviet salesman for détente (a word Richards was said to have difficulty even pronouncing), was surprising. To find them leaving the President's office together at eight-fifteen in the morning was far more so.

Grant thought again about Jane McNary's probing for information about hot-line traffic. Apparently even the talkative Senator Sutton was in for surprises today. Grant's warning mechanisms, the instincts that had kept him alive in the sky over Indochina and sane in the camps of the North Vietnamese, were fully alert.

The intercom on Ivy O'Donnell's desk pinged, and he heard Cleveland Lambert's resonant murmur. Miss O'Donnell fixed Grant with a steely eye and said. "The President will see you now, Colonel."

As he walked to the door of the Oval Office, he almost collided with Christopher Rosen, the President's Special Adviser for Scientific Affairs, who was exiting in haste and with considerable agitation.

3

The heavily guarded dacha at Usovo, on the Moscow River, stood surrounded by an unbroken expanse of snow that extended on the north to the riverbank and in all other directions to the thick forest of pines that covered much of the two hundred hectares of the private park of the First Secretary of the Communist party.

The wooden house and the grounds lay under a leaden, late-afternoon sky. There had been some snow in the forenoon, and the air was bitter with the chill of deepening winter. Members of the Guards Regiment on ceremonial duty at the dacha stamped their feet as the cold bit through the boots and heavy winter uniforms they wore. Their breath steamed with each movement; moisture condensed and then froze on the metal parts of their polished weapons.

The medical changing of the guard was under way, and the doctors being relieved looked gloomy. The members of his medical teams knew that the news they gave him each day grew progressively worse—and, though Valentin Kirov was no Stalin, no ruler loves the bearer of grim tidings.

As the doctors going off duty passed through the checkpoints, a motorcade of five Zims, bearing the metal standards of the Politburo, the Soviet Army, Navy, Air Force, and the Committee for State Security, was passed through into the car park before the First Secretary's dacha.

Marshal Yuri Leonov, the junior member of the Politburo and the youngest man ever to hold the post of minister of

Defense, had watched the departing doctors from the rear seat of his Air Force car. He knew what the substantial size of the medical team meant. There were at least five doctors in the departing crew and, Leonov had no doubt, fully that many inside the dacha in attendance on the dying master of the Soviet Union. For Valentin Kirov *was* dying; there was no question whatever about that. All that remained to be discovered was the exact moment and the precise cause, which could be any one of a number of things. Leonov's own medical advisers had briefed him carefully on the various ways in which a man with embryoma of the kidney might die. It was typical of Kirov, Leonov thought with contempt, that he should contract a cancer of the kidney occurring almost exclusively in children. The First Secretary had a tendency to be late in everything.

In the conference room, a wood-paneled imitation of a chamber in a nobleman's hunting lodge at the turn of the century, low-ceilinged and overheated by a porcelain stove in the corner, Leonov joined the others. Old Marshal Pavel Lyudin, the Red Army's defeated candidate for the post of Defense minister that Leonov now held, barely favored his young rival with a nod. Admiral Josif Viktorov, another of the old-school officers, soon to retire as chief of the Navy, did not condescend to that slight amenity. He simply looked away and studied the closed door to the First Secretary's suite of rooms, a narrow portal guarded by two poker-faced young giants of the Guards Regiment.

The old men of the Soviet military disliked Leonov for many reasons, not least of which was the way in which he had—in their opinions—subverted so many of the best and brightest of their young officers during the years when he served as an instructor at Frunze. He had stretched their minds, that was certain, with his brilliance and daring as a lecturer. Without those years at the Military Academy, he often thought, and the disciples he had spread far and wide throughout the Soviet military, it was unlikely that he would hold the post he held now. The old men were timeservers, he thought, obsolete ornaments of a system they had allowed to soften and decompose into a nation of cryptobourgeois shopkeepers who lacked the discipline and alertness to recognize the dangers threatening the state at home and abroad.

He turned away from the old Marshal and Admiral to exchange a word with Yevgeny Zabotin and Boris Novikov. The two spymasters, generals respectively of the GRU and the KGB, were more eager for the young Marshal's good opinion. Zabotin had attended Leonov's famous Crisis Confrontation Lectures at Frunze as a relatively senior officer of the General Staff's Intelligence Directorate, and both he and the KGB man were supporters of the aggressive policies Leonov represented in the deliberations of the Politburo.

Zabotin had brought a bearded civilian with him, and the man now sat alone (awed, perhaps, by the high rank around him and the unseen but ever felt Presence behind the guarded door). He was so near the stove that his florid face was shiny with sweat. He held on his lap a sheaf of papers, extracts, and what appeared to be computer print-outs. His briefcase had, of course, been confiscated by the security militiamen who reinforced the men of the Guards Regiment in protecting the person of the First Secretary.

Leonov was vitally interested in the material Zabotin's civilian had brought with him. It was this, after all, that had been missing at the last meeting of this nameless executive committee of the men who ruled Russia. But Zabotin, a roundheaded, balding man with thick features and small porcine eyes, was far more anxious to scratch for rumors about First Secretary Valentin Kirov's health.

"How is he? Has there been any change?" He spoke in a stage whisper, a paradigm of solicitous concern. He meant: Has there been a change for the better?

Leonov was tempted to repeat to the Army Intelligence chief the words his own medical staff had given him when he had asked approximately the same question. "The First Secretary's disease is highly malignant. It metastasizes early to the lungs, liver, and brain. And since the First Secretary has delayed overlong the matter of a nephrectomy, the prognosis is poor." How magnificently objective doctors could be, Leonov thought, when the subject of their observations was someone other than themselves. But there was no point in repeating this to Zabotin. If the man was worth a damn at his job—and he was—he would have consulted his own team of medical advisers.

In fact, Leonov thought, glancing at the other men waiting in the overheated room, not one of them could have failed to make similar investigations. The time left to the First Secretary, and his ability to use it intelligently, despite pain, growing weakness, and, yes, fear, was of vital importance to each one of them.

Novikov, whose sallow complexion was made even yellower by the shade of his KGB uniform, murmured confidentially, "I understand there will have to be an announcement that he will not attend the NATO–Warsaw Pact conference in England. He will send Krasin instead." He paused, weighing the wisdom of making any further disclosure. Then he continued. "The President will leave Washington sometime tomorrow, so the First Secretary has already called him to express his personal regret that they will not meet at Sissinghurst."

Leonov felt satisfaction at the near-confirmation of what he had already discovered. Kirov would *not* attend the disarmament talks at Sissinghurst. Leonov was against the purpose of the conference on principle. It was madness to speak of reducing nuclear forces at this time, even if one assumed—as he did not—that the Americans could be trusted to reciprocate. His sources told him that there had been heavy hot-line traffic with Washington since the last meeting of this group. He wondered if he dared allow himself to hope that Kirov's incapacity would bring an American delegation to the Soviet Union. Perhaps even the President himself?

Marshal Yuri Leonov had not become the youngest minister of Defense in the history of the Soviet Union by relying on luck. Still, he knew that chance was always a factor in politics. And if, out of a sick First Secretary's anxiety and an American politician's desire to act as a peacemaker, the dialectic of history was to synthesize a *moment,* Leonov was the man to seize it. A kind of savage joy warmed him at the thought. It was just possible that—here and now—his years of working and planning, his total devotion to Soviet power, and at least a decade of his scheming to create the right circumstances for a final solution to the Chinese question, all were coming to their inexorable climax.

A civilian aide, a small man dressed in the sober, ill-fitting clothes affected by the new Stalinists, said politely: "Come in, *tovarishchi.* The Comrade First Secretary can see you now."

An hour and a half later, Marshal Leonov and General Zabotin stood in the lightly falling snow before the dacha. The others had already departed, depressed by the report delivered by Zabotin, and by the obvious deterioration in the First Secretary's condition.

Stepping a distance away from the guardsmen at the door of the wooden house, Leonov spoke quietly to Zabotin. "Balsan did well. Have the Chinese killed him?"

Zabotin replied, "We don't know."

"He was supplied with everything he needed?"

"He was. We don't know whether or not he used it. He may not have been able to."

Leonov shrugged his greatcoated shoulders and changed the subject. "I was disappointed in Comrade Kirov's reaction to your report. I hoped for something more than a plan to run whining to the Americans."

Zabotin looked furtively toward the guardsmen, stolid and motionless at their posts. "His sickness—it makes him fearful."

"That device in the Turfan should make him more so," Leonov said coldly. "But you did well. He's been warned."

Zabotin disliked the sound of that. He knew how hard a man the young Marshal was, how given to strong and direct actions.

Leonov said, "Is your car secure?"

"Of course." Zabotin thought it insulting that the Minister of Defense should ask such a question of the chief of the GRU.

"There's no 'of course' to it, Zabotin," Leonov said flatly. "My technicians removed a device from my vehicle this morning. We are all being spied upon, Comrade General."

"Novikov?"

"Possibly. Though I think it unlikely. The order to watch us comes from higher up, I think. Our excellent Foreign Minister Krasin, or maybe even the sick man himself."

Zabotin's expression showed his alarm.

Leonov said, "No matter. I think it is too late for silly games like that. Ride back to Moscow with me. We have matters to discuss."

Zabotin inclined his heavy head in the direction of the dacha. "Won't *he* think it strange?"

"After what we have seen today, nothing will seem strange."

"Perhaps he feels he has to consult with the Americans."

Leonov's eyes were icy, steady. "Of course. He made that very clear." A cold smile deformed his lips as he said scornfully: "Détente is still the official doctrine. Everyone must support the official policy of the party and the state, Comrade General."

Further talk was forestalled by the arrival of the Minister's Zim. The two men got into the heavy car, and Leonov signaled the driver to proceed. At the gate they returned the salutes of the Guardsmen who flanked the roadway, their AKs held across their chests.

When the Zim reached the highway along the Moscow River and increased speed, Leonov spoke again. "How does it happen that the Chinese have begun to work on a weapon our academicians assured us years ago was impossible?"

Zabotin, whose job included the overseeing of advanced weapons research, mopped the sweat from his face before answering. "There has always been a difference of opinion on the feasibility of a chemical laser antimissile device, Comrade Marshal."

"And we have been accepting the negative view," Leonov said, "while we should have been taking a positive position." He regarded the Intelligence chief speculatively. "In Stalin's time such a misjudgment would have been treated as sabotage." Before Zabotin could protest, he silenced him with a gesture. "No matter. Perhaps it is just as well. The First Secretary has made a decision and we will all abide by it. We will work with the Americans, who will come here filled with good will and in the spirit of world peace." He gave a short, unpleasant laugh that startled Zabotin. "What is our situation in London?"

"Thin," Zabotin said. "Voronin has not been replaced yet." He hastened to add: "That is not my fault, Comrade Marshal. I have been waiting for you to make a suitable replacement available."

Leonov sat in silence, his eyes fixed on the flat white landscape between the road and the river.

Colonel Aleksandr Voronin, of the Soviet Air Force, the Assistant Air Attaché in London, had once been one of Leonov's most promising students and disciples. But he was in deep disfavor with the Marshal now as a result of his involvement with a British woman—"a Welsh ballet girl," Zabotin called her. For several weeks the Minister of Defense had been on the verge of ordering Voronin home. Zabotin, whose GRU investigators were watching Voronin carefully, suspected the Colonel was a security risk, a candidate for defection to the West. But he had not yet reported this suspicion to Marshal Leonov. His information was too equivocal and the need to have a Leonov-trained man in the British capital too essential to rush to hasty judgment.

"Are Voronin's contacts inside the British Foreign Office still active?" Leonov asked abruptly.

"Yes, Comrade Marshal."

Leonov continued to study the snow-covered countryside.

Stands of birch and elm grew along the riverbank, their leafless limbs dark traceries against the white sky.

"Kirov says he does not yet know the Americans' secret itinerary. I do not believe him. He is indulging in secrecy for secrecy's sake," Leonov said. "We can be sure they will use that charade at Sissinghurst as a cover for their visit here. So the English must know what their movements will be."

Zabotin remained silent. He had the uncomfortable feeling that the Minister of Defense was coming to some sort of decision.

"Order Voronin to find out exactly what the American schedule will be. Do so at once."

"Yes, Comrade Marshal."

"I shall make an inspection of the missile base at Aral'sk tomorrow."

Zabotin's face remained impassive though the statement startled him. It seemed a politically unwise time for the Minister of Defense to leave Moscow. He also remembered that the ICBM complex at Aral'sk, one of the most secure bases inside the Soviet Union, was commanded by still another protégé from Leonov's Frunze days.

"You will report to me at Aral'sk—in person—with Voronin's information."

"Yes, Comrade Marshal," Zabotin said.

Leonov rested his head against the deeply padded seat back and half closed his eyes. It was odd, he thought, that suddenly he had no doubts—no doubts at all. What had begun long ago as a kind of military intellectual's exercise and had grown over the years into a plan—a doctrine—was swiftly becoming a genuine possibility. The Chinese and the Americans, it appeared, were doing their part. Now I must do mine, Yuri Leonov thought.

"And after Voronin relays the information, what then?" Zabotin asked.

"We will not need him again," Leonov said coldly, and turned to look at the wintry scene that stretched away for flat mile after mile to an indistinct twilight horizon.

4

The President of the United States had regarded his Scientific Adviser with barely suppressed irritation. Cleveland Lambert had been up since two in the morning, awakened from a sound sleep by still another urgent hot-line message from First Secretary Kirov in Usovo. His eyes felt grainy, there was a foul taste in his mouth, and his tolerance was nearing its limit.

The President was not a patient man. He realized, of course, that it was not always possible for a politician to attract and hold men with really good minds in a troubled and beset administration. But he had hoped, when he nominated Christopher Rosen, a Nobel Laureate in physics, to be his Special Adviser for Scientific Affairs that within the area of his expertise, at least, Rosen would provide him with useful advice and counsel.

For four hours he had been engaged in a series of discussions about the developments in the Turfan with Rosen at his side. The man held a dozen impressive awards and titles in physics and allied fields and had been selected for his present post on the basis of his ability to confront new developments with calm competence. But it appeared to Lambert that Professor Rosen regarded the Russian reports—all of them backed, to a degree, by data received by American Nathan Hale spy satellites—as attacks on his scientific veracity.

Rosen, a jowly, red-faced man with an aureole of dry, silvery hair, was nine years younger than the President. Puffy-eyed and unshaven, he looked ten years his senior this morning. In the presence of the Secretary of State he had informed Lambert that the Russians were alarmed about nothing. In company that had included Secretary of Defense Richards and Soviet Ambassador Baturin, he had voiced the opinion that the intelligence evaluators working on the Nathan Hale data were misinterpreting the Turfan read-outs. To the Chief of Naval Operations and the Chairman of the Joint Chiefs of Staff, he had acidly suggested that it was to the advantage of the Department of Defense to believe the unbelievable—that the Chinese were developing a chemical laser weapon that could upset the nuclear balance of power—because the time for consideration of the defense budget was rapidly approaching.

In the interval between the departure of the angry officers (both of whom Rosen despised with all the force of his deeply pacifist convictions) and the entry of Three R Richards and Ambassador Baturin, he had given the President a concise lecture (simplified to suit a layman's limited comprehension) on the impossibility of anyone doing what the Russians claimed the Chinese had done. "Beyond a certain level of energy projection, Mr. President, any laser beam encounters the phenomenon known as 'thermal blooming.' In simple terms, this means that the coherent energy transforms the atmosphere through which it passes into an ionized plasma that impedes the passage of the beam and reduces its force below the MHPL—the 'mean hull-penetration level.' Theoretically, laser warfare would be possible in the vacuum of space, provided powerful generator-converter satellites capable of targeted HPL laser emissions could be launched into orbit. Even if they could be, consider how vulnerable to attack such large-size power plants floating in space would be. Lasers have been on weapons-development lists since the '70s. Progress has been made in ground laser guidance systems, and every major power has a stand-by satellite blinding program no one dares to implement. I don't downgrade the value or the potential of the military laser, Mr. President. But this— this land-to-space death ray the Russians are talking about—is simply science fiction. It cannot be done."

The President had remembered that once, long ago, an American Secretary of Defense, "Engine Charlie" Wilson, had called satellites and missiles "science fiction." The resultant lag in American research had caused one of the most embarrassing and dangerous rivalries of the Cold War.

Even the information, supplied by Baturin, that the Turfan project was under the guidance of American-born Li Chin, a man Rosen had known at the California Institute of Technology in the middle 1960s as a genius in the then primitive field of laser technology, had failed to convince Christopher Rosen.

"I must say one thing more, Mr. President," Rosen remarked as he prepared to depart. "It is precisely because of this kind of scare tactic and assumptions of the worst possible case that Li Chin left this country to work in the People's Republic. His interest was always in humanitarian and medical research, and I venture to say, Mr. President, that if I were permitted to travel to China and speak with Professor Li personally, this entire matter could be cleared up in record time. But I suppose that would be quite impossible in this climate of fear and hysteria."

"Hardly hysteria, Chris," the President said dryly, "but you are correct in your assumption that we do not think this is the time for you to visit your old colleague."

"In that case, sir," Rosen said, his reddened eyes angry and indignant, "I should like to withdraw from this business completely. My standing in the scientific community will be seriously compromised if it is to be the administration's position that the Chinese are building some sort of superweapon to upset the balance of power."

The President's expression was stony as he said, "You will withdraw from this evaluation when you are prepared to resign your post as my scientific adviser, Chris, and not before." He waited for Rosen to take the proffered escape, knowing that he would not. Cross-grained and irritating Rosen might be, but he valued his post too highly to return to the relative obscurity of the laboratory now. Power corrupts us all, the President thought, even the would-be saints of science like Rosen. "All right, then," he continued, more gently now that the Professor's crisis of conscience was past. "I don't like to pull rank on you, Chris, but I must insist that you take this Turfan business seriously. It is possible, I grant you, that your friend Li Chin is simply playing with medical lasers up there in the Turfan. But there are forty Soviet divisions massed along the Amur and at least that many Chinese facing them. You know what the Soviet Minister of Defense has said repeatedly about the inevitability of war with China. His predecessors started saying it as early as the 1950s. So anything the Russians take seriously, we must examine very, very carefully."

"Just as you say, Mr. President," Rosen answered sourly.

The President rose from behind his desk as the intercom pinged. "The Nathan Hale data will be delivered to you, Chris. Give me a report by noon today." To dismiss the about-to-protest Rosen, the President spoke into the intercom. "Is Harry Grant there, Miss O'Donnell? Good, send him in now." He nodded to Rosen. "Give it your best shot, Chris," he said. "I rely on you."

"Of course, Mr. President."

Grant, the misty rain still beading his uniform, stood aside as the scowling academic departed.

"I have three minutes for you, Harry," the President said. "Sit down and listen."

Grant did as he was told and waited for the President to speak.

Cleveland Lambert stepped from behind the desk and began to pace the room. "You won't be flying on Air Force One, Harry. I'm going to delay my start for England by at least an hour or two, but I want you on your way just as soon as you've talked to—" he lifted a paper on his desk top to refresh his memory— "Emil Jessanek, at State Department Intelligence. He is on the East European Desk and he will be expecting you. After you are briefed, you'll fly directly to Heathrow. You'll be met there by a Major Ian Ballard, of British Intelligence—the Secret Intelligence Service, to be precise." He paused to look down at Grant speculatively. It seemed to Grant that the President was considering how much more information to impart to him just now. Presently Lambert said, "This is a personal assignment, Harry. If you are wondering why you instead of someone from the Agency—don't."

Grant, well aware of the leaks in the Central Intelligence Agency, leaks that had diminished the organization's efficiency to a dangerously low level, made no comment.

The President suppressed the thin smile that came to his lips. The Iron Colonel, he thought. He must have given his North Vietnamese jailers nothing, nothing at all.

"You will report back to me in seventy-two hours. At Hurn airport. That time and place are classified, by the way." He watched to see if Grant showed any surprise and was gratified to note that he did not. "You know where that is?"

"Yes, sir."

"That's it, then. One thing more. If you need anything while in London, get it from Ballard. Leave the Embassy and the Agency out of it."

Grant stood and said, "Yes, Mr. President."

Lambert smiled and said, "I'll watch out for Ms. McNary, Colonel. You go carefully. I'm not sure what I'm letting you in for."

5

For a number of days, in fact since the capture of the Russian spy, a half-frozen rain had been falling on the high Asian plateau. The snow flurries had ceased, the temperature had risen slightly, and the result had been a general rise in the level of the water that flooded much of the basin known as the Great Turfan Depression.

Li Chin, a pale man in his late fifties dressed in the quilted cotton clothing issued by the People's Liberation Army, was both cold and impatient. The council of workers, peasants, and soldiers which oversaw the work he was conducting in the Turfan had last night made a decision to assign ten of his most highly trained technicians to the menial and useless task of sandbagging the low ground around the workers' housing area. It was the latest in a series of decisions made by the council that had kept Li in a state of irritated frustration for months. The men—now slogging through the marshy damp in a fruitless attempt to prevent the flooding of the shacks where the labor force was billeted —were desperately needed to complete the installation of the Q-switching cell, the next-to-last step in the construction prior to the beginning of full-power field tests.

Li put aside the schematic drawing he had been studying and stared moodily through the streaked window of his quarters at the bleak scene beyond. He could see the lines of power poles shaking in the wind, the skeins of cables swaying with each frigid gust from the north. From his position on the slope of the Depression he could not make out the camouflaged dome of the reactor. That, at least, had been done well and thoroughly. It would take repeated infrared and visible-light photography performed under ideal conditions for a satellite camera to pinpoint the location of the plant that supplied the installation with electrical power.

He had no doubt that certainly the Americans and quite possibly the Russians were working on that problem at this very moment and he was positive that they would succeed. He had, with great difficulty, managed to stay current with the state of the art in the West and across the border in the Soviet Union. The technological problems of locating and interpreting the activities he had been conducting for the last year and a half in the Turfan were solvable. It was the political implications that would take time to unravel, and by the time that a definite course of action was decided upon in Washington or Moscow, the laser ("the Dragon," the peasant laborers called it) should be in operation.

Should be. Li frowned as he watched a work party plodding down the slope into the marsh. It was unbelievably trying to work under these conditions. Despite his years in the People's Republic and his still-fervid loyalty to the party and the principle, he found it exasperating to conduct scientific work under the authority of an ever-changing, totally politicized group of ignorant laymen. Only last night he had been summoned to a self-criticism session called by Colonel Yu Tien, the head of security for the project. For three hours he had been forced to sit and listen to Yu describe his own failure to capture the Russian spy before the intruder managed to get his radiosonde launched. The student cadre had been particularly vicious in their ideological attacks on the Colonel, who was no particular friend of Li's, but whose long service and age deserved better treatment at the hands of the council.

Yu Tien had called the meeting himself, as required, and Li, though he had other, more important, work to do, had been forced to join in the ceremony. Chou Tsing-wen, the current Chairman of the Turfan Workers, Peasants, and Soldiers Council—a round-faced little fanatic all of twenty-two years old—had used the opportunity to warn all the scientists and technicians

38

present against the sin of bourgeois elitism, quoting from the writings of Chairman Mao and then announcing the committee decision to put the technicians to work on the flooding problem.

Li Chin was reminded of the sympathetic students he had known at Cal Tech in the 1960s. Would they, as arrogant and self-righteous as Chou Tsing-wen could ever be, have behaved in exactly the same manner given the authority and opportunity? The thought was disturbing, unsettling, infuriating!

A flurry of sleet smeared the glass, blurring the gray-lighted vista at the bottom of the slope. The buildings were minimal: wooden shacks with tar-papered walls and corrugated-iron roofs. The streets were little more than paths spread with gravel to discourage the mud formed by the constant oozing of the marsh water from below. Yet the installation was the result of immense labor, and Li felt an almost proprietary pride in it. Within the space of eighteen months the indigenous population had been either moved away or impressed into the labor force. A thousand soldiers and twenty-five hundred peasant laborers had been moved from the south. A massive nuclear reactor with its attendant generators and transmission lines had been built—with American technology, Li thought with a grim smile, imported during the brief heyday of Sino-American amity in the 1970s.

The chemical laser itself, however, was unique and his own. He chided himself for indulging in that bourgeois elitism Chou Tsing-wen liked to criticize. But it was a fact that the great laser would not have been built—*could* not have been built—without the pioneering work in the field done by Li Chin, onetime professor of physics at the California Institute of Technology. The Dragon was the result of one man's dedication, one man's genius. He could never voice such sentiments, of course. Quite the contrary. The conventions of life inside the People's Republic demanded that he acknowledge that all success flowed from the wisdom of the deified Chairman Mao. The very absurdity of such a belief was the thing that made it so intellectually fascinating to a man of Li's mental agility.

He stood and walked to the window for a better view. Now he could see the revetments protecting the acquisition radars, the microwave antennas, and, far down the marshy floor of the Depression, the focusing mirrors of the laser itself. Like Archimedes, he thought, I can move the world. But the laser desperately needed testing, and soon. The field experiments against ground targets had been satisfactory—as far as they went. The thermal-blooming problem seemed under control at terrestrial ranges up to five thousand meters. Since those tests were completed, however, the third-stage intensifiers had been added to the Dragon—devices based on the etalons devised in the 1960s by Fabry and Perot. With a suitable increase in power, the theoretical range of the device was now nearly a thousand kilometers.

What was needed now was a field test on a genuine target at suborbital or even orbital range. Li raised his eyes toward the thick gray overcast. Beyond that impalpable barrier the Americans and Russians were spying on the People's Republic. Yankee Nathan Hale and Soviet Svoboda satellites crossed the high desert of the Talimupendi a dozen times each day, probing, snooping, stripping away the Dragon's blanket of secrecy.

Li caught sight of Chou Tsing-wen leading still another shovel-bearing detachment of technicians in the direction of the workers' barracks. His thin lips tightened. His only hope was to protest to the Central Committee in Peking that his valuable technical personnel was being grossly wasted in such projects. No, not personnel—that Western capitalistic term. People. Yes, much better. But first it would be necessary to complete the plan for the tests that would transform the Dragon from a scientific curiosity into that Archimedean lever that would change the balance of power in the world. The Central Commitee, collective and faceless though it might be, must surely see that.

He strode swiftly across his bare office into the computer-terminal room. The two programmers at work looked up and nodded respectfully as he seated himself at a terminal. The plaque on the terminal was in English: Transiac XII. Another offering from the Americans, who imagined they could buy friendship with lavish gifts. For a moment Li was overwhelmed by the memory of mild bright days on a peaceful, comfortable campus. He felt an almost unbearable longing for the easy security and luxury of his native land. He put the thought sternly aside, remembering that America was venal, crass, vulgar, and racist. He had the means to bring that white Sodom down, and with it the revisionist bandits in the Kremlin.

His slender fingers began to tap out his requirements: an orbital ephemeris projecting the tracks of the American and Soviet satellites that would cross over the Turfan Depression in the next seven days.

6

At sixty-five thousand feet over the North Atlantic the sky above was shaded to a deep blue. The sun had been low in the east when the flight had begun, but as the Navy Tigercat, swing wings tucked against its slender fuselage, fled eastward, the fiery ball appeared to climb swiftly. The Mach meter on the instrument panel in the radar-observer's cockpit, where Harry Grant rode, showed that the aircraft was traveling at three times the speed of sound. At this speed, the journey from Washington to London would take slightly more than one hour.

The voice of the pilot, a young lieutenant commander assigned to the Special Flight Section at Anacostia, said in Grant's headphones: "We've got a jet stream. That's good for a few extra knots."

Grant tapped the R/O's stick in response and turned his attention to the pelagic view far below. The clouds that had sheathed Washington and the east coast of the United States were a broken blanket of white twenty thousand feet below the airplane. The sun glittered from the undercast and from the occasional patches of cobalt-blue ocean that could be seen. Grant had the pleasant impression of being totally alone, suspended between sea and sky in a softly whining capsule of shining metal. The sound of the twin jets was left far behind at this speed and all that could be heard were the gentle hummings and breathings made by the Tigercat's life-support systems.

It was sometimes difficult to come to terms with the harsh fact that this brilliantly conceived and cleverly constructed machine was a weapon, and a deadly one at that. Armed for war, the Tigercat was a city-smasher, a launching platform for fifty megatons of nuclear destruction.

Like many soldiers, Grant had always been fascinated by weapons. His reading of history and his own experience had taught him that weapons, from the Macedonian *sarissa* to the Tigercat, tended to dominate those who possessed them. But a lifetime of military experience had taught him that the real dangers inherent in this domination were surpassed by the dangers of deliberate weakness. One day, he sometimes mused, the lion and the lamb may sleep together. But that day remained far off. His bitterest scorn was reserved for those politicians who used the understandable revulsion of ordinary people against war as a tool for political advantage and even against the interests of the nation.

DeWitt Sutton was such a man, in Grant's opinion. Sutton and others like him had all but destroyed the Central Intelligence Agency and thus had made necessary the sort of makeshift mission on which he, Grant, was now embarked.

Jessanek had briefed him at the State Department less than two hours ago. In five minutes, Jessanek had outlined the President's proposed secret journey from Hurn to Moscow and Peking. He needed less time to state the bare facts, stripped of conjecture, about the Chinese installation in the Turfan. Then, after a calm warning that there was possibly no connection between those two situations and Grant's assignment, he launched into detail.

"There is a military attaché in the Soviet Embassy in London named Aleksandr Voronin. A colonel in the Air Force," Jessanek said. "SIS has been interested in him for a couple of years, particularly since they discovered that he was a former star pupil of Marshal Yuri Leonov, the present Soviet Defense Minister. SIS believes there is a chance Voronin would be willing to defect. We don't know what evidence they have for that— our allies have been reluctant to reveal their sources to us ever since the first Committee on Intelligence established the precedent of deciding what secret information should be made public. With that kind of erratic exposure possible, even our closest allies must protect themselves. So we have to take what SIS says on faith if we intend to do anything about it." Jessanek, a bearded young man with deep-set, sad eyes, paused to puff alight a fantastically large meerschaum pipe, and then continued. "We do know that Voronin has been having an affair with a British woman—a Welsh girl named Bronwen Wells—ballet dancer—something like that. Not exactly star quality, you understand. We also know that the Soviet authorities are not pleased about it." He shrugged at Grant's questioning expression. "I know that sounds like a situation out of a Cold War movie, but SIS confirms it. As far as they know, the objections are not yet official, but appear to be harbored by Defense Minister Leonov." He shrugged. "Don't ask me why, if that is so, Voronin is still in London, or even still alive. But you should know Leonov is an enigma to our local Kremlinologists. He's young for his job. He's as tough as old Grechko ever was, maybe more so. Grechko was mostly talk. Leonov is something else again." He opened a file and passed it across the desk. "Yuri Ivanovich Leonov, Marshal of the Soviet Air Force, Hero of the Soviet Union, et cetera, et cetera. Note this." A narrow, nicotine-stained finger tapped a red-flagged paragraph. " 'Though not well known outside the Soviet Union, Leonov is a highly regarded military strategist and intellectual. He served two tours of duty as a teacher at the Soviet Military Academy at Frunze, during which time he was allowed to select his students from the Army, Navy, and Air Force as well as from the Committee for State Security. Former students of his are now established in many key posts throughout the Soviet military and diplomatic hierarchy.' "

Jessanek sat back and relit his pipe, wreathing himself in bluish smoke. "Now I find that interesting, don't you, Colonel? Particularly at this—ah—point in time, as some crew-cut pols used to say."

Grant, though he remained silent, decided he liked Jessanek, who was obviously not the usual sort of State Department bureaucrat.

Jessanek continued. "Leonov is the primary exponent of"—he ticked off the items on his fingers—"an end to détente, or at least a go-slow on it; the old Brezhnev Doctrine, meaning that the USSR has a right to interfere anywhere in the world where its interests are at hazard; a hard line on the Chinese—some of our brain trusters claim he wants to indulge in a bit of nuclear castration. And yet—" he paused to stare distastefully at his giant meerschaum and put it down on the desk—"and yet not one of the hot-line messages has given any indication at all that he is even aware that the Chinese are up to something in the Turfan. I don't believe it—do you?"

"What has this to do with a possible defector?" Grant asked.

"I don't know. Maybe nothing at all. That's what the President wants you to find out. Ballard, of SIS, has been cultivating Voronin. He thinks he may be ready to harvest. But he wants us to do it. I think it's the tactful British way of offering us some help without compromising their own covert operations. One can't blame them, really. Congress is still playing with its mud bucket and shovel. Some good senators discovered back in the mid '70s that blowing covert operations was a sure-fire way to get their names in the papers and their faces on television. They're still at it. So Ballard contacted State Department Intelligence instead of the Agency. Voronin's ours if we want him and if you can make a deal with him. Ballard has arranged a meeting for you."

Jessanek leaned forward again and spoke with some intensity. "What I think is this. Voronin is one of Leonov's protégés. But a possibly disillusioned one. The Welsh girl is important to him. Maybe more important than his old teacher. If so, he could be very useful to us." He thrust himself back in his chair, took an unopened package of cigarettes from the desk, looked at them hungrily, and, with an effort, put them out of sight. "That's it."

Grant looked down at the open file before him. So the mission did not merely concern a possible defector named Voronin. What it was really about was something quite different. It was an attempt to gain some small insight into the man who controlled the total might of the Soviet armed forces: Marshal Yuri Ivanovich Leonov. The code name stamped below the SECRET, EYES ONLY bands on the folder caught his eye. The name was BOYAR.

The voice of the Tigercat's pilot interrupted Grant's musings.

"Take a look down there, Colonel." He rolled the aircraft slightly to the right to give his passenger a clearer view of the sea below.

The undercast had broken into scattered clouds now, a pattern of white that shadowed the cobalt-colored water of the North Atlantic. Grant raised his shielded visor and looked through the bubble canopy. A trio of spearhead wakes could be seen. From this height, he guessed that the surface ships could not be traveling at less than forty knots, possibly more.

The pilot had activated the on-board computer, and the machine was digesting the electronic data supplied to it by the Tigercat's identification and target systems. The cathode-ray tube on the radar-observer's console showed the targets clearly. The screen beside it was displaying information in short, succinct bursts. PRIMARY TARGET SVERDLOV CLASS USSR MISSILE CRUISER KRONSHTADT DISPLACEMENT 19,200 TONS. MAIN ARMAMENT TWIN GUIDELINE LAUNCHERS, 12 152MM GUNS IN THREE TURRETS, 12 100MM DUAL-PURPOSE GUNS, 32 37MM ANTIAIRCRAFT. TARGET SPEED 43 KNOTS. COURSE 122 DEGREES. RADAR DEFENSES ACTIVE. The computer reduced the informational paragraph, stored it in the right upper corner of the display screen. More information appeared as the Tigercat's systems continued to scan the squadron sixty-five thousand feet below. ESCORTS KRIVAK CLASS USSR GUIDED-MISSILE DESTROYERS. DISPLACEMENT 4,400 TONS. ARMAMENT . . . The on-board computer completed the description in terse words and numbers.

Grant, unfamiliar with the Tigercat's intelligence-gathering and interpreting capabilities, was impressed.

"The old computer reads them pretty good, wouldn't you say, Colonel?" the pilot said proudly. "Look now."

Though the Russian ships had already fallen far astern, the computer display continued to provide information to the Tigercat's crew. The amber-green printing changed to red as the computer informed the two men in the Tigercat that the *Kronshtadt* had launched two VTOL fighters, presumably to investigate the high-flying intruder aircraft.

"They have two chances of getting a look at us, Colonel," the pilot said. "Slim and none." The elation faded slightly from his voice as he added: "But there are one hell of a lot of them out in the Atlantic now, Colonel. I never make this trip without seeing at least a couple of Reds. Big, new ones."

Grant understood the pilot's apprehension. Over the last ten years the Soviet fleet had outbuilt the United States Navy by a factor of three to one. Their ships were new, fast, and powerful. The American domination of the seas was a thing of the past. In the U.S. Congress, the concept was labeled "New Insularity"; the rationale relied on the argument of overkill.

The Tigercat's computer wiped the display screen clean and began to print out new information. Grant watched it with fascination.

The amber-green letters appeared in a neat line across the surface of the screen: SUBMARINE TARGET BEARING 180 DEGREES RELATIVE COURSE 122 DEGREES. There was a submarine tracking the Soviet flotilla.

Grant touched the intercom button and asked, "One of our boats, Commander?"

The pilot was busy querying the computer. He said, "I don't think so, Colonel. If it were, the brain here would have recognized it. All the deep-turbulence and radiation signatures of the Polaris and Trident boats are in the memory."

The display changed swiftly. TARGET HAINAN CLASS CHINESE NUCLEAR SUBMARINE.

"Goddamn, Colonel, what about that? A slope boat," the pilot said. "There's a Chinese submarine trailing that squadron." He paused, and then asked, "Okay if we do a one-eighty and let my baby get a look at the sub, Colonel? We don't have much on the Hainan-class nukes."

As a former combat flier, Grant could understand the pilot's interest and the Navy's curiosity. But his own mission, ordered by the President, had to take precedence. "Negative, Commander. Get me to England," he ordered.

The tone of the pilot's acknowledgment told the Iron Colonel what he thought of that decision.

But for the remainder of the flight to Heathrow, Grant found himself wondering about the significance of the minor naval puzzle he had witnessed out in the frigid North Atlantic.

7

It was forty minutes past noon. A thin, watery sunlight shone through a ceiling of high cloud as Bronwen Wells drove her three-year-old Audi into the car park at the Dover Hovercraft Terminal.

She was a small woman, only two inches above five feet tall, with a lean, almost thin, dancer's body and a fine-featured face framed by black hair drawn back in the traditional ballerina's knot. Her eyes were deep brown, almost black, widely spaced, and seemed always vaguely perplexed by the complexities she saw around her. Alek had said that she had the eyes of a Kirghiz woman, and she had looked up the name to see whether or not he had been paying her a compliment. She felt her education was lacking: she had left a shabby comprehensive school in Cardiff with the bare minimum of exam certificates and had gone to London to make her way as a dancer. She had had six years of ballet training (paid for with great sacrifice by a father dying of the black lung disease), but it had taken ten more years for her to reach her present rank in a second-rate company, the Ballet Celeste. Though her teacher, Madame Zelinskaya, had not said so, Bronwen knew that she had reached her zenith with the Celeste.

She had met Aleksandr Voronin at a reception at the Soviet Embassy for a visiting Russian dance troupe. A man of great charm and some tenderness, he brightened her life; approaching thirty, she had become lonely, increasingly steeped in Welsh melancholy. Three weeks later she had become his mistress. It appealed to her sense of theater that she, a ballet dancer, should become the mistress of a Russian officer. Sometimes she fantasized that these were other, more glittering times, that she and her lover danced under the crystal chandeliers and reflected candlelight of a St. Petersburg palace. The contrasts between her balletic fantasies and the realities of the world in which she actually lived deepened her sadness.

There was a touch of theater about Alek too, which appealed to her. He was a colonel in the Soviet Air Force, and if his uniforms were not so splendid as those of the slipper-shod hussars who partnered her on stage, at least his affection for her was not the creation of some choreographer. She believed, with dramatic intensity, that she loved him. She hoped, with the same intensity, that he loved her.

There was an air of mystery to his comings and goings. She did not understand what, exactly, he did as an attaché at the Soviet Embassy. But he was of some consequence, of that much she was quite certain.

Recently he had been distracted, withdrawn. It was typical of Bronwen that she wondered if he had tired of her already and wished to end their liaison. An officer of the St. Petersburg Guards would have discarded a mistress without remorse. She worried that Alek might do the same.

The night before, he had informed her that he must journey to Calais and that he would not be taking her with him. It was to be a short visit to the Continent, to meet with a foreigner who could not, for reasons he did not specify, come to London. Perhaps distressed by the submissiveness of her response, he had told her the time of his return at Dover by Hovercraft and suggested that she meet him.

Now she hurried across the half-empty car park, across the walkway that spanned the approach to the Eastern Docks, and into the new steel-and-glass slab built to accommodate the Hovercraft passengers.

To the north, through the broad windows, she could see the stone piles of the Castle, the Pharos, and St. Mary's Church and the Keep. She had the Welsh affinity for gloomy, ancient stone-works and she wondered if Alek might possibly allow them the time to walk up to the Castle. But perhaps there would be another time, she thought, and hurried along through the sparse group of welcomers toward the seaward wing of the building.

The Eastern Docks had been extended southward to expand the docking facilities for the larger Hovercraft, and now she could look seaward to where one of the great bustling machines was approaching in a flurry of spray and propeller-driven wind. The thin sunshine caught the mists and turned them into a rainbow of color that delighted her. Alek was returning in a watery aurora of light that shaded from deep violet through green and yellow to red. She paused at the window to watch as the Hovercraft maneuvered to approach the dock directly below where she stood.

The transport officials were announcing the arrival, and people began gathering near the passageway from the dock area. She watched the Hovercraft turn, sidle into its slip, and then settle deeper as the air-cushion fans slowed. The gangway was secured in position and the passengers from Calais began to dis-embark.

Bronwen caught sight of Alek moving in the crowd flowing toward the terminal. He was hatless, dressed in a dark suit, and he carried a canvas overnight case and a dark Burberry folded over his arm. As he passed from the dock to the gangway, he raised his eyes and caught sight of her at the railed window above. He did not wave, but smiled briefly. She raised a hand in greeting as he passed under the entry port and onto the ramp leading to the upper level of the terminal.

She turned to watch the passengers emerging from the ramp. Alek appeared, walking swiftly. She started toward him, and then paused reflexively as two men in the waiting band stepped forward between her and Alek.

They wore workmen's clothes. One carried a leather jacket over his arm, concealing his right hand. Bronwen was startled to see the expression on Alek's face—surprise mingled with stark terror.

The first shot sounded flat, like the popping of a blown-up paper bag. Bronwen did not recognize the sound, nor did the passengers moving around Alek into the terminal. But Bronwen saw Alek flung backward as though by an unseen blow, and a nameless panic took her.

The second shot was unmistakable. It crashed, resounding through the steel-and-glass enclosure of the building. Alek, strangely on his knees and crouching as though in pain, held a short-barreled revolver in his hand. He had dropped his travel case and Burberry. As Bronwen watched, the weapon discharged again, and the man carrying the leather jacket sprawled on the tiled floor, twitching and kicking and smearing the white surface with red.

Passengers were shouting, pressing back. They fled from Alek and the two strangers, pushing and shoving to get clear. The second man now stepped closer to Alek, and this time Bronwen saw the gun in his hand. It was silenced, though she did not know the purpose of the heavy cylinder attached to the muzzle. The weapon popped five times in rapid succession. Alek slumped into a supine position, his leg grotesquely bent under him. Bronwen saw the puff of torn fabric as each bullet struck, and she screamed and ran forward, her mind a jumble of terrorized impressions.

Everywhere people were running and shouting. The man who stood over Alek turned and collided with Bronwen, struck at her with the automatic in his hand, shoved her aside. She stumbled and fell, tearing her stocking and scraping her knee. The floor felt slimy and cold beneath her hands. She crawled toward Alek as the man who had knocked her down ran toward the exit. A uniformed constable, running into the building across the elevated walkway from the car park, moved to stop the escaping man. There were two more soft pops, and the constable sprawled, his face a mask of brilliant blood. Then the assailant was gone.

Bronwen came to her feet, staggering, fell again, and managed to reach Alek. His shirt was bloody, his eyes half open and glazing. She could hear, to her horror, the sound of his breathing bubbling through the terrible wounds in his chest. His hand opened, and the small revolver clattered to the floor.

It seemed, as she cradled his head, that he recognized her briefly. His lips moved, and she strained to hear what he was saying to her. It was three words without meaning to her. He whispered: "Yellow—case—yellow—" She held his lolling head against her breast. She could hear herself sobbing hysterically. It was as though she were outside her body, watching and listening—as though this horror were unreal, a part of some ghastly theater.

A heavy-faced man, pale and wide-eyed, said: "What did he say? What was that he said?"

Bronwen made no response. She was oblivious to everyone, everything, except the torn body she clutched. Then her gaze rose.

There was a sea of faces around them now, white faces, mouths and eyes open, gaping. *"Help him—"* Bronwen heard her own voice, shrill and distant.

The heavy-jowled man touched two fingers to Alek's neck. "He's dead," he said thickly, and turned away.

Bronwen bowed her head almost to the floor and was sick.

8

The man on the pallet seemed barely alive. His injuries had been treated, but roughly. This was not due to any particular animosity felt by the medical attendants, but, rather, because the facilities at Turfan were limited.

The hospital scarcely deserved the name. It consisted of a corrugated-iron shed of less than fifty square meters. It was hot in the summertime and bitterly cold in the winter. Now, beyond the pair of windows facing south, a steady fall of snow blanketed the marshy ground in the Depression, and the temperature inside the hospital was nearly freezing.

Comrade Dr. Soong, an aging man with sad, deep-set eyes, had done his best with the spy. But conditions at Turfan and the extent of the man's injuries—incurred in what Dr. Soong had been told was a remarkable resistance to capture—made survival unlikely.

At this moment the doctor was unwillingly engaged in a procedure that he felt certain would remove whatever possibility existed that the man on the pallet might recover. Under his direction, a medical orderly had replaced the plasma drip with a flask of sodium amytal solution.

For the last twenty-four hours the spy had been semiconscious and had periodically been subjected to interrogations by both the Chairman of the Workers, Peasants, and Soldiers Council, young Chou Tsing-wen, and the director of the Turfan project, Comrade Engineer Li Chin himself. The results of the questioning sessions had been unsatisfactory, as Dr. Soong had warned them they would be. The man was not only gravely injured and near to comatose, but he was obviously a trained agent who had been prepared to die in the event of capture. Only the sudden violence of the final assault on his position out in the Talimupendi had prevented his using the cyanide needle Dr. Soong had found on his person.

But now, on Comrade Li's authority, the spy was to be drugged and interrogated under narcosynthesis. The doctor had warned that it was far more likely that the man would die than that he would produce useful information. But Li had insisted, and Comrade Chou, the only person at Turfan to whom Dr. Soong could appeal, supported the decision. "It does not matter if the revisionist dies, so long as he provides us with the answers the Comrade Engineer requires," he said.

Dr. Soong noted that the Chairman was phrasing his permission in such a way as to make clear that it was Li Chin's decision and responsibility. That could be important if the manner of dealing with the Russian spy should ever become a matter to be examined by the Central Committee in Peking.

In fact, young Chou had absented himself the moment the sodium amytal drip was put in place on the rack by the spy's pallet. Dr. Soong was reasonably certain that the dispensary was wired, and that, in addition to the electronic surveillance, the Chairman would have a firsthand report from the medical technician administering the drug.

Soong, his fingertips on the spy's weak pulse, looked soberly up at Engineer Li and said, "I make one final protest, Comrade Li. I do not think you will obtain anything useful by this method, and it is very likely that the depressant effect of the amytal will kill him."

Li, his American-tainted Mandarin sounding strange to Soong's ear, replied, "Perform your function, Comrade Doctor, and allow me to perform mine."

"My function is to heal him if I can," Soong said. He sounded argumentative, he knew, but he could not suppress the sense of outrage he felt at what he was being forced to do. "He has multiple fractures, a head injury of unknown severity, internal bleeding, and he shows signs of increasing pulmonary edema. The best you can hope for is some delirious nonsense. The worst is that the questions he might answer for you if he should be allowed to recover will remain unanswered forever."

Li's black eyes glittered with anger. "Do your job, Comrade Doctor."

Dr. Soong shrugged his thin shoulders and nodded to the technician to start the drip. In the cold air of the room, the occupants' breath condensed. The slow, liquid sound of the spy's respiration grew slower still.

Choy Balsan lay on a dark, icy plain in the small hours of a windless night. Fragmented images floated through his brain:

He rode his shaggy pony in a dimly seen caravan. The others all wore fur parkas and the skin hats with the upturned cheek-pieces that he remembered his father and uncles wearing when he was a child in Kazakhstan.

In those days his people had still lived in felt yurts on wagons. They drank kumiss, the fermented milk of the mares in the horse herds, and they had been free to roam across the steppe where the wind never ceased to blow and the sea of grasses rippled underfoot.

He remembered the shore of the Caspian Sea, the round pebbles in the muddy plain of the beach, and the small, swift waves—tideless, dappled with thin sunshine and cloud—lapping at the shore. In the distance lay the snowy heights of the Hindu Kush and the high passes through which the tribe moved each change of season, driving the horses from the desert banks of the Caspian to the beaches of the Sea of Aral and on to the east, across Kazakhstan and through the lands of the Kirghiz to the Chinese border.

In those days the people moved freely, far more freely than the more civilized citizens of the Soviet Union. They moved, in fact, with almost the same deliberate ease as their ancestors had, for a millennium or more, across thousands of leagues, as simply and as naturally as the winds or the seasons.

Then again, much later, already a man and a soldier, he seemed to remember that he had made that journey once again. He, Choy Balsan, who had learned about supersonic aircraft and tanks and weapons that burst like the sun breaking the dawn sky, had once again made that journey across the old lands astride a shaggy pony with a spear and a bow across his back. Someone, somewhere, seemed to be asking him *why*. He felt a darkness growing inside him and wondered if he was dying. If so, he wished that the insistent voice would grow silent and let him deal with his mortal memories in an orderly way, as befit a warrior with the blood of conquerors in his veins.

Now he sat in a brightly lighted room, and there were others. No Mongols. These were men from the far west. Blond, blue-eyed, some of them. He had known many of these Russians and yet they remained strange to him—but not the man who stood before them speaking. There was nothing strange about Leonov.

He remembered now. He was in Frunze. The light was summer sunshine slanting through high windows into the lecture hall. The Russians around him hung on Leonov's words. He did, too. The man was magnetic, harsh, brilliant.

"Who is he?" The intrusive question was spoken in faulty Russian.

Why, he was Colonel Leonov, of course. What sort of fool could ask such a question at the Frunze Academy? Officers from all the forces, from all over the Soviet Union, came to hear Colonel Yuri Ivanovich Leonov lecture. They came by invitation. It was an honor to be chosen.

"Do you mean Marshal Leonov? The Minister of Defense?"

Leonov, *Leonov,* that was all. That was all anyone needed to know. He was delivering one of the Crisis Confrontation Lectures. They were famous in the Air Force and the Army. The man had a way of twisting and turning chance and possibility and opportunity so that the facets glittered like the facets of jewels. To recognize opportunities, to grasp the moment—that was what Leonov held out before his pupils, the ability to act with swiftness and daring.

It was said that once one had been a student of Colonel Leonov's, one never need be concerned about advancement in the forces. Men and women trained by Leonov, men and women who would always know and advance a fellow-disciple, were everywhere in the Soviet Army, the Air Force, the Navy. They formed a brotherhood.

The darkness inside him swelled, blotting out some of the memories, but there was still Leonov.

Comrade Dr. Soong tugged at the skirt of Engineer Li's quilted jacket. Li, bent over the spy, turned impatiently.

"The man is dead," Dr. Soong said.

"Impossible. He can't be. He was speaking."

"Dead, Comrade Li," Soong said again, despising the American, the foreign devil with a Chinese face, the man of no refinement, the bourgeois. "The man is dead. Depart. *Go.* There is nothing here for you now."

9

Overton's, in St. James's Street, was experiencing its hour of quiet. The dinner crowd had not yet collected. Harry Grant and the SIS man Ian Ballard were in almost sole possession of the dining room. A waiter, who evidently knew Ballard's habits, hovered near the door with his trolley of liqueurs and cigars.

Grant regarded his companion with barely suppressed anger. Ballard was a handsome man, youthful-appearing despite the streaking of gray in his longish hair. His blue eyes seemed innocent and veiled the mockery conveyed by his casual pose and affected use of old-fashioned expressions. His jaws worked steadily on the excellent Dover sole he had ordered at Grant's expense. He had also ordered a second bottle of Pouilly-Fuissé and he sipped at the wine appreciatively. British civil servants, he explained, were on short rations and it was a pleasure to meet with an American functionary who could still afford a good table. "Bashing the old expense account is about the only way we poor cloak-and-dagger wallahs can still get a decent meal," he'd said with an engaging smile.

Grant, on the other hand, had scarcely been able to eat his dinner. His stomach was knotted with frustration.

"I truly am sorry, old man," Ballard said again, putting down his wine glass. "But there it is. I suppose we should have guessed someone would chop the fellow. But we are awfully short-handed these days, you know. There are more people keeping track of tax evaders than there are in Special Branch and our shop put together. And, frankly, it simply didn't occur to us that it might happen—at least not so quickly. He only spoke to us a fortnight ago."

"But you *had* a man on him," Grant said.

Ballard wiped his lips carefully. "Yes, we did. The fellow's earned himself a rocket and he shall get it. But realistically, old man, there wasn't much he could have done about it. These two gunmen simply walked up to Voronin and opened fire. The dead one, by the way, we've identified as a peculiarly nasty sort who learned his ways during the troubles in Londonderry and took it up as a career after we gave the place back to the bog-trotters. Anyone could have hired him."

"Anyone?"

Ballard signaled to the waiter at the trolley. "Yes, I suppose you're thinking of the KGB." He fell silent until he had made a selection of a Cuban cigar and a balloon glass of Courvoisier from the trolley. "Sure you won't join me, old man? The cognac is first-rate." When Grant shook his head in irritation, Ballard dismissed the waiter and puffed the cigar ceremoniously alight from a meticulously held match. "Yes, well, that would be the natural assumption. Their Wet Operations boys found out Voronin had the wind up and was considering a change and so they chopped him. It is possible, of course—though it's not their style in this country to hire ex-Provos. Former members of the Provisional Irish Republican Army, that is. Too unreliable, you see. You might give one of those fellows a pound of gelignite to terminate a defector and find out they'd touched it off at Covent Garden—" he looked around the quiet dining room—"or here, for that matter."

He swirled the cognac in the glass and put his thin, high-arched nose over the rim appreciatively. "Still, they could have done it. Except for one thing. There was a known KGB agent on the scene—at the Hovercraft terminal—when Voronin was shot down. Now that is definitely *not* their style. Our man saw him step up to the girl and ask something of her. I'd give several quid to know what he wanted to know, by the way. The point is that he *was* known, and the people in the Embassy here aren't stupid. They pretty well know which of their muscle men we can identify. So my guess is that he was simply there to follow Voronin and see what he could see. Probably someone else was on to him in Calais and on the Hovercraft." Ballard smiled grimly, and suddenly his blue eyes looked anything but innocent to Grant. "According to our man, he looked almost as startled as Voronin did when the shooting started."

"What about the second gunman?" Grant asked. "Any chance he might be found?"

"Unlikely," Ballard said. "A constable tried to stop him and got his head shot off, poor sod. We still haven't got round to arming our policemen, you know, though I doubt it would have made a difference. If he was a Provo—and I suspect he was—a constable had no chance with him." He sipped cognac and savored a puff on the cigar. "Nor would we, for that matter. Even if we could catch the fellow—which we can't—and drug him—which is illegal, of course—or connect him to the house current—which would be immoral—we still wouldn't get anything out of him. I'm sure someone simply hired him by telephone, sent him and his teammate to Dover with a good description of Colonel Voronin. It would be simple to arrange, don't you agree? Surely it could even happen in America, Grant, old man? I mean, in spite of the Teachers of Righteousness who supervise intelligence work for your Congress?"

The heavy irony did little to improve Grant's dark mood. "Why did Voronin suddenly take off for Calais? Did anyone from your department follow him?"

"Good Lord, old man, no. Britain's a poor country these days. We can't afford to have people doing that sort of work when they can make more money being shop stewards. Voronin was yours. We gave him to you. I would have assumed the local Agency people would take care of him, at least until you arrived.

But I suppose you had your own reasons for not handling it that way."

The thrust was well aimed, and below the belt, Grant thought. This Ballard could be a proper bastard. But he was exactly right, of course. The London Station Chief of the CIA had not been informed about Colonel Voronin's potential defection, and the reason was as obvious to Ballard as it was to Grant. From London CIA, the wires would have hummed to that Miniluv in Virginia. Within hours, or perhaps even minutes, the word would have reached the Senate Overwatch Committee and Senator DeWitt Goddamn Sutton. Who would stop him from leaking it without a moment's hesitation to Grant's own good friend Jane McNary, or if Jane was unavailable on Air Force One, to Jane's staff of young destroyers? By morning the information that a Colonel Voronin was considering flight to the West would appear on the press-service teletype and Voronin would be dead, or in protective custody, another way of saying the same thing.

But, damn it, Grant thought, Voronin *was* dead. The difference was simply that it was not the KGB who had killed him. Then who? And why?

Ballard was watching Grant alertly. "I suspect you are asking yourself some rather sticky questions, old man."

"I am. Old man," Grant said.

Ballard grinned, and for the first time Grant grudgingly found that he liked him a little. "That is a poser, isn't it? If the uglies from State Security didn't chop Colonel Alek, who did? And, much more to the point, why did they? Oh, he was doubledealing and looking to run, that's true enough. But in this day and age of glorious détente, people don't always get shot down for considering a change. In fact, defection isn't really popular now that we have all decided the Russians are really only misguided socialists. And then there's always a chance a defector will be shopped back at some high-level conference. But something had Voronin upset to the point of taking that chance."

Ballard shrugged his shoulders in a very non-English interrogative.

"Colonel Voronin had some exalted connections," Grant said.

Ballard nodded and tapped the brandy snifter with a fingernail. It made a mellow, ringing sound. "Yes. Minister of Defense Marshal of the Air Force Yuri I. Leonov." A rueful smile played over his regular features. "I believe your people refer to him as 'Boyar.' "

Grant was caught by surprise and showed it.

"I'm sorry, old man. But there is no such thing as a secure American secret since you appointed that commission or committee or whatever you call it," Ballard said. He continued apologetically, embarrassed for his American visitor. "That is why we have to be so careful in dealing with you. The chaps in SIS and DI-6—Defence Intelligence does sound less provocative than Military Intelligence—are not so certain as you that openness is the way to salvation." He paused, as though considering whether or not he could continue in this vein without offending. Finally he said evenly, "Have you considered the possibility that the word on the good Colonel's intentions leaked somewhere on your side of the pond?"

Grant held back an angry retort. The trouble was that he was not at all certain. In recent years too many dissident junior officials in the government seemed to feel justified in transmitting privileged information. Reward was as much a possibility as censure. What mattered most was *who* was told and on *what* terms.

"Sorry about that," Ballard continued, "but it needed to be said. You may want to consider the possibility, anyway." He relighted the cigar and drew on it carefully. "Sad, isn't it?" he said, looking at it. "We can have things like this, but our great-hearted socialist leaders have seen to it that no one can afford them—" again the rueful smile—"unless there's an American capitalist on hand to pay for them." It was, Grant realized, an elliptical and rather gracious apology for his criticism of the American mania for self-destructive disclosure.

Grant said, "The girl. What can you tell me about her?"

"Voronin's mistress, you mean. Well, not a great deal, actually. I'm not so sure there's much worth knowing. She dances with a tuppenny company. The Celeste. Know much about the ballet?"

Grant shook his head.

"Pity," Ballard said. "Marvelous spectator sport. I believe you chaps would call it girl-watching. And since so many of the male dancers are limp-wristed—by repute, at least—one can be envious of them without being jealous, if you get my meaning."

"I think I do."

"Bronwen Wells is her name. Thirtyish. Good, but hardly a great dancer. Not *prima ballerina assoluta* material by a long chalk. Mostly does things like the *pas de quatre* in *Swan Lake*. Too small, actually, to do the really demanding roles. And, as I say, not really that proficient."

"So much for her professional qualifications," Grant said dryly. "What else?"

"I think Voronin loved her. In his fashion, as Dowson would have said."

"Do you think she influenced his decision to defect?"

"We don't know for certain that he had made such a decision."

"Someone did."

"Touché. You may well have something there. Actually, I'd wager he never discussed the possibility with Miss Wells. That is not to say that his relationship with her didn't affect his loyalty to—to whomever he was, in fact, loyal. A man can get lonely, displaced. Then suddenly a woman moves into his life and he takes a fresh look at things. There was never any suggestion that Voronin might change sides before he took up with Bronwen Wells."

"How long had he served in the London Embassy?"

"Something over two years. He was due for reassignment. It has been suggested by some of our thinkers that that was the reason for his sudden journey to Calais. But I don't agree." Ballard looked speculatively at Grant. "You work for the President—personally, I take it?"

Grant hedged. "I work for the President's Air Force Aide."

"But this is hardly a routine assignment for an ordinary Air Force officer," Ballard said. "Ergo, you are not an ordinary Air Force officer."

Grant remained silent. It could do no good to admit that he had often performed tasks mightily resembling intelligence jobs for President Lambert. Let Ballard think what he liked.

"The reason I ask is that the good Colonel Voronin had a connection—well, perhaps that overstates the case—a few, let us say, contacts in the Foreign Office. I could never understand how persons of good education, favored by society in every way, the sort that often find their way into the Foreign Service—and your State Department, for that matter—can convince themselves that Communism is the wave of the future. But they do, and men like Voronin always manage to find them. I sometimes wonder if—but never mind what I wonder. The point is that Voronin had a meeting with one of our FO ideologues—chap who, perhaps coincidentally, perhaps not, was in charge of co-ordinating your President's itinerary for this Sissinghurst conference. We collected the fellow immediately Voronin got the hammer." He gave Grant a half-challenging look. "We can still do that in this country, you know. Assuming such things as the movements of a visiting Head of State can be classified as Official Secrets. So far he hasn't admitted to giving Colonel Voronin anything more sensitive than lunch conversation, but we are holding him just the same. We worry about presidents who travel in Britain, you see."

Grant frowned, knowing that he should be alarmed and yet feeling that despite what Ballard was suggesting, Aleksandr

Voronin, a Soviet military attaché, would not involve himself or his country in some obvious plot against the President of the United States.

"If you think there could be some sort of assassination plan, say so," Grant said.

"I don't think so," Ballard answered. "Oh, of course we are taking precautions. A great many of them. But my instinct says no. It is simply something I thought you should know. This FO person *was* in charge of travel arrangements. As I say, it could be pure coincidence that he met Voronin, and that Voronin rushed off to Calais and then got himself killed rather melodramatically in the Hovercraft terminal."

The situation had turned into a closed circle, Grant thought, a shape impossible to penetrate. But this was illusion. There was always a way.

"In any case," Ballard said, "you may feel your job is finished. Obviously there's nothing to be done about Colonel Alek."

Grant instantly recognized a probe. Ballard certainly felt that his job was far from done.

"Have you spoken to the girl? To this Bronwen Wells?"

Ballard said, "Not yet. I rather thought I'd offer you first innings with her. That is, in case you don't feel your job is finished. In view of our unfortunate lapse at Dover, I think we owe you that."

Grant could not avoid remarking on Ballard's choice of words. "Is that what it was? An unfortunate lapse?"

"If it's any satisfaction to you, Grant, I'm as bloody annoyed as you that it happened."

"Well, I have some time before I have to report to the President at Sissinghurst," Grant said, watching Ballard to see if he could detect any reaction to the misdirecting phrase. He could not. Either Ballard was extraordinarily good at his work or he didn't know that Grant would be meeting the President at Hurn, not Sissinghurst. "Is she being watched now?"

"Rather too well," Ballard said. "Special Branch have her

under surveillance. There is nothing, actually, she's suspected of, by the way. But Special Branch are interested in the people who *also* are watching her. These things can get complicated."

Grant considered. It was logical, at least to the Russian mind, to set the local KGB *rezidentura* onto Bronwen Wells. She had, after all, been the mistress of a Russian official. It was highly unlikely that the Soviets at the Embassy had been delighted with Colonel Voronin's personal arrangements. So it would make sense to a Russian to keep the girl under close surveillance.

"Will you go and see her?" Ballard asked.

"Yes," Grant said. It was a meeting he had little stomach for. The girl would be in shock, or at least deeply depressed. But there was no avoiding it. It would have to be done, and promptly.

"I rather thought you would, so I came prepared," Ballard said. He took out his billfold and extracted from it a small photograph. "Bronwen Wells," he said.

The print was a reduction of what may have been intended for use in some promotional publicity for a ballet tour. The face that looked back at Grant from the photograph was oddly appealing, though verging on plainness. The narrow brows were framed by a straight black cap of hair that accentuated the spacing of the solemn eyes. There was a sadness in Bronwen Wells's face that seemed to fix her expression into a signature of melancholy, despite the fact that the photographer had probably told her to smile as he took the picture.

"Unremarkable face, wouldn't you say?" Ballard commented. "Yet there is something appealing there. I've seen her dance at the Festival Hall. Something comes across. It isn't talent—but something. Poignancy, perhaps. If you don't know the form, it might not strike you." He shrugged in that almost Gallic way again. "There are dozens like her in every Welsh mining town. There's a couple of hundred years of malnutrition behind those eyes."

"Seems an odd choice for Voronin," Grant said. "I understand he had something of a reputation as a womanizer."

"Pre-Wells, old chap. *Le coeur a ses raisons que la raison ne connaît point.*"

"Yes," Grant said thoughtfully, less than twelve hours out of brittle Jane McNary's bed. "The heart does have its reasons." He handed the photograph back to Ballard, who put it away in his billfold.

But, Grant thought, they were dealing with the now very still heart of Colonel Aleksandr Voronin. And, more to the point, with his now unplumbable mind. Seeking an answer through the labyrinth of a grieving woman's emotions was not a task that appealed to Harry Grant. He was suddenly reminded of something his former wife had said to him once. One of the pilots in his squadron had died in an accident, and it had fallen to Grant to carry the news to his young widow. He had done it badly, more brusquely than he had intended, and Bethany had said, "Love makes you uneasy, Harry. Is that why you are so cruel?" He had not intended to be cruel, never that.

"I'll see her tonight," he said.

"With respect, old man," Ballard said, "I'd suggest you let it rest until tomorrow. She's had a very bad time today."

Ballard was right, of course. Grant felt a sense of urgency, of time slipping away. But he could not logically say why this unease. He would not meet the President at Hurn for almost three days. And now he realized that he was weary, achingly tired. He signaled the waiter to bring the bill and settled up. The price was shocking. He had not been in London for more than three years, and in that time the inflation had boosted prices by thirty percent or more. He wondered how someone like Bronwen Wells—or Ian Ballard, for that matter—could live in England. Yet they, and millions of others, did. It was a quality the British had, a quality he admired. They coped.

"Splendid meal, Grant. I thank you for it," Ballard said. "It's back to bangers and beer for me until you call again. Still, it's better than wormy rice and slop tea."

The obvious reference to the sort of rations prisoners of the North Vietnamese received aroused Grant's interest.

"Oh, we know quite a good bit about you, Colonel," Ballard said, smiling grimly. "We have a few things in common, you and I. I spent a year and a half in the bag in Korea. First the Koreans and then the bloody heathen Chinee had a go at me."

"I didn't know that," Grant said.

"No reason you should, old man. Just a point of mutual interest. I daresay you don't care to dwell on it any more than I do. Those nasty unfriendlies are not the best hosts in the world."

"No," Grant said with feeling.

"They had a good go at me, I must say. When they couldn't change my social outlook, they decided to starve me, and when that didn't work, they spent most of the day and all the night working out ways to impress me with their four-thousand-year-old civilization." He held up his hands. The immaculately clean fingernails were ugly and deformed. "But you know all about that."

"Yes," Grant said, thinking of his own scars and how he got them and not really wanting to remember too well. Still, it was interesting that Ballard's experiences and his should parallel this way.

"Anyway, thank you again for the feast," Ballard said, cutting off the discussion. "Shall I hear from you soon?"

"Count on it," Grant said.

He walked back to the Stafford Hotel through Blue Ball Yard strangely disturbed by his talk with the Englishman. For a moment he had seen the feral light of a real, consuming hatred there. Perhaps that was why Ballard had found his way into SIS, where the war, cold or hot, had never stopped.

10

The Chairman of the Central Committee of the Communist party of the People's Republic of China sat alone in a room that had once housed the porcelains of a dowager empress.

Chung Yee, a man in his late fifties, had survived a half-dozen "cultural revolutions" to become the most powerful man in a cabal of powerful men in Peking. As a student, he had marched in the first Great Proletarian Cultural Revolution. At the head of a Red Guard cadre he had overturned a university faculty, driven "bourgeois" teachers into the countryside, and helped to shout the demon Lin Piao into the flight toward Russia that had ended in the burning wreckage of a shot-down airplane in Sinkiang.

Chung had learned the lessons of power early, and learned them well. In the most recent, the so-called *New,* Cultural Revolution, student and soldier cadres had attempted to unsettle the Central Committee and drive Chung (an "old man" with "revisionist thoughts") out of the Forbidden City. He had reacted with a violence that would have done credit to Chairman Mao. Students disappeared; soldiers were summarily shot. The committees, councils, and cadres formed in the enthusiasm of the New Cultural Revolution's beginning remained, but Chung saw to it that they limited their discussions to such matters as working conditions, ideology, and self-criticism. Decisions relating to national policy were made here, in the mural-decorated Porcelain Room of the old Imperial Palace of Peking.

Chairman Chung, in common with many of his countrymen, was an inveterate gambler. Unlike most gamblers, he was also lucky. His thirty years of upward movement in the leadership of a society that rewarded failure with exile or death was, to him, proof of good fortune.

Now he sat at a Tang Dynasty lacquered table thoughtfully considering the report—and request—from the American renegade Li Chin.

The decision to fund the Dragon project at Turfan had not been a popular one in the Central Commtitee. Chung's gambler's instinct had convinced him that the garrulous bureaucrats on the Central Committee were wrong.

Earlier that day, Foreign Minister Teng Chou-p'ing had reported that the Americans proposed to visit Peking, secretly, in the interest of a peaceful settlement of the long-standing Sino-Russian quarrel. It was a measure of the Americans' immaturity and naïveté that President Lambert assumed that he could interpose himself and his country between the combatants in history's deadliest struggle. Since the break with the Soviet Union in the 1950s, the People's Republic had been involved in a contest for the Marxist leadership of the world. For Lambert to imagine that he could mediate this death struggle was the wish of a political child. But even children, when they commanded the nuclear power of the United States, had to be handled with care.

At another time, the intervention of the Americans might serve Chung's purposes. But it happened that a "peace mission" now—a mission that must, in the interests of world opinion, be received—was not convenient. Chinese troops had recently moved into northern India, challenging the growing Soviet influence in Delhi. A quiet infiltration of Burma was under way, and a Chinese-supported faction—the Front for African Liberation— had begun, after ten years of effort, to drive back the Soviet-sponsored forces in those Third World countries. A mission arriving in China now, bearing "concessions" from the revisionist bandits in the Kremlin, would expect balancing concessions from the government of the People's Republic.

Chung had not spent five years advancing the cause of World Maoism so that his gains could be squandered by the Americans in exchange for worthless Soviet promises.

Chung considered Li Chin's request against this background. The room was still. Outside, in the gray light, old women were sweeping the newly fallen snow from the streets leading to the Square of Heavenly Peace. Sometimes the Chairman had the unsettling feeling that despite all that the party had done, despite all that it could do, nothing would ever be very different in China. It was a very un-Marxist thought, he knew, but the things that made the nation and the people unique were immutable. Once a dowager empress had sat in this room, fondling her rare porcelains—and old women had swept the snow from the streets of Peking. In those days, people had starved in the mountains when the crops failed in the south. Today, in spite of what the New China News Agency told the world, they still starved in the north when the crops failed in the south.

China, Chung thought, would never be different until it could dominate not only all of Asia, but all of the Third World as well. There was not enough land to support China's industrious millions. Expansion was the only answer for the future. And he, Chung, successor to Hua Kuo-feng and the sainted Mao, had made a start. He had no mind to bargain it away to the Americans.

Therefore, he thought, they must not come. Not now.

He raised his opaque black eyes to the mural on the wall facing him. It was a painting of the Long March. A youthful, powerful Chairman Mao pointed the way. Soldiers in immaculately clean quilted uniforms marched against a backdrop of steep mountains and, in the distance, burning villages. Who burned the villages, Chung wondered: was it the Japanese, the American puppets? Or was it we who burned the villages, as once Greeks had burned their boats, so that there could be no return?

Such gambles formed the linchpins on which history turned.

The Russians had managed to penetrate the Dragon project's

security with a spy. How much they knew of the capabilities of Li's device could only be surmised. But they must be frightened. The Dragon could make China invulnerable to nuclear-missile attack. Some in the Kremlin might now be arguing that it was only a single, experimental, *untried* device.

The elements of a coup, a stunning gamble, were all present. Chung felt the familiar thrill of recognition, the inner joy of a run of cards at fan-tan, or a lucky throw of the dice. Here, on the table before him, were the cards he could play to sabotage the presumptuous American mission, and to make the criminals in the Kremlin tremble with fear and suspicion.

Li proposed to "test" the laser on a Russian Svoboda satellite, one of the half dozen or so that passed insolently over Lop Nor and Turfan each day.

Let it be done, Chung thought, while the Americans are in Moscow.

He took a brush from a jade holder, dipped it into a handsome porcelain inkpot. With great delicacy and some pride in his ability to form the beautiful characters, he wrote on Li's report the single word "Proceed."

11

The men from the Soviet Embassy, three of them, came just after dawn. They pressed the bell impatiently until Bronwen, her mind dulled with the residue of the sleeping pills she had taken, opened the door to her Hampstead flat.

Outside, in the still-dusky street, she saw but barely noticed the Metropolitan Police Ford sedan and the two uniformed men watching. She did not know, or care, why they were there. It seemed unimportant. Everything seemed unimportant and clouded in her mind.

She came to the door in a carelessly tied robe, her feet bare, her hair uncombed. Her eyes were red and shadowed, but she was done with weeping now. She staggered slightly as she walked, her dancer's balance upset by the barbiturates she had used to blunt the grief and horror of Alek's murder.

"You are Bronwen Wells, please?" The tallest of the three spoke in accents that reminded her of her lover, but his command of the language was imperfect. He was young, with short blond hair and a round, flat-featured face. The room seemed to pitch, and she supported herself with a hand on the doorjamb. One of the others made a comment in Russian and the blond man said something to him in a harsh voice.

Again he spoke to her. "You are Bronwen Wells?" His manner was patient, but his voice was flat and impersonal—the sort of voice one heard in a welfare office or at some harassed National Health Service doctor's surgery. "You are she, please?"

Bronwen nodded. "Yes. Bronwen Wells."

The young man took a paper from his pocket and held it out for her to inspect. She could not read it through the barbiturate haze.

"Examine it, please."

She touched the paper, stared at it and then up at the Russian's face.

He said, "We are from the Embassy of the USSR. We have come for the private possessions of Aleksandr Voronin. We have this paper from a British magistrate."

Alek—she could see him falling, his leg twisted beneath him. She could see his blood on the floor of the terminal. Her stomach tightened as she staggered, and she would have fallen had not the Russian caught her by the arm and held her steady. His hand felt hard and cold on her bare skin.

One of the policemen from the black Ford had got out of the car and walked up to the entrance to the flat. "Is everything all right, Miss?"

The Russian held out the paper, and the policeman read it through, slowly and carefully.

"This says that these three gentlemen are authorized to collect the personal belongings of a Mr. Voronin, deceased, Miss."

"Alek," Bronwen said. "Yes."

"They are from the Russian Embassy, Miss," the policeman said, his tone guarded and disapproving.

"Yes," she said again. "I understand."

"May we please proceed?" the young Russian asked.

Bronwen stepped aside and leaned against the wall of the narrow hall. The policeman was looking at her intently. "Are you ill, Miss?"

She shook her head slowly. "Not ill, no."

The policeman returned reluctantly to his car. The Russians moved past her into the flat, ignoring her now that their authority was established.

They were going into Alek's flat, she thought. Alek's and

hers. Into the living room where he kept his books and music albums, past the electric fire where she had sat with him listening to *Swan Lake* and the *Firebird*—

One of the men walked down the passage to the bedroom, where the bed stood unmade and rumpled. Her clothes lay strewn about. They are going to take it all, she thought, and leave me nothing, nothing— It was all because Alek was dead. Her thoughts jostled against one another in panic.

The blond Russian said something to one of his men, who then went out to where a black Jaguar stood at the curb. He took out some metal suitcases and returned with them.

"Which, please, are his books?" the blond man asked.

Bronwen tried to collect herself. The blond stood by the bookcase, examining the volumes. She remembered Alek putting his library into the tall narrow shelves. ("I will teach you to read Russian," he said. He never had. She was poor with languages. And there stood Pushkin and Gogol in the original, unread.)

"You will see that we do not take anything that did not belong to Colonel Voronin, please."

Slowly Bronwen began to understand that these were men who worked with Alek, who were now gathering his belongings to return them to Russia. To his family? It was strange how little she had really known about Alek Voronin.

Her own books they had kept on the lower shelves. ("Because you are not so very tall," he had said.) Some novels, a few poems by sad Welshmen. The Russian poets were on the top shelves: Kirsanov, Voznesensky, Novella Matveyeve—

> The willow's crooked roots beneath the slope
> Are shaggy like a worn and tattered rope.

Alek's translation. (He was so pleased when she said it had a melancholy Welsh lilt.) She looked at the young Russian and asked: "Must you take his books?"

"I do not understand, please."

He understood well enough. They were taking everything.

They had never been pleased that Alek had been her lover. They did not share gracefully. Alek had told her that. But now everything belonged to them again. She gathered her robe about her and stared at the floor. Her head ached abominably. She did not remember the return from Dover. Someone had driven her back in her own car, but she did not know who. She had taken sleeping pills, remembered now that she had been tempted to take them all but she had been afraid.

The men in the bedroom had finished packing Alek's clothes. They came into the room with the steel cases and Alek's Vuitton suitcase (her gift). The blond young man told the others to open them.

"You will look, if you please, to see that nothing here belongs to you."

Bronwen looked blank-eyed at the open cases. Shirts, suits, some underwear, two pairs of shoes and one of galoshes. ("Your climate is good for frogs and salamanders," he said. They had laughed about the galoshes and the rain.)

"Nothing there belongs to me," she said. "He had some other things. With him. On the Hovercraft."

"Yes," the Russian said. "That has been taken care of." He paused expectantly and then said, "Is there another suitcase? A yellow one, perhaps?"

"Only that one," Bronwen said. "And the things he took to Calais."

"But not a yellow case?"

She shook her head.

The Russian turned abruptly to the bookshelves. He took the Russian copy of Gorky down. "These are his, of course?"

Bronwen, sick now with weariness, nodded.

The books came off the shelves in twos and threes, leaving lonely bare walls.

"Not that one," she said with an effort. The Russian held a book of poems. "That is mine," she said.

"Soviet poems?"

She took the book, a collection of verses of Kirsanov, and opened it to the flyleaf. "There," she said. "What does it say?"

The blond young man examined the Cyrillic writing. He nodded somberly. "It is inscribed to you from Colonel Voronin. My apologies, please. I did not know you spoke Russian."

"I don't," Bronwen said. There was no time to learn, she thought.

"Yes," the man said indifferently.

Bronwen closed the book and held it against her breast, pressing it hard into the flesh until the edges hurt her. This man felt nothing for her, for Alek. She could sense his emptiness. It struck her that the blond and his two silent helpers were from the KGB. Alek had told her once what sort of men worked for the secret police.

One of them closed the case containing the books. He spoke in Russian to his companions, who nodded. The blond said to Bronwen, "Papers. There are personal papers?"

"No." Why did she feel that these men were Alek's enemies, she wondered. She no longer wanted them in the flat. She wished they would go.

"Are there papers? Documents?" the man said again.

"None," Bronwen said. "Colonel Voronin never brought documents here. He said it was not permitted."

The blond Russian's gaze remained flat, impersonal as a basilisk's stare. "Very well, yes." He took a paper from his inside coat pocket together with a pen. "You will please sign this."

"What is it?"

"It is a paper saying that we have taken nothing of yours."

Nothing of mine, Bronwen thought. Only everything that Alek owned or wore or touched in this place—except me. Yes, they've left me me— She gave a short, broken laugh, and the young man seemed alarmed, perhaps fearful that she might become difficult or hysterical.

"If you please now," he said, thrusting the paper at her.

She wrote her name at the bottom of the page. The pen

slipped from her fingers. The Russian folded the paper and put it in an inside pocket before stooping to retrieve the pen. He made a sign to his men, who closed the remaining cases and carried them out.

"You are certain there is nothing more?" he asked. "Another—" for the first time, he fumbled for a word and used the Russian—"*portfels*—another piece of luggage?"

Bronwen said wearily, "You have everything."

"Yes, then." He nodded curtly and started for the door.

Suddenly she did not want him to go. She wanted him to stay and explain to her what had happened, and why. She said unsteadily, "Tell me, please—why did it happen?"

"I do not understand."

"Who did this to Alek?" Her voice sounded high-pitched in her ears, near to breaking.

The Russian shook his head abruptly. "That is the concern now of your English police. It is not a diplomatic matter." He walked to the door and opened it.

"I could bear it if I knew why, I think," Bronwen whispered.

"Good day. *Do svidaniya.*" The door closed behind him.

Bronwen stood in the empty hall. The cold chilled her feet, rose through her legs into her loins and belly. It was a polar, desolate cold. She began to tremble and she hugged herself with shaking arms, but she could not stop. She pressed her narrow back against the wall, and the wall was cold, too. Her legs would no longer hold her erect; she slid down against the wall to the floor, where she sat like a child, knees drawn up against chest and chin, eyes closed against the frigid morning light filtering through the thick beveled-glass panes of the door.

Grant found her that way.

12

Jane McNary sat in the press section of the new Air Force One and impatiently watched the daylight fade over Andrews Air Force Base. Her instincts told her that the press was being had by Cleveland Lambert, President of the United States.

The thirty or so members of the Washington press corps who had been invited to travel with the President had already turned the press section of the giant aircraft into a boozy, smoky shambles. Departure had been postponed and postponed again. Now the take-off for Heathrow was scheduled for sometime in the evening. There had been more than the usual speculation at the delays, but Lambert's stroke of genius—the generous and "open" gesture of allowing the White House correspondents actually to travel with him on Air Force One—had effectively subdued the reporters. They waited aboard the airplane, weary of speculation about what Lambert might be doing.

McNary's natural suspicion had been aroused earlier in the day when she had arrived at Andrews to discover that Grant was not among the White House staff people standing by for the President's arrival. Paul Lyman had appeared in the terminal press room to shepherd the reporters on board Air Force One with the story that there would be a short hour's delay because the First Lady had, of all things, twisted her ankle. The story was absurd enough to be true.

There would be a press conference, informal but on the record, Lyman said, as soon as Air Force One was airborne. Communications facilities for the reporters on board would be made available.

In response to McNary's pointed question on the whereabouts of the Iron Colonel, he had explained with deceptive frankness that Grant had gone on to London ahead of the main party "to confer with members of the American delegation to the Sissinghurst meeting." It was a typical Lyman statement, McNary thought, implying much but stating nothing at all. She was reasonably certain that when Grant left her he had had no intention of going to England ahead of the Presidential party. Unless, of course, there was some special significance to his early departure. In which case he had dissembled, a capability she was certain he had but seldom used with her, even though they were, in a sense, adversaries.

The second delay had been announced at four o'clock. Lyman was apologetic; the President was involved in an unexpected last-minute meeting with Secretary of State Kendrick and Soviet Ambassador Baturin. Air Force regulations would be relaxed enough to allow him to open the bar on board, the reporters who still smoked could, and food would be served forthwith.

McNary was now convinced that something unusual had happened. She considered deplaning and investigating, but there was the unspoken threat of being left behind should the President and his party suddenly arrive. The Lamberts could be leaving the White House by helicopter "at any time now."

The reporters' restlessness had risen to impatience. But with food and liquor, they had settled down to a noisy, quarrelsome, and bored wait, their suspicions blunted. McNary found this irritating and contemptible. It had not always been that way. A few years ago a delay would have had the Washington press corps reacting to every guess or rumor. McNary's eyes hardened with scorn. If these were the best adversaries the press could summon to watch Cleveland Lambert, the news media had come upon bad times.

She wondered about Harry Grant. It was unusual for him not to be traveling with the President. When she thought about

Grant, it was with an ambivalence she found unsettling. On the surface, Grant was a prime example of a person living by the values that she had long ago rejected. She still retained the contemptuous disdain for patriotism of her student days. Yet Grant was nothing if not a square-cornered patriot. She could—and did—excuse this as being a result of his lifelong association with another of her personal *bêtes noires,* the military. In her Marxist youth she had been exhorted to hate the American military. With the passage of years she had grudgingly modified this prejudice—the imperialist-military coups and oppressions she had been schooled to expect had failed to materialize. Her considerable intelligence, badly encrusted with slogan and Marxist dialectic began to re-emerge as her burgeoning career exposed her to the abrasive events of real life.

She still clung to the fantasy of American radicalism: that the world's evils sprang from capitalism. But she had begun to regard the Marxist world with increasing suspicion. It was undeniable that the ordinary citizen had little freedom in the people's democracies. She had imagined that she knew a great deal about the "People." They had obsessed her, filled her with guilt and indignation. But she knew, now as then, that the "People" were a collective abstraction. She would never know them. Her talent, her intelligence—and her arrogance—made such understanding a virtual impossibility. Grant taxed her with this. ("What do you really know about ordinary people? You can't stand being around people who aren't as clever as you, or who aren't as well educated, or who don't wash as often. Face it, McNary. You despise the common man.") When he did, it infuriated her, because it flicked her on raw nerves. What he said was disgustingly true.

Yet her dislike, amounting often to hatred, of the American middle-class values that had produced her—and her privileged world—was genuine.

McNary's ability to pick and choose the targets of her fury was not remarkable. Only the intensity of her invective made her unique. That, and her passionate, if transitory, sincerity. She found her relationship with Grant both satisfying and disturbing. She understood that she was, and always had been, a lustful woman. She made no apologies for it. She believed that if Grant had not been good in bed, she would express contempt for him and his bourgeois ways. Instead, she almost loved him, and this often angered her. She would be beholden to no man, in bed or out.

As a penance, at least in her mind, she made certain that President Cleveland Lambert, the man the Iron Colonel served so assiduously, received no charity in her philippics. And as the Washington winter evening approached and she, with all her disgruntled colleagues, waited in the air-conditioned cavern of Air Force One's lounge deck, McNary considered with acid pleasure the treatment she would give in her column to these unexplained delays.

13

The officers currently on duty within the pod stood rigidly at attention. The captain in nominal command was a Ukrainian, no more than twenty-five years old. His round, ruddy face was set into an expression of what he assumed, Leonov thought, must be stern, militarily correct resolution. The second officer, a senior lieutenant with a thin Semitic look to him, stared fixedly at the far wall of the pod, where the motto of the missile wing had been painted above the banks of instrument racks. It said, simply enough: DUTY, HONOR, OBEDIENCE. It was a motto strangely similar to that of the once-terrible Nazi Schutzstaffeln who had occupied and terrorized this land during the Great Patriotic War. Leonov wondered sardonically if the young men of the Aral'sk Strategic Rocket Regiment realized this. Probably not. The study of history was not a requirement for qualification as a missile officer. Perhaps it should be, he thought.

The Marshal nodded to General Oblensky, and the inspection party moved out of the control pod, through the six-foot-thick blast doors, into the silo proper.

The Americans had given these pits that name, and it was not really suitable. They contained not life, but death. A rather magnificent and overpowering form of death, to be sure, Leonov thought, but death nonetheless.

He stood with Oblensky and his aide on a narrow catwalk at the level of the SS-19's warhead. The unpainted metal of the missile's upper stages had a dull sheen under the fluorescent lights. By leaning forward, Leonov could look down along the fifteen-meter length of the rocket into the blast pit. The concrete well was pristine, painted a flat, nonreflective gray. No missile had ever been fired from the silos of the Aral'sk Regiment, even as a test. The place had a sterile odor of metal and new paint and ozone.

"What is your best fueling time, Comrade General?" Leonov asked.

Oblensky, a stock man with large blue eyes and a small, pursy mouth, said, "Twenty-three minutes, Comrade Minister."

Leonov returned to his scrutiny of the large missile. The SS-19 had been developed during the hiatus between SALT II and SALT III. The Americans, some of them, had quite rightly claimed that the new weapon violated the spirit, if not the letter, of the treaty; nevertheless, development and deployment had gone forward without delay. The official Soviet position had been, and remained, that the SS-19, despite its far greater throw weight than any American missile, was a defensive weapons system because it was liquid-fueled and could therefore not easily be used for a first strike.

Leonov had prepared the briefs on the SS-19 for the SALT III meeting himself. He had assured the Soviet negotiators that the position was reasonable. "You may argue with conviction and honor," he had said. "The Americans may even believe you."

The Americans had, of course, not believed the negotiators. A new missile capable of carrying five fifty-megaton warheads was difficult to present as a defensive device. The talks had bogged down on the matter of the SS-19, just as SALT II had foundered on the strategic bomber the Americans called "Back-fire."

The Marshal regarded the missile speculatively. The time required to prepare it for flight was, he thought, actually excessive. It did, in some degree, lessen its value as a pre-emptive strike weapon. But Soviet military science, even with the massive infusion of American computer technology détente had brought, had not been able to perfect a really reliable solid fuel for rockets of this size.

Leonov turned to Oblensky and nodded once more. The inspection party proceeded out of the silo to the underground railway that connected this missile and its pod with the regimental command center ten miles to the north.

Seated in the electric car, Leonov considered. The Aral'sk base could be closed for "security" when the President's airplane crossed into the Soviet Union. The fueling could begin when the American aircraft entered the air space of the Smolensk Air Traffic Control Center, three hundred and fifty kilometers from Moscow.

He knew that the time was near when he must brief Oblensky completely. The commander of this base must know exactly what was required of him.

While in the southernmost pod, Leonov had been notified that General Zabotin had arrived from Moscow and waited for him in the command center. General Oblensky's Junoesque second-in-command, Colonel Louisa Feodorovna, one of the last of Leonov's protégés from Frunze, waited with him.

Oblensky, Leonov thought, might be a problem. Of Polish descent, he was given to more emotional judgments than a proper Great Russian might be. At Frunze he had been a brilliant student, and Leonov had guided his subsequent career with the same purposeful benevolence he bestowed on all his chosen officers. But Oblensky showed some of the same character flaws that Aleksandr Voronin had had. The life of a general officer of the Soviet armed forces, more specifically of the Strategic Rocket Forces, was a favored one. And with privilege came always the threat of inner rot.

As long as a year ago, the Minister of Defense had sent Louisa Feodorovna to watch Oblensky. She had asked for, and received, carte blanche as to method. Women, Leonov often thought, were actually more ruthless than men could ever hope to be. They were as firm—or firmer—of purpose, and they were totally amoral in their selection of weapons. Oblensky had a reputation as a womanizer—just as Voronin had had. Major—

then, swiftly, Lieutenant Colonel and Colonel—Feodorovna had quickly contrived to share the General's bed *and* his confidence. Leonov considered himself fortunate to have her among his protégés. She was in her late thirties, not young but not old, voluptuous as only a Russian woman could be, and her intelligence was formidable. Though not what one would call beautiful, she had regular features and eyes as clear, blue, and innocent as any Komsomol maiden's.

It was a pity, Leonov thought with a twinge of regret, that he had never enjoyed Feodorovna himself. She, and a number of other women almost as gifted, had passed through Leonov's screening, training, and career guidance. He had never touched any of them. A man of strong sexual appetites, he had sublimated them all to his duty to the state. His life had been bleak, yet strangely, painfully rewarding. Oblensky might have Feodorovna to warm his bed, but he paid a price for the privilege. It was the way lesser men allowed themselves to be known, overseen, and, in the end, dominated. It must be so, Leonov thought. The Aral'sk post was absolutely critical and must be guarded.

Leonov had scheduled a security "exercise" to take place soon. The exact time was as yet unspecified—security drills were always unannounced. The orders necessary to seal the base were drawn; they had only to be implemented.

What now remained was to inform Oblensky that the missiles would be retargeted, and that he, Leonov, would be at Aral'sk when the exercise began.

A man of more imagination and less emotion than General Oblensky would require very little additional information to construct the scenario in military-political terms. He had, after all, heard the Crisis Confrontation Lectures with the others. But what nervous Polish fears might be aroused in the man at the moment of decision still remained to be discovered.

Leonov relaxed against the hard-cushioned seats of the underground tram. The machine traveled in a tunnel a hundred feet below the surface, and the sound of the wheels echoed in the cavernous space. From time to time the electrical connections would spark, sending flashes of blue-white light into the darkness ahead.

The Aral'sk complex had been begun during the regime of Defense Minister Marshal Grechko. Construction had slowed during the warmer periods of détente with the West, but it had never ceased. When Yuri Leonov became minister, construction had been accelerated and the original installations expanded and strengthened. The missiles were now almost impervious. Certainly there was nothing in the American arsenal that could crack the hardened sites of the six SS-19s. The command center was still vulnerable, but only to a direct hit by a nuclear weapon of twenty megatons or more. This displeased Leonov, particularly so because the sick old man in the Kremlin himself had vetoed the further expenditures needed to bring the entire base up to Leonov's standard.

To divert money and scarce technical labor into the production of automobiles and television sets when it was needed for military purposes was, in Yuri Leonov's view, absolute folly. It was the kind of decision that would be made differently, and by different people, very soon.

The tram completed its journey, and the inspection party walked through another blast door into a lift. The command center stood at ground level, heavily buttressed and protected by thick walls of ferroconcrete. In the plotting room, the target-selection crews leaped to attention as the Minister of Defense appeared. These troops were all officers, carefully selected and trained to use the Aral'sk Regiment's missiles independently in the event of the command center in Moscow being destroyed in a surprise attack. They stood stiffly around their plotting table, an electronically controlled display consisting of two polar world projections and four polygonic projections showing all of Western Europe and Scandinavia, the United States and Canada, China and South Asia, and Africa. On the walls of the windowless bunker a series of television screens carried changing computer read-outs that gave the position of major American units and ships at sea and the estimated state of readiness of American, British, French, and Chinese missile bases.

Leonov gave the plotting crews and their equipment only a cursory glance before moving on to the steel ramp leading to the upper, and undefended, level of the bunker. Another blast door, this one less substantial than those below (on the theory that these surface structures would not withstand the heat and blast of an attack in any case, and that their mission should be accomplished before weapons targeted on Aral'sk could arrive), separated the plotting room from the administrative offices of the base.

In Oblensky's office, Zabotin and Feodorovna stood as Leonov entered.

"Sit, sit," he said impatiently. Oblensky and his aide followed him into the room. He turned to speak directly to the Aral'sk commander.

"The regiment is in a state of satisfactory readiness, Sergei Vissarionovich." The use of the given name and patronymic was intended to assure Oblensky that he was still privileged among the Leonovites. The statement brought a relieved smile to Oblensky's round face.

"You may go," Leonov said to Oblensky's aide. He gestured to Feodorovna, who had made a move to withdraw as well. "You stay, Comrade Colonel."

To Oblensky he said, "Zabotin and I will speak in your alert quarters. Wait for us here." He nodded to Zabotin and stepped into the small room adjoining the office, the private cubicle where Oblensky slept during times of extreme readiness. Zabotin, his face sweating above his blue-tabbed GRU collar, closed the door behind them.

Leonov said, "Well?"

"Voronin reported that the President and his party would arrive at Heathrow before midnight, British time. But our Embassy in Washington advises that take-off has been delayed. If the flight is canceled, they will send word in code. Voronin said the President will go directly to Sissinghurst, have one day of privacy and rest, another for informal meetings, and address the NATO–Warsaw Pact delegates at 1000 hours the following morning. His party will include his Press Secretary, the Secretary of State, and the First Lady—"

Leonov's rock-hewn features showed animation for the first time. "He is bringing his wife? Excellent. Better and better."

"Voronin also reported that an aircraft has been dispatched secretly from Washington to Hurn. This is an airfield near the resort city of Bournemouth."

"I know the place. Go on."

"After he has addressed the delegates, the President will leave Sissinghurst secretly by motorcar. He will drive to Hurn and board the Boeing waiting there. The Secretary of State will not accompany him. His wife will. From Hurn the President will be flown directly to Moscow to confer with Comrade Kirov. His arrival in Moscow is scheduled for 0600 hours, Moscow time, but that is subject to his route, speed, and the weather. He will then—"

Leonov halted Zabotin with a shake of his head. "He will then be taken to the Moscow Center shelter, where great care will be taken that no harm comes to him. Because by that time we shall be at war with the Chinese."

Zabotin's prominent eyes widened and he licked his lips nervously. "Voronin's British contact stated that the Americans are prepared to take a hard line with the Chinese about the antimissile laser device. He believes that the Americans are even prepared to take military action if necessary—"

"Don't be a fool, Zabotin. There *is* no American 'hard line.' That is precisely why it is so necessary that we do what we must do ourselves. Do not allow yourself to dream of ways to avoid our responsibility."

"No, Comrade Marshal. Forgive me. I only thought—"

"There is very little room for maneuver, Zabotin," Leonov

said coldly. "Either you are for the plan or against it. There is no real middle ground."

"I am for it, Comrade Marshal. For it completely."

Leonov thought for a moment, and then, almost as an afterthought, he asked, "What about Voronin?"

"Dead, Comrade Marshal. As you ordered."

"As *I* ordered? I don't recall giving any such instructions, Zabotin."

General Zabotin, a man who had imprisoned thousands, heard the gates of Lubianka clanging behind him. There was a glint of real cruelty in Leonov's eyes. Zabotin wiped the sweat from his face and held his voice steady with great effort. "You said that you had no further use for him, Comrade Minister. You said that his liaison with the Englishwoman made him unreliable."

Leonov said slowly, deliberately, "Voronin was one of my best pupils at Frunze, Zabotin. Was it necessary to murder him?"

Zabotin fought down the rising tide of panic, of nausea. "I assumed that your meaning was clear, Comrade Minister. You said, 'We will not need him again.' Those were your exact words, Comrade Minister."

Leonov regarded Zabotin speculatively. The GRU man realized with horror that there had been no misunderstanding, that Leonov was simply baiting him, playing on his fear. It was done for a reason, Zabotin thought suddenly. It was meant to stretch his nerves a little tighter. A test. With the hour of the plan about to arrive, Leonov intended to put all the conspirators under extreme stress and discard instantly any who showed the slightest sign of breaking or even wavering.

He said again, in a stronger voice, "Your exact words, Comrade Leonov."

Leonov's eyes were steady and stony. Presently he said, "Very well. We will assume it was necessary. How was it done?"

A small increment of relief warmed Zabotin's blood, which had seemed to be growing chilly with fear. "He delivered the required information to Calais. When he returned, two Irish Provos—hired gunmen—met him in the Hovercraft terminal."

"Only two?"

"He managed to kill one of them."

Leonov nodded approvingly. "Ah, Aleksandr. Not all his training was wasted, then."

"The other killed a policeman and escaped. The British police may eventually identify him, but that will take time, my friend in London says. It need not concern us, in any case."

"*Was* Voronin about to defect?" Leonov asked.

"We have only London's word on that, Comrade Minister."

"You place a great deal of reliance on your London contact, Yevgeny Danielovich."

"He is the best of our deep-cover men, Comrade Minister. And his motives are flawless and genuine," Zabotin said. He hesitated. Perhaps he should simply let the matter rest, but he could not. Maybe it was only bad luck that a KGB man had seen the shooting. The point was that General Novikov would have the KGB report on his desk by now and no one knew where Novikov stood. If he sympathized with the Leonovite faction, well and good. If he did not, he might logically want to know why a Russian diplomat had been murdered and by whom. It was risky to deceive the Marshal.

"A man from the London KGB *rezidentura* was at the terminal, Comrade Minister," he said.

Leonov's expression sharpened. Like a wolf smelling blood, Zabotin thought.

He rushed on. "London KGB has been watching Colonel Voronin—the man at the terminal was to pick him up and follow him to London. One of Novikov's Frenchmen was on him in Calais and apparently lost him. The London man was very relieved when he re-established contact in Dover. Until the shooting started, that is. I was told that he witnessed the incident."

"An agent of KGB *saw* Voronin shot?"

"Yes, Comrade Marshal."

"Novikov has said nothing to me."

Zabotin remained decently silent. It might be totally insignificant that General Novikov had so far said nothing to Leonov about the Dover incident. There could be many explanations, almost all of them innocent. A failure of communications, perhaps. But Novikov, and the way he would jump when the action began, had always been one of the unknown factors in the plan. He was not a friend of the GRU, being more a policeman than a soldier. "Perhaps he doesn't know yet," Zabotin suggested.

"KGB has no shortage of communications. If a KGB man was there, Novikov knows. If he knows, then Kirov knows, too. I must return to Moscow at once."

"There is something more, Comrade Minister."

"Yes? Get on with it."

"The agent who saw the shooting heard Voronin say something strange to the woman before he died," Zabotin said. "He told her to search out a bag, a briefcase, something of that sort. At least that is the way the agent reported it. Is it possible that Voronin was so disaffected that he could have prepared documents, something with which he could have bargained with the British or Americans for asylum?"

"Unlikely," Leonov said. "He would only have to ask for asylum to receive it. And I am certain that Aleksandr Voronin was no traitor—to his country or to me."

Zabotin momentarily considered the irony of this endorsement from a man who had ordered Voronin's death less than two days ago. He had no doubt that when the plan succeeded and it was time to name heroes, Aleksandr Voronin would be one.

Zabotin said, "I am glad to hear that, Comrade Minister. Because the KGB *rezident* in London got the Ambassador to approach a magistrate, who issued an order permitting the removal of all Voronin's belongings from the flat he shared with the dancer."

"And?"

"Nothing. They found nothing."

Leonov regarded Zabotin speculatively. "But your spy's mind, Yevgeny Danielovich—it tells you something. That something might actually exist. Something the men from the *rezidentura* might have missed, perhaps."

"I don't wish to contradict you, Comrade Minister. But any man, no matter how loyal, has a price. There could have been something. Voronin was growing unreliable; you said as much yourself in Usovo. Yet there was no briefcase, and no documents of any kind among his effects that were collected by the Embassy."

"Another search, then?"

"Yes, I think so. To be safe, Comrade Minister."

"Arrange it. And if Voronin did turn traitor to the plan, the dancer may have to be eliminated. Your London friend is to see to it. But a search first."

"Yes, Comrade Minister."

"Now send Oblensky in here. It is time to test his Polish loyalty."

Zabotin's breath felt thick in his chest. It was one thing to theorize, as they had done so cleverly, even brilliantly, at Frunze. But here at Aral'sk were the weapons themselves, the means by which those theoretical wars fought so many years ago in the lecture room would become a terrible reality. "Yes. At once, Comrade Minister," General Zabotin said.

But today other voices are heard in the land —voices preaching doctrines wholly unrelated to reality . . . doctrines which apparently assume that words will suffice without weapons, that vituperation is as good as victory. . . .

—John Fitzgerald Kennedy, undelivered speech, scheduled for presentation in Dallas on 22 November 1963

PART TWO

14

The Senator from California sat in his study facing the President's Special Adviser for Scientific Affairs. Much of what he was hearing was technical, beyond his understanding, but he sensed that he was being presented with useful information that could be exploited against the administration.

The office in which the two men sat was a subtle copy of the Oval Office at the White House. This was only one of the eccentricities that so amused DeWitt Sutton's political enemies.

Sutton was a man in his sixties, and inordinately vain. A millionaire by inheritance, he had entered politics during the Kennedy years as a champion of the poor and disadvantaged. His detractors said that his vanity exceeded his intelligence by a wide margin, that he yearned for a new Camelot. They were correct about his yearnings, wrong about his intelligence. He spoke with a broad New England accent he had acquired at Harvard Law School. He was trim and fit—at what cost in effort, time, and money only his intimates knew.

He had been working out in his extravagantly equipped gymnasium when Christopher Rosen had been announced. Now he lounged in his replica of the Presidential chair, dressed in a warm-up suit, a towel around his neck, his transplanted hair touseled and falling boyishly across his forehead.

Rosen, whose appearance stimulated Sutton's latent and carefully controlled anti-Semitism, rubbed a finger on his thick, prominent nose and said, "I hope I am not making a mistake in coming to you, Senator. But I am at a loss to know what I should do."

Sutton's least attractive gesture was a smile. His teeth were long and prominent ("Like the screaming horse in the *Guernica,*" McNary had once said cruelly), but he risked smiling now as a sign of sympathy for the President's concerned Scientific Adviser. "I have too much respect for you, Chris, ever to compromise any confidences you choose to share with me," he said.

"Thank you, Senator. I really appreciate that," Rosen said. "My problem is that I am afraid the President is committing a serious error in judgment. I am for détente, believe me. I think I represent the opinion of most of the scientific community in this. The free exchange of ideas is the breath of life to science, and we can't afford ever to return to the days of the Cold War."

Sutton, who as a young New Frontiersman had been a dedicated Cold Warrior, nodded his warm agreement.

Rosen rubbed the palms of his hands along his trousers, as though to dry them, then continued. "But it seems to me that we are in danger of reviving the Cold War against the Chinese. The President seems convinced that they are up to some fantastic plot in the Turfan. The absurd thing about it is that, even if they were, there is absolutely no threat to us—or anyone else. What the President has been told by the military is impossible. There can be no such thing as an effective laser weapon. It is technically unachievable."

"You know this, Chris? It is a certainty?"

Rosen's manner became pedagogic and tinged with impatience. He spoke to Sutton as to a backward student. "I explained the thermal-bloom effect, Senator." He fumbled in his rumpled suit for his notes, written on scraps of paper. "The power requirements are astronomical. I have the numbers here—"

"Never mind the numbers, Chris. What I want to be certain about is whether or not there is even an outside chance that your Li Chin might actually have made some sort of gun that will stop missiles and satellites."

"Not a *gun,* Senator," Rosen said. "A chemical *laser.* There is a vast difference. And he isn't *my* Li Chin. I knew him at Cal

Tech—not personally. But I do know that he is brilliant, and totally dedicated to peace."

Sutton's eyebrows arched at that. "You know this?"

"Why else would he have left this country in the middle of the Vietnam war, Senator? But all this is academic. No such device can be built. I guarantee it. What Li must be doing is refining his medical-laser techniques. But the Pentagon—you *know* how they are, Senator. General Devore and Admiral Muller see a Red menace in everything they don't understand."

Sutton removed the towel from around his neck and mopped his face lightly. Rosen's manner was irritating. He wondered if Rosen irritated the President as well. Probably he did. But was he right? He searched his memory for an all-but-forgotten fact and came up with it. "Didn't the Soviets use a laser against one of our satellites—in 1974? No, in 1975, it was. I seem to remember something being written about that."

Rosen made a shrugging, dismissive gesture. "They did. A test, a probe. Nothing more. They had the notion that they could blind the heat sensors on the satellites of the Midas series—the devices that detect the heat and infrared radiation from missile launchings. There was never any idea that they could actually damage the satellite itself."

"Wasn't that a violation of the terms of SALT I?"

"Senator, what does it matter? It didn't work. What I am trying to get across to you is something very different, sir. The Pentagon people are using this so-called laser-weapon affair. The President is going to Moscow, sir, *secretly,* to confer with Valentin Kirov—"

Sutton came alert. Lambert to Moscow in secret? Now that was fantastic, if true. He held himself in check. Rosen, he saw, assumed that because he was a member of both the Armed Services Committee and the Senate Select Committee on Intelligence, he knew all about the secret journey. Good God, he thought, the political potentials of this piece of information were limitless.

"That troubles me, too, Chris," Sutton said cautiously. "Particularly the secrecy angle. There's been entirely too much of that in recent years."

"Exactly, Senator," Rosen said. "Exactly what I told the President. But Devore and Muller are resolved to see a threat in the Chinese experiments, and of course the Russians do, too. The President thinks he can mediate the problem between them. But there *is* no real problem—at least not because of Li Chin's work. In the end he will make unnecessary and dangerous commitments."

Sutton controlled his rising expectations with difficulty. He disliked and envied Cleveland Lambert; they had been rivals for the Presidential nomination twice, and Lambert had won both times.

"What does he expect from Kirov?" he asked Rosen. "Do you know?"

Rosen spread his hands. "What can he expect from Chairman Chung, Senator? This sort of shuttle diplomacy and summitry went out of style with Henry Kissinger. It is the secret dealing I object most strenuously to—this doing the nation's business in the dark instead of in the light, where the people can see."

"But the weapon is genuinely no threat? That is vital, Chris. So you must be certain," Sutton said.

"I tell you, Senator, it is not possible to build a—a—death ray. Not from a laser. That is the sort of cheap, shoddy sensationalism that gives science and scientists a bad name." The little man seemed to vibrate with the strength of his conviction. "I have been instructed—no, *commanded* would be a better word— to produce a report on the possibilities. The *military* possibilities, though the President didn't say so in so many words. I shall, of course, do so. But I feel totally justified in coming to you and expressing my deep concern about this outrageous disregard of scientific fact and this resort to melodramatic secret journeys. I expected better of Cleveland Lambert."

Sutton felt a glow of satisfaction as he listened to Rosen.

Since the bitterly divisive days of the Vietnam war, he had espoused the philosophy of total disclosure in government. He had supported the right of Daniel Ellsberg to steal and disclose the contents of the Pentagon Papers. In a dozen lesser cases, he had encouraged disgruntled bureaucrats to leak, transmit, and expose every sort of government secret. He was convinced that the damage such disclosures might do was far outweighed by the moral considerations involved. And if such disclosures tended to discredit one's own political rivals, so much the better.

"Lambert, I fear," Sutton said, "yearns for the days of a more imperial Presidency. Thanks to men of integrity like you, Chris, those days won't return."

For just a moment, Rosen experienced a pang of apprehension over what he had done. A suspicion was growing in his mind that Senator Sutton had *not* known that the President was using the NATO–Warsaw Pact meeting at Sissinghurst as cover for a flight to Moscow and Peking.

Sutton, his instinct warning him of Rosen's doubts, said soothingly, "Chris, I can't tell you how much I admire you. Cleveland Lambert can be an intimidating man."

"Yes, he certainly can be that, Senator," Rosen said. "But one must do what one knows to be right."

"Thank you, Chris. I appreciate your confidence in me."

Sutton waited to see if Rosen had more information to impart. When the Professor remained edgily silent, he stood and extended a well-manicured hand. "Thank you again, Chris. I'll have to consider what I—what the Senate—should do about all this. Your information is invaluable. It will help us to make the proper decisions and recommendations." That meant nothing, cost nothing, committed Sutton to nothing. Professor Rosen accepted it eagerly and allowed himself to be shepherded out.

Only moments after Rosen had left, Senator Sutton picked up his telephone and punched out the number of his legislative assistant. A young voice answered.

"Allan?"

"Sir?"

"Has the President's flight left Andrews?"

"Ten minutes ago, Senator. Way behind schedule."

Sutton pondered for a time and then said, "Where in London will Ms. McNary be staying?"

"Most of the press will be at the Hilton until the President is due to speak at Sissinghurst. But Jane is staying at the Stafford, sir."

"Send a cable, Allan. I want Jane to telephone me as soon as possible. Mark it urgent."

"A Sutton cable or a Cranmer cable, sir?"

"The Cranmer address, Allan." Sutton half smiled. When they wished their correspondence or meetings to be secret, he and Jane used a flat in Chevy Chase that his staff rented under the fictitious name of Thomas Cranmer. It was Jane's choice of pseudonym. She said Sutton had much in common with the accommodating Archbishop.

He put the telephone back in its cradle and walked to the tall windows overlooking a lawn that sloped to a quiet, exclusive street in Georgetown. The evening was clear and cold. The north wind had blown away the overcast that had covered the city for days, and the stars shone brightly over the distant lighted monuments and office buildings. Sutton shivered, perhaps feeling the chill outside.

Recently, his constituents had grown restless. The people of California, politically more fickle than most, had been showing signs of an irritating conservatism. Sutton had been wondering if his great days were now drawing to an end—the days of activism and sensational disclosures, the days that had begun with the public chastisement of the Central Intelligence Agency and the Federal Bureau of Investigation. Sutton had made political capital of each exposé and, quite literally, had made his face a familiar feature of the evening television news. But of late there had been less to disclose, less chance for self-aggrandizing exposure, and a perverse skepticism among the voters. It had even been mentioned in the party's inner circle—as a possibility, no more—that a new face might enhance their hold on the Senate seat DeWitt Sutton had occupied for over twenty years.

It could be, Sutton thought, that Professor Rosen's visit would change all that. Jane's support, and that of the news people and academics who followed her, had been growing lukewarm of late. This was more like old times, Sutton mused with a toothy grin. Jane would sell herself—and her readers—for the kind of leverage Rosen's information would give her. Let Cleveland Scott Lambert look out for himself.

15

Grant was surprised when he found Bronwen huddled like a child on the floor of the hall, indifferently exposed by a door partially ajar. He had expected that she would still be shocked, perhaps even tearful: after all, her lover was not yet twenty-four hours dead. But he had not been prepared for the forlorn waif-figure he encountered as he walked into the flat.

He helped her up and guided her into the parlor, as he supposed that room would be called. It was too long, too dark, a gloomy and ill-proportioned room that had a curiously abandoned look to it. Cluttered, but empty. The bookshelves were bare except for a few volumes on the lowest shelves.

He sat Bronwen down on the threadbare couch and told her his name. He received no immediate reply. She nodded vaguely, as though to indicate that she had heard him but that she had no comment, no questions, no interest.

"I'm intruding," he said. "I am sorry. I wouldn't if it were not necessary."

She made a small gesture that Grant could interpret only as one of assent. She now held the robe she wore closed over her breasts with a small, delicately boned hand. Grant studied her face. The vulnerable quality he had seen in the photograph Ballard showed him was more pronounced in life. She had a pleasant face, or one that would have been so if it had not been drawn with grief. A wide forehead, eyes soft and dark.

Grant was struck by a series of rapid impressions of Bronwen and of the place where she had lived with her Russian colonel. A man might willingly trust Bronwen Wells, he thought, aware that it was a strange notion to form so easily about a stranger. It had been a long time since he had held such an idea about any woman. Yet Bronwen did seem the sort of woman who would not deliberately injure—or betray—a man. Or his memory. Grant thought suddenly of Jane McNary. This woman was the antithesis of that one. He resolved that the strong sympathy he was feeling would not influence his judgment. If Bronwen held any information from Aleksandr Voronin, he must take it from her: she would never offer it.

He saw an open cabinet and a bottle. He said, "Could I fix you a drink, something?"

It took her a full half-minute to respond, as though she was only slowly becoming conscious of his presence in the drab room. "I'm sorry. What did you ask me?"

"I thought perhaps you could use a drink?"

"No. Thank you. I—" She frowned, making an effort at recognition. "I am sorry. You told me your name."

"It is Grant. Harry Grant." Shading the truth a little, he added, "From the American Embassy."

"The American? I don't understand. Were you here before? No—those were Alek's people."

He decided not to question that right away. He said carefully, "I shouldn't trouble you so soon. I wouldn't normally. But it is important that I speak with you."

Becoming conscious of herself, she stretched the hem of the robe over her bare knees and ran a hand over her dark hair. She sat with her feet primly together. They were slender, oddly misshaped, probably from years of dancing, Grant realized.

"Forgive me," she said uncertainly. "I am being rude." She looked about, as though she were trying to orient herself. "Would you like a cup of tea?"

The British, he thought. Even with her world in fragments—tea. "I'd like that," he said. He disliked tea, particularly the way the English made it. But it was something for her to do, something to hold onto during these first bad moments. She stood, and he followed her into the tiny kitchen and watched while she made the tea in an electric kettle. The water took a while to boil, and all that time they stood close together in the narrow, bleak kitchen, not speaking. He caught the scent of her. Perfume and a musty unwashed woman smell that should have been unpleasant but wasn't. He had an errant, personal thought: she wasn't like Bethany, who used to rush for a hot tub whenever she was upset or injured—which was often.

She poured the tea into his cup with a hand that shook so badly he had to restrain his impulse to steady it for her. He held his cup while she poured her own.

Presently, he decided that it was time to make her face the question and that first direct mention of Aleksandr Voronin. He said, "I want to talk to you about Colonel Voronin."

Her eyes widened, filled. She did not actually weep. Maybe, he thought, she was almost done with that. She said, "I told the police everything I know. Everything I saw." Her voice went to a higher key, pitched perilously near to hysteria, but she controlled it. "I saw him killed. I was there, you know."

He felt swamped with pity. "Yes, I know. It was bad for you."

"It's finished," she said. "What's the good of talking?"

Grant said, "It isn't the end of everything." He hadn't meant to say anything so supportive. Whether or not Bronwen Wells's life recovered and went on from here was nothing to him.

"No," she said, the vagueness creeping into her tone again, "I suppose it isn't."

"Can you talk to me about Colonel Voronin?" he asked.

"Did you know Alek?" she asked.

He shook his head. "I had an appointment to meet him. I came from Washington to speak with him. But—" He stopped, unwilling to say that he had come too late. If Bronwen knew anything at all, she knew that.

"You said you were from the American Embassy." She

sounded perplexed. I shouldn't wonder, Grant thought. What could she really know about her colonel and his plans to defect?

"I was going to try to help Colonel Voronin," he said. "Now perhaps I can help you."

"Why should you want to do that, Mr. Grant?"

"Let me put it another way. Maybe you can help me," he said.

She remained silent for a time, the tea growing cold in her cup. She said quietly, "Alek was frightened before he went to Calais. I wonder if he knew someone would do this to him—"

Grant said, "Did he tell you he was worried about something?"

"He didn't want to go. It was sudden. His having to go to France, I mean."

Alerted now, Grant said, "Colonel Voronin was going to give us something, Miss Wells. Did he leave anything here with you?"

"Clothes. Books. Things like that—personal things." She was withdrawing from his intrusive questioning, but Grant felt he had to press her now. "Forgive me for asking, but may I see them? I dislike putting you through this, but it could be important."

"Three men came early this morning. I think they were policemen. They took all of Alek's things away."

"British policemen?" Grant asked.

She shook her head slightly. "No. From the Soviet Embassy, they said."

Grant's disappointment was leaden. "They took everything?"

"Yes. They had an order. From a magistrate. They packed all of Alek's clothes. Everything. They took them away to send back to Russia."

Grant's lips tightened. This morning, he thought. If he had not attempted to be considerate, if he had come right away, he might have been in time. But he hadn't. The Iron Colonel had been concerned about intruding too soon into Bronwen Wells's life and personal tragedy. What would McNary say about that?

What would the President say? Then he thought about Bronwen coming here, to this cold flat. To be alone with her thoughts and her grief and, certainly, with her fear and bewilderment.

"They even wanted to take away the books Alek gave me," she said. "I asked them not to and they left them."

"May I see the books?" Grant asked.

Bronwen nodded and he followed her back into the gloomy living room. She took a book from a lower shelf. It was a collection of Semyon Kirsanov's poems. It fell open in his hands to a poem with lines underscored.

> Frost kills the twigs with silver stings;
> Slush chokes them in a miry snare.

Voronin must have done that, he thought. He doubted that Bronwen could read Russian. He returned the book. She held it, as though she could not think what to do with it.

Then she said, "You won't take it?"

Her manner was so defeated, so devoid of hope, that Grant felt clumsy. He thought, We play our brutal games and seldom have to face the human wreckage we leave behind. He wondered if Voronin, who lived by the dark games of power and intrigue, and who must have guessed that he might one day die by them, had ever thought of what would become of Bronwen when and if the blow fell.

He said, "What will you do now?"

"I haven't thought— Work, I suppose. Start again. When the ballet season begins again, I will go back—" She broke off helplessly. It seemed too much effort now to organize her thoughts, to construct a future. Grant wondered, Did she love Voronin that much? Or was it simply that he had been kind to her and had given her her only anchor in a world swept by cold winds and treacherous tides?

She seemed to be trying to remember something. Her small teeth bit on her colorless lower lip, making her look very like a child again. She said, "The men from the Embassy—it was strange—" Her voice trailed off for a time, and in the silence Grant could hear the ticking of a clock somewhere in the flat. Then Bronwen said, "They asked if Alek had a yellow suitcase. They particularly asked for that—"

Grant said carefully, "And did Colonel Voronin have anything like that?"

Bronwen shook her head. "No. At least I never saw one. But the odd thing is that there was a man at Dover—" It became more difficult for her to speak as she went back, in her mind, to the scene in the Hovercraft terminal. "At Dover. I—I saw Alek fall and I went to him—" She struggled on, frowning with the effort, her voice thinning again, so that Grant could hear the panic in it. "I went to him. I—think—I think he said something to me about a yellow—a yellow case. And a man asked me what he had said. He didn't seem to care that Alek was hurt—that he was dying. He only wanted to know what he had said to me—" She looked at Grant with eyes that were suddenly cavernous, shocked. "Is that what you want, Mr. Grant? Is that the reason you are here?"

"It may be," Grant admitted heavily. "I don't know. Colonel Voronin wanted to speak with me about something that he thought was very important. Maybe what he said to you means something. Maybe not."

She said, "Alek liked Americans, Mr. Grant. He said they were foolish, but fair."

Grant decided to be a little bit honest with her. There was small chance that anything could now be retrieved out of the Voronin affair, but he felt the need to make a try, and without Bronwen's co-operation it would be hopeless. He said, "I believe Colonel Voronin was coming over to us. I think there may have been something he wished to warn us about. That might well be why he was killed, Miss Wells."

Bronwen looked at Grant, seeing him, really seeing him, for the first time. She saw a slender man of middle age, middle height, hair graying, with a good face. Not handsome the way

Alek had been handsome, but more open, less guarded, and kinder. Alek had not always been kind. Perhaps it was because, she thought with a flash of tardy insight, he was often frightened.

But right now it was too soon to think, to make decisions, to understand anything. "Please—" she said, gripping the book. "I don't—not now, Mr. Grant. I don't want to talk any more—" She desperately wanted Grant to go and not talk about Alek and what he might or might not have done had he lived.

Grant sensed her withdrawal. It was sudden and complete and he understood it. "I will want to speak with you again," he said gently. "May I do that?"

"If you wish."

He took the book from her and replaced it on the shelf. Then he put his arm about her narrow shoulders and held her for a moment. He didn't know why he did that, except that some instinct insisted that she desperately needed to feel some human warmth, to have some contact with another creature of her own species.

"Thank you," she said. "I will be all right."

He stepped away from her but took her hand and held it for a few seconds longer. It felt fine-boned and fragile between his fingers. "Good-by then," he said. Close by, Grant could see the tiny wrinkles in her skin, the shadows under her eyes. She had touched him, and he was not accustomed to that.

As he walked down the steps to the sidewalk he looked carefully at the black police car parked down the block. Ballard was still having her watched. But that hadn't prevented the early-morning visit by the Russians. From the KGB *rezidentura*, Grant had no doubt.

He walked slowly down the street toward Hampstead Road. It was an odd neighborhood for an Embassy attaché to have lived in, he thought. The flats were shabby. There were posters in some of the windows enjoining passers-by to "Vote Labour." Some of the entrances were decorated with designs and paintings obviously done by the tenants. What must Voronin, a colonel in the Soviet Air Force, have thought of his bohemian neighbors? In Russia they used bulldozers on street artists and their work. Here, where Voronin had lived with his little ballet girl, they made a cult of such art. Voronin had been too long in the West, Grant guessed, and somehow that had cost him his life.

In Hampstead Road, Grant found a telephone box. He dialed Ballard's private number.

"It's Grant," he said.

"You've spoken to her?"

"There were three men from the Soviet Embassy around this morning," Grant said. "They had a magistrate's order. They cleaned out Voronin's things."

"Oh, bad luck, old man," Ballard said sympathetically. "But I suppose one might have foreseen that."

"One of us might have," Grant said coldly, "old man."

"What do you suppose they found, if anything?"

"I wouldn't have any way of knowing that, would I?"

"You sound annoyed."

"I'm bloody annoyed, Ballard. It's damned odd that a British magistrate couldn't wait twenty-four hours before letting the KGB scoop up Voronin's belongings."

"No help for it," Ballard said. "This is England, you know. Even the Bolshies have rights in the eyes of the law."

"Horseshit, Ballard. What's really happening is that you couldn't—or didn't—keep Voronin alive and now SIS is having second thoughts about getting involved."

"That's rather a rough judgment, Grant." Ballard sounded injured.

"We both know who is responsible for what happened to Voronin. He was one of Marshal Leonov's protégés and the Marshal doesn't like defectors. Has he a license to turn Britain into a shooting gallery?" Grant's voice was heavy with contempt. "If that's the way of it, Ballard, I'm going to have to recommend to my boss that he make his stay short."

"Point taken, old man," Ballard said placatingly. "All right, how can I help you now?"

"You can start by putting a tail on the local KGB. They didn't get what they wanted and they may well be back. The Wells woman might be in danger."

"How is she holding up?"

"Well enough, considering she's been through hell."

"You sound as though she rather impressed you," Ballard said.

Grant pointedly ignored that comment, because it was true. He said, "She told me Voronin said something before he died that could mean he did have an insurance policy. If he did and he had, I want it."

"I don't suppose you are going to tell me what it was he said."

"Not on the telephone."

"Maybe not at all, old man?"

Grant smiled grimly. "You can buy it with some help. Voronin's dying declaration—if that's what it was—has reached the Kremlin by now. The KGB man at the Dover terminal heard it. Didn't you know that?"

"We can't know everything," Ballard said ruefully.

"Then get some protection for Bronwen Wells and we'll talk."

"Right. Just as you say."

"I'll be in touch," Grant said. "Old man."

He broke the connection, hailed a taxicab, and told the driver to take him to Grosvenor Square. Even though the Agency wasn't a part of all this, he intended to use the secure line to Langley to query the CIA computer there, asking it to expand on the connection between Colonel Aleksandr Voronin and Marshal of the Soviet Air Force Yuri Ivanovich Leonov.

16

Viktor Krasin liked to think of himself as a member of what was now known as the Kremlin Old Guard. He had stepped into line for his present post of foreign minister long ago, in the regime of Leonid Brezhnev. Under the personal guidance of the then First Secretary, Krasin had written the White Paper, a document circulated among members of the Supreme Soviet, establishing the tenet of the Brezhnev Doctrine that the USSR had a right to intervene in nations where "socialism was imperiled." To write such a document in terms that would not damage the contradictory policy of "coexistence and détente" with the United States was a task that few young diplomats in the Soviet Union would have relished. Krasin's Byzantine mind proved more than equal to the task, and from that time onward his career was assured.

Krasin was a devoted student of Americans and American government, and he believed—not without reason—that the foremost ally of Soviet expansion in the world was the United States Congress, in particular the Senate, where pacifism had spawned, first, isolationism and, now, the policy of New Insularity.

He had seen committees of the Senate diminish the United States intelligence community, discredit United States foreign policy, prevent American opposition to Soviet intervention in Portugal, Africa, and the Middle East. He had seen Pentagon budgets attacked and slashed until clear Soviet superiority at sea and in the air became facts of life. He did not pretend to understand how it was that American statesmen should so occupy themselves, but he had devoted much of his career to encouraging them.

For a time, Krasin had served as ambassador in Washington and observed at first hand the phenomenon of divisiveness among American liberals. Of particular interest to him was the Senator from California DeWitt Sutton. At one time Krasin had wondered if the Senator were not some sleeper planted long ago by Soviet Intelligence, but he had finally come to the conclusion that Sutton was a genuine, indigenous American phenomenon: the rich politician driven to joyous lunacy by a heady compound of guilt, power, and self-righteousness.

Krasin was now wondering about a different American. President Lambert had committed himself to a secret journey to Moscow and Peking—and to a course of action that would, if Krasin and Kirov had their way, result in a joint declaration condemning the new Chinese weapon in the Turfan. He turned his chair so that he could look out across the snow-covered roofs and courtyards of the Kremlin. Moscow lay under a pall of icy winter. A communicator pinged on his wide desk, and he touched a button.

"Yes?"

"The First Secretary, Comrade Minister," a secretary said. "On the telecom."

Valentin Kirov's haggard face appeared on the large television screen beside the Foreign Minister's desk. He looked even worse than he had at the meeting in his dacha day before yesterday. Once he had been a heavyset, robust man with the build and constitution of a Georgian peasant. But the embryoma ravaging him had melted away flesh until he looked to Krasin like a Christ image on an ikon. That he was dying, everyone knew, but recently it had become a question of whether or not he had enough strength left in his emaciated body to fulfill his last duty—the meeting with the Americans.

Lambert knew that Kirov was ill. He did not know, because it had suited Soviet policy not to have him know, that he was fatally ill. It was going to come as a shock to the American,

Krasin thought, when he saw this ravaged death mask of a face.

"Krasin," the First Secretary said in a faint, rasping voice, "General Novikov is here with me."

Krasin contained his surprise. Novikov was thought to be a member of Marshal Leonov's faction, though he had not been one of the pampered protégés from Frunze. The post of commander of the Committee for State Security did not make a man particularly popular with his colleagues. The ghostly ranks of all the grim, notorious forerunners—the Cheka, the OGPU, the NKVD—standing, unseen but ever present and dreadful, behind the chief of the KGB, tended to daunt even the most powerful.

Krasin studied the scene on the television screen before him. The sickroom in the dacha was darkened and, he had no doubt, suffocatingly hot. The sensitive microphones in the audio-visual link picked up the shallow, labored breathing of the ruler of the Soviet Union. There was a promise of death in the sounds.

"Yes, Comrade First Secretary," Krasin said automatically. Once, he and Valentin Kirov had been close friends, and they were still on familiar terms. But the urgency in Kirov's tone warned Krasin that this was not the time to presume on old friendships.

"Yesterday an attaché at our London Embassy was murdered," Kirov said. "Shot down at the Dover terminal by gunmen in broad daylight."

"Yes, Comrade First Secretary," Krasin said again.

"You knew about this?"

Krasin considered carefully before replying, but he could think of no way to avoid the direct question. "Yes," he said.

"Why was I not informed about it immediately?" Kirov demanded. "I am not dead yet, Viktor Stepanovich!"

"I assumed that Marshal Leonov would give you a complete report, Comrade First Secretary, when General Zabotin's investigation is completed."

"Zabotin? What has the GRU to do with this?"

"I don't know, Comrade First Secretary," Krasin said uneasily. "I suppose the Army's Intelligence Directorate would investigate because the attaché was a member of the Air Force."

"Novikov came to tell me. He says he does not know why the man was killed."

"There is still a great deal of lawlessness and hooliganism in England, Comrade First Secretary. The Irish Republican Army—"

"Don't talk nonsense, Viktor Stepanovich. The man was not killed by accident."

Krasin could not resist a thrust at Novikov, the policeman. "General Novikov's report is not complete then?"

In the background Krasin could hear the KGB chief's muttered comment.

The First Secretary said, "The man's name was Voronin, Aleksandr Voronin. He was a colonel in the Air Force, but he had been seconded to the diplomatic corps. What do you know about him?"

Krasin pressed a call button hastily as he replied, "Let me examine his file, Comrade First Secretary. I will tell you in a moment." He cursed himself for having allowed the press of preparations for the Americans' mission to make him negligent. The name Voronin meant nothing to him, and he had not taken the time from his other duties to examine the file on the murdered man. That had been a mistake.

A secretary entered, and Krasin, leaning away from the television camera's eye, whispered savagely, "The file on Voronin. *Quickly!*"

The secretary, a moon-faced young woman, conscientious but slow-thinking, said, "Voronin?"

Krasin snapped in irritation, "The air attaché who was killed in England yesterday. Aleksandr Voronin. *Move!*" To Kirov, he said, "One moment, Comrade First Secretary."

There were further murmured comments behind Kirov. The

sick man's face contorted with agony, and Krasin's bowels contracted with sympathetic pain. Kirov looked like a man having a blade twisted in his gut. When the spasm passed, the First Secretary mopped his damp forehead and said, "I want to know how Voronin came to be seconded."

The secretary returned to Krasin's office running, a green folder in her hand. Krasin felt a start of surprise. Only officers of the diplomatic service with the highest clearance to handle secret material rated green files. He took the folder and untied the sealed ribbon. He searched swiftly through the pile of information, searching for Voronin's diplomatic-qualification summary. His blunt finger ran down the closely typed lines, stopped. His mouth felt dry. He looked up at Valentin Kirov's electronic image.

"He came with a special recommendation from Marshal Leonov, Comrade First Secretary."

More murmurs from Novikov, now indistinctly seen behind Kirov. "He was one of Yuri Ivanovich's students at Frunze?" Kirov asked.

Krasin found the confirmation in the green file. "Yes, Comrade First Secretary. A brilliant one, apparently. He was a member of one of the last classes Marshal Leonov taught at the Military Academy."

The First Secretary sat silently before the television camera in his dacha. It seemed to Krasin that Kirov was suddenly weakened, brought almost to the point of exhaustion. He could not tell whether it was the cancer in Kirov's kidneys or the information he had received that was the cause of his near-collapse.

Presently Kirov said with a great effort, "I will hear what Novikov has to say. Then I will send him to see you, Viktor Stepanovich. I will want you to go through the diplomatic-personnel files together—and alone. I want to know how many more of Yuri Ivanovich's special protégés you have in our embassies abroad." He leaned forward and said, "Alone—do you understand me? You and Novikov. No one else."

"Yes, Comrade First Secretary. I understand."

"Before you leave for England, Krasin. Without fail."

"Of course, Comrade First Secretary. I will attend to it at once. As soon as General Novikov returns to Moscow." But Krasin was speaking to a diminishing point of light on the television screen. The First Secretary had broken the connection, leaving Viktor Krasin alone with his unanswered questions.

17

Patrick Sullivan had been dreaming of America when the phone woke him, which was strange enough, because he had never been in the States. His picture of the place was a scrambled mixture of old Irish immigrant legends, the stories Sean had told him, and the muck one got from the films. Sean had traveled in the United States to raise money from the rich Paddies who salved their revolutionary consciences with dollars. But that had been long ago, and now Sean was dead and probably still lying stiff and cold in the Dover morgue.

There was the taste of stale whisky in Sullivan's mouth and his eyes felt gummy. The girl sleeping beside him had belonged to his brother Sean. Karen, her true name was, but she called herself "Bridget" because she thought it sounded more fitting for a girl shared by Provos. She was American and not more than eighteen, though she claimed to be twenty-five; a bitch and no mistake, with big talk about how she could fight for the Cause like any man, given the chance. What she didn't seem to understand was that the bloody Cause was in a bad way these filthy days. It wasn't a simple thing any longer to throw grenades and packs of gelignite into London restaurants. The fascist English were getting clever, giving way just enough here and there to pacify the Regulars, who claimed to be the true and only IRA. It came to this: a Provo was reduced to killing on a hired basis just for the money to stay alive and buy guns. There was still money from the States, but not nearly enough of it.

Sullivan swung his feet to the floor and sat, head down, throat half clogged with foul-tasting phlegm. The telephone kept ringing, and the girl had begun to stir and complain. She stank of pot, which was an abomination in Sullivan's eyes, but Sean had always let her smoke, and Sullivan had not yet decided whether or not he wanted to keep her, whether or not he cared enough about what happened to her to try to get her to drop the dirty habit.

He picked up the receiver and said, "What is it?" in a thick, soggy voice.

"This is Caspar." The familiar voice, with its English public-school accent, jolted him awake. Sullivan had stopped trying to imagine what Caspar might look like. He imagined him as thick, with beefy cheeks and little, nasty eyes. Despite the upper-class Britishness of the voice, Sullivan was sure his control was a Russian. It was Caspar who had sent him down to Dover with Sean.

The girl (Sullivan refused to call her "Bridget," or even think of her that way; she was always "you" or just "the girl" to him) sat up in the bed. She was naked, her breasts bruised by what she had bitchily called his "chauvinist love-making" in the night. Her long hair was tangled and not too clean. It was hard to credit that she came from what Sean used to call "an elegant family of Yank fascists." She said: "Christ, who's that?"

"Shut up," Sullivan said, his hand over the telephone mouthpiece.

Caspar said, "Are you awake now, Sullivan?" The son of a bitch liked to torment a man by using his right name—or what came as near to being a right name as any hand-to-mouth Provo ever had these days. And of course there was no such person as "Caspar." Damned silly name it was. A Russian, though. Sullivan was sure about that.

"How the hell did you find me?" Sullivan asked. He really wanted to know. He had collected his money for the Dover hit—Sean's, too—and posted the organization's share to the money drop in Oxford. With what little was left, he had gone to ground with the girl in the most inconspicuous place he could think of, Portsmouth, where an Irishman would be common-place.

"Does that matter?" Caspar asked.

"It matters," Sullivan said. "It bloody well matters." Provo security was a shambles these days. *These days*—shit, he thought, that was a phrase he had to use too often. It hadn't always been so. In the good times, when it was all setting bombs in Ulster or killing English with Bangalores as they sat filling their English guts at expensive restaurants, the organization's security had been good. It had been worth a man's life to break ranks then. But that was years back. Now Sullivan felt old and strained to the point of exhaustion. His hair, what was left of it, was gray. His face looked like that of a man three days dead, and yet he was barely forty.

He had been a science student once and had almost made another choice when the Provos came to him with their fine fiery talk about freedom and a United Ireland. Sometimes, when he was drunk, he admitted to himself that he hadn't joined for that, or even for the Marxist convictions he held, which were sincere enough. No, he had joined for the killing, for the simple joy of it. The organization had given him plenty of that, all right.

He had even had a few months of the soldiering thing, when the Movement had seemed about to win in the fighting in Portugal. But that hadn't worked out the way the organization promised either, and he had come back to Derry first, and then into England to take calls from voices like Caspar's and do odd jobs for hire because the Movement needed money and it was getting hard to come by.

But they bloody well owed him some protection. What had happened to his brother Sean at Dover—well, that was part of the risk. Who could have guessed that the target would suddenly take out a pistol and start shooting back? That was one of the chances you had to take. Sean knew it, and that was why he had said, before going out on the job, that if he should be taken or killed, brother Patrick could have the girl. "Maybe she'll be good for more than fucking one day, Paddy-boy," Sean had said, "and in the meantime she has a cunt hotter than the fires of everlasting hell." Well, that was true enough. Not much that Sean used to say was worth the hearing, but that was.

Sullivan brought himself to hand with a start. He'd been wandering again. One minute frightened and angry from hearing Caspar's voice, then off and meandering about the old days and the dead and how things were bad now when they used to be fine.

He said again, "It bloody well matters how you located me."

"I called Dublin."

"Jesus, Mary, and Joseph! You talked about me on an international call? What are you, bloody mad?"

"This is important."

"So is my bloody life important," Sullivan said hoarsely.

Caspar disregarded the complaint and said, "The Dover job isn't finished."

"What does that mean—not finished? We put him down. It cost Sean, but we put him down. What more is there?"

"Two hundred pounds more," Caspar said.

Two hundred pounds, Sullivan thought. Christ, there was a time when the likes of Caspar would have had to pay a thousand just to get Patrick Sullivan's name. Now the mention of an extra two hundred brought the blood to his cheeks. But he said, "Not for two hundred thousand, you bastard. It's too soon for another hit."

"Not that. Not unless it is necessary, that is. No, this is a two-hundred-pound piece of work."

Sullivan remained silent, groping for a cigarette on the table beside the soiled bed. The girl put a filthy roach to his lips and he spat it out, raising his arm to slap her across the mouth. She laughed and put her hand in his crotch.

Caspar said, "The Dover target had a woman. He left something with her that we want. Very badly. You'll get it for us."

"Not for two hundred bloody pounds, I won't," Sullivan said angrily.

"Yes, you will, Sullivan. It's either that or a word to the English police. You can't get out of the country, you know."

Sullivan's stomach knotted and he felt as though he was going to get sick. He thrust the girl's hand away and found the cigarettes he was looking for on the table. He struck a light with a shaking hand. His wrist watch had stopped at three o'clock. Afternoon or morning? How the hell could he know. He had been in bed with Sean's Yankee slut since going to ground after Dover.

"Sullivan? Are you still there?"

"Yes," Sullivan said dully.

"Don't sound so unhappy. It won't take much effort. All you have to do is find what we want. You may not even have to touch the woman."

But it was never like that, Sullivan thought. You always had to touch them, hurt them, kill them. And the old joy wasn't there any more. There was only the fear of being caught. The British refused to hang you. They just kept you locked up for years and years. Unless some policeman, sick to death with temporizing, decided that you had resisted too hard and blew you to bloody rags with those guns they sometimes let them carry on hazardous special assignments.

The girl was back at him again. God, she was insatiable. She sensed that whoever was on the other end of the telephone connection had frightened him and that there could be killing. That seemed to excite her, just as Sean had said it did. She moved against him, spraddle-legged, her narrow shins pressing against his thighs. He could feel the damp heat of her against his hip. She whispered into his ear, using language that still shocked him, tonguing the back of his neck and his cheek.

Caspar said, "Pick up the key to the same Paddington Station locker we used before. You will find half the money and instructions. Do it right away."

"I have no car," Sullivan said.

"Hire one." A pause. "Don't make difficulties where there are none."

"What am I looking for?"

"It will be in your instructions."

"Five hundred pounds," Sullivan said desperately.

"Two. Good-by, Sullivan." Caspar was gone.

The girl said, "Tell me."

"Bugger off," Sullivan said angrily, pushing her away.

She fell back, laughing, against the sweaty pillows. Her legs were still folded under her, her thighs spread wide. She said, "That was your Russian friend."

"What the hell do you know about that?"

"Sean told me."

"Stupid bitch," Sullivan said, wanting to hit her.

"Let me do it."

"What? What the hell are you talking about?"

"Whatever it is. Let me do it." Her pale-blue eyes were wide, crazy. Where the hell did they come from, these lost Movement bitches, Sullivan wondered.

"No," he said.

"Let me," she said. "I can. Whatever it is. Probably better than you. You're old, used up. You're afraid."

He hit her, hard. She closed her eyes and sucked at the blood on her bruised lip. She said, "Let me do it, Patrick. I want to." Her eyes opened again, wide and still laughing. "You don't want to end up like Sean."

He drew back his hand to hit her again, but she caught it and guided it between her legs. "I can do anything," she said.

He caught her, squeezing until he was sure she would cry out, but she did not. She only thrust against him. She was hot with the idea of killing.

Well, he thought, maybe. Why not? If she botched it, what would it matter? He'd still have half the money and he could run. God, how he longed to run and keep running. "For the Cause, you bitch?" he said.

"That's right, for the Cause," she said. "I'm Bridget. I'm Leila. I'm Bernadine and Bernadette. I can do anything. Let me do it, whatever it is."

He sat on the edge of the bed staring at her. Succubus, he thought. The Jebbies knew all about you and creatures like you. Though he had not been inside a church for ten years, and though never in fifteen years of murdering strangers had he had a real qualm of conscience, he felt a sudden shivering fear of damnation. Burning with cold terror, he fell upon her, wishing with all his soul that he could pin her to the bed, to the earth, with the stake of his body.

"All right," he said in a rasping whisper, *"all right*. You can do it. God have mercy on her, whoever she is."

18

It was still dark over the south coast of Iceland. At the altitude Colonel Ortiz had been flying Air Force One, the outside air temperature was fifty-six degrees below zero and the west-to-east jet stream added one hundred and fifty knots to the six hundred knots of the C-9. He had just revised his estimated time of arrival at Heathrow to 0400 GMT and passed the information to the President.

In the communications section of the mammoth aircraft, the captain in charge had been engaged in sending bulletins filed by the news people on board—bulletins originating from the impromptu press conference the President had just completed in the midship lounge on the lower deck.

Two decks above, in the Presidential suite, Cleveland Lambert and Secretary of State Margaret Kendrick sat in conference. Ivy O'Donnell, the President's personal secretary, had just added to the stack of decoded dispatches on the table by Lambert's chair and retired to the office section of the suite. In the private quarters beyond the bulkhead, the First Lady was attempting to get a few hours of sleep before facing her own crowded schedule of visits and appointments in London and at Sissinghurst.

Kendrick, her gray eyes somber behind the rimless glasses that had become her trademark, studied the latest communication from Secretary Richards at the Pentagon.

"What do you make of it, Margaret?" the President asked.

"How much does Colonel Grant know?"

"Only what I thought he needed to know to make the contact."

The Secretary of State favored the President with the ghost of a grim smile. "He's too intuitive, then, Mr. President. I suggest you instruct the Agency to disregard his request, or at least delay it."

"I trust Harry Grant, Margaret."

"I didn't mean to suggest that you shouldn't, Mr. President. But this—" she touched the dispatch from Richards with a blunt fingertip—"this could develop into a terrible mare's nest. Marshal Leonov is, after all, the Soviet Union's Minister of Defense and the nearest thing to an heir apparent we know about."

The President frowned. "I don't want to embarrass or compromise him, but if he is up to something, we had better know about it."

"You may have to deal with him when you get to Moscow. Kirov is a very sick man."

The President's frown deepened. "The British should have taken precautions, damn it. Voronin had something to tell us."

"We didn't share our suspicions, Mr. President. Under the circumstances, we can hardly blame them."

"Some more of your well-known Anglophilia, Margaret?" the President said, shaking his head.

The Secretary of State shrugged. "Maybe, Mr. President. But they are about the only friends we have left. We could have called them in and consulted with them."

"To tell them what, Margaret? That we *think* that *maybe* there is a danger of some kind of coup in the Soviet Union? We have nothing solid to go on, and even if we did have, our policy must remain one of strict neutrality in their internal affairs."

"Then you are going to allow Colonel Grant to continue this line of inquiry, Mr. President?"

"Until I leave for the Soviet Union, yes. I know Grant. He may turn up something to make up for the loss of this Aleksandr Voronin."

Margaret Kendrick looked through the window near her chair. The airplane was flying very high, and the sea below was lost in darkness. She was tired. She had not slept more than three hours out of the last twenty-four. And she was filled with intuitive apprehension. She had the feeling that neither she nor anyone else in the government had a really sound idea of what was happening in the Soviet Union. A change such as the one she and the President had been discussing could be cataclysmic. There was simply no way of knowing. Valentin Kirov, sick unto death, must surely relinquish the reins of power—but to whom? To Krasin, the Foreign Secretary? Krasin was no greater friend of the United States than any other dedicated Russian Communist. But he was a diplomat, and not a soldier. Leonov was a soldier, by all accounts a brilliant one, and not the sort of antagonist the United States needed. Yet she felt certain she could deal with Leonov if she must. Provided no incident was allowed to force him into some premature action. She liked the Iron Colonel well enough, but she fervently wished that the President would shorten the leash on which he was running at this very moment.

The President said, "I can tell by your expression, Margaret. You are disapproving."

"Yes, I am, Mr. President."

"You'd like me to call Grant in."

"I think that would be the wisest course."

"Did you read General Devore's evaluation of the thing the Chinese are building?"

"I did, Mr. President. I deplore it. I think we should take an open stand against it. Perhaps in the UN."

Lambert regarded his Secretary of State stonily. "The United Nations, Margaret? You aren't serious."

"I know, I know, Mr. President. But it *is* a world forum. People listen to what is said there."

"The UN is hopeless, Margaret. It lost its credibility with the American people when it took in murderers and terrorists. There's no help for it. It is simply *so*."

Kendrick remained silent. She knew what the President was saying was a fact of life. The great hopes on which the United

Nations had been founded had been swamped in prejudice, envy, and anarchy. The Communists had, in the forty years since the San Francisco Conference, turned all the values upside down and, with the help of the turbulence and blatant self-interest of the Third World, made the UN a travesty. Save for the British and a few others, the United States stood alone in the glass tower on New York's East River. To take a complaint about a Chinese weapons system there would be to invite scorn and laughter and, in the final roll call, rebuke. Lambert would never risk such a fruitless action.

"Tell me, Mr. President," the Secretary of State said, "unofficially and personally. Do you believe a coup is imminent in the Soviet Union? And does the Chinese development have anything to do with it? I'm serious, Cleveland," she said, taking the liberty of using his Christian name to assure him that what was said here would remain between the two of them.

"I see you are," the President said. "Yes, I think there will be a coup in the Soviet Union. It will take place one hour after Valentin Kirov is dead. And yes, I think the Chinese business will affect it. Marshal Leonov will do his best to use the threat as a justification for setting aside whatever choice the Presidium makes of a successor to Kirov. He may even pull it off. I would hate to see that, Margaret. I think it would be bad for the United States and the West to have a man like Yuri Leonov in the number-one spot in Russia. And that, more than any other, is the reason I am allowing myself to become involved in this rather melodramatic skulking about from Hurn to Moscow to Peking." He leaned back in his seat and folded his hands across his chest. "Did you really need to be told this, Madame Secretary?"

"No," Kendrick said deliberately. "We have been through this kind of shuttlesmanship before, Mr. President, and not too long ago."

The President smiled at her with real affection. "Let no one say my Secretary of State is afraid to speak her mind."

"You didn't appoint me to the Cabinet to serve the coffee,

Mr. President," she said tartly. "Wasn't it Oliver Cromwell who said: 'I beseech you, in the bowels of Christ, to think it possible you may be mistaken'?"

"If it wasn't Cromwell," the President said, still smiling, "then it must have been Kendrick."

The Secretary of State stood, wearily. "Very well, Mr. President. I've had my say. Now I think I shall try to get an hour or two of sleep."

The President watched her thoughtfully as she went down the stairway to the quarters on the second deck of Air Force One.

Lambert was as tired as his Secretary of State, but the presence on board Air Force One of a large part of the White House press corps made him wary of displaying so simple a human weakness as a need for sleep.

He found it surprising, as some of his predecessors had, that though he had once been the darling of the press—the charismatic leader, some proclaimed, that the nation had been yearning for—his inauguration had changed that. There had been the customary honeymoon, during which the opinion-makers watched him with the expectation of children awaiting a trip to the seashore. But "openness" and "obvious integrity," so often mentioned during his successful campaign, were discussed less often after Inauguration Day, and the "compassion and sensitivity" that seemed apparent to the media people in November were less so in January. He was too much of a realist to suppose that the newspapers and television networks would not, to some degree, become his adversaries as well. It was the duty of a free press, he believed, to view elected officials with—if not suspicion—at least some healthy skepticism.

But over the years Lambert had watched what he considered a dangerous growth of the journalism of advocacy, a tendency to attack without conscience or too much regard for equity those who failed to do what the press consensus regarded as right. In his first State of the Union message, he had made the serious error of chiding the news media and reminding them that in a democracy politicians were elected to do, in so far as they were able, the bidding of the electorate and not what an elite—even the fourth estate—felt was best.

From that moment on, Lambert's relations with the news media had become tense. In a short time as President he had learned that Lord Acton's admonition about power applied as much to the men and women whose faces appeared nightly on millions of television screens as it did to politicians. Perhaps, he thought, even more so.

Tact, learned from caution, saved him from all-out war with the news media, and he took solace in the knowledge that there were members of the Washington press corps who liked him personally. Still, he dare not, even aboard his own airplane, show a tired face, or stumble, or speak an ill-considered word. He was the President of the United States. He had given up the simple privilege of being an ordinary, fallible man. But he thought, That's what I am—an ordinary, fallible man.

"Mr. President?"

Lambert looked away from the darkened sky outside the aircraft to Paul Lyman, who had just come into the compartment with a sheaf of Telex copies.

It had been Lyman's idea to allow the top rank of the Washington press corps to travel with the President on Air Force One. At first there had been some comments that the President was trying to "buy" or "bribe" the press with this courtesy. But soon the more reasonable Washington correspondents had come to see that this method of traveling vastly increased the availability of the President. The informal press conferences that had lately become a regular feature of Presidential travel severely curtailed the amount of time available to Lambert for his work, but Lyman had been certain that the practice was steadily improving the President's relationship with the men and women who covered the White House. At the moment, however, Lyman was not so sure.

The President, mildly displeased at having been interrupted while getting some little rest, said, "All right, Paul. What is it?"

"The press conference went rather well, I thought, Mr. President."

"But what?" The President noted that Lyman was holding the Telex sheets as though they were warm to the touch.

"McNary, Mr. President."

"Ah, Comrade Jane. What now, Paul?"

Wordlessly, the Press Secretary handed the President the Telex copy. It was a short piece, obviously written in some haste, but with McNary's typically acid touch, about the airborne press conference. Datelined Air Force One, it was headed "Is This Trip Necessary?" The President's eyes ran swiftly down the page. One phrase in particular caught his attention: "Since the administration is committed to satisfying every whim of the Pentagon generals, one wonders what, precisely, we carry aboard this luxurious airplane that we propose to offer the Warsaw Pact powers in return for the socialist retreat we seek in Europe."

"Has this gone?" the President asked.

Lyman nodded. "She stood over Captain Wheeler's shoulder until the transmission was complete."

The President grinned ruefully. "Not that I would like to interfere with First Amendment rights, but it's a damned shame we couldn't have had a communications failure."

"She has something to say about that, too," Lyman said sourly.

The President read: "This aircraft is more impressive than the politicians who travel in it. Connected, as it is, to our nuclear overkill by a dozen redundant systems, there is no way to separate us from the millions of megatons which back up our trivial proposals."

Lambert pursed his lips in suppressed irritation. "The lady has the charm and graciousness of a cobra. I do wonder what Harry Grant sees in her."

"Should we do something to sweeten her up, Mr. President?" Lyman asked. "If she keeps on in this vein, she'll make the Sissinghurst conference look like a disaster before it begins. And if, God forbid, she should get wind of the trip to Moscow and Peking—" He broke off, as if the enormity of the thought overwhelmed him.

"How do we do that, Paul? You can't buy what isn't for sale. You can't win what has been given elsewhere."

"I know that, Mr. President. But I thought a little special treatment might get her to take *some* of the edge off."

The President grinned. It rather shocked Lyman to realize, as he did often, that Cleveland Scott Lambert was a bit of a lecher. "Harry isn't available, Paul," the President said. "You aren't suggesting that you or I—?"

"I was thinking more along the line of an exclusive interview, sir. I could have her up here in two minutes."

The President's eyes quickly hardened. "Not a chance, Paul. I don't offer myself up to her sacrificial knife quite that easily. She takes her turn with the rest of the press corps." The President, his smile gone and his flinty texture exposed, regarded the harried, rumpled man standing before him.

Lyman shivered inwardly, aware of his own vulnerability.

"McNary is your problem, Paul," the President said. "I haven't the time for her. So handle it."

"Yes, Mr. President."

Lambert heaved himself to his feet and favored his Press Secretary with a squeeze on the shoulder. "Don't look so grim, Paul. It isn't the end of the world. Not yet."

Lyman watched his chief go into his private quarters. When he was alone, he sat down in the seat Lambert had just vacated and tried to imagine what it would be like to be President of the United States. The simple presence of the Army warrant officer sitting in the crews' quarters, the case containing the nuclear codes chained to his wrist, put the fantasy out of his reach. For which he was silently grateful.

19

In Room 2E294 on the second floor of the Pentagon, the Joint Chiefs of Staff sat in one of their thrice-weekly conferences. The gold-colored drapes had been drawn aside, and the steel map case behind the walnut paneling had been opened to expose a large-scale chart of the central Asian land mass.

The Chiefs of Staff of the Army and the Air Force, the Chief of Naval Operations, and the Commandant of the Marine Corps sat at a sixteen-foot hexagonal table. At the head of the group sat General Clinton Devore, the current chairman. Before each man lay a yellow pad, pencils, an ashtray. The red light indicating a meeting in progress glowed over the locked door.

Beyond the door of the Gold Room lay the War Room. The larger table dominating that chamber was empty, but the tiered areas surrounding the "Pit" were manned by a full complement of military personnel working at desks, computer consoles, and communications equipment. The displays on the wall, changing once every six minutes, gave the watchers a running tally on the disposition of United States military forces everywhere in the world. The telescreens that had once carried information on the American dispositions in Southeast Asia were dark, as were the screens devoted to information from Greece and Turkey. In these areas, American forces had been either withdrawn at the insistence of the Congress or invited to depart by the local governments. The gap that these omissions left in what the Joint Chiefs called the "Operations Perimeter" was evident: an attempt at filling the breach with satellite data and information from picket ships and aircraft had been made, but the coverage was incomplete, painfully and obviously so.

The data screens in the War Room were duplicated on a bank of screens in the Gold Room. Messengers and technicians worked in dumb show, the audio turned down, behind the officers at the hexagonal table.

A second bank of monitors carried similar duplications from the National Command Center, a much larger and more active room connected to the War Room by a short corridor and a flight of descending stairs. In the Center lay the main terminus of all military communications systems connecting Washington to the military and naval commands, including the Looking Glass airborne command center, the Polaris and Trident nuclear-submarine fleet, the North American Air Defense Command, and the National Satellite Tracking, Command, and Control Center.

That portion of satellite tracking and control devoted to the Nathan Hale system was on full alert, all consoles fully manned and all evaluators present.

It seemed to Admiral Muller, the Chief of Naval Operations, that the intensity of activity increased in direct proportion to the distance from the military commanders in the Gold Room. The Nathan Hale section was fully operational and alerted; the Joint Chiefs silent and, Muller thought bleakly, indecisive.

The Admiral doodled a series of stars interspersed with explosions on his yellow pad. Devore was once again going through the report handed to him earlier in the day by Christopher Rosen, the President's Special Adviser for Scientific Affairs.

It seemed to the Admiral that Professor Rosen's main purpose in composing the report had been to deny that the Chinese had accomplished a feat that American scientists had not been able to accomplish. Rosen insisted that it was impossible to construct a chemical laser capable of directly inflicting damage on military targets. Devore, like Muller, remained unconvinced, though the implications were unsettling.

Devore finished the second reading of the report and looked around the table at his colleagues. He knew that Muller was considering the possibility that Rosen and his ad hoc committee were dead wrong and what this might mean to the Navy's beloved cruise missiles. These were subsonic air breathers with highly sophisticated ground-avoidance radar guidance systems. The Navy had developed them after SALT I because, though slow, they could not be detected by Soviet radar and therefore had the capability of turning almost every ship of the Navy into a strategic weapon. An effective laser would make cruise missiles obsolete.

General William Steyning, the former fighter pilot who was now Chief of Staff of the Air Force, was thinking approximately the same thing about the pitifully few B-2 bombers the Air Force had been able to cajole from a hostile and "insular" Congress.

General Lawrence Lazenby, the Marine Commandant, was trying to imagine an amphibious landing against a coastline defended by what amounted to a lattice of death rays. He would have liked to believe the conclusion of Christopher Rosen's study group.

General Herbert Dahlberg, the Army Chief of Staff, was thinking of tanks—of massive tanks glowing cherry red under the probing of threads of coherent light. It was a possibility so far from any that he had ever considered that it brought a thick dryness to his throat.

General Devore had worked closely with these men for more than a year and understood them. They were good men and soon they would make the jump from concern about their individual services to concern about the welfare of the nation.

"You don't share Professor Rosen's opinion, Clint," Muller said, still doodling on his pad.

"I can't afford to," Devore said. He placed a well-manicured hand on the thin stack of papers on the table before him.

"What does Advanced Weapons Research say?"

"They hate to commit themselves, but they don't give a categorical 'no.' The technical problems are substantial, but the thing might be done," Devore said. "They think it might be tested on satellites. Possibly passive birds like Transit—"

"Christ," Muller said. "I hadn't even got round to thinking about that possibility. Could a laser knock out a Transit? The inertial-guidance navigation for Trident and Polaris-Poseidon depends on those birds."

"AWR thinks that if it works at all, the range would be limited. Synchronous birds at thirty thousand kilometers might be far enough out to be safe."

"Might be?" Muller asked. "That's hardly reassuring."

Devore smiled bleakly. "Well, Rosen says it won't work, can't work. But he might be doing what I suspect we have all been tempted to do. That is, think in terms of our own private preserves. If it turns out the Chinese have done it, then Rosen and his team have let the country down badly. So naturally he thinks it is impossible."

"So you disagree with Rosen," Steyning said.

"I do," Devore said. "What's more, so do the Soviets."

"All right," Dahlberg, a scholarly, balding man with steel-rimmed glasses, said, "let's assume Rosen and his group are wrong. What then? What does the President intend?"

Devore glanced at Muller. Only they, of the Joint Chiefs, had been fully briefed on the President's plan to go to Moscow and Peking. Earlier in the day, Defense Secretary Richards had instructed Devore to inform his fellow Chiefs and prepare a recommendation concerning the military posture to be assumed during the negotiations.

Devore said, "The President is going on from Sissinghurst, gentlemen, to Moscow for a meeting with the Soviets. There may be a joint declaration about the Chinese threat to the peace."

"Jesus Christ," Steyning said, "the press will go wild."

"The press doesn't know, and won't. Not until the thing is

done," Devore said. "The President will carry the declaration to Peking personally and offer to mediate between the Chinese and the Soviets."

"This is risky as hell, Clint," Dahlberg said. "Did you recommend this policy?"

"The President makes foreign policy," Devore answered. "I was informed, not consulted."

"I don't see that defusing the Sino-Soviet quarrel is in our interest anyway," Lazenby said. "As long as it exists, we have leverage."

"As long as it exists there is a danger of war," Muller said quietly.

The Marine fixed Muller with a cold glare. "Are you so sure a Sino-Soviet war would be such a bad thing, Admiral?"

"It would be a nuclear war, General," Muller said evenly, "and *any* nuclear war would be a bad thing."

"Comments about the President's decisions are not within our purview, gentlemen," Devore said. "The fact is that he is on the way. The Secretary now directs that we make the best dispositions possible to back him up. Without alarming the civilian population."

"The voters, you mean, Clint?" Lazenby asked. The Marine Commandant was not an admirer of the President, or of any of the current crop of Washington politicians.

"When the declaration is made, whether to the Chinese in private, as the President hopes, or to the world in general, as may be necessary, our dispositions are to suggest that we are both capable and willing to take action," Devore said.

"Military action?" Dahlberg asked. "Against the Chinese?"

"In concert with the Russians?" demanded Lazenby.

"That should be the impression we give," Devore said. But it would be a false one, he knew. The Secretary of Defense had made that very clear. "We won't make direct threats, because we can't carry them out," the Secretary had said. "All we can do is apply psychological pressure."

It would have been fruitless to tell Richards what he already knew, that the installation in the Turfan could be surgically excised with a single flight of B-2 bombers. But the age of "sending a gunboat" was gone. Devore often wondered at the bitter irony of great nations impotent to affect the course of events because they feared to strike a light to the fuse that could blow up the whole bloody world.

"There can be no question of military action," Devore said.

"Then we are talking about a bluff—and not a very convincing one," Lazenby said. "Is this wise?"

"From a military point of view, not entirely," Devore said. "It is never really wise to threaten something you have no intention of doing. But as you gentlemen know, not all the decisions reached in this room are purely military."

"If it is to be a political decision, General," Lazenby said, "why doesn't the Secretary give us a clear directive?"

"Because," Devore said dryly, "there has to be a cutout between the President and the military command. If the decision is the wrong one, we can be cut adrift. I shouldn't have to tell an officer who has been around Washington as long as you have, General, about the way the system works."

A heavy silence fell on the men around the table. Devore realized that he was making their task difficult. That was all right with him. A man didn't rise to command of his service by shirking unpleasant duties. Now he intended to press them further.

"I am recommending that as of tomorrow at 0100 hours, our time, we go to Red One," he said. In the current jargon of the Defense establishment there were six stages of readiness for war. Green for no threat on the horizon, Yellow One and Two for situations in which some action by United States forces abroad might be indicated, and Red One, Two, and Three for situations of increasing hazard up to and including an imminent attack on the continental United States.

A wave of surprised alarm ran through the room. Red One

was the highest stage of alertness that could be ordered by the Joint Chiefs without authorization from the President. Red Three (absurdly, in the opinion of every member of the Joint Chiefs since the law was passed by a militantly pacifist Congress) required the authority of the President *and* two-thirds of the Senate. Since it would be virtually impossible to get sixty-six senators to agree to anything concerning the military, Red Three was considered an unattainable stage of readiness until after an attack. This made Red One a single step from putting the armed forces of the United States on a war footing.

Even Muller was shocked at General Devore's suggestion. "That's one hell of a dangerous suggestion, Clint," he said.

Devore snapped off the recorder in the table. "I have been authorized to say this—off the record. The President needs Red One to give him credibility with the Communists. I think you all know it has to be this way to counterbalance the image given by our Congress among the Reds. It's extreme and we might be giving Senator Sutton and his friends our heads on a chafing dish. But it has to be, so let's face up to it. I can't order Red One on my own authority. It has to be unanimous among the Joint Chiefs. Make up your minds, gentlemen." He waited for an objection. The silence in the room grew oppressive. "All right," he said. "That's it, then."

He snapped on the recorder again and said, "Your comment is noted, Admiral Muller. Anyone else?" Again the heavy, ominous wait. Again no spoken objection. "I call for a vote on Red One as of 0100 hours, tomorrow's date." He called the roll deliberately. There were no dissenting votes. "Very well, gentlemen, I will notify Secretary Richards so that he may keep the President informed. This meeting is now closed." He gathered up his papers and thrust them into a briefcase.

As the Joint Chiefs filed silently out of the Gold Room, Muller murmured to Devore, "What would you have done if I had voted no, Clint? On the record."

"I would have relieved you," Devore said without hesitation.

"That's what I thought," the CNO said quietly. "But I still think it's a dangerous situation."

"I agree with you," Devore said. "And I hope to God the politicians know what they are about."

Muller looked out across the empty Pit of the War Room. At 0100 hours tomorrow, the plotting tables would be manned, the room would be alive with tension and a kind of horrifying, fascinating excitement that only the threat of human conflict could bring.

"Amen to that," he said fervently.

20

Grant was finishing breakfast alone in the small dining room of the Stafford when the porter appeared to tell him that he had a telephone call.

He took it at the porter's desk, thinking the caller might be Ballard or someone at the Embassy. Instead, it was Bronwen Wells. She sounded much more animated than he remembered, and for the first time he detected the strange, to him, Welsh cadences in her speech.

"I hope I am not troubling you, Mr. Grant."

"No, of course not." He had offered to help her, and he did want to speak with her again.

"I've remembered something. It may be nothing at all, but perhaps it could be important."

"What is it, Miss Wells?"

"You remember I told you about Alek saying that odd thing about a yellow case. And then there was that other man who asked me about it. I did mention that to you yesterday, Mr. Grant, didn't I?"

"Yes, you did. Have you found anything like that?"

"No. But I remember now that *I* have something that one might call a 'yellow case.' I keep my practice things in it. You understand, a leotard, slippers, that sort of thing."

"Where, Miss Wells? At home?"

"No, not here. It's at Madame Zelinskaya's. It's a loft, you see, in Chelsea. Some of the company practice there in the off season." She hesitated and then rushed on, the words tumbling in a kind of hysterical elation. Grant realized that this was the second stage of the shock she was undergoing, but anything was better than yesterday's dull despair.

"It isn't truly a yellow suitcase, Mr. Grant. It is only a canvas holdall. But it could be the thing Alek meant. I mean, it might be, surely?"

"It's worth a look," Grant said.

"Yes. Yes, I think so, too. I'll go and collect it straight away, shall I?"

Grant made a snap decision. Time was growing short. He could hardly justify chasing yellow cases in company with Bronwen Wells. He decided to do just that and felt better for it. He said, "Give me the address. I'll meet you there." They could pick up the case, and if it contained nothing but Bronwen's practice clothes, they could take it to Ian Ballard's men for a more complete inspection. It was just about time now, Grant thought, for some transatlantic co-operation.

"Thank you," she said in a suddenly quiet voice. "I don't think I want to be alone any longer."

Grant was surprised by the intensity of his reaction to that simple statement.

The address was in Hobhouse Close, a dead-end street somewhere off the King's Road, and not really the sort of loft he had expected. Rather, it was the top story of an old town house that had been opened up to contain Madame Zelinskaya's ballet school.

Grant arrived in a taxi, being unwilling to waste time finding his way through the maze of London streets. A steady rain was falling out of a dark sky, and the temperature had dropped to near freezing. As Grant alighted and stood bareheaded in the close, a frosted-glass door opened and Bronwen stood there, wrapped in a belted raincoat, a beret on her rain-damp hair. He was touched again by the effort she was obviously making to give him the impression she was in command of herself.

Her hands were cold in his; he hoped that it was only the cold of the winter morning and not the dead cold of despair. She had taken a long look at hell, and the courage with which she had faced it deserved to be rewarded with an end to grief. He found himself wishing that he had more time, that he had met Bronwen under different circumstances.

"Is something wrong?" she asked. They still stood in the open doorway. On the floor above Grant could hear someone playing a Tchaikovsky melody on a piano and the soft thudding of ballet shoes on a hardwood floor.

"Wrong? No, why?"

"You were looking at me so strangely just now," she said. Her small even teeth caught briefly at her lower lip, giving her the air of a perplexed child.

"I'm pleased to see you looking better," he said.

"Do I? Seem better, that is? Maybe it's too soon for that," she said. She let the door close behind them but did not move toward the stairs. In the semidarkness of the hallway she stood head down, as though she was trying to compose herself, to formulate some idea that kept evading her. Her hair and the damp beret held a faint scent of flowers, or some elusive, delicate perfume.

Presently, she said, "Perhaps I am not a good person. It suddenly seems that Alek has been gone a very long time." She raised her eyes to him, and something seemed to turn over inside him, stunning him with the intensity of his reaction. She said, "I want to live. No, that's wrong. I want to start living again. That's wicked, I know, with Alek dead—" She broke off and looked pleadingly at Grant. He had the impulse to take her in his arms and he realized that it was not the first time. All his life he had suspected that there were people drawn to one another by some sort of instant chemistry, an unexplained and unexplainable intimacy that existed outside logic. He had never known it at first hand, and yet here it was, battering at his common sense and incredulity.

He touched her cheek lightly with his fingertips and said, "No, there is nothing wicked about it, Bronwen. Don't think there is." He might have added that the dead were dead and that all the grief in the world would never revive them. If he had learned one thing as a soldier, it was certainly that.

She caught his hand and held it. They stood so for a long moment, until the door burst open and a group of four young girls carrying canvas bags ran, laughing and talking, up the stairs.

Bronwen smiled faintly and said, "I was like that once. We are all Fonteyns and Makarovas at that age." She took his hand again, but lightly now, and said, "Let's go and find my yellow bag."

The ballet mistress was a thin, steely-bodied woman with red hair gone to gray, a face like a hawk's, and immense pale-blue eyes. She burst into a dazzling smile at the sight of Bronwen and moved across the floor of the long room to embrace her.

Grant, who had never been inside a ballet school before, looked about with interest. At the far end of the room, which ran the length of the house, a long-haired young man sat at a piano piled high with scores. The walls were lined with mirrors, and at waist level a practice bar ran down one side of the room. Along the far wall, two young male dancers exercised at it. Three girls in grubby leotards and toeshoes practiced pliés to the Tchaikovsky melody, which was played again and again in metronomic rhythm.

"This is Mr. Grant, Madame," Bronwen said.

Madame Zelinskaya, with a positively royal presence even in her threadbare lavender leotard, extended a hand, and Grant had the impression he was expected to kiss it. He shook it instead and was favored with a smile.

Bronwen said, "I'll go and collect the bag. Look after him, please, Madame." She moved away toward the hallway.

Madame Zelinskaya said, "She is one of my favorites, the little Welsh girl. Are you a friend, Mr. Grant?" Her voice was British, but heavily accented. Russian or Polish, Grant guessed.

"We have only just met," Grant said.

"Ah. I see." The old woman paused before saying meaningfully, "You are not a friend of the Russian, then?"

Grant had difficulty understanding what she meant, before he remembered: Voronin, of course. She had not heard about his death at Dover? Unlikely, he thought, though possible. Probably these ballet people paid little attention to news outside their own demanding world.

"No," Grant said carefully, "I never met Colonel Voronin."

"He has not been good for the little Welsh girl," Madame Zelinskaya said positively. "He distracts her from her dancing."

Before Grant could comment, the girls who had passed them in the hallway came in from the dressing room. They were still chattering and laughing as they walked by in the peculiar splay-footed way of dancers in toeshoes.

"Excuse me, if you please, Mr. Grant," Madame Zelinskaya said. "I must attend." She clapped her hands imperiously for the girls' attention and began giving them instructions.

Bronwen reappeared. She was carrying a scuffed canvas carryall. It could be called yellow. She looked pleased, almost excited. She started to open it. "Why don't we wait until we are in the taxi, Bronwen," Grant said.

She looked about quickly, "Yes. All right." She spoke her farewells to Madame Zelinskaya, and the two women embraced again.

"Good-by, Madame," Grant said formally.

"Perhaps we will meet again, Mr. Grant," Madame Zelinskaya replied with equal formality.

In the street, Bronwen said suddenly, "Madame did not like Alek. She is a Russian refugee, you see."

"Yes," Grant said. "I understand."

Bronwen slipped her arm through his and, holding the canvas

bag to her chest with the other, lifted her face to the rain. As they walked out of the close, she said softly, "This isn't it, is it? I mean, this bag isn't what Alek meant."

"Perhaps not. But we'll make sure," he said.

"I looked inside. Only my old practice clothes are in it." There was disappointment in her tone, sadness in her manner. Grant took it from her and held it under his free arm. She walked very close to him. "I wanted it to be important, I wanted it to be something that would explain why Alek had to die."

"I know," he said. "We *will* know why." That much, he thought, I can do for you.

They walked in silence toward the Thames, Grant looking for a cruising taxi to take them to Westminster and Ballard's office.

In a small room off the practice hall in the house on Hobhouse Close, Madame Zelinskaya dialed a number on the telephone.

"She was here to collect her practice clothes," she said in Russian.

The male voice on the other end of the line asked, "Was the American with her?"

"Yes."

"Very well," the man said, and broke the connection.

He turned to his companion and said, "No wonder we found nothing. The woman had it at Zelinskaya's."

"What do we do now?"

The KGB man stood at the window and watched the rain falling on the street before the Soviet Embassy. "We wait," he said.

21

General Sergei Vissarionovich Oblensky lay supine on the bed in his quarters and regarded the voluptuous buttocks of his second-in-command as she stepped out of her uniform. Louisa Feodorovna was certainly the most enticing Soviet Air Force officer in Aral'sk or anywhere else, he thought.

She folded her skirt neatly and placed it on the leather chair across from the bed. Oblensky watched her with anticipation. Her flesh was white, still marked with the imprint of her underclothes. Her thighs were full and firm, the inner surfaces warm and smooth as velvet to the touch. The patch of hair covering her pubic mound was reddish-gold and thick, and her round belly was covered with a faint golden down.

She smiled under his scrutiny and asked, "You like what you see, Comrade General?" She enjoyed teasing him with mention of his rank whenever they went to bed: it was her own form of coquetry. Later, she would become wanton and her talk would run to vulgarisms from her native Ukraine. Oblensky enjoyed that, too. Louisa had been a revelation to him. He had had no idea that such women actually existed in the Soviet state. The lady colonel, he thought, was a born courtesan. She belonged in the court of Peter the Great.

"I like what I see very much. Come to bed," Oblensky said. He was erect and taut with watching her. But she delayed longer, knowing that he was not yet completely ready for her. She stretched and cupped her large breasts. The dark nipples stood hard and contracted as she moved toward the bed. Oblensky reached out for her, and she let him feel the smooth skin of her buttocks.

It was nothing short of miraculous, Oblensky thought, that such a woman should be one of Marshal Leonov's special protégés. He wondered, as he had many times, if the Marshal had ever had her. He did not think so. The Marshal was not like ordinary men. It was difficult to think of him humping and pounding between a woman's thighs.

He felt himself slacken. The thought of Yuri Leonov had done it.

Louisa looked at him and raised an eyebrow. "Perhaps this is not a good time, Sergei?" she said.

Oblensky heaved himself into a sitting position and reached for the vodka on the low table near the bed. "I thought about *him*," he said, frowning.

Louisa sat on the bed beside him and held out her hand for a glass. "My poor general," she said.

Oblensky gave her a drink and tossed down his own. He held the glass thoughtfully and then refilled it. "What did you make of his visit yesterday, Louisa?" he said.

The woman shrugged her naked shoulders and sipped at the glass of vodka she held. "A routine inspection," she said.

Oblensky shook his head. "No. There was nothing routine about it." He hesitated, not certain that he should continue in this vein. The example of Aleksandr Voronin stood there for all Leonov's protégés to see and ponder. "We have changed the fail-safe procedures. On his orders. Did you know that?" As second-in-command, Louisa would *not* normally know about such a change unless she should have a *need* to know. But under Marshal Leonov's command much had been changing.

Louisa's white hand caressed her own thighs and belly. "Are we going to spend the night talking about that?" she asked.

"It is important, woman. Don't you understand what's happening? The changes he ordered effectively put this base under his personal command. The Kremlin is out of the launch procedure."

"Kirov is a sick man," Louisa said. "A dying man, according to what I hear."

Oblensky wondered suddenly what else she heard, and from whom. He wondered, too, what had happened to him in the years since he had been at Frunze as one of Leonov's chosen few. In those days he had craved action, high risks, excitement. When had the doubts begun? Certainly he had had them even when his appointment to the Aral'sk missile complex had been announced. But they had grown to frightening proportions since his arrival in this place. Perhaps it was the proximity of the actual weapons that had unmanned him: the nuclear warheads that could scour a million square kilometers of all life.

He leaned back against the pillows and reached for Louisa. The woman was what he needed, he thought. He needed to bury himself in her, not thinking about what he was almost certain now Leonov intended.

The Marshal had ordered a reprogramming of the target list. Had the order come from anyone else, Oblensky would have been on the line to the Kremlin instantly. And had the order been given to anyone but one of Leonov's protégés, the result would have been the same.

But Oblensky had not reported the target changes.

He closed his eyes and thought: The man is the Minister of Defense. And: He may well be the next ruler of the Soviet Union. There was no reason to assume, as many did, that Valentin Kirov's successor must come from the party or the bureaucracy. Why *not* the armed forces? Was that not where the power really lay?

He remembered the Crisis Confrontation Lectures as though they had been delivered yesterday. They were aggressive, nakedly so. They dealt with the realities of power. And they served to separate the wolves from the jackals. If he were truly honest with himself, Oblensky thought, he would admit that he had always known that it would come to this.

But what, exactly, was *this*?

To start a war, possibly the last war men would ever fight?

He shivered, as though a cold wind had touched his naked flesh.

Louisa's hand was on him. She smiled, showing white, even teeth. "Am *I* frightening you, Comrade General?"

How well the man knew his creatures, Oblensky thought in a rush of self-hatred. With some it was liquor, or privilege, or worse. With Sergei Vissarionovich Oblensky it was women. Women like Louisa Feodorovna. Richly ripe, voluptuous, white-skinned, and dark-nippled women.

He forced himself to smile. "A Soviet man fears nothing. Least of all his woman," he said, reaching for her. His own sexuality was the antidote to doubt, to timidity, to *sanity,* he thought. He rolled Louisa over roughly, spread her legs, and entered her, letting sensation destroy fear.

Louisa Feodorovna left General Oblensky's quarters in the early hours of the morning. She moved with an unhurried pace out of the senior officers' compound, across the service road that led to the command center and across an expanse of lawn damp with mist from the Sea of Aral'sk. In the distance she could make out the faint sky glow of the city of Aral'sk, in the foreground the sharp line of lighted towers that formed the first security cordon around the missile base.

She had enjoyed her hours with Sergei Oblensky. The man was physically unattractive, but he was strong and driven by his fears to really remarkable sexual performances. He was an athlete in bed. An athlete without finesse, to be sure, but a man no woman like herself could fault.

He was, however, a fool, she had concluded. It had been clear to all from the beginning at Frunze that the time would come for decisive action. Now that it was near, Oblensky was weakening. The Marshal would be disappointed in him, but not surprised. Her own instructions made it plain enough that the Marshal believed in—she smiled in the chilly, wet darkness—backup systems.

The reprogramming of targets was under way. The junior officers, the pod crews, would not have to be informed before launch time. The targeting was all controlled from the central command computer, and she, Louisa Feodorovna, would be in charge at the computer center.

Beyond the reprogramming, what remained was the positioning of additional security. General Zabotin had promised a full battalion of GRU troops. The personnel were already on the move and would fly in aboard six special Tupolevs during the morning.

She allowed herself to consider the possibilities that seemed to frighten Oblensky. She could not see them as so terrible. There might well be some Russian casualties, but the important thing was that the Americans would, at worst, be immobilized, and, at best, active participants. The years of planning by Marshal Leonov took all possibilities into consideration. The nation would recapture some of the spirit and discipline it had lost since the death of Comrade Stalin. And women could once again be proud of their role in the new society.

At the command center a soldier of the GRU saluted and demanded her identification. The boy saw her every day, she thought approvingly, yet he acted correctly. She presented the coded card, then walked swiftly through the quiet corridors to the lift. At the third level she emerged into a hallway where blast doors stood open. Another GRU guard asked for her identification and again she presented it. She moved through a radiation-proof, lead-lined chicane in the corridor and arrived finally at her destination, a small office reserved for communications by senior officers. She had to unlock the door before she could enter. Once inside, she had to unlock the scrambler phone.

This done, she tapped out the code for General Zabotin's headquarters. She listened to the signal and was given the combination of the day for Zabotin's home. She punched the five-digit series into the scrambler's console and waited. Presently Zabotin's voice, thick with sleep, answered.

"Louisa Feodorovna here, Comrade General."

"Go ahead."

"In my opinion, Oblensky is unreliable."

There was a momentary silence. Feodorovna understood that Zabotin was considering the possibility that her statement was an attempt to remove Oblensky so that she might take his place. He would have to think about that. But she was certain that he would remember that such self-serving was extremely rare among Leonovites. The Marshal picked his people more carefully than that. Still, she was implying that he had made a mistake of sorts with Oblensky.

Zabotin asked, "Have you facts to back up your opinion?"

"None yet. It is just my opinion."

A touch of sarcasm in the reply. "Woman's intuition?" The man was a chauvinist, after all.

"The Comrade Marshal said that I was to be completely frank. I have given you my evaluation. What is to be done about it is up to you. I am ready to carry out your instructions."

Another silence, more prolonged this time, Feodorovna noticed.

Presently Zabotin said, "No immediate action. But watch him carefully. If he shows *any* signs of informing Moscow, kill him."

"Yes, Comrade General."

"You have the means?"

Feodorovna smiled at the locked door. "I have the means, Comrade General."

"Good, then."

"When may we expect the troops?"

"No later than 1100 hours."

"And the Comrade Marshal?"

"That has not yet been decided exactly. How soon will the retargeting procedure be completed?"

"As soon as we have exact co-ordinates from Baikonur."

"Then good night, Comrade Colonel," Zabotin said, and broke the connection.

22

Approaching the age of seventy, Marshal of the Soviet Army Pavel Semyonovich Lyudin had learned patience. He had lived more years than the Soviet state and he had served it diligently and with distinction. As a military cadet he had escaped the purges of the mid-'30s, and as a company commander he had survived the black early days of the Great Patriotic War. His rivalry with Marshal Yuri Leonov was not of his choosing. He avoided political conflicts whenever possible, and left to his own devices, he would never have allowed himself to be used in a challenge to the younger man.

But Leonov was the sort of officer who aroused great loyalties—and great antagonisms. The older men in the Politburo had proposed Marshal Lyudin as their candidate for the post of minister of Defense as much because of their instinctive distrust of and aversion to Leonov as because of any reliance on Lyudin. The old Marshal had no brilliance. He had a certain talent for survival and a loyalty to the older members of the Kremlin leadership, men such as First Secretary Kirov and Foreign Minister Krasin. These qualities had not been enough to win him the support of the more activist members of the Supreme Soviet. He had been defeated in the contest for the post of Defense minister, a post that carried with it supreme command of all the armed forces of the Soviet Union.

Since Leonov had taken the post, Lyudin had momentarily expected a command to retire. It was improbable, he thought, that the younger man would permit him to remain in his position as chief of staff of the Soviet Army.

Leonov had not, however, relieved him or forced him into retirement. At first, Lyudin considered the possibility that Leonov feared to replace him with one of his ubiquitous protégés from Frunze and therefore risk the opposition of the Old Guard. But it soon became apparent to Lyudin that Leonov withheld the stroke for less fearful reasons—perhaps only because he did not think it worth the trouble. A blow to Lyudin's pride, but he was realistic enough to accept it. Though not to forgive it.

Through the whole of Leonov's tenure as minister of Defense, Lyudin behaved with military punctilio and with great discretion. His position was at risk to begin with and the deteriorating health of his most powerful supporter, Valentin Kirov, increased his vulnerability each day. The USSR no longer retired its military commanders with a pistol shot in the back of the neck, but with a man like Yuri Leonov in command of the armed forces, the practice just might be reinstated.

In these circumstances it was a measure of Lyudin's concern that he had crossed official channels to deliver personally to Kirov a piece of information that had mightily disturbed him.

Since the meeting three days ago in the First Secretary's dacha, during which the developments in the Turfan had been discussed, Marshal Leonov had made a number of peculiar—to Lyudin the word should be "suspicious"—military dispositions.

The entrenched divisions of the Far Eastern Army—the units facing the Chinese along the Amur and Ussuri rivers—had been alerted to participate in a series of winter maneuvers. This periodic action was a reasonable enough decision from the military point of view, though it came at a time when great stretches of the border rivers were frozen and capable of being crossed by infantry. The maneuvers, code-named Task Red Glory, seemed ill-timed to Lyudin. Leonov had also moved a number of Soviet naval units, including three of the newest Allende-class missile ships, into the China Sea from their bases in Haiphong. And lastly, most suspiciously, Lyudin thought, he had ordered a series of *manned* Svoboda satellite launches from Baikonur. It was the unmanned satellites that flew over Lop Nor and the Turfan daily and these Svobodas that had supplied the first indications of the new installations in the Turfan Depression.

Yet the Svoboda had not been able to supply the specific information required by the Soviet Air Force staff. It had been necessary to send a GRU agent to the local site. The agent had done his job—and paid for it with his life, Lyudin guessed accurately. Then why was it now necessary to man Svobodas? To the old Marshal it seemed that Leonov was intent on refining his data on the laser installations at Turfan.

At the Soviet Army Command Center outside Moscow, the Chinese Target List in the central computer now carried a "Temporarily Withdrawn for Update" flag. This was a procedure that was run at irregular intervals of from thirty to ninety days. The last target update, however, had taken place no more than eleven days ago.

None of these oddities was certain evidence that anything out of the ordinary was taking place, but all of them—coming when a secret meeting was about to take place between Valentin Kirov and the American President—had set Lyudin to thinking.

At the dacha he had been greeted by one of the First Secretary's aides, a young naval officer. Before being allowed to speak to Comrade Kirov, the aide said, it would be necessary for the Comrade Marshal to speak with the resident physician now on duty. Lyudin was led through the crackling snow to the residence building and there passed through the cordon of Guardsmen into the medical facility and office. The duty doctor was a middle-aged Georgian woman who introduced herself as Academician Lisavetta Lazarova.

The atmosphere in the dacha compound had grown grimmer, or so it appeared to Lyudin. There were many more KGB troops evident, the medical facility seemed more heavily staffed, and the faces of all the First Secretary's household aides were drawn with concern.

"Has he grown worse, Comrade Academician?"

The woman, tired and irritable, frowned. "Is that what is being said in Moscow?"

Lyudin unbuttoned his greatcoat and frowned back at the physician. "Nothing is being 'said in Moscow,' Comrade Academician. Yesterday's bulletin stated that the First Secretary was improving, and that his temperature was down. Was the bulletin incorrect?"

"Forgive me, Comrade Marshal," Lazarova said. "I didn't mean to imply anything improper. But, yes, the bulletin was incorrect. At least it was not completely accurate. The First Secretary is still very ill."

"I wish to speak with him. It is necessary."

"Are you absolutely certain, Comrade Marshal? He desperately needs to rest. General Novikov was with him through much of the night."

Lyudin's sense of unease grew. Why would the commander of the KGB have been with the First Secretary through much of the night?

"Novikov is here?"

"No, Comrade Marshal. He left for Moscow early this morning."

"Is Comrade Kirov too sick to see me, then?"

"Comrade Marshal, I hope you will understand what I am saying to you. The First Secretary is an extremely sick man—"

"I know that. Do you take me for a fool?" Lyudin spoke sharply.

"No, I do not, Comrade Marshal. But I must emphasize once again that the First Secretary's embryoma—"

"If he saw Novikov last night, he can see me today. I am not here to discuss idle matters, Comrade Academician."

The woman looked distressed. Lyudin guessed that he was forcing her to make a judgment—and a statement of that judgment—that she most definitely wished to avoid.

He said harshly: "The First Secretary will have to make a

great effort during the next few days. You must know that the Americans will be here very soon."

"I do, and I am appalled, Comrade Marshal, to think of my patient facing such an ordeal."

"Your medical concern is commendable, Comrade Lazarova. But Comrade Kirov will do his duty. My question is: can he perform as he must? This is a matter of great importance to the state."

The doctor's dark eyes seemed suddenly liquid and sad. Deep lines of fatigue and concern etched the plain, Georgian face. "Comrade Marshal Lyudin, the First Secretary is dying."

Lyudin felt some of the tension leave him. What remained was a strange sort of lethargy, a hopelessness that he could not precisely define except that it was an emotion connected with his secret vision of a world run by ruthless men much younger than himself, men to whom his years of service and devotion to the state and the Revolution were worth nothing.

He stirred himself to act. "I thank you for your frankness. It does not come as a surprise to me to know that Comrade Kirov's illness is that severe. We all know it will kill him. The problem is when? And how much can he be expected to do between now and the time when the inevitable happens? I have a great many matters to discuss with him—matters that require *his* decision."

"Come," Lazarova said.

She led the way down the pine-paneled hall toward the reception room outside the sickroom. As Lyudin walked, he could feel the temperature rising. It was suffocating outside Kirov's door.

The doctor signaled the KGB guard to stand aside and then said to Lyudin, "He was given a sedative when General Novikov left him. He may be asleep."

"Wake him, woman," Lyudin said impatiently, suffering in the heat.

"That may not be easy," she said, and opened the door.

First Secretary Valentin Kirov lay on the bed, propped erect.

A nurse stood when the doctor and the Marshal appeared, but Kirov gave no sign. His gray, sunken face seemed more wasted than before, Lyudin thought. Was it possible that he was failing that fast?

The man's breathing was shallow and slow. His eyes gleamed, half open, but he lay in a drugged half-sleep with his lips apart to show gold-backed, nicotine-stained teeth and the tip of a thick, gray-furred tongue. The smell of rotting was in the air of the room.

"He exhausted himself last night while General Novikov was here," the doctor said. "He needs to rest."

"You shouldn't have drugged him," Lyudin said angrily. "His mind must be kept clear."

Lazarova's eyes flashed with an anger to match his own. *"The man needs rest,* Comrade Marshal! You are all killing him with your urgent messages and worries."

"Very well, Comrade Academician," he said. "But I must try to speak to him."

The doctor shrugged despairingly and signaled to the nurse to leave the room. The old Marshal moved to the bed and leaned over the ravaged face of the ruler of the Soviet Union.

"Comrade First Secretary, it is I, Lyudin."

There was no response from the sick man. The odor of illness made the old soldier want to gag. Kirov smelled like a day-old battlefield.

"Valentin," he said more softly, "can you hear me?"

The stupefied eyes opened slightly, but there was no comprehension in them. Lyudin turned exasperatedly to the woman standing behind him. "How long? For Christ's sweet sake, how long will he be like this?"

"Several hours, Comrade Marshal. He must rest, believe me. He is exhausted."

Lyudin straightened abruptly. "Very well, I will wait, then."

He went to the door of the room and turned to scowl at the physician. "Are you here all the time now?"

"Since yesterday, when we decided that a physician should always be here."

He studied the woman's face carefully. He had the feeling—amounting to a suspicion—that she was withholding information from him about Comrade Kirov's true condition. That was one of the problems with doctors when one dealt with matters of a leader's health. Their fear of blame made them cautious, and when their patient failed to respond to their treatments, the caution became fear and they began to lie. Was it desperation he saw in Lisavetta Lazarova's face now, he wondered. He could not be certain and he dared not make accusations. At least not yet. Perhaps Valentin Kirov *was* only resting.

He nodded his grudging acquiescence to the woman and went back into the only slightly less overheated anteroom to wait.

He stood for a time staring unseeing out of the double-glazed window at the snowy whiteness outside. He thought carefully about Yuri Leonov. Was he being overly suspicious, he wondered. After all, there had never been a successful coup in the Soviet Union. In the early days of the Revolution there had been palace revolts that might be thought of as coups, but they had not been—not actually. They had been carefully planned assumptions of power by men who were, in the final analysis, most suited to hold it.

Stalin had succeeded Lenin by virtue of his ability to command loyalty in those bitter and terrible days. It was fashionable now to think of Stalin as some sort of mad butcher, and certainly his toll of dead and exiled was enormous. But the times had been incredibly difficult, and Josif Vissarionovich had only done what needed doing. And who but so strong a man could have saved the Motherland from the fascists? Still, there was a stench of sickness in the land now, and it did not all come from the First Secretary's rotting kidney.

The old Marshal sensed that the Soviet state, that Russia herself, was in danger. And he could do nothing but wait for Kirov to waken from his thick sleep.

Sweating in his woolen uniform, Pavel Semyonovich Lyudin sat down near a window overlooking the frozen Moscow River and wished that he and that all the Old Guard were still physically and mentally strong enough to deal with what he sensed was nearly upon them.

23

The plain-clothes man sitting in his unmarked car near Bronwen Wells's flat was bored. He had seen her leave earlier in the morning and had duly reported it by radio. He had not been ordered to follow her, but to wait near the flat instead. It seemed to him that the surveillance plan was lax, but he was not the sort of man who caused trouble by complaining to his superiors. He was told to wait on station and wait he did, his alertness dulled by the wet cold and his boredom.

He did notice a couple walking up the street: a middle-aged man in work clothes and with longish gray hair and a bird of the sort that were growing less common in London these days—thin, dressed in scuffy men's jeans and leather jacket, hair straight and stringy (and none too clean, he thought idly).

The pair walked in a peculiarly entangled manner, the man's arm around the girl's waist, his hand under the leather jacket (and under her shirt, too, the policeman guessed disapprovingly). The girl walked with her hand jammed into the man's waistband, and they kept their heads together, with much nuzzling and mouthing of necks and cheeks.

The policeman looked away. He did not fancy sex as a public exhibition, but there was nothing to be done about this sort of thing. The couple were breaking no laws—except the laws of good taste, he thought sourly.

They had come up the street from the direction of Hampstead Road, walking slowly, as though they had nowhere in particular to go and no reason to hurry along. The policeman wondered darkly how people like that managed to live, obviously not working. They lived on the dole, of course, collecting money that other people had to work to earn and then pay over in taxes. That was your bloody welfare state for you. Some men had to sit in the cold, doing boring and nasty jobs so that blokes like that one could spend the day wandering about feeling their birds in public—and probably having a good laugh about it in the bargain. For a moment he was tempted to accost the pair and make some sort of trouble for them, but it wouldn't do, of course. It wasn't against the law to irritate London citizens, even plain-clothes men.

Near the Wells girl's flat the pair got into a laughing and grabbing scramble, acting like teen-agers, though the man, at least, had to be in his forties. The girl said something to him and he laughed and said something back. They were both looking in the direction of his car, and he knew bloody well that they were putting on their act to irritate him, and succeeding, particularly when the man put his hands on the girl's braless chest and had himself a fine old feel.

The policeman felt a flush of anger and looked away. He could hear the pair laughing. At him, he hadn't a doubt.

When he looked again, they had moved on past a line of flats, several of which had signs on the windows: peace symbols, old CND posters, and admonitions to "Vote Labour" (which the policeman always had done, of course).

He ducked his head to light a cigarette. He was on duty and should not be smoking, but the conduct of the "liberated" couple on his beat had aroused a resentful rebellion. He sat low in the seat, cupping the smoke in his hand, feeling the boredom returning. He did not know why he was watching Bronwen Wells's flat and by now he didn't really care. There had been a flurry of excitement when the Russians had come to collect some luggage, but that had been on someone else's shift.

When he finished the cigarette, he conscientiously rubbed off the coal, broke the paper to scatter the shreds of tobacco outside the car window, and balled the remains into a pellet.

He sat up straighter and looked for the man and girl, but they had gone. The street that he could see from one end to the other through the rain-streaked windscreen of the car was silent and empty.

24

Like many of his predecessors, Harold Hood, Vice President of the United States, was a person of little political consequence. He had been Cleveland Lambert's fourth choice as a running mate, selected only after it had been concluded by the party powers that if Hood could add little to the ticket, he was at least unlikely to embarrass anyone.

Students of American politics had pondered for many years the anomaly of the Vice Presidency. It was a position of absolutely no authority, and yet it was a position of potentially supreme authority. For the past decade politicians had been promising to select only men suitable for the Presidency to fill the office, this due to the fact that many Vice Presidents had actually been called upon to do so. But their success upon assuming the Presidency had been, and would remain for the foreseeable future, a matter of chance. The second position on the ticket still fell to the lot of the Harold Hoods, party loyalists, and liberal or conservative stalking horses, as needed.

In the Lambert administration there had been no attempt even to give lip service to keeping the Vice President involved in the business of the nation. In Cleveland Lambert's opinion, the times were too difficult, the problems too complex, for the mental equipment of Harold Cassius Hood. It was a standard joke among White House staffers that Vice President Hood did not know the private number of the White House telephone and that he had never thought to ask for it.

Hood had served twenty-five years as a senator, and in that quarter-century he had never challenged the conventional wisdom of the party—whatever it might be. In the time of isolationism that followed the defeat in Vietnam, he had become—quite sincerely—a pacifist and antimilitarist. He had embraced at one time or another during his political career the New Frontier, the Great Society, the New Federalism, the Reasonable Alternative, and the New Populism. When the electorate gave notice that they would accept no more grandiosely named plans and policies, he was heard to declare that he had never believed in bloated schemes and unfulfillable promises.

Hood was now in his late sixties and he was tired. He had accepted the Vice Presidency gratefully, aware that he would be ignored, and secretly grateful for that, too. He scarcely knew Cleveland Lambert; Lambert the man made him uneasy, and Hood avoided him. But the prerogatives of the Vice Presidency seemed to him a suitable reward for years of devoted service to the party and the nation, and he wanted nothing more than to finish his political career full of years and honors.

In the book-lined study of Admiral's House, the residence of the Vice Presidents of the United States, he received his late-night visitor uneasily. Senator DeWitt Sutton's infrequent appearances in the Vice President's circle always presaged trouble and unwanted decisions. Though he had never been so unwise as to say in public that he doubted the soundness of the policies established by the Senate Overwatch Committee on Intelligence, it seemed to him an elementary truth that the eager public disclosure of covert activities conducted by American agencies gave much aid and comfort to the nation's enemies. His silence on the subject was simply his notion of proper Vice Presidential reticence. And surely, he often told himself, United States senators could never be governed by any but the most patriotic motives.

Hood, a plump-bodied man with a high-domed forehead and soft brown eyes, sat behind his leather-covered—and empty—desk. The library of Admiral's House was a warm room, gracefully proportioned, but without the Georgian grandeur of similar rooms in the White House. In a way, the room and the house were symbolic of Hood's reduced, but comfortable ambitions. The Vice President had once dreamed of moving up, but repeated rebuffs in the primary elections had taught him that the Presidency was (and probably always had been) beyond his reach. Now he was content, here in Admiral's House. And he had no wish at all to be disturbed and confused by the implications of what Senator Sutton was saying.

"I think it is unconscionable, Mr. Vice President," the Senator from California said, baring his long teeth in his characteristic grimace of disdain, "that the President has flown off to Europe this way leaving you totally unbriefed."

Hood bridled at that, though it was near to being the simple truth. "I *did* speak to the President, Senator."

Sutton, suspecting correctly that the conversation had been brief and probably on the telephone, said, "And did he show you Chris Rosen's report, Mr. Vice President?"

"No. That he did not," Hood said, deflated.

"Well, sir. It happens that Chris and I have gone very carefully over his preliminary findings. He assures me that whatever the Chinese are building up there in Sinkiang, it *isn't* a weapon. Good God, a *death* ray? The thing is absurd."

The Vice President, a garrulous man, made an effort to begin talking, but the Senator interrupted him. "Hold on just a moment, sir. Let me make my point." He directed a long, well-manicured finger across the desk. "The plain fact is that Cleveland Lambert is using this fantasy for political purposes. You know as well as I that his performance in office hasn't pleased some of us. He was elected as a liberal, as a man with some compassion for the poor and the minorities, and look at the record! His last budget message called for a twenty percent increase in the Pentagon's appropriations. He's trying to revive the Trident submarine building program. *After* the battle we had with the opposition about paring it back to some reasonable size. The Air Force wants a whole new generation of missiles. *New* missiles, when the Minuteman force is capable of pulverizing the Soviet Union *and* the People's Republic *three times over—*"

The Vice President, whose understanding of the technical points governing missile obsolescence was minimal, had heard that the Soviets had been hard at work deploying increasing numbers of immensely powerful ICBMs capable of neutralizing the Minuteman force with a pre-emptive strike. But to hear an important member of the Committee on Intelligence mouth the conventional wisdom about American overkill capacity tended to reassure him.

"The point is," Sutton said, "that Lambert has not lived up to the promises he made to the party or the people. He has allowed himself to fall into the same trap that other Presidents have stumbled into so stupidly. He wants to play the power game, and the only way that can be done is by using scare tactics." He leaned forward to give emphasis to his words. "This secret trip to Russia and Peking, sir. By God, it's almost an impeachable offense if he intends to make commitments without the advice and consent of the Senate."

Hood made a placating gesture. He hated to hear words like "impeachable offense" and "secret commitment." That was the sort of thing the *other* party did, not Harold Hood's. "I don't think the President would risk antagonizing the Senate in the way you suggest, Senator. The President isn't perfect; good Lord, who of us is? But you make it sound as though he were going to appear in Moscow with Valentin Kirov and start sending out ultimatums. I can't even *imagine* that happening—no, it is just too impossible to consider. Why, Lambert is too good a politician to take such a chance, Senator." He was absolutely convinced of this. Politics was the prime mover in Hood's life: the politics of the ward, the county, the union hall. To imagine that there might be overriding national interests that could modify a politician's behavior into that of a statesman was a concept Harold Hood's mind could not encompass. It was this political tunnel vision that had brought him the comfortable sinecure of the Vice Presidency, and it was the same limitation that had prevented him from ever being seriously considered as a Presidential possibility.

"I can't emphasize too much, sir. Lambert is on a secret trip to Russia. He is lying to the Congress, to the press, to the *People*." The capital letter was in his voice, in his expression.

Hood's conception of the People was different from Sutton's. The difference was apparent in everything the two men did and their manner of doing it. Hood, for all his attempts at keeping up with the times, would never say the things Sutton did, would not wear the clothes Sutton did, or cut his hair as Sutton did. He realized (and it frustrated him) that all of these things made a statement about Sutton's life style and politics. What he did not realize was that Sutton's rather Mod manner was as out of fashion as his own dated machine politician's kind of plastic liberalism. When Sutton spoke about the People, he meant one thing, and Hood, listening fearfully, heard something else. The People, to Hood, were ward leaders, party volunteers, precinct workers, union organizers, and political-action committeemen. DeWitt Sutton connected a number of frightening words: weapons, lies, secret commitments. Implicit in what he was saying were other, unspoken, words: outrage, protest, demonstrations. That was enough to frighten Hood badly indeed. The picture of his President as a secret saber-rattler distressed him greatly. It could well be true, he thought; Lambert could be using a scare dreamed up by the generals in the Pentagon to make all sorts of entangling, dangerous deals with the Soviets against the Chinese—or, for that matter, with the Chinese against the Soviets. How could one be certain? He did not really know Cleveland Lambert that well, he thought, and whose fault, really, was that? Not Harold Cassius Hood's.

"I have spoken to some of my colleagues on the Overwatch Committee, Mr. Vice President," Sutton said, formally. "I am not at liberty to disclose who, or even how many, but you may be sure I represent a consensus when I speak. We ask that you stand with us in this."

"Stand with you? I don't think I understand you," Hood said uneasily.

"Nothing public, sir. Nothing like that. We understand your position and sympathize with you. But what we would like to have is your assurance that you will back us should it become necessary to block some rash move on the President's part." He held up his hand to forestall the inevitable protest. "I don't say that he will make any ill-considered moves. I certainly hope that he will not. But *if,* Harold. If he should—"

"What sort of moves, DeWitt? What do you think he might do?" Hood asked, now thoroughly frightened.

Sutton shrugged. "I can't be sure of anything, Harold. But it isn't outside the realm of possibility that he might want to issue some sort of warning to the Chinese about this so-called weapon of theirs. The Joint Chiefs are in a stew about it. A phony stew, I think. But nevertheless you can't ignore the possibility that they might prevail upon the President to make some threatening gesture to back up his moves. I want your personal assurance that you will resist this."

"What can *I* possibly do?"

"Oh, for heaven's sake, Harold," Sutton said. "I only ask that you side with us, as presiding officer of the Senate, if it becomes necessary to invoke our Constitutional privilege of advice and consent."

"But you said the JCS—"

Sutton held up a placating hand. "I assure you, Harold, the Joint Chiefs are not going to misbehave as long as they know we are watching them. It is Lambert who worries me, and what he may commit us to do about the absolutely phony danger." He spoke in a lower, more confidential voice. "I sometimes wonder if the strain of the job hasn't been too much for him. It is something to think about before the convention next year."

The mention of the party convention put all matters into perspective for Hood. Everything that had been said now made sense. Sutton was talking about *politics,* not about fantastic weapons and international crises. That made all the difference. All this talk was really about a possible reason to weaken or possibly even discard Lambert as the party's leader. Naturally, Sutton, who had never completely lost his Presidential fever, would view matters in a way that would most enhance himself and damage Cleveland Lambert. Politics, that was what it was, Hood thought with a sudden, beatific smile. *And politics is what I best understand.*

He was old, and he was tired. But he was neither so old nor so tired as to leave the political game he had played for most of his life. This was something he could handle.

"Senator," he said, "I take your meaning. You can rest assured that if and when the occasion arises, you can count on me."

25

"Nothing," Ian Ballard said. "I'm sorry, old man, but the thing is absolutely nothing more than what it appears to be—a rather scruffy canvas holdall." He glanced again over the work sheet from the laboratory before handing it over to Grant. "As you can see, we can tell you where it was made, where it was purchased, how much the bloody thing cost, what it's made of, and even—with a fair degree of certainty—where it's been for the last six months or so. But that's all. There's nothing hidden in it. No tapes, no microdots, none of that cloak-and-dagger nonsense the boffins love to dream up. Sorry."

Grant looked at the sheet and nodded. "I didn't think you'd find anything, but I thought we should make certain." He glanced at the door to the anteroom where Bronwen waited. "She was trying to be helpful."

Ballard withheld comment. It was obvious to him, as a rather shrewd judge of human nature, that Colonel Grant's view of Bronwen Wells was not unprejudiced. This both surprised and concerned him. He tended to think of Americans in the field as rather hard-bitten creatures, but perhaps he was wrong. It was possible that they were all—even the men who operated out in the cold—as naïve as their legislators. Grant had obviously been touched by the Welsh girl, and therefore was vulnerable to errors of judgment.

Grant said, "I keep having the feeling that we are off the track somehow. I'm not sure any longer that what we are looking for actually exists."

"You mean you don't think Colonel Voronin left an insurance policy?"

"Something like that," Grant said, frowning. "The man Bronwen describes wouldn't have taken such a risk. And there's something else—this is purely subjective judgment on my part, but I feel it's right—the man Bronwen knew might have come over, but he wouldn't turn traitor."

"That's a fine distinction, old man," Ballard said skeptically.

Grant stood and walked to the grimy window overlooking a dark and rain-dappled Thames. "Yes, it is, isn't it." He stood thoughtfully for a time. "What I mean is that it would take something terribly important to make a man like that defect. Something that he felt was as important to the survival of his own country as it might be to the West." He turned toward Ballard and added, "But all we know for certain is that someone thought it was important enough to kill him. Is there anything new on the gunmen?"

"As a matter of fact, we have identified the dead one," Ballard said. "That is, we have identified him—more or less. Provos take on so many aliases sometimes it's hard to know which one is the right one even for the moment of truth." Ballard unlocked a drawer in his desk and withdrew a thin folder. "The dead man was Sean Xavier O'Neill. He was arrested twice in County Derry, three times in County Armagh, and twice by the Irish Republic, both times in Dublin. The charges were suspicion of planting explosives, of course, and murder. He was never brought to trial and was released twice in general amnesties. This all happened from 1968 to 1975. We've known him as a suspected Provo since his first arrest, but—" Ballard's shrug was expressive. "It isn't easy to keep these people behind wire, Grant."

"Definitely a hired hand, then."

"Without much doubt. The Provos get most of their arms from the Soviet Union, as I'm sure you know. Often they actually buy them from Continental arms dealers—with money contributed in the States, as I am also sure you know. New England still seems to be populated by second- and third-generation Irish who hate the British enough to contribute several millions of dollars a year. We've tried to enlist the aid of your government in stopping this, but so far no luck. It appears that buying guns and gelignite for the Irish is an inalienable civil right in your country."

Grant had no reply to that and attempted none. He knew that what Ballard said was true.

"O'Neill—alias Gresham, Graham, Kennedy, Grogan, Sullivan, MacMurtry, and Maguire, just to give you a few names—usually worked with an older brother named Patrick. We are going on the assumption that Patrick was the second gunman, and there is a warrant out for him. But I haven't much hope that he will turn up, old man. These types are professional killers and they don't take chances unless they are on a job. My guess would be that Patrick O'Neill, Gresham, Sullivan, Maguire et al. has collected his pay and is long gone to ground. Probably in the Republic, but he could have gone anywhere." Ballard regarded Grant cynically. "I think it obvious that the gunmen were hired, though by whom, I'm not prepared to say. It could have been anyone. The KGB, of course, though they usually have their own assassins and prefer to use them. Or it could have been someone else entirely." He gave Grant a hard smile. "The CIA, even. According to the statements coming out of your Congress for the last six or seven years, the Agency still likes to keep its hand in."

"That's pretty goddamned absurd, Ballard," Grant said tiredly.

"I suppose it is, old man. But I only know what I read in the American papers."

"I thank you for your help, anyway," Grant said.

"My pleasure. I owe you for that magnificent feast at Overton's. Which I hope we can repeat before you leave London."

Grant ignored the not-very-subtle probe concerning his plans. He said, "We'll do that, Ballard."

Ballard placed Bronwen's carryall on the desk. "I suppose Miss Wells would like this back. I'm sorry it wasn't what you were looking for." He zipped the case shut and stood. "By the way, we will be taking the surveillance off Miss Wells's flat now. I don't think there's much point in it now, do you?"

"Probably not," Grant agreed reluctantly.

"Will I see you down at Sissinghurst?"

Grant evaded the direct answer. He did not know whether Ballard and other SIS people had been informed of the President's plan to fly to Moscow. The Prime Minister knew, but there was certainly no point in offering Ballard information. "Possibly," Grant said. "If my boss doesn't send me off somewhere on another wild-goose chase."

"I'm sorry this one has turned out badly, Grant," Ballard said. He sounded sincere and probably was, Grant thought. But he was right. The mission was a total failure. The man the President had wanted him to see was beyond interviews. If he had planned to defect, if he had know something worth learning, neither Harry Grant nor anyone else would ever know now.

In the taxi with Bronwen, he said, "It's your yellow case, Bronwen. Not *the* yellow case."

"I am sorry. For a bit I thought it might be something important."

Grant felt the light pressure of her hand on his arm. He was intensely aware of her and he wondered if his awareness was not damaging his objectivity. He said, "I hate to ask about this again, but it could be important. I think we've taken a wrong turning somewhere. When Alek spoke, was it in English or Russian?"

Bronwen's narrow face became pale, pinched.

Grant said, "I mean, Bronwen, did he speak of a *portfels zholtye* or did he actually say, in English, 'yellow case'?"

"In English. I don't really speak Russian, you see. I did tell you that, didn't I?" Her eyes looked enormous in the tarnished silver light of the dark winter day.

"You must have picked up some Russian," Grant said, "surely a few words."

"Well, yes. A few words. But not those. What you said."

"*Portfels zholtye.* Yellow case."

"No one said that at the Hovercraft terminal. I'm quite sure of that. I would have remembered it."

"It's all right," he said. "We've gone wrong somewhere, that's all. We might be looking for something that never existed. Now let's look for some lunch. Then I'll see you home."

They fell silent as the taxicab inched through the London traffic toward Hampstead. Grant watched her solemn profile silhouetted against the rain-smeared window. He thought how amused Jane would be if she could see the Iron Colonel now— the man who could take women or leave them, as the occasion and opportunity demanded. And never any entanglements, never an emotional tie or a sense of need. That was Jane's picture of him, and, in truth, he had done nothing at all to convince her that he was not that way. Because since his last miserable days with Bethany, he had thought of himself in just those aloof, self-contained, and in-control terms. Had McNary, with her brittle feminist intuition and her sharply focused intelligence always known what a fake he was? Had she ever guessed that he was as vulnerable as any man?

Sometimes, he knew, you caught a glimpse of someone—a stranger passing, lost instantly beyond any hope of a second encounter—and you had the strange certainty that *if* you were to meet again, and under different circumstances, you might love one another. You even saw the flash of recognition in that other face and guessed that she felt it, too. And all this from a glimpse of a face seen through a taxicab's window, or in an airport waiting line for some other destination.

The Iron Colonel would never have put such insights into

words for a Jane McNary. One didn't even risk the use of words such as "love." Yet here it was, it seemed. Bronwen Wells was that face glimpsed in the crowd that brought the swift sweet pang of an almost unbearable poignancy and sadness and sense of loss. Was it possible that it could all be retrieved, all made right in one moment?

Bronwen had said little during lunch. All the way to Hampstead she sat silently close to him. He found himself hoping that she derived some comfort from his presence. He was beginning to believe that she did.

When the taxi pulled up in front of Bronwen's flat, Grant took note of the absence of the police Ford. Ballard had wasted no time in passing the word. Perhaps he was right: there seemed little point now in having Bronwen troubled by policemen. Or watched by them.

Bronwen said quietly, "You'll be going away now?"

"Yes," Grant said reluctantly. While he and Bronwen had been at Madame Zelinskaya's and at Ballard's office, the President would have launched his day of informal meetings at Sissinghurst. Tomorrow the first plenary session of the Sissinghurst conference would hear his keynote speech. By late morning he would be on his way to Hurn, where Major George Barrow and the stand-by crew would be waiting with their 767 to fly him to Moscow. And Harry Grant would have to be at Hurn to report to the President that his mission was a complete washout. Whatever Voronin might have had in the way of information for the Americans was now lost.

Bronwen got out of the cab holding her shabby yellow bag.

Grant said, "I'll see you in." To the cab driver he said, "Wait. I'll be back right away."

At the door, Bronwen asked, "Will I ever see you again, Harry Grant?"

"Yes," he said. "I don't know exactly when or even how, but yes."

"I'm glad," she said and opened the door.

The interior of the flat was a shambles. Bronwen drew a sharp, suddenly frightened breath. "Oh, God," she said.

The rugs had been pulled up and thrown aside. The pictures on the walls had been smashed, the backing ripped away. The furniture had been slashed and torn apart, its foam and metal entrails thrown about. The lamps had been overturned and the bases shattered. The books were lying about in a confusion of torn pages.

Grant pushed past Bronwen and went down the hallway to the bedroom. It was even worse there. The mattress had been systematically cut to shreds; the dressing table had been overturned and the drawers upended. There was a thick smell of perfume in the room. Bronwen's toilet articles had been emptied onto the confusion piled on the floor. Even her clothes had been taken from the closet and ripped and cut into ribbons. On the mirror above the dressing table someone had written in lipstick: FASCIST WHORE.

Grant turned and saw Bronwen in the doorway. She was staring at the message on the glass with shocked, disbelieving eyes.

"Don't come in here," he said, and took her by the arm back to the door.

"Oh, my God, Harry," she whispered. "What is it? *What's happening to me?*"

Grant could not remember feeling such a surge of anger and hatred since his days in the POW compound in Hanoi. "Leave it alone," he said harshly. "Don't touch anything."

He gripped her arm tightly as he led her back to the waiting cab. The driver stared curiously. Grant snapped, "Stay here. Keep her here."

Back in the flat he looked around again. The place had been

searched, but the search had been tinged with a kind of madness. He found the telephone in the ruins. It had been ripped from the wall and smashed. He did not touch it.

He walked out of the flat and closed the door. To the cab driver he said, "Stafford Hotel, St. James's Place."

Grant held Bronwen giving her what comfort and reassurance he could. She was like the sleeper who has awakened from a nightmare with relief—only to discover that the awakening was false and that the phantasms of the night are still all around. The terror of the dream within a dream was something Grant himself had experienced, and this understanding of what the girl was going through aroused his pity and his anger.

In St. James's Place, Grant released the taxicab and took Bronwen into the Stafford's intimate lobby. At the porter's desk he ordered his rented automobile to be brought around; at the registration desk he requested that his bill be made up. The clerk, solicitous, as were all the staff, asked: "Is the young lady ill, sir? Is there anything we can do?"

"Thank you, I don't think so," Grant said. "She's had a shock, that's all."

Bronwen sat in the alcove just off the entry, feet together, shoulders tightly straight, face pinched and pale, eyes dry and unseeing.

"It *is* Miss Wells from the Ballet Celeste, isn't it, sir? I've seen her dance several times. I hope she isn't unwell, sir."

Grant managed a smile. At some other time, he felt reasonably certain, Bronwen would have been surprised and pleased to be recognized. It was a thing, he suspected, that usually happened only to better dancers of prominent companies. Yet Ballard had seen her dance and admitted that something special came through. Ballard and this man must be—what were they called?—balletomanes.

He took Bronwen's arm and raised her gently. "Come," he said. He led her to the lift. The Stafford had been made, over the years, of a series of town houses around St. James's Place, and the hallways were complex, turning right and left, rising two or three steps and then dropping back to their former level, forming alcoves and culs-de-sac from which the hotel's elegant rooms opened. Grant's room, one of the smaller ones, overlooked a quiet inner court. He let himself and Bronwen in, locked the door behind them, and poured two stiff whiskies from the bottle in his luggage.

"Drink it," he said.

Bronwen obediently swallowed the neat liquor, making an involuntary, bitter mouth.

"Better?"

She nodded. "Whisky isn't the ballet's drink," she said faintly.

"In there, if you want to freshen up." He nodded toward the bathroom.

"Yes. All right."

When she had gone, Grant picked up the telephone and called Ballard. After the SIS man had heard Grant's angry description of the flat, he said, "We shall have a word with the Yard, I think."

"Do that," Grant said.

"Perhaps we were premature in removing the surveillance."

"It didn't happen after the police were called off. Someone just got by," Grant said in a harsh voice.

"Yes. I suppose that is what happened. I am very sorry. But it may give us a lead." For once, Ballard sounded genuinely contrite. "How did she take it?"

"How the hell do you imagine she took it?"

"Yes. Well. We'll put some Special Branch people on it now, Grant. We'll keep the place under close surveillance."

"What the hell for, now? If there was anything there, whoever it was has it. If there wasn't, it will be Bronwen they come after," Grant said. "And she won't be there."

There was a long silence on the other end of the wire. Then Ballard said carefully, "I don't suppose you would care to tell me where she will be."

"I haven't decided yet," Grant said.

"Old man, I wouldn't take her with you to Sissinghurst. I really wouldn't do that if I were you."

"Advice noted, Ballard," Grant said. "I'll be in touch."

He replaced the telephone receiver and almost immediately the bell rang. He answered curtly and impatiently, "Grant."

"Colonel Grant, there is a message for you at the porter's desk."

"All right. Is my car there yet?"

"It's waiting, sir."

"We'll be down right away."

He hung up again and began to pack. He was putting his uniform into his suitcase when Bronwen returned. She looked at the blue uniform and said slowly, "I didn't know you were a soldier, Harry."

"Does it matter?"

She shook her head vaguely. "I don't know—" A strange, stunned smile touched her pale lips. "I—I'm not lucky for soldiers, Harry—" Her shoulders began to shake and her eyes filled.

"Don't," he said, going to her. "Don't cry. Please don't." He held her.

"I thought it was all over," she said in a muffled voice. "But it isn't. I don't know what's happening, but it isn't over."

He said, "I'm taking you with me."

"I don't understand. Where? How?"

"We'll decide where when we get out of London. I want you out of here, somewhere where you'll be safe."

"But, Harry, how can we do that?"

"Simple as hell," he said roughly. "We just go and we find a safe place for you in the south. Somewhere you can stay until we begin to make sense out of all this."

She leaned against him gratefully—or was it simply that there was no more resistance left in her, he wondered.

She said something that he couldn't catch, her voice muffled against his chest.

"What?"

"Why did they write that on my mirror? Why did they call me that?"

"I don't know. But we'll find out. I promise you that."

"I'm not a whore, Harry."

"I know that. Forget it. It isn't important."

"It is to me." She looked up at him with her eyes glistening and, he hoped, with the beginning of anger in them.

"Good," he said. "Get mad."

"And a *fascist* whore—I'm not like that."

"No," he said. "You aren't."

"What sort of animals do things like that?"

"Not animals, Bron. People trying hard to frighten other people."

Surprisingly, she smiled. "My father used to call me that—Bron. I'll be all right now, Harry. Or should I call you Captain or Colonel or whatever? I hardly know what I'm saying now. Whatever's the matter with me?"

He sat her down in a chair and poured another whisky for her. "Drink that. Slowly."

"I'll get drunk."

"Not very," he said. "Slowly, now. While I finish packing."

He had his valise closed and didn't wait for a porter. He carried it down to the lobby, Bronwen close behind him. He could hear voices in the lounge. He went to the desk, settled his bill, and gave the porter the bag to take out to the rented Volvo parked in front of the hotel steps. It was growing darker, though there was still a watery light outside.

The porter handed him a note. It was from McNary and read: "The press expects the Iron Colonel for drinks in the lounge."

The porter said, "The young lady is inside, sir, with some other people."

Grant hesitated, then said to Bronwen, "I'll be just a moment."

As he turned toward the lounge, Jane McNary and a man named Cotter, whom Harry knew slightly as a correspondent for the Associated Press, appeared in his path.

McNary was dressed in one of her pantsuits. She began to smile at him, but her expression froze when she saw Bronwen.

"Hello, Jane," Grant said.

"I see you haven't been wasting any time—Colonel," she said in an icy voice.

Grant ignored the thrust. This wasn't the time for one of the all-too-frequent McNary-Grant sparring matches. "I'm sorry I wasn't here to meet you," he said.

"Oh, I can see that."

If Grant was not already angered by the afternoon's events, not concerned about Bronwen's emotional condition, he might have reacted differently to this greeting. But Bronwen, surprised and offended by McNary's bad manners and hostility, became tense and withdrawn. Grant felt the change immediately. He said, "Will you wait for me in the car, Bronwen?"

"Yes, all right," she said, and walked out into the rainy twilight.

Grant turned on McNary in a cold fury. "Who the hell do you think you're talking to, Jane?"

McNary prided herself on never retreating. "Been cruising Piccadilly, I see. I wonder what your boss would think about that."

Grant felt the blood draining from his face. It had never occurred to him that McNary would ever behave in quite this way. Her insult to Bronwen, whom she did not know, was obviously calculated to infuriate him.

There had been a number of things he had wanted to say to her. Now he would say none of them. He turned abruptly and walked out to the Volvo. Through the curving glass of the entrance, McNary saw him get into the car beside Bronwen. Jim Cotter, the AP man, followed Grant out and leaned over to speak to him through the car window.

"Hey, Colonel, listen. She's had a bit to drink." From the smell of him, Grant concluded, so had he. "Listen," Cotter said. Grant remembered that he had a way of beginning almost all his sentences that way. "Tomorrow we're going down to Sissinghurst in a BBC chopper. We—I—was hoping I'd get a chance to talk to you. Listen, *she*—" he nodded toward the hotel—"she said we could count on you."

"Well, I'll tell you, Mr. Cotter," Grant said grimly, "she was wrong."

Grant put the car in gear. Cotter stepped back, watched the Volvo make the turn toward St. James's Street and Pall Mall. Presently he turned and went back inside the hotel.

He said to the hall porter, "The young lady with Colonel Grant. Do you know her?"

"That was Miss Wells, sir. Bronwen Wells, of the Ballet Celeste," the porter answered.

"The what?"

"The Celeste, sir. It's a small dance company. Miss Wells is a featured artist."

"Real nice," Cotter murmured, and headed back into the lounge. McNary was there, her thin face white and angry.

"You made the Iron Colonel mad, Janey-girl," Cotter said.

"Tough shit," McNary said.

"Never thought I'd see you jealous."

"Shut your mouth, Cotter."

"Want to know who she is?"

"Get fucked, you fat prick," McNary said quietly.

An English couple sitting in a far corner of the lounge glanced up uncomfortably, and McNary fixed them with a steady glare. They signed their tab and left, abandoning the lounge to the Americans.

"That's our Jane," Cotter said, "an ambassador of good will." He signaled a waiter on the way to the bar. The waiter nodded and said, "Right with you, sir."

McNary said, "Well, you son of a bitch, who is she?"

"Bron-something Wells. A dancer with some cruddy little ballet outfit."

"Jesus Christ. I always knew Harry Grant was a nineteenth-century character."

"Damned pretty, though."

"So long, Cotter," McNary said, standing up, and managing deliberately to spill a drink so that the liquor ran over the small table and onto his lap. He dabbed at himself, cursing, as McNary left the lounge.

When she closed the door of her room, McNary moved toward the telephone. It was time, she thought, to call Sutton and see what the old fool wanted. She'd kept him waiting long enough. And perhaps she could say some damaging things about Grant. "The bastard," she muttered. "The unmitigated bastard."

26

At almost the same time that Harry Grant and Bronwen Wells, in London, had left Ballard's office in Parliament Street, two young men sat down to breakfast in a fast-food restaurant on the outskirts of Washington, D.C.

In their self-conscious images of themselves, they believed such a plastic place was so anomalous that it afforded protection from discovery. Who would search them out in this niche of the American scene?

They did require privacy, even secrecy, because their conversations frequently involved the exchange of classified information. The more sophisticated of the two, Senator Sutton's assistant Allan Dalland, occasionally considered the irony of his need to indulge in secret, hole-in-the-wall tactics in order to balk the government's tendency to do the same.

His companion, Gerald Ransome, a GS-10 in the Soviet Intelligence data-processing unit of the Computer Section at CIA headquarters in Langley, Virginia, never had such thoughts. He was twenty-nine, two years younger than Dalland, and had transferred to the CIA from the space program. He was now one of those the old hands called "the punch-card crew." These were primarily technicians—evaluators and programmers—who had come into the Agency on the waves of reform that followed the congressional investigations of the mid-'70s.

The most obvious result of the congressional dismemberment of the Agency's covert capabilities had been a drastic reduction of field operatives and a heavy dependence on satellite intelligence and computer decision-making. It was owing to this basic change in the means of accomplishing the CIA mission that Ransome and others with his qualifications now inhabited the guarded Langley buildings.

Ransome did not believe in governmental secrecy. Like his companion, he grew up to an approximation of maturity in the confused decade of the '70s. He bitterly regretted having missed the activism of the '60s, but there were still enough echoes and legends of that time to affect his political views. Meeting Allan Dalland at a Washington cocktail party two years earlier had opened up social and political opportunities for him.

Dalland had gone to a better prep school than Ransome. Dalland had gone to Harvard Law School, while Ransome had received technical training at a small college in the Pacific Northwest. Dalland was, in Ransome's eyes, an important man, one to be cultivated.

Dalland would not have been surprised to know of Ransome's feelings: he had carefully nurtured them. But he regarded Ransome as a resource of great value, and that would have surprised Ransome very much. Ransome had access to a wealth of material that Dalland could use to help Senator Sutton's activities.

Dalland did not love the Senator, but he recognized him as a suitable employer for an ambitious man of ability and principle. Dalland was heavily committed to his principles. These included absolute and total opposition to anything that could, however remotely, be linked to American militarism, American imperialism, American secrecy in government, and American interference in the affairs of other nations. Armored in such righteousness, he drew classified information from Ransome, and others like him, and passed it on to Sutton. If questioned about this practice (and he never had been), he would have protested, quite sincerely, that surely a U.S. senator was entitled to know what the intelligence community was doing.

One day Allan Dalland planned to run for elective office

himself. He suspected that even now he would make a better senator than his patron, but he felt that he could afford to wait. He was learning—as a senior member of a senator's staff—how to exercise power and influence. That was essential to long-term political success. Moreover, like the Senator, Dalland was wealthy by inheritance. This not only smoothed his path in expected ways, but also made possible a political stance fashionably left of center.

Dalland's ultraliberal convictions were taken by Ransome as indications of a generosity of spirit, a tolerance that permitted an East Coast Brahmin to be friends with a grind of a technician from the hinterlands of the Northwest. Ransome had been deeply grateful—and therefore easily subverted. For what he regularly did—discuss with Dalland the activities of the Computer Section of the Central Intelligence Agency—was still, under any interpretation of federal law, illegal.

This morning, as they sat near a grotesque plastic statue of the white-bearded founder of the fast-food chain, the two men were a study in contrast. Ransome wore a denim leisure suit tailored to resemble the work clothes of a ranch hand. This garment had been purchased at considerable expense from a New York boutique recommended by Dalland—who had never bought, and would never buy, a single article of clothing anywhere but at Brooks Brothers.

Ransome's soft face was outlined by a silky black beard. Dalland's was clean-shaven. Both men conceded something to the current style in the length of their hair, but Ransome was secretly pleased that his hair was thicker and more plentiful than Dalland's, who sprang from a long line of balding aristocrats. This mild vanity about his appearance was possibly Ransome's only arrogance. Though a splendid scientist and technician, he was not the possessor of a rounded education; and like many specialists, he had a tendency to be muzzy about things outside his particular discipline.

Largely because of Dalland, he was an admirer of Senator

Sutton and the other "Insularists" in the Congress. He now accepted as fact that the United States did not face any particular threat from international Communism; from his limited experience, he had never seen any indication that such a threat even existed. The Cold War, which he remembered only vaguely, he regarded as a mythical conflict created by the military-industrial complex (which Dalland assured him *did* exist). The Vietnam war, in which he had been too young to take part, he connected in his mind with "Nixon and Watergate." History was not his subject.

The "openness in government" that a succession of Congresses had thrust upon the intelligence community could be measured by the fact that Ransome's political opinions, as shallow as they were, had never been examined before he was given access to highly sensitive information. As a member of the SovInt data-processing unit at Langley, he found himself in charge of processing all inputs about high-echelon Soviet policy. He was, as well, responsible for output for American officials and agents in the field.

It was to Gerald Ransome that Harry Grant's request for a computer run on Marshal Yuri Leonov and Colonel Aleksandr Voronin had come.

Dalland had been telling Ransome over coffee that the Senator's staff had been working overtime collecting material to be used by his committee when it called Margaret Kendrick, on her return from England, to explain exactly what was being bargained away by the administration at the Sissinghurst conference.

Dalland's work was more important than his, Ransome thought with a touch of sulkiness, and far more interesting. Dalland was privileged to deal directly with people who had the power to check even the President, while he, Ransome, dealt with routine demands from overseas—case officers, mostly, seldom even station chiefs.

But there had been one request within the last twenty-four hours that he had found intriguing: Harry Grant's. It had been to tempt Dalland with this that he had suggested a breakfast meeting. Dalland had put him off by spending the better part of half an hour talking about how he and his fellow-staffers were digging into the business of the Secretary of State. Presently, however, Ransome realized that Dalland was marking time, talking simply so as not to be placed in the position of asking directly why he had been requested to appear this morning. Ransome was so pleased with himself for having discerned this that he smiled broadly.

Dalland stopped talking about Secretary Kendrick abruptly. "What are you grinning about?"

"I have something for you," Ransome said.

"I thought you might," Dalland replied.

"Unless you're too busy investigating the Department of State?"

"All right, Gerald. Stop the game-playing now. I rely on you. You know that."

Ransome regarded his friend's narrow, rather fine-featured face. He enjoyed hearing that Dalland relied on him, that he had something useful to offer.

"What do you know about the White House staff people, Allan?"

"Quite a lot."

"Have you ever met a Colonel Grant?"

"I may have. It's hard to keep track of all those people over there. What is Colonel Grant's claim to fame?"

"I thought Senator Sutton's staff knew everything," Ransome said, piqued by Dalland's manner.

"As it happens," Dalland said, helping himself to coffee, "I *do* know Harry Grant. He is Deputy Air Force Aide and he fucks Jane McNary."

Ransome flushed. He disliked vulgarity and thought it unworthy of a person like Allan. The swift reversal was typical of Dalland's habit of trying to confuse and disorient the people with whom he came in contact—even his close friends. To indicate it was time to stop these silly games, Ransome said: "Grant is in London."

Dalland waited, simulating a touch of weariness. Ransome knew the gambit well.

"Do you want what I have or shall we just drop it?" he asked irritatedly.

"Get on with it, Gerald. Please?"

"All right, I will," Ransome's momentary rebellion collapsed. He could never win these petty contests. "Did you know that Colonel Grant raced off to London well ahead of the President's main party?"

"As it happens, I heard that. Do you know why? *That* would be something interesting to hear about." Dalland's interest was stirring but he kept it masked. When Ransome got to thinking of himself as important, he could become unmanageable.

"Maybe I don't know it all, but I do know something about what he's been doing in London," Ransome said.

"Are you going to tell me?" Dalland asked, fingering the check impatiently.

"This is secret, Allan."

"Everything is, according to the Agency."

"Well, I won't argue that point. But I could be in trouble with this one if it gets out you learned about it from me. Will the Senator protect his source?"

"Has he ever failed to do that, Gerald?"

"No, but I'm liable to get some White House people very angry this time."

"If you are concerned about Grant, don't be. He's just another ironhead soldier." Dalland did not like military men, and the information, derived long ago from the Senator, that when the President had something confidential and personal that needed doing, Grant, the Iron Colonel, got the job, did nothing to improve Dalland's opinion of him.

"That may be," Ransome said. "But remember, Allan, I'm trusting you."

"Don't stroke me, Gerald. I said I'd watch out for you, and I will."

"Well, it's something the Senator probably ought to know about," Ransome said. He paused for dramatic effect and then said, "Did you know that Grant was briefed by State before he went tearing off to England?"

"By State?"

"Department of State *Intelligence*." Ransome leaned forward and spoke intently. "He was personally briefed about a Russian air attaché named Aleksandr Voronin."

Dalland's interest surged. The Washington papers had carried the news about the murder of the Russian diplomat in the Hovercraft terminal in Dover. The story had been brief and buried, but he had seen it and wondered. He fantasized for a delicious moment the possibility that Colonel Grant had killed the Russian on the orders of the President. Regretfully, no; the timing was all wrong. Someone else had killed him. But had it been *because* he was about to meet with the Iron Colonel?

"I see I have your attention," Ransome said dryly.

"Yes, Gerald. You have indeed. Did State request anything in particular from the Agency?"

"No, but Grant has. That's why I called you, actually. I thought Senator Sutton ought to know," Ransome said.

"Grant is in London asking for Agency help?"

"More information than help," Ransome said. "He is requesting a full computer summary on the dead Russian. Well, that makes a kind of sense if we assume he was supposed to meet him. But that's not all. He has asked for a special search run on any specific connections between this Voronin person and Yuri Leonov—the Soviet Minister of Defense. Our Colonel is building something, Allan. You don't ask for—and get—authorization for this kind of service from the Agency unless someone very important wants you to have it."

"Lambert," Dalland said.

"Of course. But isn't that all fascinating?"

"You did a complete retrieval on both men?"

"SovInt dropped everything to authorize the computer time."

Dalland's intent stare betrayed his excitement. "What did you find out?"

"That's the thing. I really don't know what I found out."

"For Chrissakes, Gerald. Don't play the fool. This could be important."

"I *said* that. But if you're going to ask me to produce a copy of the print-out, Allan, the answer is *no*. Absolutely *no*. If it got into the wrong hands, there wouldn't be any doubt at all about who leaked it."

"What did the computer say?"

"Voronin was a student of Leonov's at the Russian Military Academy."

"What about it?"

"This about it. The run included the names of over two hundred other former students of Leonov. Specifically those in his course in something called 'Military Geotechnics.' Then something really strange came up. About two-thirds of those former students attended a series of lectures he conducted in the '60s and '70s—called the Crisis Confrontation Lectures—whatever *that* means."

"Well, what about it?"

"I'm *telling* you, Allan. Let me finish," Ransome said reproachfully. "The people who attended these lectures were very, *very* carefully selected by Leonov *personally*." He showed his small teeth in a brief smile. "The best and the brightest, you might say."

"Jesus, Gerald. What did the goddamn computer *say?*"

"It *said,* Allan, that Marshal Yuri Leonov's pets are—every one of them—spotted in extremely sensitive positions all through the Soviet military and diplomatic establishment. It *said,* my friend, that if the good Marshal should suddenly decide to stage a coup, *the probability of success would be better than forty-three percent.*"

"Are you telling me that goddamn machine predicts a coup in the Soviet Union?" Dalland demanded.

"The 'machine,' as you call it, doesn't predict anything. I wish you would try to understand computers, Allan. Data processing is my work, after all. I've tried to explain to you—"

"Shut up, Gerald, and let me think."

A whole maze of possibilities was opening up before Dalland. A special envoy of the President's—a military man—was sent ahead to make contact with a Russian air attaché, a man closely associated with an extremely high Russian official who might be, possibly was, planning some move against the legitimate government of his country. That made American meddling in places like the Congo, Chile, and Angola look like child's play. With growing excitement Dalland imagined the reaction of the committee—of the whole Congress—to such a disclosure. God, the audacity of the bastards in the administration was staggering. And the uproar that would follow would be explosive. Cleveland Scott Lambert was playing with impeachment. What a gift, what a splendid, incredible, magnificent gift to Senator Sutton! A staffer who brought such riches could name his own reward.

He deliberately made himself slow down. He would have to have proof. Ransome would have to produce the request from the station chief in London, naming Colonel Harry Grant as the originator. And he would also have to smuggle out of the Langley compound a copy of the actual computer print-out. That was essential. The run-of-the-mill transgressions of the executive branch could be pumped into the news media with hints and innuendoes, but something this big needed proof—a "smoking gun" in the administration's hand.

Dalland studied his companion speculatively. This might well mean the end of Ransome's career in government service. The information would have to be pedigreed, attributed beyond the shadow of a doubt. The customary "leak" would not do. Not only would Ransome have to produce the request and the print-out, but he might even have to appear in public session before the committee and testify. To nerve plump and skittery Gerald Ransome, bureaucrat, to such a performance would take some doing. But he could be managed. What was needed was a little time to plan, to consult with the Senator and others on the staff, and, finally, to act.

"How long can you sit on Colonel Grant's request?" he asked quietly.

Ransome's soft eyes widened. *"Sit* on it? Good God, Allan, do you know what you're saying? The man is the *President's personal aide."*

"Seventy-two hours?"

"Seventy-two hours? Allan, you're insane."

"Forty-eight. You could easily hold it up for forty-eight hours."

"Listen, Allan, you don't know what you are asking." Ransome looked genuinely frightened.

"Two days, Gerald. Just two days. You can do it. Lose the print-out."

"Lose it? Allan, it just isn't possible. Do you know what's involved?"

"You could manage it, Gerald," Dalland said relentlessly.

"People in my section don't just lose things like that, Allan," Ransome said. "You don't know how many cross-checks are made on secret material—"

"You could manage it," Dalland said again. "I know you could."

"Allan, *please,"* Ransome protested. "It would be *incredibly* dangerous for me to do something like that. Why, I'd have to check the document out again, get permission to move it from the computer room, sign my *life* away. And then I'd have to delay returning it—think of some reason to make another run. That's the only way I could delay sending it off to London, Allan, and I just don't see how I could make it *reasonable.* They watch us, Allan, they really do. You don't believe that, but it is the truth. The supervisors who are still around from the old days. They are

just waiting to catch someone doing something really wrong—"
His voice grew shrill at a sudden thought. "Why they might even
accuse me of being a *spy,* Allan. Oh, no. No *way.* I can't do
it."

"You can. You just explained how," Dalland said intently.

"Allan, you can't make me do this." The younger man's eyes
were near to brimming.

"I don't have to make you do it, Gerald. You are going to do
it because it is right. You know that. It's your duty."

"Allan, for God's sake—"

"You'll be protected, Gerald. But that doesn't matter. You
are going to do what you have to do because we have to. *We*
have to, Gerald. The People have a right to know what's being
done in their name."

"Oh, Jesus, Allan," Ransome said miserably.

"It'll be all right, Gerald," Dalland said. "Everything will be
just fine."

27

Comrade Dr. Soong was in deep despond, his mood as melancholy as the icy wind that blew over the frozen marshy bottom of the Turfan. Since the Russian spy had died under his ministrations, the old physician's spirits had fallen to a new depth. He looked around his cold and barren quarters and through the grimy windows at the rattling reeds protruding, sere and brittle, from the ice, and wondered what had happened to all the hopes and dreams of his youth. He had always been a good Communist—at least he liked to think so—and in the beginning he had been elated at the progress of the people under the regime. The flies, as Western visitors always liked to notice, had vanished from China. But recently he had wondered if much else had not vanished as well. It seemed to him that life was gray and joyless, that discipline had replaced freedom, and that he, personally, was no longer given the respect his position as a healer and an educated man deserved.

Since the arrival of the courier plane from Peking, young Chou Tsing-wen, the council leader, and the abominable Engineer Li Chin had been in a state of high excitement. There had been a flurry of activity at the Dragon installations. The laser was obviously being prepared for a major test.

The doctor went to the door of his quarters and looked outside. The bitter wind carried the deep winter of the terrible, ice-sheathed Altai, and the cold seemed to settle into the Great Depression of the Turfan, to remain, it seemed, forever. Soong shivered in his quilted cotton trousers and jacket and rubbed his delicate blue-veined hands together for warmth.

From where he stood he could see the projecting muzzle of the laser—rings of machined alloy that glittered like precious gems even in the dull afternoon light. He considered the effort that had gone into making those massive rings, each at least a meter in diameter and finished to the tolerances required for microsurgery.

The technicians were raising and lowering the laser head from its ferroconcrete bed, testing the synchronous system with the radar installation in the adjoining bunkers. There was activity at the reactor building as well, and at the camouflaged steam-turbine building. The technicians had been given instructions to bring the electrical generators up to capacity; the day and the night had been filled with the almost hypersonic whine of the massive machines.

A sudden and gigantic drive was being made to "wake the Dragon," as the laborers said. The same laborers, Soong thought, who lived under conditions far more primitive than his own. These were the people to whom the regime had promised a better life; yet they lived like animals and worked like slaves. In the past week, two of the women in the labor force had been discovered in their barracks frozen to death. Still, these stolid, loyal people worked on. He looked again at the gleaming metal rings of the laser head. There were five of them, and the cost of each one would have built warm houses for a village full of people, would have fed a thousand workers for one year. This, he thought bitterly, was what it meant to become a Great Power.

Soong had become a Marxist as a young man for genuinely humanitarian reasons. He regretted the loss of liberty this entailed, but he sincerely believed the step was necessary to improve the material lot of the long-suffering Chinese people. Now he was no longer so certain as he had been. But had someone told him that he was becoming a counterrevolutionary, he would have been shocked and angry.

28

Yuri Leonov arrived at the new Ministry of Defense building overlooking Sokolniki Park in the late afternoon. A steady fall of snow had covered the grounds with a white blanket, the icy crust of which reflected the lights of the buildings along Sokolniki Prospekt, golden in the swiftly deepening winter dusk. The Marshal was alone and went swiftly through the doors, returning the salutes of the Guardsmen on sentry duty with a preoccupied brevity that was unlike his usual military punctilio.

The new Ministry was designed on the American plan, with large open spaces on the ground level and acres of glass behind a geometric concrete façade on the upper levels.

In his private office, the Minister of Defense seated himself behind his broad, bare desk. He still wore his greatcoat and cap, and snowflakes melted on the fine, thick cloth. His lean face was thoughtful as he removed the cap and placed it on the desk.

Beyond the door four young aides waited, each with a sheaf of papers that, to judge from their attitudes, demanded instant attention. Leonov smiled ruefully. The new breed of soldier was not to his liking. It was just as well he had stopped lecturing at Frunze. The purpose of the Crisis Confrontation Lectures had been recruitment, and he seriously doubted whether the latest classes out of the Academy would have supplied many real Leonovites. However, he thought, it no longer mattered. The tool he had labored so long to forge was ready at hand.

He picked up a telephone and a voice a continent away replied instantly, "Naval Operations Center Haiphong."

"This is Conductor."

The tone changed subtly at the mention of the code name for the commander in chief of all the Soviet armed forces. "What are your orders, Conductor?"

"Give me a position report on the vessels on station in the South China Sea."

The reply came with commendable swiftness: "Beech, Oak, and Elm are on station along the line Sigma-Omega." Beech, Oak, and Elm designated the very new, powerful eighty thousand-metric-ton aircraft carriers: Sigma-Omega was the patrol zone whose northern corners were Da Nang and the former American naval base at Cavite, in the Philippines. "Serpent and Crocodile are on station submerged in Zone Omega." The nuclear-missile submarines *Molotov* and *Zdhanov* were patrolling the Gulf of Tonkin. "Adder and Cobra will arrive on station to reinforce them at 0500 GMT." The nuclear submarines *Vishinsky* and *Ho Chi Minh,* traveling at flank speed on his, Leonov's, personal orders, would arrive before local sunrise.

"Notify the commanders that they are to stand by to participate in Task Red Glory. The exercise will begin at any time after 0900 hours GMT tomorrow. They are to maintain radio silence until then."

"Yes, Conductor."

He considered for a moment and then said, "My compliments to Naval Operations Haiphong. Your efficiency is noted."

"Thank you, Conductor." The sailor on the other end of the line did not attempt to conceal his pride and pleasure at being praised. Leonov had learned long ago that soldiers and sailors would do a great many more things well if praise was mingled with discipline.

He replaced the telephone in the holder and pressed a button on his television console. The screen beside his desk came to life and displayed the interior of the office of the Chief of Staff. There was no one behind the desk. Almost at once the picture changed and one of Marshal Lyudin's junior aides, a paratroop captain with a pale, moonish face, said, "Yes, Comrade Minister?"

"Where is Marshal Lyudin?"

The paratrooper licked his lips before replying. "He is not in the office, Comrade Minister."

"I can see that," Leonov said. "Where is he?"

"Ah, I believe he is in Usovo, Comrade Minister."

Leonov sensed danger. What would Lyudin be doing at the First Secretary's dacha? It was highly improper for the Chief of Staff to deal directly with the First Secretary without first asking permission from the Minister of Defense. He was tempted to demand an immediate explanation, but stayed the impulse before speaking. The dish-faced captain would know nothing. The old Marshal certainly would not discuss his moves with junior officers. Instead, Leonov said, "Transfer me to the Operations Officer."

"At once, Comrade Minister."

The television picture flipped and the interior of the Moscow War Room appeared. It was lightly staffed, Leonov could see. Just as well. The burly figure of Lieutenant General Anatoly Boyko, an old tank commander well known in the Soviet Army for his dogged stupidity and bluff manner, appeared.

"At your orders, Comrade Minister."

"I will be departing at once for Aral'sk. I intend conducting a personal inspection of the base there. Take the regiment off standby status. It will be necessary to seal off the post."

"Take Aral'sk off the line, Comrade Minister?"

"Those are my orders, Comrade General. Shall I repeat them?"

"No, sir. I understand, sir."

"I can't tell you how much that pleases me, Comrade General," Leonov said softly.

The Operations Officer changed color. Leonov fancied the bright boys, the clever school soldiers. He did not suffer fools gladly, or, for that matter, at all. And though Boyko did not consider himself a fool, he suspected that Leonov did. He stared as the Marshal's image faded from the television screen. By the balls of Lenin, he didn't envy Oblensky, down at Aral'sk. The Marshal had only just come from there and must have seen something that he didn't like to conduct an immediate personal, closed-base inspection. The sort of thing that got senior officers relieved of command—and sometimes much worse. No, General Boyko thought, I wouldn't be General Sergei Vissarionovich Oblensky for all the slivovitz in goddamn Poland.

29

In her room at the Stafford Hotel, Jane McNary poured herself a strong drink of Scotch and sipped it while she waited for Paul Lyman to come to the telephone. She had had some difficulty in reaching the Press Secretary. Lyman had to be located and disengaged from the British and other foreign news people who had been converging on Sissinghurst as the last diplomats gathered.

She set the glass carefully on the telephone table and held her hand up. It was amazingly steady, considering the raging currents of anger, elation, and excitement that filled her. The anger was directed at Harry Grant, who had treated her as no man could without suffering a reprisal. The elation stemmed from the sure knowledge that she was about to blackmail Lyman into giving her the greatest news beat of her career. She deliberately savored the knowledge that she had the power to humble the President and the President's men—including Grant. DeWitt Sutton had put it all in her hands with a single transatlantic telephone call.

Her Cranmer had been more excited than she as he talked. Sutton obviously saw his information—and the McNary touch—as a tremendously potent political weapon. And well he might, she thought. It wasn't often a member of Congress caught the President of the United States in quite so compromising a situation.

Cleveland Lambert, Sutton had said, was planning to slip away from the conference for a secret flight to Moscow and Peking. The excuse was some new weapon that the Chinese were said to be developing.

About weapons McNary knew little. But about politicians she knew a great deal, and about the American political climate she knew all there was to know. Sutton had said that his "source" (who very likely was Christopher Rosen) discounted entirely the possibility that the Chinese might actually be building something dangerous to peace. She cared next to nothing about that. What was important was that Lambert intended to conduct a high-level secret mission without even consulting Congress.

To know this would, in itself, give her considerable leverage with Lyman: the threat to expose the secret trip would be enough to send more than a shudder through the administration, she was sure.

But Sutton's information had not stopped there. Far from it. He had talked, foolishly, she thought, over an open line about possibilities that made her breath catch in her throat. On Air Force One she had wondered why Grant had been sent on ahead. The reason was supplied by the talkative Senator. Grant had come to England alone to meet with a Russian diplomat, one Colonel Voronin. Voronin had been murdered at Dover in some sort of cloak-and-dagger action—apparently before Grant could see him. But Voronin was a protégé of the Soviet Minister of Defense, who, according to Sutton, was in the process of planning some sort of political takeover in Russia, presumably when old Valentin Kirov died.

Sutton had, rather insultingly, she thought, tried to explain to her the implications—as if she didn't know them far better than he. "You see what Lambert is doing, Jane? He is allowing the United States to become involved in something really dangerous. It's like the disastrous meddling of the '60s and '70s all over again, only this time we are tampering with the internal affairs of China and the Soviet Union!"

"Are you sure of your facts?" she asked crisply. Sutton had been known to be careless.

"I am. And I shall have documentary proof within twenty-four hours. A copy of Harry Grant's request for information on

Marshal Leonov and this Voronin fellow. My God, Jane, you do see what they are up to, don't you?"

She saw very clearly that if Sutton's information was correct, the administration was involving the United States in some sort of coup in the Kremlin. A shiver ran down her back. Her spare knowledge of weaponry included the fact that more than five thousand nuclear weapons were at the ready in Russia.

"Then let me wrap it up for you," Sutton said. "I learned two hours ago that Clinton Devore and his hotheads in the Pentagon have ordered a *Red One.*"

"My God." The comment was torn from her by a sudden surge of anger and outrage. She abandoned herself to a moment of pure hatred, directed against Cleveland Lambert and all those who served him, the creatures of the corporations and the fat-cat bourgeoisie who ruled the United States. She had returned to the Marxist fury of her student days, and it felt *good*. Then she controlled her emotions and said, "Thank you, Cranmer. I'm going to use this."

"I expect you to," Sutton said stoutly.

"I may have to give my source."

"Wait just a moment, Jane. That has never been the way we worked together," Sutton said, now alarmed.

"It is a matter of credibility, Senator," McNary said, and broke the connection on his protest. It was typical of Sutton that he could make no distinction between a news person "protecting a source" in the case of some petty graft or misdeed within the government and the absolute need of convincing Lyman, and, if need be, Lambert himself, that she had sound information and would use it—*if* she was not given exactly what she wanted.

And what she wanted, she had decided, was a seat on that secretly dispatched 767 at Hurn. A seat on the airplane, the entire story of the mission—*all* of it—with no other media people about, and the right to publish it in her own time and way, without harassment. That, she decided triumphantly, is the Jane McNary interpretation of the New First Amendment.

30

In a room in a grimy hotel in Woolwich, the telephone in the hallway rang. The American girl who called herself "Bridget" snatched the receiver off the hook before it could ring again. Sullivan, who lay drunk on the bed upstairs, had told her that Caspar might call. It was a measure of how Sullivan had deteriorated since Sean was killed that he had allowed himself to get so sodden that she would have to take Caspar's call.

Bridget's face was bruised, her lips cut and battered. The Irishman, great hero that he was, great soldier of the Cause, had beaten her up after they had ransacked the Welsh girl's flat. The lipsticked message on her mirror that Bridget had thought was fine and clever and would really blow the English pigs' minds had instead blown Sullivan's. He had been angry and frightened, sure that she had left her prints everywhere scrawling that message.

"You're *stupid,* you goddamned Americans!" He started screaming at her the minute they'd gotten off the street and into this dirty fleabag. Screaming, literally, with flecks of spittle flying from his lips. "You *ignorant* bitch! What's the matter with you?"

Then words had failed him and he'd started beating her with his big fists. At first she'd liked it; it had started to turn her on. But he wouldn't stop, and now her swollen, blotched face defied recognition. And he had started soaking up gin, which was all he had, until he got so falling-down drunk that he couldn't stand by for Caspar's call. Sean would never have behaved this way, Bridget thought, but Sean was dead, blown away by an English fascist cop, thanks to Sullivan.

Caspar's cultivated accents made Bridget want to laugh.

Stupid Sullivan said he was a Russian. No Russian Bridget had ever heard had sounded like Caspar.

"Who is this?" he asked.

"Bridget."

"Where is Sullivan?"

Bridget considered lying and then decided against it. What the hell, let the drunken son of a bitch get what was coming to him. What kind of a revolutionary would do what he did?

"He's upstairs. He's drunk. Did you pick this place as a safe house? It smells like shit."

There was a momentary pause after this outbreak, and then Caspar said, "You were Sean's girl, I think?"

"You think? You're fucking right I was. Now I'm Patrick's." She winced when she started to smile. "I'm not doing so well, Mr. Caspar. How about me being *your* girl for a while?"

The son of a bitch almost sounded amused, she thought. He said, "Ah, I don't think so, Bridget. That wouldn't work out." The tone had changed, all business again. "I want you to give Sullivan a message. When he sobers up." This last was said with a distaste Bridget could understand. And there was something in Caspar's voice. Dismissal. Jesus, the bastard was turning them out!

"Are you listening?" Caspar sounded impatient now.

"I'm listening."

"Tell Sullivan that the job he was to do is no longer necessary. Tell him the object we wanted is valueless, not worth any risk at all. Do you understand?"

"Yes." She didn't, but she was damned if she was going to give the owner of that Limey voice any satisfaction.

"Tell Sullivan that we are satisfied. He can keep what he has been paid. Have you got that?"

"Yes."

"Tell him that he is to stay where he is. *Stay,* is that clear? We are arranging safe passage to the Republic. When that's done, he will be told."

"How?" Bridget wanted to know. Somehow all this wasn't right. There were lousy vibes in the air.

"He has another telephone number. This one is going out of service. Permanently."

"And we aren't to do anything about the Welsh girl?" God, she'd been counting on that. The thought of doing it had stoked her. And Sullivan had *promised* that she could do it.

"Nothing. *Do nothing.*" The words were carefully and grimly spoken. "Tell him that."

"But listen—"

The line went dead, and Bridget held the receiver for a moment before slamming it onto the hook. Sullivan would like this, she thought. The great hero of the Cause would just love lying about, doing nothing, and being paid for it. She started to climb the stairs, a slender figure in flared denims that had once been expensive and now were stained with body secretions, blood, and food. The sweater she wore was expensive, too, and as grimy as the rest of her clothing. From time to time, when she needed money, she would call her parents in Pennsylvania and tell them that she was tired of living underground and that she needed air fare home. They always sent it. She never went home. It was, she thought, a kind of game they all played. She despised them and they couldn't have borne to have her near them for a day. Yet they pretended that there was still love among them, pretended that they didn't understand what had happened to their little girl at that exclusive college where she had become radicalized.

Bridget walked down the littered hallway to Room 9, where Patrick Sullivan, soldier of the revolution and quondam hero of the Provisional IRA, lay on the sweaty, creaking bed in a fearful, drunken, open-mouthed stupor.

Chief Inspector Alfred Owen, of the Special Branch, New Scotland Yard, was on the firing range when the telephone call from SIS came. He had just placed six out of six in a ten-centimeter bull at a range of forty meters. The weapon he favored was an American Smith & Wesson .357 Magnum revolver with a fifteen-centimeter barrel. It was a difficult weapon to fire accurately, but Owen was a marksman, one of the best in Squad Alpha.

The average British citizen was unaware of the existence of Alpha, a fact rather resented by Chief Inspector Owen and his men. It seemed to him that after twenty years of terrorism, the ordinary citizen of the British Isles would be pleased to know that there was a group of men trained to deal with gunmen and terrorists in the only language they understood.

After the police psychologists, the lightly armed constables, and the sympathetic bleeding hearts had a go at barricaded terrorists—and failed—they sent for Alpha. And Alpha, flak-jacketed, heavily armed, and totally devoid of tolerance for bombers, kidnappers, and murderers, simply went in and either took them or killed them. Most often the latter. Authorities never sent Alpha if they hoped to take the terrorists alive.

It was a unit made up of men like Alfred Owen: young, aggressive, and *angry*. Men came to Alpha after being touched in some personal way by acts of terrorism. In Owen's case it was a young sister, blown to bloody bits by a bomb in an airline terminal in America. It had happened years ago, but Owen's fury had not abated.

He unloaded his weapon, laid it on the shelf of the firing position, and removed his ear muffs. The uniformed sergeant at the desk held up the telephone receiver. Owen walked across the soundproofed concrete floor and took the call.

"Is that you, Chief Inspector?"

"Yes." Owen was a laconic man, and his long service with Squad Alpha had made him even more so.

"Major Ballard here."

"Yes, sir."

"We've had a possible break in the Dover terminal matter, Chief Inspector. An anonymous tip."

"Yes, sir." Owen's tone gave no indication of the satisfaction he felt. Since the identification of the gunman the Russian had killed at the Hovercraft terminal, he had wanted very much to take the other. The bombing that had sacrificed his sister had never been solved, but Owen had always known in his own mind that the blast had come from an IRA bomb in transit. He also knew that anonymous telephone calls were the best source of information in cases involving terrorists and political killers. The bloody-minded bastards could never get along among themselves, and one was always turning in another—in the name of peace, freedom, and God only knows what else.

"The word is that the second gunman has gone to ground at a hotel called the Dartford Arms in Woolwich."

Owen's thin lips curled into a smile. He was coldly amused at the way Ballard used hunting terms. So bloody posh was Major Ian Bloody Ballard of Winchester and Sandhurst. Next he would be offering to let Alfred Owen have the brush.

"I've talked to the Home Secretary just now. He will permit an Alpha action. Provided it is quick and not too noisy. We don't want a great flap while the Yanks are in town."

"Understood, sir."

"The word we have is that he has a girl with him. And they are both heavily armed."

"Yes, sir."

"I have the hotel under surveillance. The girl is in and out a good deal, but she's not too important. I think about eight o'clock tonight?"

"With respect, sir," Owen said, "I think such things are better handled in the early morning. When there are not many people about on the streets." Owen hated it when these intelligence types tried to tell Alpha how to run its business.

"Just as you say, Chief Inspector. I'll instruct my man to keep a very loose cover on the place. We don't want our bird flying."

"Will you be joining us, sir?"

"I think not, Chief Inspector. The Home Secretary would prefer that it appear a domestic police matter. The Yanks, you understand."

"Very well, sir."

"I will be going down to Sissinghurst this evening, Chief Inspector. I would like a report from you as soon as the action is completed. My deputy will be available here to let you know exactly where I am."

"Very good, sir."

Owen replaced the telephone receiver and returned to the firing line. He reloaded his weapon, placed the protectors over his ears, and fired six times at the head of the human outline on the target. Six more hits. He smiled. It had not been necessary to ask whether or not he should try to take the gunman alive. That really wasn't Alpha's job. Chief Inspector Owen wouldn't have it any other way.

In his office in Parliament Street, Ballard turned from the telephone to look out the window at the roofs of London. He was wondering now, as he often did, if he were, in fact, a traitor. He rejected the idea, as he always had. A double agent, yes. Or even twice a double agent. But certainly not a traitor to England, and maybe not even to that amorphous and sadly impotent entity that people thought of as "the West." Objectively, he thought, one could make a case for the proposition that he was serving the West better than it deserved, helping to set in motion events that might prove its salvation.

Breeding, almost as much as personal experiences, had turned Ian Ballard into a man of ambiguous loyalties. He was one of the last products of the old British society, the society of imperial pride, and he had never come to feel at home in the drab egalitarian structure imposed on Britain by successive Labour governments.

His torture and interminable sufferings as a prisoner of the

Chinese during the Korean war had ingrained a deep hatred of the Communist Oriental. But he might well have learned to live with that had it not been for what he considered the slavish ease with which English statesmen had accommodated themselves to the reality of a Communist China. On the day Britain recognized the People's Republic, he had, for the first and only time in his life, drunk himself into bitter insensibility.

During those years, while he was working his way quietly upward in the weakened and diminished branch of British Intelligence designated SIS, he had regarded the Russians as a threat little different from the Chinese except in power. And while the Americans fought the Cold War with Yank ferocity, his admiration for them—an admiration learned in the icy school of POW camps—remained unflagging. If others had suggested to him then that he would betray his trust as an Englishman, it would have been at their peril.

Ian Ballard became susceptible to subversion with the great schism in the Communist world: the moment when Russia and China abandoned the charade of ideological community and resumed their roles as imperialist enemies. Even this might not have been enough to render him vulnerable had it not coincided with a sharp decline in British willingness to share with the Americans the task of opposing the spread of what Ballard thought of as the Communist virus.

It was in that discouraging period of his life that he met the then Colonel Yevgeny Zabotin. Over a period of two years, while Zabotin served as a military attaché in London (though it was common knowledge that he was more: the *rezident* for the GRU), Ballard learned—was *allowed* to learn—that there were officers in the Soviet armed forces resolved to precipitate a confrontation, not with the West, but with China.

The knowledge gave Ballard a cautious hope. For many months he considered what should be done with the information. He was, like most intelligence officers, a realist. He knew the substance of his many conversations with Zabotin would be rigorously questioned. The gradually developing conspiracy the Russian described was too fantastic to be accepted without corroboration. To obtain this meant the risk of a mistake and a silent purge in Russia, with the followers of Marshal Leonov, the man the Americans so appropriately code-named Boyar, either dead or buried alive in the labor camps of Novaya Zemlya. And Ballard, out of experience, knowledge, and instinct, had realized he might be a pawn of the Russians in a more complex and dangerous game than even this appeared to be.

Gradually he formed the conviction that the conspiracy, if it did in fact exist anywhere but in the devious mind of the GRU man, Zabotin, was too potentially valuable to England and the West to risk by disclosure.

This had been the key decision. From the moment Ballard decided against informing his superiors of Zabotin's talk—and, more important, the Russian's attempt to recruit an officer of SIS as a coconspirator—he became a traitor.

Even then, he remained a passive traitor: a traitor by omission, as it were. Until Richard Nixon, that Cold Warrior nonpareil, betrayed the weakening West with his policy of détente. In Ballard's mind, no betrayal ever loomed so large as the act of an American politician selling his lifelong anti-Communism to the Kremlin for political advantage. That the same President had compounded his infamous sellout by extending an olive branch to the Red Chinese merely raised the order of magnitude of the threat to Western values and culture.

It was then Ballard resolved to assist in any way possible the Byzantine maneuvering of Yuri Leonov and his followers. If their aim was the insane one of precipitating a nuclear exchange with the Chinese Reds, well and good. Ballard was a soldier in the old mold. In his mind, nuclear weapons were not too dissimilar to the weapons with which he had worked during his active-duty career. They were larger and more conclusive. Nothing more. And it was fortuitous, he thought, that the Russians and the

Chinese—Orientals, both, actually—had the kinds of mentalities that would allow them to spend themselves savaging one another while the West waited safely at a distance.

Ballard was relieved that it would not now be necessary to distress Bronwen Wells. Until Grant had so innocently brought the yellow case to him for examination, there had been the real possibility that Sullivan might have killed her in his brute's search. If it had been necessary, Ballard would have ordered it without hesitation. But the girl, with Grant's blundering Yankee assistance, had saved herself and that was a good thing. Ballard could kill, and had, and he could order others to kill, and he had done that, too. But he seldom took pleasure in it. He had been saddened by the need to have Voronin eliminated. But the order had come straight from GRU Moscow—and, in any case, he would have recommended Voronin's termination once it became apparent that his affair with the dancer had turned him.

Voronin *had* been about to defect. He, Ballard, had enticed him, cultivated him, offering a new life among the Yanks. It was a dirty business, of course. The poor sod had no way of knowing, when he was talking to Ballard, that he was simply enmeshing himself in still another fold of Boyar's maturing conspiracy. But intelligence work wasn't done with white kid gloves on the hands. Voronin knew this as well as anyone else involved in the profession.

Ballard returned to his desk and studied his schedule. He allowed himself an ironic smile. The poor bloody Yanks were going to be involved, but it was as much for their good as for the rest of the world's. That fancy Leonov bastard was going to use them, neatly, as cat's-paws. And the best of it was that he, Ian Ballard, having been detailed by the PM himself, was going to join the American party to "co-ordinate special security matters." Whatever happened now, he would have a ringside seat.

Chief Inspector Owen and his Alpha thugs would take care of the Provo and his girl while Major Ian Ballard, MC, of Her Majesty's Secret Intelligence Service, reported to his American counterpart at Sissinghurst Castle to offer his assistance and his respects to the President of the United States.

He carefully cleared the top of his desk and locked the drawers before informing his secretary that he was leaving for the day. Ballard liked to have things tidy.

31

___

It was late evening when Harry Grant drove the rented Volvo up narrow, cobbled Mermaid Street in Rye. They had stopped in Maidstone for dinner and to buy Bronwen some necessities and a brown canvas flight bag and to telephone the Mermaid Inn for a room for her.

"Why are we going to Rye?" she had asked.

"It's a place for you to stay until I get back," he said. He might have added that it was somehow a place where it seemed unlikely she would be troubled by whoever had ripped apart her flat. Rye, with its half-timbered houses and medieval charm, was an environment in which twentieth-century violence could not prosper. That, Grant knew, was nonsense, but it was as true an answer to Bronwen's question as he could muster at the moment. He knew only that he wanted her safe. He had stopped questioning his motives.

He remembered the Mermaid kindly from another trip to southern England. He was worried that perhaps it had changed, as so much seemed to be changing in Britain, but it had not. The hall porter met them in the car park. The wet sea wind from the Channel was blowing. They could see the lights of Winchelsea and a single trawler moving slowly across Rye Bay toward Dungeness.

The porter said, "The kitchen is closed, sir. But I could probably find you a few sandwiches if you're hungry."

Grant said, "Just some coffee and biscuits, please."

The woman at the desk offered the register. Bronwen signed "Hilary Grant," as Grant had coached her to do.

"You won't be staying, Mr. Grant?" the clerk asked politely.

"No. I will join my wife later. In a few days. That will be all right, I suppose?"

"Quite all right, sir. We are seldom filled at this time of year."

Grant and Bronwen followed the porter upstairs, through the low-ceiling, timbered hall to Cadman's Room. All the rooms at the Mermaid had names. Bronwen asked, "Who was Cadman?"

The porter, a young local with long hair and a pleasant, toothy smile, said, "A smuggler, mohm. He stayed in this house before it was remodeled. In 1411, that is, mohm."

In spite of his weariness and concern, Grant couldn't help smiling at that. The implication that it's having been redone in 1411 somehow made the place into the *new* Mermaid Inn was so typically English. This calm acceptance of a long history was one of the things Grant admired most in these people. It gave one the hope that no matter what, four hundred years from now a boy very like this one would be showing somebody to Cadman's Room in the still-new Mermaid Inn.

The smuggler's room held a fourposter, a dressing table, a wardrobe, and a desk. It overlooked Mermaid Street. Grant walked to the window and glanced out at the steep cobbled street. It was quiet, not entirely deserted at this hour. At the foot of the hill lay the more modern part of the town. There wasn't a great deal of it. One street and, beyond, the placid water of the inlet of the Royal Military Canal, another piece of somnolent history that had once carried barge traffic to the northeast between the Isle of Oxney and Walland and Romney marshes. A few small boats rode to moorings in the inlet, their white hulls limned by the reflected lights of the town.

Grant drew the curtains closed and turned to Bronwen. She was sitting quietly on the bed looking at him.

"I don't know what to say," she said softly.

Grant essayed a thin smile. "I don't mean to be taking over

your life, Bron," he said. "But I want you to stay here for a bit. A while—until we can get things sorted out."

"Yes," she said. Then: "But I can't hide forever, can I? I mean, I'll have to go back to London soon."

"Ballard will tell me when it's safe."

She closed her eyes and drew a deep breath. "I am so tired, Harry. I'm confused, too. Sometimes I wonder if it matters at all—"

"It matters," Grant said roughly. And then he added, more gently: "It matters to me."

Bronwen turned up her hands in her lap, a gesture of helplessness and perplexity. "You don't even know me, Harry."

"I suppose not."

"We have only just met."

"That's right. But it still matters to me. *You* matter." The admission seemed torn from him. It wasn't his way at all, he thought. For years he had led a self-contained, untouched—yes, cold—life. Why this? Why now? Little wonder McNary had behaved like a fishwife. He supposed that if any woman had a claim on him, it was Jane. Yet here he stood, having abducted Bronwen Wells because suddenly he was afraid for her. His actions were not those of the Iron Colonel. He had no doubt that he would be in for a first-class reprimand from Lambert; God knew what the President's political enemies, or the news media, might make of what he was doing.

None of that seemed important. Bronwen's safety was vital. If he could be certain she would come to no harm, he could do the rest of his job in good conscience.

The young porter came and went, leaving a tray of biscuits and small cakes and a pot of steaming strong coffee.

Grant ate, thinking that he still had to drive a quarter of the way across southern England tonight to be at Hurn when the President arrived. Bronwen drank coffee and watched him with dark, troubled eyes.

Presently he said, "I had better leave now." He took several ten-pound notes from his wallet. "Take these. You are not to write any checks or make any telephone calls. Do not reveal your name—just be Mrs. Grant. I will call you as soon as I know it's all right."

She took the money, looking at it strangely as she held it. "Harry—"

He held her by the shoulders. "Bron. I don't want anyone to know where you are. Anyone."

"I should let Madame Zelinskaya know—"

"No. Not *anyone*."

She looked up at him: a gamine face, broad across the brows, narrowing through hollow cheeks to a small chin. He could imagine how she looked onstage, her slender, dancer's body in the tightly fitted bodice and traditional tutu. Like a Degas painting, he thought. He touched her softly feathered temple with his fingertips. Then he kissed her.

She held him lightly, not refusing his kiss, but not accepting it either. It was like holding smoke in his arms.

"That doesn't help the situation much, does it?" he said.

She closed her eyes and smiled, pressing her forehead against his lips. "It makes me feel—safe," she said.

Grant doubted that he had intended that. "I'm going now. Before I really make a fool of myself," he said.

"No," she said, and lifted her mouth to his again.

32

In Moscow, at four-thirty in the morning, the temperature had dropped to ten degrees below freezing. The vast emptiness of Red Square glistened as the harsh lights that were kept burning there reflected from the ice on the pavement. The Kremlin wall, with its funerary decorations and wilted flowers, was also illuminated by the hard, cold light.

Viktor Krasin, bleary-eyed with fatigue, stood at the window in the Foreign Ministry staring out at the bleak, lonely prospect. Behind him, at a broad table covered with dossiers, General Novikov, his KGB tunic opened at the throat, sat wolfing down cold chicken and drinking vodka.

Krasin was frightened. His last instructions from the First Secretary had been to discover how many of Marshal Yuri Leonov's personal protégés were now in sensitive positions inside the Soviet diplomatic corps. He had done so, working privately and with only Novikov's assistance. What he had discovered had shocked him. There was hardly an embassy in Western Europe or in South Asia where a former student of Leonov's had not been located in a strategic position. They were military attachés, air attachés, naval attachés, intelligence officers, advisers, and even deputy ambassadors. The peculiar subservience of the Soviet bureaucracy to the military had apparently made possible an incredible penetration of the diplomatic corps. In all, there were over six hundred former students of Leonov's in capitals surrounding the USSR.

When Novikov had telephoned the dacha at Usovo to pass this alarming information on to First Secretary Kirov, he had been told that the First Secretary was sleeping. What this meant, exactly, Krasin had been unwilling to guess until old Marshal Lyudin, the Army Chief of Staff, had come on the line to tell him that he had been waiting for more than ten hours to see First Secretary Kirov and that he had been "sleeping" all that time. "Something is very wrong," the Marshal had said. "If I'm kept out of his room by these sawbones much longer, I am going to do something about it."

Precisely what Lyudin meant by "doing something about it" was a thing that Krasin wished devoutly not to know. But he was afraid that he would not be permitted ignorance. Novikov, invoking his authority as head of State Security, had called the headquarters of the Moscow Military District to demand a computer run of Leonov's protégés in the Army, Navy, and Air Force. "If they've saturated the diplomatic corps as they have, Krasin," he said roughly, "we'd better have a look at the armed forces."

Krasin, tired and frightened as he was, could not withhold a waspish suggestion that the General should investigate the KGB as well. Novikov hadn't like that, and his gross manner showed it. He was eating and drinking like a peasant, spitting chicken bones on the floor, because he knew how much it would offend the Foreign Minister.

But he had given the order. The computer run was now under way.

Meanwhile, they waited for Marshal Lyudin to call back. Krasin wished that he had some notion of why old Lyudin had felt it necessary to go directly to Kirov at Usovo instead of passing whatever he had through the proper channels. Since the channels would include the Minister of Defense, as commander in chief of the Soviet armed forces, Krasin had a sinking feeling that Lyudin's complaint, whatever it was, directly concerned Marshal Yuri Leonov.

Novikov, his mouth full, studied Krasin with a feeling of

contempt. The Foreign Minister was not a weak man; a weak man could never have survived the last twenty years of maneuver and combat inside the bureaucracy. But Kirov had not made it his habit to surround himself with associates who could threaten his position of leadership. Yuri Leonov was surely an exception—and Novikov, in his capacity as the top Soviet policeman, had told the First Secretary so. But Kirov had been ailing then, and Leonov had marshaled ample support from the Politburo to assume the post of Defense minister. Krasin was a diplomat, not a proper gutter fighter. He was the sort of man the First Secretary allowed near the levers of power, Novikov thought flatly, because he had known that Krasin could never be a threat.

First Secretary Kirov had, in fact, chosen all of his close associates for their inability to construct an opposition; even, Novikov conceded, himself. Only Leonov did not fit the pattern. Now, the policeman wondered, with Kirov sick and immobilized, were they going to pay the price? He was not yet certain, but this whole affair was beginning to stink like fish rotting in the sun. His instinct told him what the computer would show about Yuri Ivanovich's precious protégés from Frunze. The question was: were they in a position to do some immediate mischief, or was the Defense Minister still building himself a power base? Plot it was, Novikov was certain. Power was the "why" of it. But what was the "how"? And the "when"?

He had been particularly explicit in his orders to the Moscow Military District that GRU was not to be informed that any investigation was under way. But he had little hope that order would be carried out. The officers at the Military District were, after all, Red Army and not KGB. It would be too much to hope for that the GRU would not get wind of his demand for so peculiar a computer run. That was what came of allowing the putrid military to have its own intelligence service, he thought. At least a dozen times during his career in the KGB he had written confidential reports recommending that the GRU's functions be incorporated into the Committee for State Security. But no First Secretary had ever seen fit to take his recommendations seriously. Well, now see where they all were, he thought with bitter satisfaction.

He looked again at Krasin. The diplomat was Comrade Kirov's choice to be his successor. Novikov had his reservations about that. Krasin lacked the essential personality, the ability to decide, to command. Well, I couldn't do it, he thought sourly. I don't really *want* to do it.

Kirov was a shrewd judge of human nature. He had been at his best when it came to manipulating others. Even the Americans. He had just manipulated their President to come and take half the responsibility of demanding that the Maoists stop their development of a weapon that could seriously imperil the military balance among the three megapowers.

But Kirov had made an error, it seemed. He had allowed himself to grow old and ill without, apparently, watching his bright, bloody-minded genius in the Ministry of Defense closely enough. And such mistakes could still, in the Soviet Union, be fatal. How long could the nervous and tentative Krasin hold on to power once his patron was dead? Which seemed likely to be soon, perhaps a matter of hours. Shit, Novikov concluded, Krasin must take over, even if only for a short time. There had to be authority.

"Comrade Foreign Minister," he said abruptly, "I think you should convene a meeting of the Politburo. At once."

Krasin looked startled by the thought of what was an obvious necessity. "That could be extremely dangerous, Comrade General."

Novikov tapped the dossiers. "We are in the midst of a crisis, Viktor Stepanovich."

"It looks suspicious, I agree. But we cannot yet be certain."

"Comrade Kirov is not capable of carrying out his duties," Novikov said relentlessly. "It is understood by all that you are empowered to step into his place."

"Comrade General, you forget yourself."

What madmen we are, Novikov thought, to have created a system in which the mere mention of a change in the regime brings such panic. Even the tsars had a semblance of logical succession.

"Every member of the Politburo has been instructed at one time or another that you are to take command when Comrade Kirov cannot act. Well, he cannot, Comrade. He is dying."

"The doctors do not say so."

"The doctors are frightened. They are shitting in their pants. They are waiting to be told what to do."

Krasin's eyes looked like those of a hunted fox. "I am leaving for England almost at once."

"That is now out of the question."

"Those are my instructions from Comrade Kirov."

"It is out of the question and you know it," Novikov said. "Your place is here." His expression hardened. *"And you know it,"* he repeated.

Krasin sat down and stared at the dossiers. Was there a chance, he wondered, that all this was a terrible mistake? That the men and women whose records lay before him were merely what they seemed to be, bright, young minds culled and trained by an even brighter mind to be of service to the state?

Novikov cut to the core of his doubts. "You must convene the Politburo. Lyudin and I will support you, and if we do, then so will all the others."

A bleak, frightened smile touched the Foreign Minister's lips. He asked: "Including Yuri Leonov?"

"We don't need Leonov."

"He commands the armed forces, for God's sake, Novikov."

"An hour after you assert your authority, I'll have Leonov under arrest."

"There will be trouble. Zabotin is a Leonovite, I'm sure of it. He will have the GRU and who knows how many units of the Army, Navy, and Air Force. What then?"

"We deal with it," the KGB man said grimly.

"And how do we explain to the Americans when they arrive here and see Moscow under martial law?"

"To *hell* with the Americans. Tell them not to come."

Krasin leaned forward, his face a mask of strain and anxiety. "You talk like a policeman—"

"I *am* a policeman. This is a matter for policemen."

"Perhaps it is, and then perhaps it isn't. We have no real proof that Yuri Ivanovich is making a Stalinist plot—"

"If we wait for proof, Viktor Stepanovich, we may find ourselves congratulating each other on our restraint at Novaya Zemlya," Novikov said.

"But the Americans are coming. We can't tell them to stay away now. We can't display that sort of confusion and weakness before them *or* the Maoists," Krasin protested. "They simply must be allowed to come as planned."

"Then ask them to postpone the visit. The First Secretary's health."

Krasin sat thoughtfully, biting nervously at his lower lip. The man was a disaster, Novikov thought. That was what came of spending so much time out of the country among the imperialists.

"Twenty-four hours, perhaps," Krasin said tentatively. "Not more, certainly. We could delay their arrival that long."

"Then do it."

"I must wait for instructions from Comrade Kirov."

"Damn you, don't you understand the old man is *dying?* Do I have to draw you a diagram? Must you see him stiff before you admit it?" Novikov roared, pounding the table and setting the dishes bouncing.

A communicator pinged, and Novikov reached for the television switch. *"What is it, son of a bitch?"*

The startled face of the duty officer at Moscow Military District headquarters appeared. "The computer run is complete, Comrade General. Shall I present it on the screen?"

"No, you fool! This is supposed to be a secret run. Send me

the print-out by officer messenger. An *armed* officer messenger. At once!"

"Yes, Comrade General. At once, Comrade General." The officer vanished from the screen.

Novikov spoke to Krasin. "You know what that print-out will say, don't you? I'll be surprised if there is one major command that isn't polluted with Leonov's pretty faces."

Krasin made a gesture of despair. "Let us see," he said. "Let us see."

In the dacha at Usovo, Marshal Lyudin lumbered to his feet. For hours the medical people had been passing in and out of the First Secretary's sickroom. Twice the doctor Lisavetta Lazarova had paused to speak with him, each time telling him that the First Secretary was still sleeping and that she dare not disturb him. But others were disturbed, Lyudin thought. In fact, it seemed to him that the medical staff was far more than simply disturbed. He had served in the Great Patriotic War and knew well enough what an outfit stricken by fear looked like. This fancy medical team, composed of the best academicians in Soviet medicine, looked terrified, and it was time to do something about it. Pavel Semyonovich Lyudin had not become the second-ranking officer of the Soviet Army by being polite.

He stood and walked to the door. The soldier there, a young flat-faced peasant with wide blue eyes, came to attention.

"Open the door, soldier," Lyudin said quietly.

The boy looked confused. "My orders, Comrade Marshal, are—"

"To hell with your orders!" Lyudin's bull roar came from deep in a massive chest covered with medals. *"Open the door, soldier!"*

The young soldier almost vibrated with the rigidity of his stance. He stepped aside and opened the door.

Lyudin stepped into a scene out of some medical version of

hell. Valentin Kirov was almost lost amid the equipment surrounding him. Intravenous drips were tubed into his arms and thigh. A kidney machine, all glistening pumps and blood-washed plastic chambers, whirred and ticked. A tracheotomy had been performed on the corpselike figure on the bed, and the tubes of a respirator curved out of the machine and vanished into a hissing hole centered above Kirov's scrawny clavicle. Electroencephalogram leads were taped to the half-shaven head. The screen above the bed showed a suspiciously unblemished line. Another screen translated the laboring, electronically induced heartbeats into spikes of green light.

Academician Lazarova, her eyes wide above the face mask she wore said, *"Out! Comrade Marshal, out of here at once!"* Her assistants, green-robed and masked, made a row of frightened, hollow eyes.

In spite of himself, Lyudin retreated into the anteroom. As a soldier, he was accustomed to seeing unpleasant things. But nothing in his experience had prepared him for the horrifying spectacle of death being held at bay by the complex, advanced devices of modern medical science. The man on the bed was changed from a human—sometimes all too human—colleague and leader into a thing half flesh and half machine. The blood-sluiced plastic bulb and domes of the kidney machine seemed to Lyudin to have partially ingested the flesh, and the sounds of the respirator were like the iron breathing of a loathsome robot.

Lazarova followed him from the room and shut the door behind her. Her green smock was lightly spattered with blood, her hands encased in membrane-thin surgical gloves. To Lyudin, she seemed a demon, with her dark, angry eyes and her plastic-mask snout.

She pulled the mask away from her face and said in a tension-pitched voice, "That was inexcusable, Comrade Marshal. The intrusion could kill him."

The old Marshal felt his gorge rise. "The man is dead, you bitch. Admit it."

"The First Secretary is *not* dead, Comrade Lyudin. He has had a relapse, nothing more."

"You lied to me," Lyudin said. "You said he was resting." These butchers, he thought. Their power over us makes them arrogant and dangerous.

"He was resting," Lazarova said. "He took a turn for the worse. We had to put him on life-support. There was hardly time to discuss it with *you,* Comrade Lyudin. We had to keep him alive."

"*Alive!*" The word was ripped from him. Suddenly he felt angry enough to strike her. "You call that alive?"

"Yes! We are keeping him alive."

"God help you."

The dark eyes were frigid, opaque. "God has nothing to do with it, Comrade Marshal. This is a matter of science."

Lyudin gathered his papers and stuffed them into his case. His trembling hands looked old and bony and were disfigured with brown spots. He placed his cap on his head and shrugged into his greatcoat. He said bitterly, "If you ever come near *me,* you bitch, I'll kill you."

"That is an emotional remark unworthy of a Soviet soldier," Lazarova said. "My task is to keep Comrade Kirov alive, and that I will do for as long as I can."

"Spare me your loyalty," Lyudin said, and brushed past her toward the door. Once outside the dacha, he stood in the sharp, cold air and breathed the wind deep into his lungs. For a terrifying moment he was actually aware of himself: not as a human being, but as a collection of aging cells and systems with blood and plasma pumping through hardening veins and arteries, into alveolae necrotic with tars and deadly oils, driven by knotted deteriorating muscle in his barrel chest that could fail at any time and starve his bones and sinews into bluish submission and collapse, his brain into an anoxemic pulp. And if that were to happen, Lisavetta Lazarova and her familiars could gather him up out of the snow, strip his puffy body into shameful nakedness, plug him into those terrible machines, and keep him—alive? No, hardly that—*functioning,* yes, that was it—functioning, as a vegetable functions—*forever.* God, it didn't bear thinking about!

His staff car appeared, and he did not wait for the driver to open the door. He opened it himself, said "Moscow," and sat down in the shadowy light inside, aching with the effort of controlling his churning stomach. As the car began to roll, and he could hear the tires crushing the powdery, new-fallen snow, he began to think again, organizing what he had seen into a coherent picture.

No matter what the academic bitch said, Valentin Kirov was dead. That artificially supported corpse in the sickroom would make no decisions, hold no meetings, issue no orders. Kirov had planned everything with the Machiavellian nicety for which he was famous. But he had not allowed for his frailty. And now the whole structure was in danger of fragmenting.

Lyudin picked up the radiotelephone. Moscow Military Central answered at once.

"Get me the Minister of Foreign Affairs," he said. Novikov was with Krasin; leave it to the KGB to be always near the power fulcrum, Lyudin thought bleakly. He did not like General Novikov and he did not trust him. In the end he could easily turn out to be Leonov's man. He had supported Leonov's policies in the Politburo. Though that in itself need not mean that he was disloyal, it was cause for suspicion. At least he had never been one of Leonov's bright protégés. The problem was that there was no way of knowing how much time there was to take action against Leonov. There was even the possibility that the Minister of Defense was innocent of any counterrevolutionary activity, though that would matter not at all if it should come to a trial.

It was Krasin's problem now. He, Lyudin, would lay his findings before Krasin, tell him of Leonov's suspicious military moves: the naval concentration in the South China Sea, the movement of GRU security troops to Aral'sk, the mystifying decision to man the next Svoboda satellite, and the provocative maneuver called Task Red Glory by the Far Eastern Army.

He would do that which was no more than his duty. And since the vegetable on the bed at Usovo could make no more decisions—not about Leonov, not about the Americans, not about the Chinese and their laser—Viktor Krasin must decide. He thought of the old days, in the field; a few minutes' sleep were all a hardened campaigner needed. He closed his eyes.

33

From the suite on the top story of the new and glaringly inappropriate glass-and-steel high-rise Labour House the British had recently completed at Sissinghurst, the President of the United States looked down at the famous rose gardens. The castle itself, dark red in the damp morning mist, and the oast houses that still dotted the green countryside seemed to hold aloof from the new conference halls and buildings of the Labour House complex.

Cleveland Lambert was taut with displeasure, and the architectural conflicts that met his educated eye merely added to his irritation. "Why the hell do you suppose they chose to foul this beautiful place with their new monstrosity?" he asked.

Margaret Kendrick did not reply because no comment from her was expected. Lambert knew perfectly well that Labour House was among the many public-works projects instituted by the Prime Minister to blunt one vituperative criticism of the welfare state. ("We no longer have a dole; instead, we have legislated a programme of useful work in return for government subsidies," he said often.) It was, as Lambert's Secretary of the Treasury liked to say, "as though the English had rediscovered the New Deal."

From where he stood, he could see his wife, surrounded by British and American security people and accompanied by Mrs. Dalworth, the wife of the British Foreign Secretary, making an early-morning tour of the gardens. "Helena and I were here sixteen years ago," he said abruptly. "Before the PM and his ward boys took the place over from the National Trust. It was better then. Christ," he added with reawakened irritation, "everything was better then."

Kendrick waited patiently for the spasm of temper to pass. She didn't blame Lambert for being angry. It was a measure of the low estate to which the Presidency had fallen that he could be badgered—blackmailed, to call it by its real name—into giving Jane McNary special treatment.

But Paul Lyman had been absolutely correct. She *did* have vital information. She *could* cause untold harm by releasing it. And she most certainly *would* release it unless she got what she wanted—the right to go along on the trip to Moscow and Peking.

When the Press Secretary had come to her with the problem, the Secretary of State had seen clearly that there was nothing to be done but give in to McNary's demand. There would be, she devoutly hoped, a chance to make McNary regret her insolence. But that time was not yet. For now, the secret of the Moscow mission had to be kept. So Lambert could stand at the window, grumble about the English, damn the state of the world, but he would have to give in—and with as much grace as he could muster.

Of almost equal importance to Kendrick was the need to trace the source of McNary's information. The Moscow-Peking mission was vital to the foreign policy of the United States as she conceived it, and she had hoped, when they had left Washington that *this one* secret could be kept, at least until the groundwork for what she privately thought of as a "New Triple Entente" was laid. The news about the Chinese weapons breakthrough (if that was what it was—she was a political scientist, not a physicist) had been unsettling, but it had presented her, and the Lambert administration, with the opportunity to score a major foreign-policy coup. It was her dream that the United States take the lead as a peacemaker between Russia and China, breaking down old remnants of Cold War barriers and accomplishing unilaterally what the United Nations could never accomplish.

The news of the Chinese weapon and the possible Soviet response to it had come as a risky, but plausible, opportunity for the United States to assume diplomatic leadership. A peace—even a temporary one—between the Chinese and the Russians arranged by the United States would be of inestimable value in the conduct of American foreign policy. Even the British were agreed on this point—to the extent of committing themselves to send along a small, but impressive liaison group. A premature disclosure of the President's journey could be more than an embarrassment. If the tale was told by one of McNary's ideology, the trip would be made to appear another example of vainglorious Presidential interventionism.

Moreover, Lambert was certain that premature publicity implying that the USSR and the People's Republic actually needed the assistance of the United States in resolving their differences could easily cause either—probably both—governments to cancel the trip and claim that no such journey was ever contemplated by them.

Though she felt a grudging respect for McNary's energy and ability, the Secretary of State disliked her intensely. To a woman with Margaret Kendrick's reasoned approach to public affairs, the famed McNary vitriol was mischievous, petty, and ultimately stupid. Kendrick considered McNary a self-seeking trouble-maker, a person more dedicated to advancing herself and her basic Marxism than the interests of the American people. Like all elitists, McNary visualized herself among the powerful of some future, socialized America—Commissar of Truth, no doubt—the Secretary thought icily.

There was a time when Kendrick would have totally dismissed the power of the McNarys to do harm. Now she was no longer sure. The isolationist trends in the Congress that she had discounted in her teaching days had shown a disturbing tenacity. This, combined with the appalling power of the press and electronic media, must surely give the President pause. But now there was a chance to act with courage and initiative to the credit of the republic, and she was willing to pay any price to see this mission through. The President, she knew, felt the same way. He would hate paying blackmail to Jane McNary. But he would do it.

He turned now to face the Secretary of State. "Damn it, Margaret, this is a hard one to swallow." He ran a hand over his longish gray hair in an unconscious, familiar gesture. "I'm afraid I tore a bloody strip off Paul when he presented that bitch's terms."

"Paul understands, Mr. President."

"What's happening to us, Margaret? In the last four or five years we've gone soft. There used to be some sense of outrage. What the hell are we doing to ourselves?"

"I'd guess, Mr. President, that you can trace it all back to the '70s—the Vietnam war, Watergate, the recession, the intelligence purge. Confusion and disillusion bred fear, and that culminated in a demand for change. Some of it may make glorious theoretical sense, but it has raised sheer hell with our position internationally. Reform, a sane activity, was raised to a frantic obsession by every opportunist who could make use of it—including some of your colleagues in both parties. In the name of freedom and 'openness in government'—splendid ideals, by the way—we strip ourselves naked before our enemies."

The President grimaced. "I suppose this is Sutton and his friends you're talking about."

"DeWitt Sutton is a fool and a prig, Mr. President. But he is in a position to do us great harm."

"You think he's the source of Jane McNary's information?"

"I don't doubt it for a minute. Sutton and his staff. Don't ever underestimate the harm those faceless, unaccountable staff members can do. They find the information. They pass it along. Sometimes with their boss's approval, sometimes not. There is no accountability, Mr. President. You know what would happen if a senatorial assistant were to be fired for passing classified material to the press. Chances are he'd be made a hero. And, if prosecuted, a martyr. In Russia or China, or several other lands, he'd be a corpse."

Lambert looked again through the double-glazed windows at the rose gardens, now half-obscured by the thickening wet mist. "I sometimes am tempted to test that, Margaret," he said. "But in the end I find I'm just a politician like all the rest—like Sutton—"

"Not that, Cleveland," Kendrick said dryly.

"I hope not, but facts are facts. I'm going to give in to McNary. You know that, don't you?"

"Of course."

"Sometimes I wonder if a democracy can weather this century," the President said glumly. "One thing I do know: the Founding Fathers of our republic would be appalled by the license the Constitution has been used to confer. Bare-breasted waitresses protected by the First Amendment and paramilitary fascist marching clubs by the Second. Good sweet Christ, when you think about it, it's laughable."

"Hollow laughter, Cleveland."

"One thing I promise you, Margaret," the President said. "I'm not giving in without getting a pound of flesh. I'll know who leaked this trip to McNary or she doesn't go."

"She'll protect her source."

"I'll protect the country, Margaret. I *will* know before she climbs on that goddamned airplane."

The Secretary of State hesitated a long while before speaking. "Is there a possibility it could have been Harry Grant, Mr. President?"

"Come off it, Margaret."

"He is—friendly with her."

"Don't be prudish, Madame Secretary. He sleeps with her from time to time. But I don't think they are exactly friends."

"A male-chauvinist distinction, Mr. President."

"Touched a nerve, have I?"

"She *could* have got the information from Colonel Grant."

"I don't think so."

"You can't ignore the possibility."

"All right. No, I can't. If she has, I'll break him. But I don't think Harry would be disloyal. Not to the nation, not to me, not about something like this."

"How about something like *this?*" Kendrick produced a folded photostat of a page from the *Daily Express*. Lambert knew it only as a daily paper specializing in sensational stories. She opened the sheet to show a large photograph of a pretty, dark girl. Another, of the same girl in ballet costume, was inset. The headline screamed: DANCER MISTRESS OF MURDERED SOVIET DIPLOMAT VANISHES. Below, there was a short account by-lined to credit an *Express* "Special Correspondent."

In silence he read the piece carefully.

Ballet Celeste dancing star Bronwen Wells, "friend" of Colonel Aleksandr Voronin, the Russian attaché murdered by unknown gunmen at Dover last Tuesday, has vanished from London. Miss Wells, present during the crime and considered to be a material witness by the police, was last seen in the company of U.S. Air Force Colonel Harry Grant, a member of President Cleveland Lambert's personal staff. The U.S. President is visiting Sissinghurst, in Kent, to address the current conference on disarmament being held at Sissinghurst Castle.

Lambert looked up from the copy of the newspaper grimly. "The Embassy sent this down?" he asked.

Kendrick nodded. "One of our young doom-seekers fresh from home spotted it and rushed a copy to our Head of Mission." She shrugged her narrow shoulders. "It *is* a tabloid, Cleveland. We have them at home, too, you know."

The President crumpled the paper angrily. "I'm not complaining about British journalism, Margaret. Grant knows damn well we're heading for Moscow. How the hell are we to deal with those masters of intrigue if they even suspect we could be involved—in any way—with the murder of a sensitive member of their Embassy staff. And a military officer to boot. And a possible defector. And for Grant to allow this to be splashed in a London paper—" He walked to the door and opened it. "Ivy, get in here!"

Ivy O'Donnell appeared in the doorway, prim and prepared for anything, as usual.

"Is there any word from Colonel Grant?"

"Not yet, Mr. President."

"Call Hurn and tell Major Barrow he is to report the moment Grant arrives. Grant is not to leave Hurn under any circumstances, even for an hour."

"Yes, Mr. President."

Lambert turned back to the Secretary of State, his face set in lines of cold displeasure. "All right, Margaret, now what about Sutton?"

"If he leaked the Moscow story to McNary, I don't know what can be done about it, Mr. President. What troubles me most is what the Russian reaction will be if the mission becomes common knowledge before you've seen Kirov and Chung. They might deny that such a mission was ever authorized by them."

"My friends in the Senate would love that," Lambert said bitterly. "I can hear them now, talking about the 'Imperial Presidency' and my delusions of grandeur."

"There are men in the Senate who would understand that the mission is real, Mr. President. The Sino-Soviet situation has never been grimmer."

"I know that and you know it, Margaret. But what the hell do people like DeWitt Sutton know?"

There was a tap at the door, and the President said, "Come."

O'Donnell reappeared with a State Department messenger. "Signal from Washington for the Secretary, Mr. President."

Lambert snapped his fingers impatiently, and the messenger handed him a sealed envelope. He turned it over in his hands, tempted to open it, then handed it to Margaret Kendrick.

She waited until the President's secretary and the messenger were gone before breaking the seal. Inside the envelope was another, banded in red and marked SECRET. She opened it and withdrew a single sheet.

The President waited restlessly while she read it.

Kendrick looked up, a strange expression on her face. "The Russians want a twenty-four-hour postponement," she said, and extended the message.

The President read the half-dozen sentences quickly. The message had not traveled the customary route from the Foreign Ministry in Moscow to Ambassador Baturin in Washington and thence to the State Department for transmittal to the Secretary. Instead, it had come over the State Department Intelligence hot line, and it was signed by Viktor Krasin, the Soviet Foreign Minister, in his personal cipher.

"What the *hell* does this mean?" Lambert exploded. "Have they learned about our leak?"

Kendrick frowned. "I don't think so, Mr. President. Not yet, at any rate. They wouldn't ask for a twenty-four-hour postponement if that were the case. They'd make it much longer and then slip out from under the commitment to meet at all."

"And why does this carry Krasin's signature instead of Kirov's?"

"He could be much more ill than we've been led to believe, Mr. President."

Lambert read the message again. "Twenty-four hours. They have some kind of a problem, Margaret. Something they think they can clean up in a day."

"If the First Secretary is out of action, they could be wrong, Mr. President."

Lambert returned to the window. Through the thick mist he could no longer see the rose gardens, and the oast houses were vanishing as the gray moisture streaked the windows of Labour House.

He folded the message and returned it to Kendrick. "Well, we have no choice but to agree to the request. Send a signal to Peking explaining that there will be a change in the schedule. Make it clear that the delay is not our doing."

The Secretary of State gathered her papers and stood. "Yes, Mr. President."

When she had gone, he called O'Donnell back into the room and asked, "Have all our communications been set up, Ivy?"

"They are completing the installations now, Mr. President."

"Good. As soon as everything is ready, I want a television link with Richards at the Pentagon."

"Yes, Mr. President."

As if compelled, Lambert returned to the window. The countryside had vanished in the fog.

34

At the Soviet Cosmodrome near Baikonur, Colonel Valery Adanin was completing his briefing. A lieutenant colonel of the GRU was putting away his photographs and navigational read-outs. His final act was to remove from his steel briefcase a thick envelope bearing the cachet of the Ministry of Defense.

He placed this in Adanin's space-gloved hands directly. His young face was grimly official, so much so that Adanin, who was a veteran of the Soviet Air Force's military space program, was tempted to smile. He did not do so. These young-genius types from the Minister of Defense's personal staff had a tendency to be humorless; they inclined to a sort of personalized fervor in the completion of their military assignments.

"These are your sealed orders, Colonel Adanin. You are to open them when you reach orbit. I am empowered to tell you that they pertain to certain specialized photography and electromagnetic intelligence tasks. Beyond that, you will take your instructions from the GRU directly. A link will be established to your Svoboda."

Adanin nodded his head inside the plastic helmet. He wished the fellow would stop talking and leave now. He was not happy with his assignment. He had been unceremoniously removed from a team that was training for an exchange-crew mission with the Americans and he had been looking forward to a flight in the American Shuttle. Then quite suddenly, and without, he thought, suitable preparation, the GRU had ordered a manned Svoboda flight.

The Svoboda was the newest and best of the Soviet spy

satellites, but it had been designed primarily as an automatic vehicle. Its manned capability was marginal at best. A Svoboda pilot was a pilot in name only, very like the pilots of the early Voskhods, who rode their birds the way Laika rode hers. A man crammed into the tiny cockpit of a Svoboda could operate special equipment well enough, but the accommodations were unpleasant, cramped, and, Adanin thought, damned dangerous.

Adanin was too brave a man to be panicked, but he was too intelligent to minimize the danger. The GRU must want some very specific information to risk manning a Svoboda.

It was Lop Nor, he was certain. Most of the new satellites were being launched in orbits calculated to take them directly over the Sinkiang Autonomous Province where the Maoists built and tested their nuclear weapons, their new intercontinental missiles, and God knew what else they might be building to threaten the Soviet Union. Adanin accepted the need for a manned Svoboda mission, but he did not look forward to a week in space, sharing the few cubic meters of the satellite's capsule with sharp-edged equipment, and flying six times daily over the most closely guarded military area in China.

The young lieutenant colonel, resisting an impulse to deliver himself of some appropriately patriotic sentiment, stood up. "You will be under the personal direction of Comrade Marshal Leonov, Colonel. I envy you the honor."

Adanin did not reply to this comment. He disliked being preached at before a flight. He was aware of both the risks and the honors of a cosmonaut's life. He had discussed his feelings with his wife Ludmilla, when he drew the assignment. Ludmilla's father was a member of the Baikonur Central Committee, and it was just possible that he could have intervened to let this particular task go to someone else. But in the end both he and Ludmilla had agreed that it would be unwise to ask for special consideration. It was, after all, only a week's orbital mission and, they concluded, one that, since it was to be performed at the express orders of the Minister of Defense, would look well on Valery's service record.

They had talked, made love, talked again, and finally decided to make no attempt at evading the mysterious Svoboda assignment. Then they had slept, warm and secure in their comfortable apartment in Star City—totally unaware that they had just made a decision that would dramatically change their lives.

In Woolwich, Patrick Sullivan waited sullenly for the American bitch to return. He had sent her out for food and a bottle late last night and, typical whore that she was, she had stayed out until now. He sat at the grimy window looking out at the watery dawnlight trying to spread over the littered, twisting streets below. It was raining, a steady, heavy drizzle that was as much a foggy mist as a proper rain. Through a break in the block of buildings across from the Dartford Arms he could see the leaden surface of the river. A rusty freighter moved slowly upstream toward the Pool of London. It flew a Polish flag, and Sullivan wondered thickly if this, perhaps, was the transport that Caspar had promised would get him out of the country. If it was, he thought, he would use it alone. During the long, dreary hours of the night he had decided that he'd had enough of Bridget's crazy ways.

Sitting in the grubby twilight of a dirty room in a third-rate hotel, spent and alone, Sullivan had considered his doubts. What had all the bombing and killing actually accomplished, he wondered. The British were still in Northern Ireland. Even the politicians in the Republic heaped scorn and hatred on the IRA. What the hell was it all for, then? Why hadn't it all worked out the way it had for Castro and his bloody *barbudos* in Cuba?

Moving wearily, like a man much older than he was, Sullivan walked to the bed and knelt to retrieve the Russian machine pistol hidden under the mattress. He had only a single clip for the weapon. The Yank money was drying up. The Movement was running out of cash to buy guns and explosives. Instead of dollars, the stupid Americans sent their dirty daughters, he thought.

He took a rag from his knapsack and began to polish and caress the AK-57. In his mind a fantasy formed: when Bridget came through the door he would point the weapon at her, pull the trigger, and watch her smirking Yank face explode into bloody shreds. It would be a fitting finish to one of her famous nights out. She had this way of picking up men in pubs, on the street, anywhere. And screwing them anywhere, too—in alleys, in rooms grimier than this one, even on the top decks of omnibuses. The girl was quite round the bend, of that Sullivan was sure, her head turned to mush by too many drugs and too much killing.

She'd helped Sean on jobs, plenty of them, carrying explosives into women's loos in London restaurants and airports and then, crazy bitch that she was, standing by to see the bloody victims and the confusion because that was the one thing left that made her come alive. She had gone into a rage when Caspar said that there was no need now to do anything about the Wells girl. It was, she said, as though she'd been teased and brought almost to climax and then left unsatisfied.

Sullivan's thoughts, thick and gummy, flowed and eddied in his tired, used-up mind. His hands soothed and fondled the AK resting across his thighs. He heard a small noise in the hallway beyond the locked door. The bloody bitch was back, then. Why not indulge the fantasy? At least why not change her pouting expression from one of contempt to one of genuine fear.

Sullivan grinned and waited for her knock.

It didn't come.

Instead, the door was kicked in with a crash, slammed back against the wall with a force that pulled the hinges from the jamb. He caught a glimpse of shadowy figures beyond, behind the big man who came through the dimness.

Sullivan had a single moment of panic that was like the

grinding of broken glass in his guts. He started to move, to do something with the beautiful Russian weapon on his lap.

The room exploded with noise and light.

Chief Inspector Alfred Owen's .357 Magnum made a terrible sound. Sullivan was flung back across the bed, his chest and face pulped by the heavy bullets.

The plain-clothes men of Alpha crowded into the room. Owen lowered his weapon and carefully set the hammer on safe.

Someone said, "What about the bird?"

"We've bloody missed her."

"That's a pity," Owen said mildly, "but I know a few places where we may find her." He picked up the oily rag that Sullivan had dropped on the floor and sniffed it. Then he lovingly wiped his Magnum with it and returned the weapon to his shoulder holster.

Outside, at the end of the street where other Squad Alpha men had set up barricades, the girl who called herself "Bridget" stood in the gathering crowd. She had spent the night in a van with four Teddy boys she had encountered, and though they had labored mightily, she had left unsatisfied. She had come back with a bottle for Sullivan, but she had arrived as the constables were setting steel barricades in place. Her training as an urban guerrilla had been spotty, but she recognized these preparations easily enough. It never occurred to her to attempt to break through and warn or help Sullivan. The moment the barricades went up, Sullivan was as good as dead; she decided that. So she had remained in the silent crowd, her excitement growing as she saw the cars of Alpha move in toward the Dartford Arms.

She trembled so much that a woman, perhaps concerned by her nervousness, asked, "Are you all right, dearie?"

Bridget nodded, brushing the long straight hair from her face. Her lips were wet with anticipation, and when she heard the gunfire, muffled by distance, she was shaken with the aching tremors of sexual excitement. She stood, thighs pressed tightly together, as her crotch moistened and finally contracted with a deep orgasm.

Without realizing it, she had dropped the bottle in its paper sack and it had smashed on the pavement. The woman who had spoken to her cried out as the gin splashed her ankles. *"Here now, look out!"* But when she looked up again for the girl who had dropped the thing, she saw only her narrow back and tight trousers as she pushed through the crowd and was gone.

35

At 0200 hours, Washington time—0700 hours GMT—the status board in the Pentagon War Room began its quarter-hourly update. The data originated with a Nathan Hale satellite in synchronous orbit over European Russia, its antennas attuned to the ultrashortwave radiation emitted by the targeting on-board computers of Soviet ICBMs in their silos.

Since the target programs were both enciphered and multiple-coded, the actual information—that is, the identity of the targets—remained unknown. Several teams of data-processing specialists—their IQs in the "genius" range—were hard at work on this project in the United States, and had been for the better part of a year. But the research effort had been somewhat handicapped by the refusal of a number of prominent universities to allow "war research" on their campuses and by their hostility to scientists who performed such research in military facilities.

The result was that the data coming from Nathan Hale satellites, while impressive and substantial, were not yet fully utilized. The changing columns of figures on the display screens in the War Room could indicate which Soviet missile wings were ready for war and which were down for maintenance. The identity of the targets at which the missiles were aimed could be derived (with less accuracy) from other sources—statistical analysis, games theory, and simple spying. But the hope that American military planners entertained, of being able to strike, if need be, certain specific missile complexes in order to prevent attacks on specific American and European targets, was as yet unrealized.

The War Room was fully manned, owing to the alert ordered by the Joint Chiefs. The state of readiness was Red One, with all stations activated. The Pit, the large table in the center of the room, and the command stations on the balcony were occupied by their working teams, and the steel-and-concrete room hummed with the subdued noise of purposeful activity.

Captain James Creighton, USAF, the duty Missile Information Officer, whose job was to monitor the Nathan Hale data, and Captain Catharine Lane, USMC, the duty Computer Liaison Officer, who had the task of overseeing the data-processing crews who prepared the raw intercepts for transmission to the National Command Center, sat at adjoining consoles.

Captains Creighton and Lane were in the process of beginning what promised to become a pleasant and perhaps long-lasting affair. Catharine Lane was pretty, blonde, and full-figured, all of which qualities James Creighton considered remarkable. He was in that stage of incipient obsession that made the mere fact of Captain Lane's existence remarkable, even marvelous. It was this preoccupation that accounted for the fact that ten full minutes passed before Captain Creighton looked away from his new beloved and at the status board, where he noted that the Aral'sk Regiment of the Soviet Strategic Rocket Forces was down.

"Hey, what the hell," he said softly.

Captain Lane was in the same love-soaked state of inattention, and his comment startled her. "What's the matter?"

"Look at the board. The Russkis have taken Aral'sk off the line."

What the display showed was that the targeting computers on board the Soviet SS-19 missiles had been powered down—a certain signal that retargeting was in process.

Lane, recovering from her romantic bemusement more quickly than her partner, reached for the *Soviet Procedures Manual* racked above her console (a volume once, before détente filtered through the Defense Department, known as the "Intentions of the Enemy Manual"). She riffled through the pages to the section devoted to the facts known about the Aral'sk Regiment.

"They aren't due for a retargeting stand-down for eighteen days," she said, puzzled.

Creighton pressed a call button on his console. On the balcony above, the Defense Co-ordinator on duty, Air Force Brigadier General Paul Young answered, "Defco."

"Aral'sk is down for an unscheduled retargeting, sir," Creighton reported.

"When did they power down?"

Creighton flushed and glanced guiltily at Catharine Lane. "I'm not certain, sir. I'll have to query Nathan Hale Memory."

"I'll stand by." Young's voice was chilly with disapproval.

"There goes my next fitness report," Creighton said. "Get NHM for me."

Lane punched out the query code. "You're hooked in," she said.

Creighton's fingers raced over the keys of the terminal on his console. The screen before him lighted with a single line of electronic print: ARAL'SK POWER-DOWN 0703 GMT.

Creighton was reaching for the call button to notify General Young when Catharine lifted her eyes to the big display above the Pit and said, "They are coming back on the line." She checked the digital-time read-out on her console and said: "Retargeting completed at 0712 GMT."

Creighton relayed the information to Young on the concrete balcony overlooking the Pit.

General Young, an austere black man with four rows of ribbons under his command pilot's wings, allowed himself a single comment: "Unusual." He marked the log tape that recorded all internal communications and sat for a moment, his long and slender fingers poised over his communications console.

He reached a decision swiftly and pressed a button. The single member of the Joint Chiefs on duty at this hour, Admiral Muller, appeared on the General's television screen.

Without preamble, Young said, "We've detected an anomaly, Admiral. Aral'sk has just retargeted. They were not due for eighteen days."

The CNO pursed his lips. If the War Room had not been on Red One, it was likely that the retargeting would not have been noted until the next scheduled review of Nathan Hale Memory.

"Any similar activity elsewhere?"

Young's eyes swept the displays along the perimeter of the Pit. "Negative, Admiral."

Muller considered. He was thinking that some of Nathan Hale's capabilities were a mixed blessing. It was wonderful and remarkable to be able to detect power changes in the on-board computers of Soviet missiles. But it was maddening not to be able to interpret them accurately enough to unscramble the program and identify the targets.

He glanced at the polar projection that covered one entire wall of his office. He pressed a call-up button and the Soviet SS-19 missile installations became a series of red lights scattered across the Soviet Union.

Aral'sk. What the hell was unique about Aral'sk? He stared at the map. "Thank you, General. Keep me informed," he said. Young's face vanished from the TV screen, and Muller leaned back in his chair, still studying the map. Why Aral'sk?

The Russians never retargeted oftener than every twenty days. Never. There was seldom a need to retarget at all. For years now, the ICBMs of both the major powers had been zeroed in on selected targets: Washington, of course; and Moscow; Chicago, New York, Leningrad, Vladivostok. The opposition's missile bases, nuclear submarine bases, and communications installations. The list was well enough known so that any field-grade officer could almost recite it by heart.

Then why Aral'sk?

Muller tapped out the Defense Intelligence Agency call code. When the officer on duty there answered, he said, "Get me everything we have on the Aral'sk Strategic Rocket Regiment."

The woman's voice was prim. "We have a great deal, Admiral. Are you sure you want it all?"

Muller envisioned the thick book that would soon be placed on his desk. He glanced at the wall clock. It was 0219, less than two hours from the end of his watch. As long as the Red One remained in force, a member of the JCS remained available to the alert crews in the War Room.

"All of it, Commander," he said.

"Aye aye, sir."

Muller considered passing his fragmentary and puzzling information on to the White House for transmission to the President at Sissinghurst. But the day's activities were starting in England. The President would be awake and preoccupied with his impending address to the delegates to the NATO–Warsaw Pact meeting. The alternative was to call Admiral's House and notify Vice President Hood. Not that Harold Hood would have the slightest notion of what the information might mean. No more than I have, Muller thought with characteristic honesty. He decided against it. After reviewing the available data on Aral'sk, perhaps then.

On an impulse, he called up the map lights that indicated the known position of missile bases in the People's Republic of China. There were far fewer of these, and they were all oriented for a swift strike to the north and west. Toward the Soviet Union.

Muller sat for a long while staring at the sprinkling of lights on the polar chart.

He added to the display the lights that indicated other military installations in China—including the Lop Nor nuclear-test range and the new construction in the Turfan Depression.

On this small-scale chart, the lights marking Turfan and Aral'sk were less than a centimeter apart.

Muller was not an imaginative man, nor was he given to rash assumptions. But there was something in the juxtaposition of those tiny lights that bore thinking about.

It was a totally absurd notion, he knew, but he could not ignore even the most fantastic possibilities. He pressed the DIA call button again and said quietly: "Add to the book on Aral'sk: computed SS-19 flight time between Aral'sk and—" he took his spectacles from the inside pocket of his beribboned and gold-braided jacket and put them on—"forty-two thirty north, eighty-nine fifty west. Got that? Good. Thank you, Commander."

36

It was midmorning and snowing heavily by the time Marshal Lyudin joined Foreign Minister Krasin and General Novikov at the Ministry of Foreign Affairs. What he discovered there was a distraught diplomat and an angry policeman.

The conference room was a shambles of papers and records; dirty dishes were still on the table, and the outer offices were a confusion of hurried activity. Krasin, badly shaken by the extent to which Leonov's Frunze protégés had penetrated the foreign service of the USSR, had ordered a mass recall of the suspect officers. Novikov had approved of the move but not of the method. A general return to Moscow of all of Marshal Leonov's adherents at this critical time was not what he wished. The argument had been bitter and protracted, precipitated by the arrival of the courier from the Moscow Military District headquarters with the computer read-out demanded by Novikov.

The Military District computer had uncovered the unsettling information that Leonov's former students in positions of high command in the Army, Navy, and Air Force numbered no fewer than two hundred. Among these were two commanders of armored divisions, four of strategic naval units, one commanding the missile complex at Aral'sk, and another in charge of the Army Security Forces for the Kazakh SSR. And, of course, there was Zabotin, the top man in the GRU.

The KGB, Novikov was happy to discover, was relatively free of the Leonovite infection. Apparently Leonov's protégés were not drawn to police work.

At Novikov's insistence, a timorous Krasin had dispatched a

message to the American President in England, requesting a twenty-four-hour delay in the Moscow meeting. That much, at least, had been accomplished.

Now, here came Lyudin with further disturbing news. Novikov shrewdly studied Viktor Krasin and wondered how much more of this the man could take before collapsing under the weight of sudden responsibility.

Marshal Lyudin seemed drawn, gray-faced. "Comrade Kirov is now totally incapacitated. He may even be dead, or whatever passes for dead with those medical criminals," he said heavily. He looked directly at Krasin as he spoke.

The Foreign Minister made no reply. It seemed to Novikov that this last news was driving him into a kind of catatonic funk. He decided to act. "I want your approval, Lyudin, for a meeting of the Politburo. Krasin must take command."

The old Marshal nodded agreement. "Yes. At once."

"It will take time to assemble the entire Politburo," Novikov went on relentlessly. "Perhaps more time than we have available. An ad hoc committee will do for now—to speak for the Politburo."

Lyudin looked narrowly at Novikov. "You are suggesting that we constitute ourselves such a committee?"

"With one or two others, perhaps. Yes, I am," Novikov said.

"Comrades, you are talking treason," Krasin said thinly.

Novikov disregarded the protest. "I have alerted all KGB troops in the Moscow area. If we need to, we can have Leonov and his people under arrest in three hours."

Lyudin shook his head. "I don't think so, Comrade General. Yuri Leonov is conducting 'an inspection' of the SS-19 base at Aral'sk. The base is closed and guarded by special GRU troops he has had flown in for 'the exercise.' You might precipitate a pitched battle if you try to arrest him." He opened his briefcase and added his papers to the scatter of documents on the conference table. "He has put the Far Eastern Army on alert, again for 'an exercise.' Something he calls 'Task Red Glory.' And there are some very strange maneuvers being conducted by some of our strategic naval units in the South China Sea. There may be others involved. I have not yet had a chance to investigate."

Novikov stared hard at the Foreign Minister. "There, Viktor Stepanovich. What more do you want for proof? Leonov's actions are counterrevolutionary. He's waited like a vulture for Comrade Kirov to die or become helpless and now he is preparing to act."

"To do *what*, for God's sake?" Krasin demanded in a sudden fury. "Are you suggesting he can take over the government with a few battalions of security troops and some submarines?"

"He has considerably more than that under his command, Comrade Foreign Minister," Lyudin said heavily. "He has the Far Eastern Army, and he has the missile base at Aral'sk."

"And he has this," Novikov added. "He has our confusion, the American visit, and the damned Chinese threat. All working for him. He thinks we cannot act against him while all this is happening."

"I agree," Lyudin said. "I think he may act while the Americans are here. The opportunity would be too good to ignore."

"I say we arrest him," Novikov said, striking the table with a large fist. "There is only one way to deal with rebellion. *Smash it!*"

Krasin, driven to the wall, began to exercise his unwanted authority. "I will have no battle between Russians, Novikov. Certainly not while the damned Americans are here."

"Then at least let me isolate him," Novikov said. "We can cut Aral'sk off from the rest of the country. Block all communications. Surround the place with troops." He glanced at Lyudin. "The Red Army. Will it help the KGB in this?"

The old Marshal bridled. "You don't suggest that the Army is disloyal?"

"I suggest nothing. I ask a simple question."

"The Army will do its duty," Lyudin said angrily.

"Including the Far Eastern Army?"

The old man's face showed his pain and humiliation. To a soldier of his stature, the suggestion of mutiny in any part of the Soviet Army was a bitter anguish. "If the Minister of Defense is isolated at Aral'sk, I can relieve the officers in command. The rank and file will obey orders."

"Very well, then," Novikov said. He looked challengingly at Krasin. "Viktor?"

"There will be no attempt to penetrate the base at Aral'sk."

"Until the Americans have gone," Novikov said.

Krasin looked at Marshal Lyudin. The old man nodded assent.

"So be it. See to it, Comrade General Novikov." Krasin paused, then turned to Lyudin. "What about General Oblensky?"

"What about him?"

"Does Leonov control him?" Novikov asked.

Krasin tapped the read-out on military personnel. "He was at Frunze in '70. One of Leonov's brightest, according to this."

"But what about the man personally? Can he be had?" Novikov persisted.

"You mean," Lyudin asked heavily, "would he betray Leonov?"

"Exactly."

Lyudin shrugged his thick shoulders. "When one is dealing with people of this sort, who can tell? If what we suspect is true, Oblensky has already betrayed his soldier's honor and his responsibility as a Soviet citizen. Perhaps he can be subverted again. I don't know."

Krasin spoke carefully, "We are dealing here with fanatics, Comrades. None of the usual rules apply."

"I will try, then. I will telephone Oblensky. After the troops are in position. And before the Americans arrive here."

"He might simply alert Leonov, Comrade General," Krasin said.

"That's a chance worth taking. If Oblensky will arrest the

man, half our battle is won. Quietly." Novikov looked at Lyudin. "Don't you agree?"

The old soldier nodded slowly. The entire business filled him with anger and despair. That Soviet officers could so betray their Motherland was a terrible thing to the aged campaigner.

"It is agreed, then." The KGB man demanded their approval, Krasin realized, because even he was still uncertain about Defense Minister Leonov's intentions. What they were planning could, in different circumstances, be recorded as an act of treason as heinous as Leonov's own. But there was no other choice left to them now. None at all.

"Agreed," he said.

37

Harry Grant had been awake since dawn. Through the open window came a smell of salt marshes and the sea, a scent of dampness and growing things.

Bronwen slept fitfully, sometimes crying out softly or burying her head in the bolster. But never once had she stopped holding herself against him, her slender arm across his scarred chest.

He wondered, as he had more than once in the night, if what he was doing was shameful. The girl desperately needed safety and reassurance. Was he simply taking advantage of this because she had moved him, touched some wellspring of sexual desire in him? To indulge himself with Bronwen Wells would be the act of a savage, he thought, if that was all there was.

On her part the intimacy might be nothing more than a desperate wish to be held and comforted. God knew she was entitled to that. The last days had been a living hell for her. To stop now and make love, to retreat to warmth and tenderness, that could be a deep need in one so dependent.

He turned his head and looked at her fine profile against the bolster. Her firm dancer's body lay tight against him, her breasts against his side, her legs entwined with his. He dared not move for fear of waking her and yet he knew that he must, now and quickly. Not only had he allowed himself a dubious advantage with her, but also he was seriously neglecting his sworn duty. By this hour of the morning he should have been at Hurn waiting for the President to arrive. But last night everything had slipped, events rearranging themselves without his conscious will. He told himself again, as if the thought alone could make it true, that he had not fallen in love with Bronwen Wells.

He felt her mouth against his shoulder, lips open, wet and warm. Her eyes were open, shadowed and glistening in the half-light. "Harry," she said. Softly, as though to herself.

"I have to go soon," he said.

"Please. Not yet." She ran her hands across his belly, searching for him. He turned and held her, feeling the almost desperate thrusting of her *mons* against him. He knew that she was using everything, all of herself, to hold him. She was afraid of the time when he would be gone and she would be alone.

"Please, please, Harry—"

The hunger she aroused in him was like a fever. It made rational thought impossible.

"Don't leave me." Her legs hooked his, pulled him onto her. She spread her thighs wide, and without device or conscious effort he slipped deep inside her.

"Love me, Harry—love me—" Her voice was muffled, the words spoken against his skin. She strained against him, determined to make them into one single being. In all his casual sexual encounters, and in the years of his marriage, he had never experienced anything like this. She spent him, spent herself. It was all beyond his control.

He sat on the edge of the bed. She lay behind him, huddled against herself, her skin glistening with sweat, her hair a dark tangle. And she was weeping. Her ribs outlined themselves against her pale skin with each racking sob. "I was sickening," she said. "I tried to use you. I *am* a whore."

"No," he said. He could think of nothing to add to the simple denial. He knew what was torturing her. A lover not three days dead, and now this. Because she did not dare to be alone, unsupported.

But it wasn't the Bronwens of the world who made it what it was. It was the Voronins, the Lamberts and Ballards—and, yes, the Grants. The manipulators and conspirators. Left to her own devices a Bronwen Wells would find life as simple and uncomplicated as a fairy tale: *Sleeping Beauty* or *Giselle.*

"I have to go now. I must," he said.

"Yes. I know."

"I'll come back."

"Don't say that."

"I will. I promise."

"Don't *promise.* Alek promised."

There was that, he thought. Alek had, indeed, promised. What? Peace and quiet? A kind of security? Love? Yes, surely love. And Bronwen had believed it all; she had thought that it would all end like some silly ballet, the poverty of the Cardiff slums forgotten, her own inability to rise above her small talent forgotten, too. In the final analysis, all she had ever wanted was a life. A real life.

"I don't care what Alek promised," he said roughly. "I will come back. You'll see."

She sat up suddenly, holding her knees to her chin, her tear-streaked face so pallid it seemed translucent. "Oh, God, why should you want to?"

He managed a thin smile and caught her by the hair gently. "Do I have to have a reason?"

She held onto his hand. "Harry, what are you doing? What is all this mystery?"

"When I know I'll tell you."

"Were you really going to help Alek? I mean *really,* without a price?"

"Everything has a price, Bron. But yes, I was going to help him. If he had wanted my help."

"And me?"

"Now most particularly you. I'll be back. Here. In a week—two at the most."

"Then?"

"Then you come with me." He paused. "If that's what you want."

"I don't know. I don't know anything now."

He began to dress. "I'm not surprised," he said.

"Harry?"

He looked at her upturned face. Child and woman, he thought.

"I think I love you."

He managed a smile. How could she know?

"I think I do. That means I have no heart, doesn't it?"

"No."

"It must. I saw Alek die."

"Forget that now."

"I did, though. But I can scarcely remember—"

"Stop it, Bron."

"Only three days ago, Harry, and I can't remember it all."

"Stop. That's over."

"Is it?"

He thought of her gutted apartment and knew that he was lying to her. He finished dressing and said, "Bron, promise me that you will stay here."

"Yes."

"Don't give me a glib answer. I want your word."

"You will come back?"

"I said that I would."

"Then I'll be here."

Something in the tentative way she spoke made Harry want to take her by the narrow, naked shoulders and extract a promise from her by plain force. He had an overwhelming feeling of helplessness, of vulnerability. That was how she felt, he thought with sudden insight. That was how she felt all the time.

"Bron?"

"Yes. I'll stay here," she said vaguely.

It had to do. He couldn't wait longer.

On the empty, rain-swept roads to Hurn she filled his mind: that last sight of her, naked and lovely and lost on the rumpled bed at the Mermaid. He had the feeling that something unique had brushed against the orderly fabric of his life and was gone.

38

"Mr. Vice President, I want you to meet Allan Dalland, one of the fine young men on my staff." DeWitt Sutton presented Dalland as though displaying a particularly fine collector's item. Dalland stepped forward and took the Vice President's hand gingerly. He had no particular regard for Harold Hood. He considered him a ward politician of the most commonplace kind.

Dalland had come to Admiral's House reluctantly and with fear of the possible consequences. Sutton, if he could, intended to enlist the Vice President's sympathy in his vendetta against the President. To do so he needed to impress Hood with the accuracy—and sensitivity—of his information. And that, at the very least, would compromise both Allan Dalland and his private source within the Central Intelligence Agency. Dalland wondered what Gerald Ransome would say if he knew he was about to be credited with the release of secret information in the presence of the Vice President of the United States.

"I am delighted to know you, Mr. Dalland," Hood said smoothly. "It is always my pleasure to see a young man doing well in government service."

The three men sat in the study of Admiral's House, a handsome room, ironically enough refurbished and stocked with rare books by a dyslexic—and immensely rich—predecessor.

DeWitt Sutton, his long teeth exposed in his customary expression of pious self-righteousness, came straight to the point. "Harold, you no doubt recall what we discussed when I was last here with you."

"I do remember, Senator," Hood said, "and I wonder if it is

wise to continue discussions of that sort. You do follow me, Senator?"

"I think we must discuss it, Mr. Vice President," Sutton said. "At least to the extent of letting you hear—from the source, as it were—what else has happened since we talked."

Hood turned toward Dalland. The younger man was conscious of the Vice President's hairless, pale, and waxy dome of a forehead. He noted the tracery of bluish veins under the skin, the slick gloss imparted to the skin by the oils secreted by the pores in the white scalp. He suppressed a shudder. It was really a terrible thing to be old.

"Are you the Senator's source, Mr. Dalland?" the Vice President asked abruptly.

Dalland replied with an effort of the will. "Yes, one might say that."

Hood frowned slightly at the tone and the lack of formality. *"Do you* say that, Mr. Dalland?"

"Tell the Vice President what you told me, Allan," Sutton said encouragingly.

"There is a good possibility that a Russian marshal—the Defense Minister, in fact—is planning a military coup in the USSR. There is even a better chance that President Lambert is helping—if not to set it up, at least to make it stick."

"You *know* this, Mr. Dalland? How?" Hood's eyes were cold and hard.

Dalland said, "I have discovered that Harry Grant, the President's Deputy Air Force Aide, has been digging up CIA information on Marshal Yuri Leonov."

Hood turned to look at Sutton. "You consider that significant?"

"It is when you add that bit of information to all the others," Sutton said. He held up his soft, tapering hand and began to count away on his fingers. "One. The President is lying to the Congress and to the People—"

"How is that, Senator?" Hood protested. "Unless you call his not announcing his trip to Moscow and Peking a kind of lying—"

"Well, sir, isn't it? The sins of omission are sometimes worse than those of commission. Hear me out. Please. Two. Grant's request for a dossier on Leonov may suggest that there is dishonor among thieves and that the conspirators don't trust one another—"

"Conspirators, Senator? That's rather strong language you use to describe a group that includes the President of the United States." Hood's manner was disapproving, but Sutton gave an inward sigh of relief. He was at least back to square one. He might squirm, but he had just made a statement that implied that there *was* a group, a conspiracy, and that Cleveland Lambert was included. It would take the man a while to realize this, but now it could be reinforced. The important thing was to convince Hood of the danger in Lambert's irresponsibility.

"Maybe I'm implying too much, Mr. Vice President," Sutton said placatingly. "But the *facts* are there, sir, for anyone to see and interpret."

Hood frowned, but did not speak.

Sutton turned down a third finger. "Three. And this is frightening, Mr. Vice President. Really frightening. The Joint Chiefs have ordered a Red One. Were you aware of that?"

"Yes," Hood said. "All members of the National Security Council are normally told about practice alerts. I see nothing sinister—"

"Admiral Muller got to you, sir," Sutton said. "Or Devore did. I am certain that this Red One is no practice."

"I can't believe that, Senator. American soldiers simply don't go around making military coups, you know."

"But Russians do, Mr. Vice President. And I am not at all certain that our generals and admirals are averse to taking advantage of the confusion."

"Let me understand you, DeWitt," Hood said nervously.

"Are you telling me that Cleveland Lambert is conspiring with some Russki general to help overthrow the government of Soviet Russia?"

Sutton was about to exclaim that that was exactly what he was saying when Allan Dalland saved him from pushing Vice President Hood's credulity over the edge into an abyss from which it would never be retrieved by Sutton.

"It simply looks very bad, Mr. Vice President," Dalland said, "for any member of the President's party to be showing so close an interest in the Soviet Minister of Defense. He asked for—and is receiving, I believe—a complete retrieval on Marshal Leonov. If the President had not involved himself in this transparently phony peace mission, and if the First Secretary was not so ill, it wouldn't look quite so bad. But as it is—" He shrugged his shoulders. "What is one to believe?"

"Is yours a generally held opinion, Mr. Dalland?" Hood asked.

"Among those few who actually know what is going on, yes, sir."

"And you are sure you know what is going on?"

"My information came from Langley, sir. From the headquarters. Where all this is being orchestrated, I have no doubt," he finished.

Hood glanced at Sutton for guidance. "You have proof of all this, Senator?"

"Proof enough, sir. I have copies in my office of Harry Grant's request for a computer run on Marshal Leonov, and I have a duplicate of the read-out. It is very complete."

"I still don't understand why you think this is so conclusive, Senator," Hood protested. "If there were some sort of sinister connection between the President's men and the Soviet Defense Minister, why would Colonel Grant need information from the CIA?"

"Backup, Mr. Vice President, backup. You know—we all know—how suspicious and untrusting Lambert has become since he was elected," Sutton said. He added, almost mournfully, "He is not the same open person you and I used to know so well."

Hood fixed his attention on Dalland. "How did you come by copies of the Grant request, Mr. Dalland?"

Dalland considered making some effort to protect Gerald Ransome, but immediately realized that if he attempted to withhold his identity from the Vice President, Sutton would speak out. If Hood retained any vestige of the old-style government love of secrecy, Ransome was lost. Very likely, Dalland thought, he was lost in any case. The word of the leak would swiftly get back to those fascist bastards at Langley, and they would not rest until Gerald was cut adrift. That was a pity, a damned shame, really. But it appeared that he would have to be sacrificed—in the name of openness in government.

"A friend of mine works there, Mr. Vice President. A man named Gerald Ransome. He was concerned. He felt it was his duty to let someone know what was happening."

Hood's tiny eyes were suddenly, it seemed to Dalland, hard as chips of flint. "His duty, you say?"

"Yes, sir."

"So he brought the information to you."

"To Senator Sutton, sir. *Through* me."

"I see."

"Do you want copies, Mr. Vice President?" the Senator asked.

"No," Hood said hastily. "No need of that. I'll take your word for the content and the importance, Senator. Now what, exactly, do you expect me to do?"

"I realize your hands are, to a large extent, tied. It is your moral leadership that I want to invoke now, sir."

Sutton paused to let the flattery take effect. Then he continued. "The first thing is to take the military people in hand, sir. It is dangerous to allow a Red One under these conditions. Good God, suppose the Russians get wind of it? What will they believe?"

"I am not commander in chief, Senator." And for the moment, thought Hood, I thank God for it.

"But you could speak to General Devore and the other Chiefs, sir. Privately. Devore will see the wisdom of not presenting so aggressive a face."

"You think he believes there is some political uproar in the Kremlin?"

"I'd be surprised if he didn't."

"Then perhaps he had reason for declaring a Red One."

"I'm sure he'd say it was because of the Chinese death ray. Or that it is just an exercise. Whatever he says, Mr. Vice President, I intend to bring the whole matter before the Overwatch Committee on Intelligence in a few days. But the alert should be stopped now. At once. It is rashly provocative. Who knows how jittery they are in Moscow?"

"I have heard that Kirov is dying."

"All the more reason. You can see that they would believe we are ready to attack while they are in the process of sorting out the leadership. No, Mr. Vice President, the alert *must* be called off."

Hood remained doubtful. He wondered if the President himself had not ordered the Red One. If that was the case, to influence the Joint Chiefs to cancel it might be a very dangerous thing to do. Cleveland Lambert had a fearsome temper.

But there *was* the party convention to think about. It would be a grand thing, after all these years in politics, to be able to go before the delegates as a Man of Peace.

"It is your considered judgment, then," he said, "that there is no valid foreign-policy reason for the United States military to be in any advanced state of readiness? That is what you believe?"

"That is correct. No legitimate reason." The emphasis fell heavily on the word "legitimate" and the inference was not lost on the Vice President.

"Surely the proper course would be to discuss it with the Secretary of Defense?"

"An interesting observation—and not to be overlooked.

However, Richards has very neatly managed to absent himself from Washington, Mr. Vice President. The President may know where he is, but no one else does."

"Very well, then," Hood said. "I cannot guarantee anything, but I'll speak to General Devore."

"Soon, Mr. Vice President? The longer it goes on the more provocative it seems," Sutton said.

"This evening," Hood said. He stood up to indicate that his guests should leave. Dalland led the way. At the door of the entry hall of Admiral's House, Hood spoke quietly to Sutton. "I would warn your young man to expect some difficulties. Devore will surely want to know the source of my information."

"Everyone must make certain sacrifices for peace, sir," Sutton said loftily. The Vice President noted the egregious piety of the remark and realized that it was said in that manner for his benefit. He felt a momentary sadness that he, the second magistrate of the republic, was thought of so lightly that a United States Senator would be so transparent.

When Sutton and Dalland had driven away into the rain, Hood returned to his study and removed the cassette from his recorder. Dealing with a conniving man like the Senator, he thought, was rather like trying to fill an inside straight. It was best to have an ace in the hole.

There is a pleasure sure in being mad which none but madmen know.

—John Dryden, *The Spanish Friar*

PART THREE

39

"Comrade General Oblensky?" The voice on the telephone crackled with hostility.

The commander of the Aral'sk Strategic Rocket Regiment knew General Novikov well. He had always thought of him as a plodding bureaucrat, but the KGB chief's tone now conveyed an impression of icy contempt and threat. It did not reassure Sergei Oblensky to realize that this was the only open line to Moscow from the base, and that the executive of the Committee for State Security seemed perfectly aware of it.

"Oblensky," Novikov said without preamble, "I wish you to tell me exactly what is the situation down there."

Oblensky felt a sinking sensation in the pit of his stomach. Surely this was a clear indication that the KGB had penetrated the Defense Minister's plan. Novikov would not be mixing into Air Force matters otherwise.

"We are undergoing a combined test and exercise, Comrade Novikov," Oblensky said. "Under the personal command of the Minister of Defense." This was the day the Americans would arrive in the capital. The elements of Leonov's plan were clicking into position with military precision. The preliminary retargeting was completed and required only the refined data from the manned Svoboda that had been launched earlier from Baikonur. The missiles were being fueled, a process that would be complete within the hour. They could then be placed on hold for as long as thirty-six hours if need be. The GRU security troops had arrived shortly after midnight and were in position. The Aral'sk base was on a war footing now and, under the terms of the exercise code-named Red Glory, isolated from the rest of the Soviet Union. Except for this single line.

"Comrade General," Oblensky continued, "we are conducting our part of Task Red Glory. It assumes that Moscow has been destroyed and we must operate independently."

"That is shit, Oblensky," Novikov said harshly. "We know exactly what you are doing."

Oblensky's heart hammered in his chest as he searched for something, anything, to say. "This is an exercise ordered by the Minister of Defense, Comrade Novikov."

"Is Leonov there?"

"He is on the base, Comrade General. I do not know exactly where."

Novikov's voice grew even colder, more deadly. "Very well. Now listen to me. The Americans are delayed. Do you understand that? *They will not arrive until tomorrow.*"

Oblensky's mouth felt dry. He knew how vital to the plan it was for the action to begin while the Americans were inside Russia. Without that, the whole thing was an act of madness. Was Novikov lying, he wondered desperately. How much did he really know? And others—did they know?

"Are you there, Oblensky? Are you listening?"

"I am here, Comrade Novikov," Oblensky said faintly.

"Then hear me. Leonovite traitors are being arrested wherever we can find them. There will be no military coup in this country, Oblensky—"

Oblensky's face went white. My God, he thought, the man *knew*—but knew what? He spoke of a military coup. He didn't know about the main element of the plan. He was a policeman, and all he could imagine was that Leonov planned to take over the government. Oblensky had an impulse to laugh wildly. To discover so much and to understand so little! Novikov thought that Yuri Ivanovich was using the base as a command post for counterrevolution.

"Are you listening to me, Oblensky?"

"I am listening, Comrade General, but you can't believe what you are saying." Oblensky, shocked into swift thought by Novikov's accusation, was beginning to think more clearly.

The plan was still working. Novikov was threatening and accusing in the hope of uncovering a conspiracy that he suspected existed, but could not yet prove. The First Secretary would not relinquish command in such an emergency. He would not allow Novikov to make accusations over a telephone. Kirov would act. Kirov would send troops in to arrest the officers under suspicion. Therefore, Oblensky deduced with great clarity, the First Secretary was *not* in command. His condition must be worse. That would explain the delay in the Americans' visit.

The Politburo must be in a state of confusion, the security forces in disarray. This wouldn't last, of course, but for the next day or so, Novikov and whoever was supporting him would take no really effective action. The man was lying about Leonovites being arrested. That would not happen until the Americans were on the way home.

Who would speak for the USSR to the American President? Krasin, most likely. A diplomat, not a soldier, thank God.

It was all falling into place. Despite the unpredictable, uncontrollable events that had allowed Novikov to indulge in conjecture—the ill-advised action of the Maoists in developing a doomsday weapon, Kirov's terminal illness, the stupidity of the American President in wishing to act the peacemaker—despite all that, the elements of the plan remained staunch.

Oblensky said, much more calmly, "I am shocked at your accusation, Comrade General Novikov. I think I should locate the Minister of Defense and let him speak to you to clear up these fantastic misunderstandings."

"You son of a bitch, you listen to me."

"I am listening," Oblensky said coldly.

"Your base is surrounded. There are security units holding all roads leading in."

Oblensky felt a surge of triumph. The key word was "holding." Novikov had no intention of trying to move in with his KGB forces. *He didn't dare.* Not until the Americans had come and gone.

And the Americans *would* come. But it would take time before they could depart. And the world would have to conclude that Leonov's plan had been cleared with them, implemented with their approval.

God, Oblensky thought, Yuri Ivanovich is a genius, a military genius. The plan had always seemed vague and uncertain to him, a theoretical thing—like the plans written in answer to the situations described in the Crisis Confrontation Lectures. Now it was something very different. He wanted to shout at Novikov that he was a bloody-minded fool, a dunce-brained policeman incapable of understanding what was really happening to the Soviet Union.

He said, "I am not going to listen to any more of this, Novikov. This base is undergoing a test exercise. We are authorized to do so by the Minister of Defense."

"Oblensky, I am going to say this only once. You have a chance to save yourself. Are you listening to me?"

"I hear you very clearly, Novikov."

"Arrest Leonov."

"What?"

"Don't play the fool with me! Arrest Leonov," Novikov shouted.

Oblensky spoke into the telephone calmly. "Certainly, Comrade Novikov. As soon as I receive the order from First Secretary Kirov personally."

The line went dead, and General Oblensky sat, deeply thoughtful, before replacing the receiver of the scrambler telephone.

Colonel Louisa Feodorovna stood by the open blast door of the command center until Marshal Leonov noticed her and signaled for her to enter.

Alone, he had been monitoring the fueling of the missiles by television. He was satisfied with the efficiency of the crews; all preparations were proceeding on schedule.

Feodorovna said, "Comrade Marshal, the last land link with Moscow is broken."

Leonov's smile accentuated the swarthy good looks of his Kirghiz features. "Then we are theoretically on our own. The exercise can proceed."

"The last contact was between General Oblensky and Comrade General Novikov. I have a recording of it if you want to hear what was said."

"Is it worth hearing?"

"I believe so, Comrade Marshal," she said. "Novikov wants Oblensky to arrest you."

Leonov's expression remained unchanged, but his eyes seemed to grow harder, opaque. "What else?"

"The Americans are delayed until tomorrow."

Leonov said thoughtfully, "Krasin's doing. The First Secretary must be worse."

"Perhaps dead, Comrade Marshal," Feodorovna said.

"Possibly. What else?"

"General Novikov accuses you of attempting a coup."

"And what does he propose to do about it?"

"That's the odd part, Comrade Marshal. Nothing really effective. He claims to have moved KGB troops into position around the base. But they are simply holding the roads."

"Do you understand what is happening, Comrade Colonel?" Leonov's tone was familiar to Feodorovna; it carried echoes of the lecture hall at Frunze, the verdant pathways, the sparkling white mountains. She had come a long way from that place to this concrete burrow near the Sea of Aral'sk. It had been exciting, satisfying. Whatever happened now, it had all been worthwhile. Her life had been much more rewarding than that of millions of her Soviet sisters.

"I think I understand, Comrade Marshal," she said.

"Explain."

"Comrade Krasin and the others are unwilling to use the KGB against us until the Americans have gone."

"Correct, Comrade Colonel," Leonov said. "Does General Oblensky understand also?"

"Who can tell, Comrade Marshal?" Feodorovna replied carefully. "He has his uncertain moments."

The feral smile reappeared. "I rely on you to inform me when one of those moments is upon us."

"Yes, Comrade Marshal."

"A technical question, Comrade Colonel."

"Sir?"

"Assuming a launch within twenty-four hours, must we put a hold on fueling the missiles?"

"No, Comrade Marshal. The SS-19 can stand ready and fueled for thirty-six hours."

"Then there is nothing more that need be done until the updates on the target area are received from Svoboda."

"That is correct, Comrade Marshal."

"Now I want a low-frequency link with the naval vessels on line Sigma-Omega."

"Our links to Moscow Command Center are jammed, Comrade Marshal."

"We will use Naval Operations Hanoi. They are saving a frequency for Task Red Glory."

"Very good, Comrade Marshal. I will have the Communications Battalion set it up."

"Also a link to Headquarters, Far Eastern Army."

"Yes, Comrade Marshal."

Leonov stood, a tall, lean, impressive figure in his well-tailored uniform. "You understand what we are doing, Louisa Feodorovna? Really understand, I mean?"

"I do," she said.

"And you are not afraid?"

She looked directly into his eyes and said, "I am not afraid, Comrade Marshal. You are in command."

He placed a hand firmly on her shoulder. "I shall remember that, Comrade Feodorovna," he said.

40

Harry Grant arrived at Hurn in midmorning.

He found Major Barrow and his crew aboard their 767 parked in a remote corner of the airfield under RAF protection.

The arrival of an American military transport plane at Hurn, well off the beaten path for such events, had aroused surprisingly little interest among the regular users of the airport. The RAF detachment guarding the aircraft was small and under the command of a flying officer in battle dress.

Grant identified himself, somewhat surprised that no advance members of the President's traveling party had yet arrived. The RAF officer had obviously been told only the barest minimum of what he needed to know and had no explanation.

"Major Barrow has been expecting you, Colonel," he said. "He received a signal early this morning through our Telex net."

Grant walked with him across the parking ramp to a jeep standing on a taxiway. A steady, thin rain was falling. There was no flying activity on the field. The beacon atop the control tower showed flashing red, indicating that the airport was closed to traffic.

"A number of British Airways trips have had to overfly this morning," the flying officer said. "There have been a few queries. The weather's not that bad, you see. But we've had Admin report our main runway unserviceable. That's stopped any rumors." He paused beside the vehicle and asked, "I expect you'll be leaving soon?"

Grant turned the question away with a noncommittal murmur. The sight of the gleaming 767 standing in the rain had the effect of wrenching him back into a more familiar context. For the last three days he had allowed himself to become more and more involved in the puzzle of Voronin's death, the man's intentions, Ballard's peculiar brand of co-operation, and—above all— Bronwen Wells.

He thought about her as he rode in the jeep toward the parked aircraft. The degree of his involvement with her, the personal feelings he had so suddenly developed about her, seemed unreal in these circumstances. Yet he knew beyond any doubt that they were far from unreal. And he realized that he had failed in the mission given him by the President. Bad luck and bad timing. He had arrived in England too late to do anything about Voronin. But he wondered if he had not allowed himself to become so concerned about Bronwen that he had neglected to do his best to discover what it was that Voronin had thought to trade for his own—and Bronwen's—safety.

Away from her now, Grant could think more clearly about her murdered lover. At his briefing by State Department Intelligence, the connection between Voronin and the Soviet Minister of Defense, Leonov, had been noted. Grant had the uneasy feeling that somehow he had not probed beyond the surface of the strange circumstances surrounding Voronin's death. It was all very well to accept Ian Ballard's statement that Voronin had been gunned down by hired Irish killers. But there matters became a bit thin because, as Ballard had pointed out, it really wasn't the KGB's style to entrust sensitive liquidations to the likes of the Provos. They were simply too unreliable, too involved in their own unique need for murder. Even the soldier spooks of GRU were not really likely to handle the Voronin affair in the way it had been handled. The killing had a conspiratorial flavor to it, an almost personal touch.

An Air Force steward met him at the boarding ramp. He was wearing a side arm and inspected Grant's identification carefully. The flying officer drove his jeep back toward the light cordon of

RAF security troops guarding the taxiway. Grant carried his flight bag into the aircraft. The steward, a sergeant, closed the fuselage door behind him. "Major Barrow is on the flight deck, Colonel," he said.

Grant made his way up the aisle of the empty plane. The air conditioning made a soft whine. He detected the familiar smells of kerosene, ozone, and hydraulic oil. As he passed the leading edge of the swept-back wings, he could see, through the cabin windows, two members of Barrow's crew standing near the portable ground-power truck. The vehicle bore Royal Air Force numbers, but there were no RAF men nearby. And the two Americans were armed.

The flight deck was crowded. Barrow's second and third pilots were in the forward seats working with a checklist. Grant did not know them. The radar-navigator, Captain Stevenson, was an old acquaintance, and he smiled a greeting from where he sat studying his charts and Loran tables. Barrow, a stocky young man with reddish hair and a freckled face, was conferring with Master Sergeant Oliver, another acquaintance of Grant's, over the flight engineer's panel.

When Grant entered the flight deck, Barrow straightened and took Grant by the arm. "Jesus Christ, Harry, where the hell have you been?"

"What's happening here?" Grant asked, parrying Barrow's question.

"There's been a twenty-four-hour hold. The President will arrive here sometime before 2400 hours. But what the hell have you been doing? I had a signal from the Chief that you were to stay here, talk to no one other than the crew. I was told to detain you, if I had to. Now what *is* going on?"

Grant smiled. "I may be in trouble."

Barrow took a newspaper from a folder above the navigator's desk. "Could this be it? One of the RAF people picked it up at the terminal an hour ago."

Grant opened the tabloid and read that the Soviet Colonel's

mistress had disappeared in the company of one Colonel Harry Grant and the rest of it. His face felt frozen with a mixture of anger and apprehension. He wondered if Bronwen had read the story and, if she had, what she might take it into her head to do about it. There was simply no way of knowing.

It was doubly bitter because the only person who could have given the details of his identity to the *Express,* the one interested party who had seen him depart from London with Bronwen Wells was Jane McNary.

It was the act of an angry woman, that was true enough. But it had the unique, acid McNary touch. His personal life was impinging destructively on the performance of his job and, even worse, on Bronwen Wells's already shaken peace of mind. McNary's cheap shot was sensational and possibly dangerous.

"I have to get to a telephone, George," he said abruptly.

"Harry, the Chief said you were to stay put and talk to no one," Barrow said.

"This is personal."

"I'm sorry. I can't let you out of my sight."

"This is important to me, Major." Grant's voice had hardened.

Barrow recognized the danger. He opened the door to the main cabin and called: "Sergeant."

The sergeant steward trotted up the aisle. "Sir?"

The pilot looked at Grant pleadingly. Grant's face was set in harsh, determined lines. Barrow sighed and said, "Sergeant, Colonel Grant is under quarters' arrest by order of the President. Take him aft and put him in the President's study. See to it that he stays there."

Snow had stopped falling on Moscow. The heavy overcast had been replaced by clearing skies and a biting freeze.

The ad hoc committee of the Politburo that had gathered in the bell tower of Ivan the Terrible—the place having been chosen for privacy—consisted of Foreign Minister Krasin; General

Lyudin, representing the Army; General Boris Novikov, of the Committee for State Security; Anatoly Gagarin, the Agriculture Minister; Yevgeny Suslov, the Minister of Finance; and Lieutenant General Alexis Sheremetiev, the Chief of Staff of the Strategic Rocket Forces and Deputy Commander of the Moscow Military District.

The remaining members of the Politburo, including the Premier and the Deputy Premier, had either been unavailable on such short notice or their presence had been vetoed by either Novikov or Lyudin, who had decided between themselves that they must supply the stiffening needed under these extraordinary circumstances.

General Zabotin, chief of the GRU, had been deliberately excluded, and a secret order for his arrest had been sent to all military and police commands. Thus far, all the organs of the state under Novikov's operational command had failed to locate Zabotin.

In Soviet installations around the world, former students of Yuri Leonov were being quietly detained. A heavy security cordon had been thrown around the dacha of First Secretary Valentin Kirov, and all units of the KGB had been alerted for immediate action.

The committee, guided firmly by Novikov and Lyudin, had voted to appoint Viktor Krasin acting first secretary of the Communist party of the USSR. In a second swift vote the committee had appointed old Lyudin acting premier and Novikov his deputy. The fact that there now existed two sets of high-ranking functionaries in the Soviet Union was seen as regrettable, but none of the men gathered in the Ivan the Terrible tower could suggest a more effective course of action. It was absolutely necessary, Novikov declared, that the regime present a calm and well-organized hierarchy to the visiting Americans. The reasons for the American visit remained as pressing and important as ever, and it would be the height of folly, Novikov contended (daring anyone to contradict him), to let the visitors (who were, after all, the long-range enemy) see the regime in disarray.

An open line to Valentin Kirov's sickroom had been established so that the ad hoc committee could know the instant the First Secretary died. As a matter of policy, a special KGB detachment had been sent to Usovo to arrest Academician Lisavetta Lazarova and the other medical staff the moment their services were no longer required by the First Secretary. "Under no circumstances," Novikov ordered, "is word of Comrade Kirov's death to be released to anyone." Privately, to Viktor Krasin, he declared that he, Krasin, must make the announcement—first to the Americans in secrecy, and then, after the joint declaration to the Chinese had been agreed upon and the Americans were on their way to Peking, to the rest of the world. It was imperative, in both Novikov's and Lyudin's view, that the Chinese be made to understand that the death of a first secretary in no way altered the severe view taken in the Kremlin concerning the development of new and destabilizing weapons.

"But what are we to do about Leonov?" General Sheremetiev demanded. "He has dug himself in at Aral'sk and it might be extremely difficult to root him out of there."

Lyudin said, "At least Yuri Ivanovich does not suspect our countermeasures."

Novikov cleared his throat. "That may not be exactly the case, Comrades."

The men in the small octagonal room stopped talking to look at him. The thought that Leonov might know what they were about clearly frightened some of them.

"I spoke to General Oblensky this morning before we cut off communications from the base. I ordered him to arrest the traitor."

"By *God,* General," Krasin said explosively, "that was a *stupid* thing to do!"

There was a general murmur of alarmed agreement.

Novikov slammed the flat of his meaty palm against the table for silence. "It was a chance worth taking. It may still pay off."

Lyudin said heavily, "Oblensky refused, of course."

"He said that he would do it when ordered to directly by the First Secretary."

"Which is clearly impossible," Krasin said angrily.

"He may still reconsider, Viktor Stepanovich," Novikov said in a firm voice. "It would be to his advantage to do so. He has, after all, a choice between an act of loyalty to the state and one of loyalty to Yuri Leonov. He will consider carefully, I think, and come to the obvious conclusion."

"Which is?" demanded Suslov nervously.

"He will see that the Leonovite plot cannot succeed. The choice will be one between reward and a shot in the neck. There are no other options."

"There aren't any options at all," Lyudin said, his small eyes hard as marbles. "*All* Leonov's protégés must be liquidated."

Krasin shivered inwardly. He had lived through the Stalin era. He had not thought to hear talk of mass liquidations again in his lifetime. But what other choice was there?

"I agree, Comrade Marshal," Novikov said to Lyudin. "But we are concerned here with what Oblensky will think and do. Not with what we know must be done."

"At least we have Leonov contained and isolated," the Minister of Agriculture said. He was a thin, sad-faced bureaucrat, young for his position, but old in appearance and in attitude. Overseeing Soviet agriculture was not a task that made for joy and lightness in a man.

"Unfortunately, that is not quite so," Sheremetiev said.

"What the hell do you mean by that?" Novikov demanded. "We have ordered all communications links with the base at Aral'sk shut down. The man is deaf, dumb, and blind."

"I am afraid not, Comrade General," Sheremetiev said. "It is true we can shut down the land links between Aral'sk and the Moscow command center, and that has been done. We can also jam most of the regular VHF and UHF frequencies he might use for communications with his coconspirators. But if the communications officer at Aral'sk knows his business, Leonov can still communicate with naval units at sea by shunting his transmissions directly into the ultra-low-frequency grid in central Siberia. You will recall, Comrades, that we recently completed that twenty-thousand-square-kilometer antenna specifically so that we would have a nonjammable radio link with our nuclear submarines at sea. The low-frequency pulses travel through the earth instead of through the atmosphere."

"Are you saying that he can still issue orders?" Krasin demanded.

"If the communications personnel at Aral'sk know what they are about," Sheremetiev said calmly. He added, with a note of pride that infuriated Krasin, "And they are good, Comrade Minister—I'm sorry, forgive me—Comrade Acting First Secretary—"

"That's incredible," Krasin said. "Are you saying we can't silence him?"

"That is why the ULF grid was constructed, Comrade Krasin," the Air Force General said.

"At such staggering expense," breathed the Finance Minister glumly.

Sheremetiev glanced at the civilian with a touch of hauteur. "You may think so, Comrade Minister. But the system works. We can reach our nuclear boats—"

"And so can Leonov," Krasin said heavily.

"Well, yes. That is so. He can also reach the manned Svoboda that was put in orbit last evening—"

Krasin stared at Lyudin unbelievingly. "Do you know anything about this? A manned flight ordered by whom?"

"By Yuri Ivanovich," the old Marshal said. "Perhaps I

should have ordered it stopped, but there was so much else to do. And I was not certain the Air Force would obey me if I counter-manded an order from the Minister of Defense."

"Well, order the Svoboda down at once," Krasin said sharply.

Sheremetiev said, "We will have to wait six hours, Comrade Krasin. If we brought the man down now, he would land in the sea. We have no units deployed to recover him."

Sometimes, Krasin thought, I think I am going mad. "Then bring him down at the earliest possible moment consistent with safety." He stared hard at Sheremetiev. "Is there anything else I do not know that I should be told about?"

The Air Force General subsided, shook his head, surprised, as only a military man could be, at the never-failing ignorance of military matters displayed by civilians.

Krasin said to Lyudin, "Why isn't the Navy represented here?"

"Comrade Admiral Viktorov is at Kronshtadt. He has been summoned, Comrade Acting First Secretary."

"It occurs to me that if Leonov can communicate with the nuclear boats, he might well be able to establish a relay to Army and Air Force units through a ship or a naval base."

"That is so, Comrade First Secretary." The dropping of the qualifier did not go unnoticed in the small room. Krasin himself wondered if he had just now passed some watershed in his relationship with these men who had "elected" him to stand in for Valentin Kirov.

"Then notify all commands that no messages from Aral'sk are to be relayed."

"That will alert any Leonovites in those places, Comrade Krasin," Novikov protested.

Krasin regarded the KGB commander levelly. "Have you a better suggestion, Comrade General?"

Novikov met his eyes. "No," he said, looking away.

"Then do as I say."

A secretary tapped on the seventeenth-century door. Krasin

nodded and Finance Minister Suslov, who was nearest, opened the massive carved portal. It creaked on ancient hinges.

The secretary said, "You asked to be informed, Comrade Krasin. The American President is addressing the NATO-Warsaw conference. We have a satellite transmission coming in. Shall I tape it for replay or will you hear it now?"

Krasin looked about the room at the men who had made him, for better or worse, temporary ruler of the Soviet empire. "Is there anything more?"

No one spoke, each man now concerned with his own bit of authority and how to preserve it through the difficult days ahead.

Krasin stood up. "All right," he said to the secretary, "I'll come." To the others he said, "This meeting of the ad hoc committee of the Politburo is closed."

41

It was late evening when Madame Zelinskaya, after dinner with friends in a Soho restaurant, returned to her ballet school in Hobhouse Close. While she was unlocking the door she could hear the telephone ringing insistently upstairs in her office. As she climbed the stairs to the practice hall, it stopped.

Ekaterina Zelinskaya was what once was known as a White, or Shanghai, Russian. Her parents, members of the bourgeoisie of old Russia, had fled the Revolution to the east, as had many members of their small class.

Before the upheavals of 1917, young Ekaterina had, at great expense, been enrolled in the Imperial Ballet School in St. Petersburg and had progressed rapidly with her studies. She and her parents had entertained hopes that she might become a star of the Imperial Company. But those hopes were dashed by the Revolution and the family's flight to Shanghai. Ekaterina had been seven when she left Russia.

From Shanghai the family had drifted, in the manner of *émigrés,* to Budapest, thence to Paris, and finally to London. Like many *émigré* children, Ekaterina had been raised with longing tales of the beauty and splendor of the mother country—a country she barely remembered. Her parents despised the Reds, of course, but their love of the homeland and their fervent patriotism influenced her more than they could have foreseen.

By the time Hitler's Germany invaded Russia in 1941, Zelinskaya's parents had been dead for a decade. Her career as a dancer had flourished—to the limit of her talent, which was considerable but not great—and she had begun to teach.

The war years had a profound effect on Zelinskaya. An emotional and suggestible woman, she was deeply affected by the stories that appeared in the British press about the gallantry of her countrymen at Leningrad, in the Ukraine, at Stalingrad, and before Moscow. She understood, of course, that Russia and Russians had become a popular cause in the West. As the only ally actually facing the Germans on the ground, a people defending their homes with bravery and at immense sacrifice, the citizens of the Soviet Union were the stars of Allied propaganda.

Zelinskaya found herself often accepting and even repeating the complaints of Josif Stalin concerning the delays in establishing a second front. It seemed to her that people of her blood were bearing the terrible brunt of Hitler's war. Her hatred of the Communists, a thing learned from her parents and not from any firsthand experience of them, became submerged in her pride in Russian resistance to fascism.

In 1943, Zelinskaya, an attractive woman with many admirers, was contacted by a member of the Soviet Military Mission in London. The proposition put to her was simple and direct. The British and Americans were half-hearted in their prosecution of the war because there were many cryptofascists in high places. She, as a dancer in the then Sadler's Wells Ballet, was in a position to meet and cultivate many high-ranking British and Americans. Would she serve the Motherland? She would and did. By 1944 Ekaterina Zelinskaya was an agent of the NKVD. She remained an agent through the Cold War years, seldom used but always considered reliable.

Now as she grew older, her usefulness diminished, but she was still loyal, still willing.

As she entered the darkened practice hall, the telephone began to ring again. She hurried into the office and lifted the receiver.

A distraught Bronwen Wells said, "Madame, is that you?"

"It is I. Am I speaking to Bronwen?"

"Yes, Madame. I have been trying to reach you all evening."
The voice was unsteady, edged by hysteria.

"Where have you been, Bronwen?"

"In Rye, Madame. Have you seen the newspaper?"

Zelinskaya had, indeed, seen the *Express* story. She had been
wondering what effect it would have on her pupil and on the
American who had taken her away.

"Yes, I have seen it. I was worried about you, my dear,"
Zelinskaya said. "Are you all right? You are not harmed?"

"Of course I'm not harmed, Madame. Colonel Grant was
only trying to help me. But now I don't know what to do."

Zelinskaya had not known until reading the tabloid that the
man was a member of the President's personal staff.

The newspaper story had shaken her. Knowing, as she did,
that the *rezident* did not want to lose track of the girl, she had
been certain that the Americans had spirited her away.

Now that she knew where Bronwen was, she had no intention
of allowing her to slip away again. She said, "Where in Rye are
you?"

"I was at the Mermaid, Madame. Now I am at the Ashford
railway station. I am coming back to London. I can't let the
police think that Colonel Grant has kidnapped me. That's what
the newspaper seems to be saying."

"Come here to me, dear one. At any time."

"Thank you, Madame Zelinskaya. I didn't know where to
turn."

"Is your American with you?"

"No, Madame. He took me to Rye and said that I should
stay. Until he could come back for me, that is. But then I saw the
terrible things they were saying in the newspaper and I felt I
should come back to London and explain what happened."

"Why did you rush away? Forgive me for asking, my dear,
but it wasn't wise, you know."

Bronwen's voice was near to breaking as she told Madame
Zelinskaya about the invasion of her apartment. Zelinskaya

frowned into the darkened room. "It must have been the work of sick minds, dear one. Enemies of Aleksandr Voronin, perhaps. In any case, you must not return to your flat. You must come here straight away. Your teacher will care for you."

"Thank you, Madame. I don't want to be any trouble to you—"

"Silence, now. You could never be trouble. You are to come here to me and let's hear no more about it. What time does your train arrive in London?"

"At eleven-fifteen, Madame. At Waterloo Station."

"I will meet you or have someone there to bring you to me."

"Thank you, Madame," Bronwen said again. "You make me feel quite safe."

"Good girl," Zelinskaya said, and waited for Bronwen to break the connection.

When the line was clear, she dialed the number of her control at the Soviet Embassy.

A secretary replied to her coded query: "The Cultural Attaché is at home. I will connect you."

The familiar voice of the KGB *rezident* came on, and Zelinskaya spoke without preamble.

"The Wells girl has just called me. She was in Rye, where the American hid her, and is now returning to London. Do you still want her?"

"There has been a re-evaluation of her situation," the *rezident* said. "Moscow is no longer convinced that she possesses any useful information."

"That does not answer my question," Zelinskaya said sharply. During her many years in London, she had worked with many controllers, seen many *rezidents* come and go. She preferred direct answers to direct questions. "I have instructed her to come here to me. She will do this. Do you want her? Or shall I send her away?"

"The American who came to meet with Voronin took her to Rye, you say?"

"That is what I said."

"She must be of some value to them, then."

"Possibly," Zelinskaya said with some asperity. The *rezident*'s voice was that of a young man. One of the new bureaucrats, she thought, the baby-faced ones who did not remember the days of the Great Patriotic War.

"Then let her stay. For a time, at least. Until I get word from Moscow."

"Very well. Send a man to Waterloo to meet the eleven-fifteen from Ashford. Have him bring her here to me. Gently, as a friend."

"You want me to send a man?"

"Of course."

There was an irritated silence on the other end of the line. Zelinskaya wondered with a twinge of acid amusement if this meant that the bright young bureaucrat would have to do it himself. It was always difficult to know how important a *rezident* was in the Embassy at any given time.

"Very well," he said. "I will take care of it."

Before he could hang up the receiver, Zelinskaya threw a quick question at him. It was an impertinent question, but she wanted to know the answer. It had to do with what she would have to expect if Bronwen Wells stayed more than a few hours at the school in Hobhouse Close.

"Was it your men who destroyed her flat?"

"Certainly not."

He could be lying. But there was no logical reason for him to withhold such information from her.

"Then who?"

"I have no idea. Ask the British police," he said, and broke the connection.

For a long while Madame Zelinskaya sat at the small desk in the darkened room. The second answer *had* been a lie. She was too experienced not to know that the young *rezident* had been deliberately evasive. He *did* have some idea of who had tried to frighten Bronwen. Perhaps he was not certain, perhaps he only suspected. But it was a reasonable assumption, Zelinskaya thought, that the same people who murdered Aleksandr Voronin were trying to terrify—perhaps to kill—Bronwen Wells. That was important, since by bringing Bronwen to the school, she exposed herself to the same dangers.

This was not an English thing, she thought, or an American thing. It was Russian. She felt it in her bones. Someone in the homeland had ordered Voronin killed. If it was not the KGB, and she sensed that it had not been, then there was a second force at work. Who, why, and how powerful, she wondered.

She turned on a brighter light and looked carefully at the morning's copy of the *Times*. There was nothing in the news to suggest that anything unusual was happening in the Soviet Union. There was a small item about First Secretary Kirov vacationing at Usovo, some probably fascist-imperialist-inspired items about Soviet military moves in Siberia and in the South China Sea. Nothing else.

She closed the paper and sat quietly thinking. She felt a certain strange, yet familiar thrill of excitement. It pleased her. She had not felt quite like this since the old days during the war, when her acts of treason against her adopted country had put her in delicious jeopardy. She almost felt young again.

42

Close to midnight, the President of the United States and his traveling party arrived at Hurn airport. They traveled in three large but unobtrusive limousines and they drove directly onto the airfield and through the RAF cordon to the waiting Boeing 767.

With Cleveland Lambert came Paul Lyman, the First Lady, Jane McNary, and two secretary-interpreters. The two British observers, included at the request of the Prime Minister, were the Minister of State for Foreign Affairs and the Under-Secretary, accompanied by their personal assistants and a security co-ordinator. This last official was, again at the request of the Prime Minister, a member of SIS, Major Ian Ballard.

The remainder of the party consisted of six American Secret Service agents, bringing the total number of passengers boarding the 767 that night to seventeen.

Major Barrow, utilizing the aircraft's sophisticated communications to establish contact with Andrews Air Force Base Flight Control, filed a coded flight plan programming the aircraft's path south and east over the English Channel, northeast over the North Sea and east to a point on the Lithuanian Baltic coast, then due east through Soviet air space direct to Moscow. This route avoided land areas wherever possible and, to avoid the appearance on radar of a high-velocity military aircraft, was plotted on a deceptive zigzag pattern and at commercial airliner speed. At no time would the plane fly through the air space of countries not privy to the secret journey. The Major's flight plan included the data needed to keep the President in touch with

Washington by UHF transmission, first to Telstar 17, in synchronous orbit over Western Europe, then to Samos 23, in polar orbit. Backup communication and television transmissions, if needed, could be relayed through the Nathan Hale net. These transmissions were limited to traffic between the Presidential plane and the Pentagon War Room.

Grant, chafing in the President's study, heard faintly the arrival of the traveling party. He realized that it was a measure of the President's displeasure with him that he was not immediately allowed to join them in the main cabin of the plane.

He heard the ping of the Fasten Seat Belts signs going on. Through the window he could see the starting truck standing by, and within minutes he heard the whine of the starter-boosters. The aircraft trembled with the vibration of the engines as Barrow and his crew prepared for flight.

Grant thought of Bronwen and wondered what she would do when she saw the *Express* story. He had a feeling of deep apprehension and helplessness. Impatiently, he stood and rapped sharply on the locked door.

Sergeant Halloran opened it and said, "You'd better buckle up, Colonel. We're moving out." As he spoke, Grant could feel the aircraft begin its roll out to the end of the runway. He looked past the Sergeant at the second set of doors that closed off the Presidential cabins from the main salon of the plane. He could see no one.

"Does the President know I am here, Sergeant?"

"He does, sir. He'll probably be back as soon as we are airborne."

Grant thought grimly: I don't look forward to that.

"Will you take a seat now, Colonel?"

He threw himself into a seat and fastened the belt. Gloom dominated his thoughts. Somehow he had managed to accomplish nothing more than the grand achievement of incurring President Lambert's formidable anger. And where was Bronwen now?

With his airman's ear and instinct he followed Barrow and

his crew through the checklist as the plane stopped, turned to square with the take-off runway.

Then swiftly the 767 moved forward, accelerating. Grant watched the runway lights flashing by. He felt Barrow rotate the aircraft as it approached take-off speed. Within seconds, the plane that custom dictated be called "Air Force One" was airborne, climbing into the darkness over southern England to head for the Channel coast. The local time was 12:03.

At 1910 hours, Washington time, General Clinton Devore stepped from his staff car and into his house at Fort Myer, Virginia. As he handed his overcoat and cap to his orderly, his junior aide appeared from the study.

"Admiral Muller on the line, General," he said.

Devore, frowning as he remembered the interview he had just concluded with the Vice President, strode into the library and lifted the blue telephone that connected his quarters with the office of the Joint Chiefs.

"Clint here, Jay," he said.

The Admiral's voice was urgent. "Let's scramble."

"All right," Devore said. He pressed the scrambler button and said, "What is it?"

"I have received information that the Soviets have taken Aral'sk off the top line for retargeting. That aroused my curiosity, Clint. They aren't due for another eighteen days."

Devore's frown grew deeper. "Just the Aral'sk Regiment? Nothing else?"

"Damned peculiar, isn't it?"

"What's your guess?"

Muller spoke carefully. "A guess is all it is, understand. But I had Data Processing compute the flight time for an SS-19 between Aral'sk and the place where the Chinese are building their new toy. There would be better ways of taking out that installation, I know. The SS-19s are big birds, and they would have to be launched at a very high angle to hit the Turfan or Lop Nor. But it can be done. DP gives me a flight time of thirteen minutes—give or take a few seconds."

"Jay, you're scaring the hell out of me with that kind of talk."

"I'm not saying that's what the new target for Aral'sk is. I'm just considering the possibilities."

"Is there anything else on the board? Any new moves by the Far Eastern Army?"

"We have an intercept about some maneuvers called 'Task Red Glory.' That was a couple of hours ago, but since then there's been nothing at all. A lot of local coded radio and telephone traffic, but that's all."

"What are they doing at sea?"

"Very little. There's a funny sort of concentration in the China Sea. Some Yankee-class boats and a pair of their new carriers. But that's about it. No sign of serious activity anywhere else. A Sverdlov-class missile cruiser—we have it tentatively identified as the *Kronshtadt*—is messing about in the Kattegat, playing games with a Chinese nuke. I'm still uneasy, though, Clint. I have a bad feeling in my sailor's gut."

"Well, here's something to make your gut feel even worse, Jay," Devore said. "I've just left the Vice President. It seems that Senator Sutton and his friends are upset about our Red One practice. The Vice President suggests—in a nice way, of course—that it would be politic of us to cancel the alert forthwith."

"It will slow our reaction time, Clint. By four hours, at least."

"That's just the point our garrulous Veep is making. He wanted to know if there was any reason for the alert and, though he didn't come right out and say so, he wanted to know if the President had authorized it." When Muller remained silent, Devore added, "He didn't, you know. Not actually."

"It was implied in the instructions he gave us before he left."

"*Implied* won't cut it, Jay. Hood as much as told me to get his authorization or stand down."

"What do we do?"

Devore glanced at a world-time clock on the paneled wall. "He's airborne now. I don't want to ask in the clear. He is scheduled to make a touch with Samos 23 at—let's see—about 2030 hours, our time."

"We could use Nathan Hale. That's as secure as we can make it."

"That would mean another hour's delay. He's not due for that hookup until he's over Russian soil."

"I don't think," Muller said carefully, "that it would be a good idea to discuss a Red One over the Samos net. It's been in place for fifteen years or more, and the chances are better than good that the Russkis and the Chinese both have learned to tap it."

Devore silently agreed. It would hardly be the best advertisement for a secret peace mission to have the President discussing a Red One alert with his military commanders while en route to talk to the enemy. To Devore, as to Muller and the other Joint Chiefs, the Communists—both Russian and Chinese—were, and would always be, the enemy.

"Then we'll have to go through the motions of a stand-down, Jay," the Chairman of the Joint Chiefs said. "We have enough antagonists on the Hill without arousing Hood." He paused, about to make a political statement and therefore one he doubted a soldier should make. But it needed to be said, and Muller, of all the Joint Chiefs, could be trusted to be discreet. "I think Hood wants us to go over his head to the President. I think he wants it on the President's record that he flew off to talk about peace while rattling nuclear rockets all the way. The convention is coming up and, if the mission fails, Hood and Sutton and that lot will blame it on the President's 'lack of sincerity' or his 'threatening attitude.' Something like that."

"Then perhaps we shouldn't involve him at all," Muller said.

"And just stand down?"

"We can drop to Yellow Three."

"Two hours' reaction time?"

"We can't have it both ways. Yellow Three would be better than stand-down. There's no indication of a general move by the Soviets."

"What about that gut feeling of yours?"

"Maybe I can learn to live with it."

Devore said, "Do you really think they might hit Lop Nor or the Turfan?"

"They've been talking about it for years, Clint. This new thing the Chinese are building could supply a perfect excuse."

"The Chinese would hit back. They don't have too much, but they would use what they have."

"Unless—" Muller grew thoughtful.

"Unless what?"

"Unless they thought we were in on it and would respond if they launched against the Soviets."

"That doesn't make sense, Jay. They'd never buy it."

"But wouldn't the Russians love it if they did? Now you're going to tell me I have a dirty, suspicious mind."

"I think you do, Admiral," Devore said. "You should be in the Senate."

"I'll take that suggestion under advisement," Muller said. "Now it's been a long night for me and I'm going home. The Marine Corps will be in charge here. I'll brief Lazenby before I leave for my quarters." He paused and then added, "You'll have to decide about the stand-down yourself, Clint. I know what I would do, but I'm not chairman. You are."

"All right," Devore said heavily. "Let's go to Yellow Three. Is there any word on when the Secretary will be back?"

"The latest is that he'll be in Washington tomorrow night."

"Fine. By that time the President will be in Moscow and Richards can carry the can."

"Good night, Clint."

"I hope it is, Jay," Devore said, and gently replaced the blue handset in its cradle.

43

Colonel Valery Adanin stretched his cramped muscles and turned on the preheaters of his special communications equipment. The jam of gear in his tiny capsule almost immobilized him. Only his hands were free. The Svoboda, he thought for the dozenth time, was a poor substitute for the Soyuz birds in which he had made his previous flights.

He was tracking northeast over some of the most desolate stretches of ocean now. Unseen in the darkness below lay the seamount tips of the Southwest Indian Ocean Ridge, the tiny dots of land known as the Prince Edward Islands. Fifteen minutes before, he had crossed the Princess Ragnhild Coast of Antarctica, and ten minutes from now he would pass over the Mozambique Channel on his way toward his rendezvous with Asia. His track would carry him almost directly over the city of Bombay, where he would receive his last fix from the tracking station at Daman. From that point on he would make no transmission until he had traversed the twenty-six hundred kilometers between the coast and the Turfan–Lop Nor area.

He relaxed on his couch as best he could, watching the seconds and minutes tick away on the luminous dial of the chronometer on the instrument panel centimeters from his face. His only view of the outside was through two tiny ports on either side of the capsule. He could see a small section of the eastern horizon outlined with the loom of the distant dawn. He could see no stars. He thought about his wife, but she was far away and seemed unreal to him. It was nearly twenty hours since his lift-off from Baikonur, and this was the beginning of his ninth orbit.

As a cosmonaut and an officer of the Strategic Rocket Forces, Adanin was in possession of a great deal of classified information. He was aware, for example, that there were at least six Svoboda satellites presently in orbit, and that every one of them followed the track he was now flying. The Turfan–Lop Nor area was examined closely by these unmanned vehicles every four hours of the day and night. When the order had come down from the Ministry of Defense for a manned mission over the same ground, he had assumed that what was wanted was more specifically refined data, observations that could be made only by a pilot.

His orders, however, filled him with curiosity. Adanin was not a political man. As a soldier, he did not concern himself with the nuances of the long-standing quarrel with the Maoists. It did seem to him, though, when he considered it, that transmitting long bursts of information to the low-frequency net at the very moment of overflying an installation the Chinese must surely regard as a high-priority target was an extremely provocative procedure.

It was true that direct observations of the new facilities in the Turfan Depression would be useful to the military planners of the Strategic Rocket Forces, and it was also true that Soviet space technology was not sufficiently sophisticated even yet to provide these planners with everything they would wish to know about what was being developed in the Turfan. Still, it seemed to Adanin that he was being asked to do something to which the Maoists might take violent exception.

It was not his job to make such judgments, and he put the disturbing thoughts out of his mind. To have been chosen to work directly with Marshal Yuri Leonov, the man the military hoped would succeed Valentin Kirov when the present First Secretary stepped down, was a source of great pride to Adanin. If this meant risking a niche in the Kremlin wall—well, he thought fatalistically, so be it.

The communications gear was now warmed up to transmitting temperatures. His heavily gloved fingers snapped the switches that would keep it all on stand-by. He allowed himself the luxury of a small touch on the attitude controllers, and the Svoboda rolled slightly to the right. He caught the movement expertly and stabilized the satellite in its new position. One had to be extremely careful with attitude control in a Svoboda. The supply of attitude-control jet fuel was severely limited.

He craned a bit inside his bubble helmet and looked below. It was still deep night in the Indian Ocean, but ahead and to the right he could see through the thin cloud cover the lights of the coast of the Indian subcontinent. The towns of Mangalore, Kozhikode, and, at the tip of the dark peninsula, Trivandrum showed a few lights. The dark bulk of Sri Lanka, to the east of the Gulf of Mannar, could barely be discerned. Farther still to the east, the loom of the dawn had grown brighter, but the Bay of Bengal and the Indochina Peninsula lay under a thick blanket of storm clouds.

Adanin wondered what it was like down there on the dark, humid earth. He could not imagine it. Nor could he imagine what the people who lived all their lives in such places might really be like. He was not an unkind or vicious man, but he shared the strong xenophobia of many of his countrymen. Dark people, Asiatics and Africans, would always be mysterious to him. He knew many officers who had served as advisers in places like Angola and Mozambique, in Africa, and in India and Vietnam along the underbelly of Asia. But even through them he had never been able to derive any sense of community with blacks and Asians. He understood that it was his duty to believe that it was vital to the future of the Soviet Union that these peculiar people in hot and muggy places should carry forward the triumph of Marxism. But deep inside himself he often wished that his country were not so committed to the Revolution in these equatorial countries—which, in too many cases, were hardly countries at all.

It was not his place to have opinions, and he took care to see to it that those he had remained silent and inert. But he knew, as almost all Soviet soldiers did, that Defense Minister Marshal Leonov shared his doubts about the Marxist-Leninist devotion of the dark races, and he felt justified in his bigotry.

He stared half-seeing at the immense shadowy mass of India moving beneath him; a sweating kennel of people so impoverished as to be subhuman. Yet, he thought, thanks to us, the government of that ocean of human flesh owns nuclear weapons. It was a chilling, disturbing thought. He looked ahead at the rising ramparts of the Himalayas. In the growing half-light, the snow and ice looked blue and purple; the deeper valleys of Nepal showed patches of dirty brown.

He checked the time. The instrument-panel chronometers showed 0301 hours, Moscow time, 0501 hours, local time. The transmissions from the Bombay station began to update the on-board computer. Adanin had only to watch and to listen as the machines exchanged telemetry and corrected the Svoboda's track. He felt a three-second burst from the forward-facing retros. The satellite was, apparently, fractionally too high for the run across Sinkiang.

The earth below was bathed now in a strange silvery half-light. There was still darkness over the whole of the view to the west, but the east was lighter as the high dawn approached, tinging the thin layer of the troposphere with layers of brightness. Not for the first time, Adanin thought how fortunate he was to be a Soviet cosmonaut and to see what so few people down there on the gloomy earth would ever see.

A late moon was rising swiftly, propelled by his orbital velocity into the black sky. It was gibbous, misshapen. He felt a pang of envy as it moved into full view. The Americans had walked there. Even now, after so long, it was almost miraculous to think about. *The* technical achievement, he admitted grudgingly, of the last thousand years. But what did they do now? Even their shuttle program limped along, poorly funded and neglected by their politicians and ignored by the masses. They were a volatile, uncertain lot, the Americans, sadly lacking in discipline.

Moonlight glinted on the thin ribbon of the Ganges River. The lights of Delhi were half obscured by the clouds. Ahead, quite near now, the snowfields of the Himalayas caught the moonlight.

At 0516 hours, local time, the Svoboda passed over the central Tibetan Plateau. Ahead lay Sinkiang, the land completely covered with thick clouds. Adanin switched the radar and infrared scanners to manual control. He positioned the special antennas to search ahead and directly below.

At 0519, his instruments told him that the Svoboda was being swept with radar transmissions from the ground. His distance from Lop Nor was five hundred and twelve kilometers, from the Turfan Depression, five hundred and sixty-six. He noted with just the slightest touch of apprehension that the radar search was being originated at Turfan, rather than Lop Nor, as might be expected. The Lop Nor test site was a highly sensitive area to the Chinese. Yet the origination of a search from the Turfan suggested that those conducting the sweep thought Lop Nor secondary.

His gloved fingers activated the radar-jamming devices on the Svoboda. He studied the instruments to see what effect his defenses were having on the Chinese radar. The pulses continued to be received by the Svoboda's antennas. The jamming was ineffectual.

The cathode-ray tube of his own radar showed a clear electronic map of what lay hidden beneath the clouds. He could see the returns from the K'unlun Shan Mountains, the shape of the tiny settlements along the rivers that threaded the southern edge of the Talimupendi, the great high desert of Sinkiang.

He began his measurements, working with the optical system of the satellite, to produce an accurate grid upon which could be located the exact features of the terrain below. From such measurements, charts accurate to a meter or less could be constructed, and the Chinese installations he had come to spy on located with absolute precision.

His own sky-search radar pinged to indicate that he was receiving detection and ranging radiation from far out in space. He grimaced. That would be the Americans with their newest device, the Nathan Hale satellites they imagined were still secret. He wondered if the synchronous satellite was making photographs of him, of the Svoboda making infrared and radar photographs of the Chinese.

Now, at the edge of his radar screen appeared the distinctive shape of the Great Turfan Depression. He pressed the transmit button on his low-frequency communications system and began to call. It was a complicated way to reach Marshal Leonov's control center (wherever it might be; Adanin had no idea). But by using the low-frequency net in Siberia—the gigantic grid built to reach even submerged submarines—the transmissions from the Svoboda were very nearly jamproof.

He had called once indicating his readiness to transmit specific data, and was waiting for a response from Russia, when the thread of ruby light appeared.

It did not seem to rise from below. One moment the sky was empty. The next it was bisected by a beam of light the color of blood.

Colonel Adanin, preoccupied with his mission, never saw it. It is doubtful if he would have seen it even if he had not been engrossed in his communications procedures. It did not search for the Svoboda. The radar pulses from the aiming devices below had centered the target exactly. The laser beam appeared, pierced the skin of the satellite as though it were mist. More than ten million kilowatts of energy were concentrated in the coherent beam: the entire output of a large nuclear-power installation plus the stored energy of twenty-four banks of giant accumulators. The discharge was instantaneous. The internal temperature of the Svoboda was raised in less than a hundredth of a second to four-hundred degrees Celsius, enough to explode the satellite and its occupant into an expanding cloud of steam, melted metal, and broken plastic. Some of the lighter alloys in the Svoboda ignited, but their oxygen content was too low to sustain combustion. What fire there was, was fed by the oxygen leached from the cloud of water vapor that had been Colonel Valery Adanin. Strings and tendrils of molten aluminum and steel spun and wound themselves into strange and fantastic shapes. The larger pieces of the satellite—the engines and certain of the heavier electronic assemblies—did not melt completely. Instead, they spun swiftly out from the core of the soundless blast, some to become temporary mini-satellites, others to start their long plunge into the atmosphere and destruction by the heat of friction.

The remains of Colonel Adanin swiftly coalesced into droplets that froze hard in perfect spheres, many tinged with red.

By the time the sun rose, these marbles of frozen bloody water would have spread out across almost a cubic kilometer of space. Of the Svoboda and its equipment, and of Colonel Adanin, there remained nothing recognizable.

At 0021 hours GMT, Nathan Hale 7, on station in synchronous orbit twenty-two thousand miles above central Asia, recorded the destruction of the Svoboda. The event was captured on infrared and ambient-light tape, the power of the laser beam was measured and its point of origin charted. These data were inscribed on magnetic disks and shunted by the American satellite's on-board computer into the ultra-high-frequency transmission loop.

In the glaring bright sunlight of space the Nathan Hale's antennas glinted as they sought out and fixed upon the tracking-station array on Christmas Island. The alignment was completed at 0026 GMT, and thirty seconds later Nathan Hale began emitting bursts of high-speed coded information.

At 1927 hours EST, the teleprinters at the Nathan Hale Center at Fort Monmouth, New Jersey, began to clatter. The duty officer, a dark-haired, pretty girl with captain's bars and Signal Corps insignia on her collar tabs, studied the print-outs until the machines fell silent. Then she ripped the sheet from the roll and picked up a telephone.

At a console in the War Room in the Pentagon (once again lightly staffed after the stand-down to Yellow Three ordered by General Devore), Second Lieutenant John Steinhart, three weeks out of the Air Force Academy, received the call.

When Fort Monmouth left the line, Steinhart sat, plagued with indecision. It was now after normal business hours in the Pentagon and, though the alert status still stood at Yellow Three, he did not relish the notion of bucking the information he had received up to the office where General Lazenby, a well-known Marine Corps martinet who ate Air Force second lieutenants for supper, occupied the duty chief's chair.

Steinhart did not hesitate for long. He did not understand the significance of what Nathan Hale was reporting, but he felt certain that it was not something that could be handled in a routine manner. He picked up his blue telephone and pressed the call.

"Chief's office. Kenney." The assistant on duty was a Navy warrant officer with whom Steinhart was only recently and slightly acquainted.

"I just received something from Nathan Hale Center that I think the Duty Chief should see, Mr. Kenney."

Like most warrant officers, Kenney had an inborn resistance to anything that did not come through proper channels. "Won't it wait until the 2000 distribution? General Lazenby is running a status check right now."

"I don't think we should wait, Mr. Kenney."

Warrant Officer Kenney sighed heavily, and Steinhart could hear him speaking to someone. Presently Kenney said, "Bring it up, then, Lieutenant."

Steinhart called his relief to take over his console and walked into the Communications Section, where the teleprinter was just completing the duplicate dispatch from Christmas Island through

Monmouth. He waited until the print-out was ejected from the machine, tore it from the roll, checked it over and started for the balcony.

Three minutes later, the Lieutenant had been ushered out of the Duty Chief's office by Kenney, and Lawrence Lazenby was on the telephone to Devore's quarters.

When the General came on the line, Lazenby, a craggy, sharp-featured man with pale eyes and aggressively short gray hair, said harshly: "The fucking Chinks have gone round the bend. They've just lasered a Russian satellite."

In the study of his house at Fort Myer, Devore's expression hardened into a frown. "Nathan Hale saw it?"

"Twenty minutes ago."

"So much for Chris Rosen's theory, then," Devore said bitterly. "Did we get good measurements?"

"Nathan Hale Center says we did. We have only the preliminary report so far. The rest of the data should be arriving any minute now."

"I'll be there in ten minutes. Get someone to chase down Rosen, will you? I want that bastard there when we go over the data. I want him to tell me again it can't be done."

"What about the President? He should be notified."

"He's airborne. We'll have a secure contact with him through Samos 23 in about half an hour. We'll hold it till then."

"What happens if the Russians tap us?"

"I'm sure they know they've lost a bird. They probably know how and why."

"Clint," Lazenby said, "the early data suggest that the Svoboda was manned."

"Christ! Are you sure?"

"Monmouth says Nathan Hale heard telemetry from the Svoboda before it got greased. They're refining the material to be sure—but what do you make of it, if so?"

"Maybe," Devore said bitterly, "the Russians have been listening to Christopher Rosen. I'm on my way." He hesitated

---

and then said decisively, "General, call the other Chiefs in. I want a full house until further notice."

The extraordinary meeting of the People's Action Committee of the Politburo of the People's Republic of China had convened at precisely eight-thirty in the morning, Peking time.

The gathering took place in a small meeting room in an annex to the Great Hall of the People, and the six men who were the de facto rulers of the People's Republic all attended. Chairman Chung Yee had insisted on that, in the name, he said, of collective leadership.

Despite the polemics displayed in the wall posters throughout the city and the several speeches delivered by members of the government over the last few days, there was less "collective leadership" in China at this moment than at any time since the death of Mao Tse-tung. Chung Yee described himself as a believer in the Maoist cult of continued revolution, but he was presently near to absolute ruler. All of the men gathered in the meeting room understood this. They also understood that it was now inner-party doctrine that this particular dictatorship of the proletariat would continue until the Russian threat was, once and for all, contained and resolved.

Foreign Minister Teng Chou-p'ing spoke briefly to his colleagues, explaining to them the Marxist-Leninist significance of the expected American visit and how it was to be used to lever the Soviet revisionists to retreat from their belligerent stance along the Manchurian and Mongolian borders.

The Minister of Defense, Marshal K'ang Pei, carried a heavy briefcase filled with materials that, the Chairman hoped, would make clear to the rest of the committee—Wang Po-ling, the Minister of Agriculture; Chiang En-kai, the Minister of Internal Security; and Kuei Lin-yuan, the General Secretary of the Communist party of the People's Republic—what military moves had been ordered prior to the Americans' arrival, and why.

"As you know," Teng said, regarding the circle of intent

faces across the bare expanse of the mahogany table around which they had gathered, "on March 3rd last—almost fifteen years to the day from the first encounter on the same ground—soldiers of the People's Army fought an engagement with troops of the Soviet revisionists on the Ussuri River islands. The battle was inconclusive, as all such skirmishes have been, but I mention it here to remind all of you how little the situation has changed in the last decade and a half." He looked at each member of the committee carefully, trying to judge their reaction to the news he was about to impart. He looked last and most carefully at Chairman Chung Yee's youthful face and opaque eyes. The Chairman nodded almost imperceptibly.

"For these and other reasons, with which you are all familiar, Chairman Chung has given orders that research and development go forward on a weapon intended to neutralize the advantage in nuclear terror rockets held over us by the Soviet revisionists."

There was a slight stir in the room. The members of the committee had heard rumors of special-weapons projects before, but this was the first official confirmation of something specifically designed to nullify the Damoclean threat of Soviet nuclear attack.

"After the Chairman has addressed us," Teng continued, "Marshal K'ang will distribute to each of you copies of a report describing the weapon in question in some detail, so that you will be able to brief your subordinates on what may be expected in the coming bargaining sessions with the Americans—and, through them, with the revisionists. I suggest that simplified versions of Marshal K'ang's report be prepared and distributed down to cadre level, so that the solidarity of the people may be shown to the Westerners." He looked again at Chung, who now rose to his feet and began to speak.

"This morning, Comrades," he said, "a new weapon was tested in Sinkiang. The data are as yet incomplete, but I can tell you that the test was totally successful." He paused for effect and then continued. "The project, which is code-named Dragon, was begun three years ago under the direction of Comrade Engineer Li Chin—who is the world's foremost expert on lasers."

The mention of the word "lasers" evoked the reaction the Chairman had been expecting. Even to men who had spent their lives as political activists and who scarcely understood even the derivation of the acronym, *laser* was a magic sound.

"I will have more to say on the subject of the Dragon project in a moment. First, I want Comrade Minister Marshal K'ang to explain to the committee certain military dispositions I have ordered—dispositions that relate both to the test made this morning and to the visit of the American President and his party, which we are expecting to take place within the week. Marshal K'ang, if you please."

The Minister of Defense stood and began to speak, in a harsh Cantonese dialect. Some of the men gathered in the meeting room had difficulty understanding him easily, for they were schooled in the Mandarin dialect. In China, as elsewhere in the socialist world, the leadership of the Communist party was drawn almost exclusively from the academic and intellectual classes. But if they had problems with the Marshal's dialect, they understood clearly enough what he was telling them in terms of movement and numbers.

"Last week, in expectation of the success of the Dragon test, the Comrade Chairman ordered me to reinforce the Eighth People's Army in Manchuria with units of the Fourth and Fifteenth armies, both of which are units consisting mainly of armor and nuclear artillery. By last night, the Ussuri River border was being guarded by one million eight hundred thousand soldiers. In addition to this, we have withdrawn fifty thousand infantry from the Tenth People's Army on the Burma-Vietnam frontier to reinforce the border units in Sinkiang and Mongolia. At present, we have nearly two and one-half million men facing the revisionists from Kazakhstan to Vladivostok. In addition to these forces, we have redeployed a number of units of the People's Air Force in support, and the eighteen IRBM sites in Manchuria, Mongolia, and Sinkiang have been placed on alert." He finished talking and sat down abruptly.

Chairman Chung, who had been observing the other members of the People's Action Committee, was not surprised to see their shocked expressions. They had all grown too accustomed to the state of near-war between the People's Republic and the Kremlin revisionists. It was as well that they understand fully the risks involved in the actions necessary to resolve, once and for all, the question of who would lead the socialist world. He had a further shock prepared for them and he stood to deliver it.

"Comrades, now I will amplify my statements about the Dragon project and this morning's test. Comrade Li's laser device is primarily a weapon of defense. It was—and is—intended to protect the air space—and the space above the air space—of the People's Republic. As you know, the revisionists and the Americans have been violating our sovereignty with their orbital devices for many years. This morning, we served notice upon them both that they can no longer spy upon us with impunity."

He paused again, gauging the effect his words were having. He concluded that the effect was satisfactory. The members of the committee had reached that peculiar state of mixed enthusiasm and apprehension necessary to confirm still again his strong leadership.

"As I say, the Dragon device is a defensive weapon. It has been designed to destroy ballistic missiles. When Dragon lasers are in full production—" it would not do, he thought as he paused, to dwell on the technical problems such production would pose and how extremely difficult it would be to provide a full laser defense with power—"when in full production, they will make the People's Republic and our revolution immune from any attack by either the revisionists or their imperialist apologists. But—" he fixed his subordinates with a hard, opaque look—"in view of the negotiations we will shortly be undertaking, it has been necessary to make clear our strength. That is why I authorized, in the name of the People, the test conducted in Sinkiang this morning." He leaned forward and spoke slowly and with great clarity, his knuckles resting lightly on the carved mahogany table. "This morning, before this meeting, the Dragon destroyed a Russian satellite of the Svoboda type, one of the series the revisionists have used to spy on our nuclear-test grounds at Lop Nor."

The members of the committee sat in stunned silence. It was the reaction Chung Yee had expected. He took from his briefcase a copy of the *Red Book* and opened it. "For those of us who may fall into the error of faintheartedness, I offer these words written by the first Chairman. 'If anyone attacks us, we will wipe him out thoroughly, resolutely, wholly and completely. We do not strike rashly, but when we do strike, we must win. *We must never be cowed by the bluster of reactionaries.*'" He snapped the book closed and stood erect, his face stern and uncompromising. "I leave you with that important thought, Comrades. You will now return to your duties and organize discussion groups among your coworkers to prepare the people for the difficult days ahead. I wish to conduct negotiations with the Americans assured that the people are confident of success and satisfaction in our long-standing quarrel with the bandits in the Kremlin."

Not one of the men in the room protested the tone of the Chairman's statement. They did not even consider that, far from being attacked, the People's Republic had committed an act of war against the Soviet Union. A generation had accepted the substitution of rhetoric and ideology for consideration, which had produced the inevitable result: a power structure incapable of rational caution. Mao Tse-tung, had he lived to see it, would have been proud of his disciples.

44

The President of the United States regarded the slender, taut woman seated across the small table. Jane McNary sat on the edge of the seat, her thin face composed and filmed with hostility. The compartment where they sat alone was almost silent; the shrill sound of the jet engines muffled by the heavy soundproofing of the 767's fuselage. Beyond the window lay a heavy darkness. The plane was flying at thirty-five thousand feet above the North Sea in thick cloud. The slave instruments set into the bulkhead below the Presidential seal showed an airspeed of almost four hundred knots and a compass bearing of eighty-eight degrees—almost due east.

Cleveland Lambert had never approved of McNary, but he had never before actively disliked her. The fact that she had managed, with the assistance of Senator DeWitt Sutton, to blackmail her way aboard this sensitive flight, had changed all that. Furthermore, he had been told, no more than five minutes before, by Paul Lyman that McNary was the source of the rather calumnious story about the dancer Bronwen Wells and Harry Grant. It added to the President's considerable anger that Grant, the man known around Washington as the Iron Colonel for his austerity, had allowed himself to be put in such an equivocal position. He was aware that Grant was waiting for him in the study—waiting in a kind of informal arrest. The President intended that Grant should continue to wait. He hoped, with all the force of his irritation, that Grant was damned worried.

"In the words of one of my less than illustrious predecessors,

Miss McNary," the President said, "I want to make something perfectly clear to you. You have forced your way onto this aircraft by methods better suited to the gutter than to the conduct of international affairs. Be fully aware that it won't be forgotten."

"I never imagined it would be, Mr. President," McNary said as coldly, "though I must say I have always thought that international affairs *were* conducted in the gutter. I don't think it is necessary for me to justify my methods. The American people have a right to know what is being done in their name by their elected officials. I've always believed that, and nothing has happened recently to change my opinion. Your administration is following all the old pathways, Mr. President. When you were elected there was a feeling that some sort of new age was upon us—no more secrecy, no more covert operations. It hasn't worked out that way, and I feel perfectly content with what I've done to learn what this fantastic voyage is all about."

"Very well," the President said. "I won't comment about your opinion on the conduct of foreign policy. You are here because premature disclosure of this mission would defeat its purpose—and for no other reason. I will give you the information you need to know now, and again later. You will not have access to free communications and your story will not be released until we return to Washington. Those are the conditions. There will be no bargaining now or later. You are here—you will have to accept that as the only concession I am prepared to make."

"I suppose, Mr. President, that I should consider myself fortunate to be an observer," McNary said acidly, "but please do not expect me to be grateful or to approve of these police-state methods."

The President smiled. "You have a genuinely unpleasant way of expressing yourself, Miss McNary." He paused, eyes fixed on the woman's thin, finely made face. "Before anything else is said, I do want to comment on one thing. I understand from Paul Lyman that you were to some degree responsible for the story that appeared today in the *Daily Express* about Harry Grant and that ballet girl."

"I spoke to some of my English friends about it, yes."

"Jealousy, Miss McNary?"

"Certainly not. When a Presidential aide disappears with the mistress of a murdered Russian diplomat, that's news."

"I see. Then it is of no interest to you that Harry Grant is aboard this plane."

McNary's expression grew even colder. "Almost none at all."

"I sent Colonel Grant ahead to speak to that Russian diplomat, Miss McNary, because we had reason to believe he had information that bore directly on this journey."

A flicker of interest showed in McNary's eyes. "And did Harry speak to him?"

"Unfortunately, no. The man was killed returning from France. But Grant would have had reason to think the woman was in danger."

"Gallant Colonel Grant," McNary said nastily. "And was she?"

"I don't know the answer to that," the President said. "And frankly speaking, it no longer matters. Protecting her is a matter for the British police. I do understand that her apartment was ransacked and she was threatened in some way."

"By whom, if I may ask?"

"We originally thought it might have been the KGB."

"That again. Every time an American administration becomes involved in some covert game-playing, the old bogieman of Russian spies come up. That is really out of date, Mr. President."

"If you think that, Miss McNary, you won't be capable of understanding what I am going to tell you now."

"I'm listening."

"I wonder if you are. Your view of politics and the world is very biased, Miss McNary. You have always seemed to me to be one of those who automatically think the worst of your own country and its government, while speaking out for our enemies." He forestalled her retort with a gesture. "We *do* have enemies, Miss McNary. Sometimes it is necessary to work with them, and it is always necessary to assure them that negotiation is better than confrontation. But there are those in the world who wish us ill. Accept that, even if only for the next few moments, or nothing I say to you will have any meaning."

"I don't believe you for a second, Mr. President. I have always thought that most of our troubles have been brought on ourselves with our meddling abroad and our exploitation of the poor and helpless all over the world. But, all right, I'll listen and pretend that what you tell me is true."

"Given your background, I suppose that is all I can ask," the President said, almost sadly.

He stood and walked to the closed door, balancing against the slight movements of the plane in the mildly turbulent air.

"The situation between Russia and China has been tense for years," he said, regarding her closely, "but recently a new element has been introduced. The Chinese—with the help of an American-born scientist, by the way, a man with political beliefs not too dissimilar to yours—have built a very special sort of weapon. A laser, Miss McNary. If it works—and we think it will—it will seriously upset the balance of nuclear power between the Chinese and the Russians. I'm not an engineer or a soldier, but it is obvious to me that one of the first applications of such a device would be to use it as an ABM. In this rather insane world, Miss McNary, a nation that can defend itself against ballistic-missile attack ironically becomes a terrible threat to the peace."

He sat on the arm of a seat across the aisle and studied the newswoman's skeptical expression. "We know about your 'Cranmer' conversations, Miss McNary. The British are not nearly so sensitive about intercepting transatlantic telephone calls as we have had to become. Sutton and, indirectly, Chris Rosen, are going to have some explaining to do about the classified information they have passed to you."

McNary's lips tightened angrily. "You had my telephone calls monitored? That's outrageous."

"I'm sure that's the way you'll describe it when you write your story," Lambert said dryly, "but as it happens, it was not done at my request. SIS has had a long-time interest in you, and I can't blame them. You have been a vocal supporter of every radical cause that ever gave our British friends a headache, from terrorists in Rhodesia to the IRA in Northern Ireland. I can't find it in me to complain to them about it."

"Particularly when their spying on me serves your purpose, Mr. President," McNary said.

Lambert studied her in silence. He had to credit her with the courage of her convictions, he thought. She didn't lack for bravery.

"I suppose," McNary said in the same acid-laced voice, "that the Iron Colonel has been a useful source of information about me as well."

"I think you know better than that," the President said quietly. "It has been suggested more than once to Colonel Grant that he might find a more suitable—friendship. And yes, there have been those who thought he might turn his relationship with you to practical use. Harry Grant has never done that, as I am certain you know."

McNary's eyes grew veiled, and the President sensed that he had touched a hidden soft spot in her feminist-radical armor. It would be ironic, he thought, if she really had some tender feeling for Grant, and more ironic still if she should lose him irretrievably because of a single mistake in judgment on his part and a spiteful act on hers. But in the final analysis, both Jane McNary and Harry Grant were expendable in the service of a greater need. It didn't matter what happened between them now.

The President had the disturbing thought that such a view of life was more in keeping with the opposition's ethic than his own. Perhaps, he thought, it was not a question of the end justifying the means, but, rather, that there *were* no genuine ends. Means became the end-all and be-all. It was a damned harsh world and people were *used*—because imperfect societies had no better way to conduct human affairs.

"We are on our way to Moscow, as I'm sure you know," he said. "I have offered my services as a mediator between the Soviets and the People's Republic. There will be a meeting with Valentin Kirov and Viktor Krasin immediately on our arrival. We hope to work out a declaration on the new weapon that I will then carry to Peking, along with a plan to resolve the dispute between Russia and the People's Republic. That much you know from Senator Sutton. What you don't know—and what none of us are sure about—is what has been happening in the Kremlin. We know that Kirov is ill. How ill, we are not certain. We know that there are factions at work. One of the most militant and potentially dangerous is headed by Marshal Yuri Leonov, the Defense Minister. He is and always has been violently anti-Chinese, but we simply don't know how deeply his influence has penetrated the Soviet power structure."

The President's tone grew edged. "Perhaps we would know more, and could act with more wisdom, if the intelligence community hadn't been gutted by the Suttons—" He raised a hand. "I know what you think of that, Miss McNary, but the simple fact is that the CIA has never recovered fully from the congressional investigations of the late '70s. Perhaps some good was done by that fit of mooning—but I doubt it."

He favored her with a dour smile. "Do you know what I mean by mooning, or are you too young to remember? When I was in college, there was a fad for sticking one's bare rump out of automobile windows. God knows why, but it made some people feel 'liberated.' And that is exactly the way I think of the 'exposés' by those chaste committees. The self-righteous displays and careless disclosures turned reform into vulnerability. Since

321

that time, of course, no allied intelligence service has trusted ours. And our own hasn't been worth much.

"That is why I sent Harry Grant to London, to do a job that should have been done by the CIA. The trouble is that Grant isn't an intelligence officer."

"No, Mr. President," McNary said, "he isn't. But you've rather made him into a kind of White House 'plumber,' haven't you?"

"If I have, it isn't because I wanted to. I had to try with him. At least I knew he could be trusted."

"Yes, you would feel that way."

"I still do."

"You didn't expect him to run off with a material witness, of course."

"No," the President said, "I didn't expect that."

The light over the locked door came on and there was a soft ping. The President stood and opened the door. Lyman stood in the aisle with a Telex print-out. His face was pale. "This came with the scheduled Washington contact, Mr. President."

Lambert took the sheet and read it through twice. He frowned and remained silent for most of a minute. Then abruptly, he said to Lyman, "Confirm this. Get Colonel Grant and have him take over military communications."

"Yes, sir," Lyman said, and hurried toward the front of the plane.

McNary said, almost archly, "Bad news, Mr. President?"

"This discussion is ended now, Miss McNary," he said, dismissing her. Then, almost as an afterthought, he stopped her and said, "It may be of interest to you that the Chinese weapon that concerns us is a success. They have just used it to provoke what could be the last war this sorry planet will have to endure."

Yuri Leonov watched the heavy blast doors of the Launch Control Command Center swing ponderously closed. There was a kind of mystical inevitability to the smooth movement of the two-meter-thick portals. The Marshal's bladelike features were composed and he felt a deep inner calm.

The command center of the Aral'sk Strategic Rocket Regiment was not so complete, or so well protected, as the center in Moscow, but it would do, he thought. It would take nothing less than a direct hit by a nuclear weapon in the multimegaton range to destroy the bunker and disrupt the communications network his technicians had patched together. A smile played over his lips as he thought of the clumsy efforts the fainthearts in the Kremlin had made to thwart him. He was far too well prepared for the men who were even now gathering fearfully around Viktor Krasin in Moscow.

The control teams were quietly waiting at their consoles, the communicators standing ready. From time to time an update on the readiness of the regiment's SS-19 missiles, now all fully retargeted, flashed on the television screens that lined the walls of the deep shelter.

General Oblensky, seated with him in the center, was listening to a report on a telephone. The television landlines had been disrupted by the junta in the Kremlin, but information leaked through their dams in a flood. Leonov's painstaking plans were proving to be as foolproof as genius could devise.

Oblensky looked up and said, "The American aircraft is now over the Baltic north of Gdansk, Comrade Marshal." He paused, listening. Then: "Naval Operations Hanoi reports that Serpent, Adder, Cobra, and Crocodile are on station in Zone Omega together with Beech, Oak, and Elm. We still have access to the low-frequency net. Are there any new orders for them?"

The naval task force in the China Sea was only a backstop threat. Leonov could not be absolutely certain that the ships' captains would attack on command, since they still believed that they were taking part in an exercise, Task Red Glory. But the presence of the vessels in the China Sea was enough to support his strategy.

"Tell them to remain on station. The exercise is about to begin."

Oblensky, unusually pale, spoke rapidly into the telephone.

The call light on the television monitor linking the command center to the administration block on the surface winked. Leonov pressed the receive button. Feodorovna's face appeared. "Novikov has moved three more battalions of KGB troops into Aral'sk, Comrade Marshal. We are entirely surrounded now."

"Any movement?"

"None. They are holding their positions, that's all."

Leonov could not resist grinning. "I thought that would be their plan. They'll do nothing until the Americans are safely gone."

Feodorovna spoke with great calmness. "We have word from Usovo, Comrade Marshal. Valentin Kirov is dead. The medical teams are being detained incommunicado."

So the old man was finally done, then, Leonov thought with satisfaction. That was a bonus, something one could not have hoped for. The schemers in the Kremlin had a clear choice now. They could cancel the American visit or they could keep the First Secretary's death secret until the Americans had come and gone. If they had arrested the Usovo medical teams, their choice was clear. They were opting for the latter plan.

"Are they jamming our radio communications?" he asked.

"Yes, Comrade Marshal."

"Send a messenger out to the KGB troops. Tell him to notify Comrade Krasin or Comrade Novikov that I wish to speak to the Politburo in—" he glanced at a large wall chronometer—"in one hour. Tell him to say that if there are any attempts to penetrate the defenses of this base I will take appropriate action."

"Yes, Comrade Marshal."

He smiled at the image on the television screen. "Are you concerned, Feodorovna?"

The woman's face was composed as she said, "I have complete faith in your judgment, Comrade Marshal."

"Good, Comrade Colonel. Is General Zabotin with you?"

"He is inspecting our troops guarding the base perimeter, Comrade Marshal."

Leonov considered. "Let Zabotin be the messenger," he finally said. "If he has the stomach for it." His tone was almost boyish. "He might wish to put some distance between himself and this base for the next few hours in any case."

Feodorovna said, "We have received a report that the Chinese have destroyed Colonel Adanin's Svoboda."

"Yes," Leonov said, hiding his exultance. The idiots had taken the bait at the first cast. He would have had difficulty in ordering the full sequence of manned launches from his present equivocal position, but the Maoist anarchists had reacted with typical rashness and done exactly what he had hoped they would do.

Oblensky, still on the telephone, touched his shoulder. "The American aircraft is crossing the coast now, Comrade Marshal. They are in Soviet air space."

"Begin the countdown," Leonov said. "Now let's see what our friends in the Kremlin are made of."

Sometime after 7:00 P.M., EST, Gerald Ransome finished clearing his desk in preparation for leaving the CIA compound in Langley, Virginia.

Warned by Dalland that there might soon be trouble over the leakage of classified material from his section, he was desperately worried. Dalland had made it quite clear that if someone became expendable in the event of an investigation, that someone was going to be Ransome. Dalland had even had the bad taste to joke about it, but Ransome had the suspicion that he had not been so light-hearted in the course of his interview with Senator Sutton and Vice President Hood. Hood might be a party hack and the butt of edged humor around Washington, but there was never any assurance that the babbling man might not babble to someone who could stir up an immense storm. He could even tell the President, and God alone knew what that might lead to.

So Ransome has resolved, on his own, to rid himself of as many ties as possible to the information he had been confiding to Dalland, who was proving too faithless and too dangerous a friend for comfort.

He had deliberately stayed at work late to deliver to the Communications Section, personally and at the last possible moment, the material Colonel Grant had requested on Marshal Leonov and his protégé Colonel Aleksandr Voronin. In his anxiety to cover the delay he had caused, he had ordered a second computer run and a more detailed print-out. The result ran to several pages, and he hoped that the bulk of the material would explain the fact that it had taken him almost three days to deliver it to the President's man.

In the Communications Section, Jill Tabor, a bored GS-9, accepted Ransome's packet and reproachfully signed the charge slip.

"Does all this have to go?" she asked.

"Don't blame me. The Iron Colonel asked for it," he replied.

"Big deal," the girl said with a frown. She had a date at ten and transmitting this packet over the cipher lines to the Pentagon would take at least twenty minutes. "Is it time-stamped? I don't see any log entry for it."

"Jill, dear. Just send it—please?"

Tabor sighed heavily and set the packet of computer readouts on the feed rack of the transmitter. "Now," she said, "I have to sit here and watch this stuff while you run off home. Thanks a bunch."

Ransome smiled at her and said, "I'll make it up to you." He was heartily glad to be rid of Colonel Grant's damned packet and gladder still that it was finally in the pipeline and on the way— much good it would do Grant or anyone else.

At the Pentagon end of the cipher wire, the print-outs began to appear in replica. The duty Communications Clerk there leaned across his console to speak with his supervisor, Major Appleton.

"There's a packet coming in from Langley, Major. It is coded to Colonel Grant. Shall we send it along with the next transmission to Olympus?" He spoke the code name for the President with familiarity: he had transmitted many messages over the years to a Presidential plane via one of the military satellites.

Appleton, a pudgy man with round, prominent blue eyes, peered carefully at the world-time chronometer on the wall and said, "Olympus will be receiving from Nathan Hale in two minutes. Let me see what you have." He walked around the cipher console to look at the print-outs accumulating in the bin. "It just looks like some sort of background stuff on the Soviet Defense Minister. I don't know that we ought to send it right away. It depends on how much else has to go. The brass upstairs are in a flap over some Russian cosmonaut buying the farm—"

The duty Communications Clerk ventured an opinion. "I hear Colonel Grant can be an ironass, Major. Maybe we ought to tack it onto the transmission just in case it's important."

Major Appleton succumbed to irritation. It had been a long day and he was anxious to get home. The crews in all the departments had gone from Red One to Yellow Three, and now this flurry of activity because something happened to some stupid Russian satellite. And now here was an E/5 making suggestions about what ought to be sent on to Olympus. It was on the tip of his tongue to say that he, not a duty clerk, would make decisions about what went out on the net and what waited for routine transmission. But the clerk had been right about one thing: Grant could, indeed, be an ironass when he wanted to be. Why take chances?

"All right," he said. "When everything else has gone out, you can put this on the line. If Grant wants it, who are we to say he can't have it?" He took his cap from the rack, buckled the belt on the trenchcoat he was already wearing, and headed for the door. "Watch the store, Sergeant," he said loftily and left.

"Officers," the duty clerk muttered. "She-yit." Then he settled down to wait for the long transmission from the CIA headquarters in Langley to be completed.

45

On the flight deck of the aircraft now designated Air Force One, Grant relieved the crewman on duty at the military-communications console.

"We're in the net with Nathan Hale now, Colonel," the Sergeant said. "Telefax material will start coming in as soon as the codes are synchronized." The Presidential communications codes of the Olympus series were computer-changed at irregular intervals ranging from thirty seconds to five minutes, making it nearly impossible for unauthorized listeners on the net to intercept anything but a meaningless garble of signals.

Grant glanced forward to where the flight crew worked. Over Major Barrow's shoulders he could see the flight instruments and beyond the window, a solid darkness. The aircraft was flying in heavy cloud. The radio operator worked over his equipment, talking in a low voice to the Russian air controllers at the Pskov Air Traffic Control Center. He finished his transmission, listened for a time, acknowledged the Russian message, and leaned forward to speak to Barrow.

"They are scrambling an escort of MIG-37s, Major. They say they will keep a separation of two thousand meters."

Barrow nodded and spoke to the main cabin, then craned to look back at Grant. "Everything all right, Colonel?"

Grant ignored the peace gesture and fixed his attention on the encoder-decoder read-out. The numbers came up and vanished, changed in swift sequences. The on-board computer began to print out an intelligence update on the presumed state of First

Secretary Valentin Kirov's health. The source, Grant guessed, was some CIA station in one of the satellite capitals. Like almost all CIA reports, its accuracy initially had to be considered.

Printing one full line at a time, the computer ejected its material in swift, jerky movements. When it paused and sent the "more coming" signal, Grant ripped the sheets free and examined them briefly.

0100 HOURS GMT. SECURITY INCREASED AROUND KIROV DACHA AT USOVO. MEDICAL TEAMS ATTENDING HAVE NOT BEEN RELIEVED. IT IS BELIEVED HERE THAT FIRST SECRETARY'S CONDITION IS SLIGHTLY IMPROVED. REASON FOR INCREASED SECURITY IS BEING EVALUATED. MORE TO COME.

The information, Grant thought, was hardly worthy of the name. But he folded the sheets lengthwise and handed them to the duty sergeant. "For the President," he said.

The aircraft moved through a series of softly thumping rolls as turbulence in the clouds affected the flight path. Grant asked the radar-navigator, who sat across the narrow aisle from him, "What's our position now?"

"We are over Žagarė, Colonel," Stevenson answered. "Estimating Moscow in forty minutes."

The computer showed the Pentagon code and began once again to print. 0100 HOURS GMT. STRATEGIC ANOMALY, SATELLITE DATA CONFIRM STRATEGIC ROCKET REGIMENT ARAL'SK RETARGETED OUT OF SEQUENCE. UNEXPLAINED CONCENTRATIONS OF LIGHT ARMORED FORCES AND INFANTRY POSSIBLY SECURITY TROOPS IN ARAL'SK AREA. JCS HAVE ORDERED STAND-DOWN TO YELLOW THREE. REQUEST PRESIDENTIAL AUTHORITY TO UPGRADE ALERT STATUS. SIGNED MULLER.

The computer was silent for a dozen seconds and then printed: FURTHER ANOMALY FOR PRESIDENT'S INFORMATION. SAMOS 23 HAS DETECTED CONCENTRATION OF SOVIET NAVAL UNITS IN CHINA SEA. HEAVY ENCODED RADIO TRAFFIC ON ALL SOVIET MILITARY COMMUNICATIONS NETS. MORE TO COME.

.   .   .

"Interesting, that. What do you make of it, old man?"

Grant turned to see Ian Ballard standing behind him, swaying slightly with the movements of the aircraft.

"How did you get here, Ballard?" Grant asked sharply.

"Part of the British delegation—or whatever it should be called. I moved heaven and earth for the assignment, too." Ballard's expression was bland, but Grant detected an odd excitement in his stance and manner.

Ballard inclined his head toward the print-outs. "Do you read anything from all that?"

"This is all classified material, Ballard."

"I'm cleared, old man. All the way. If you can't trust your allies, whom can you trust?" He perched on the arm of a seat before the console and said, "You'll be happy to know that the girl you were so concerned about is quite safe now. Special Branch has tidied up the situation in London. The Provo we talked about is no longer with us."

Grant, despite his annoyance at discovering Ballard aboard the plane and snooping, felt a surge of relief. "You found him, then? The second gunman?"

"Yes. I had word just before we left Hurn."

"Did you also find out *why?*"

"Not that, I'm afraid. And the Irishman—he *was* an Irishman, by the way—won't be in any condition to tell us now. But Miss Wells is quite safe. You put yourself in hot water for nothing, old man. It wasn't necessary to spirit her away. Where did you take her, by the way?"

"To Rye."

"Ah, of course. Quaint, picturesque, and all that. One can't imagine a pretty woman coming to any harm in a place like Rye."

"If she stayed there," Grant said.

"As a matter of fact," Ballard said, "she didn't. That story in the *Express* flushed her out, I imagine. One of our people spotted her arriving at Waterloo Station on the eleven-fifteen from Ashford. She was met by a fellow from the Soviet Embassy —the local *rezident*." Ballard's eyes were bright and his expression speculative. "He drove her first to her flat and then to Madame Zelinskaya's in Hobhouse Close. What do you make of that?"

Grant's face felt frozen. "Are you telling me she's KGB?"

"Not at all, old man. But Zelinskaya is. Has been for years. Odd, isn't it?"

"What is odd is that you didn't see fit to tell me this before."

Ballard shrugged impassively. "No need, you see. I knew you'd bring whatever you found there to us for examination. Bad luck it didn't come to anything. But there was really no necessity for passing the word back to Zelinskaya that we have always known about her. We can't be sure Miss Wells wouldn't carry tales, can we? And now she's gone back to Zelinskaya's straight away. It's something to think about, surely?"

Grant ripped the sheets out of the printer and folded them. His mind was racing over the events of the last seventy-two hours. Ballard was right, of course. Bronwen *had* been Voronin's mistress. If Ballard knew the facts, she *had* left Rye almost at once. She *had* gone straight to Madame Zelinskaya. But he still could not believe that what Ballard was implying might be true. His every instinct cried out against it.

The computer began to print again. It was a routine assessment of Soviet dispositions in Eastern Europe, the sort of thing sent to the President almost hourly, wherever he might be. Ballard watched with mild interest, saying nothing.

Then suddenly the print-out stopped. The code-change lights flashed the numerical symbol for an Intelligence Alert notice. Immediately a new sequence began.

INTEL ALERT. PRIORITY ONE. FROM DEVORE, JCS. ACKNOWLEDGE CODE CHANGE.

Grant typed out the acknowledgment and waited. The computer began again.

ADDITIONAL TO EARLIER PRIORITY ONE ON DESTRUCTION OF SOVIET SATELLITE OVER TURFAN DEPRESSION AREA SINKIANG. NOW CONFIRMED SATELLITE WAS MANNED.

The computer fell silent, as though waiting for some response.

Grant turned to look at Ballard, who had read the print-out as it appeared.

The Englishman's expression was strangely, almost savagely, pleased. "So they have decided to test their toy," he said. "You wouldn't think they would be so stupid."

Grant got to his feet and tapped Stevenson on the shoulder. "Take the console. I'm going back to see the President."

He shoved past Ballard and walked down the forward companionway into the main cabin. McNary looked up, startled by his sudden appearance.

"Harry—"

"Later," he said brusquely, and moved through the cabin to the passageway separating it from the President's private quarters. He knew Martin Kroll, the Secret Service guard on duty. "I have to see him now, Martin."

"He's with the Britishers, Colonel."

"This takes precedence," Grant said.

Kroll shrugged and rapped once on the door. Lambert's voice came through the metal door. "Yes, what is it?"

Before Kroll could announce him, Grant was through the door and inside the President's quarters. The two British observers, Minister of State Vincent Sawkins and Under-Secretary Raymond Matthews, looked up from the material they had been discussing with the President. From a window seat, Helena Lambert smiled a greeting.

The President did not smile. "All right, Colonel," he said coldly, "what is it?"

Grant handed him the print-outs. Lambert's lips tightened into a thin line. After sitting in silence for a moment, he said, "Set up a three-way link with Moscow and Washington. If Kirov is not available, I want Viktor Krasin. On the Washington end I want Devore and Richards, if he's back. If not, I want him found. How long will it take?"

"Ten minutes. Less, if the Russians are awake."

The President passed the print-outs to Sawkins, then regarded Grant steadily for what seemed to Grant a long time. "We'll have a personal talk before we reach Moscow, Harry. Right now, what do you make of all this?"

"The timing is too peculiar to be coincidence, Mr. President. Something damned strange is going on inside the Soviet Union— damned strange and damned wrong."

"I think you're right." The President addressed the Englishmen. "Care to speculate, gentlemen?"

"I haven't a clue, Mr. President," Matthews said. "But it feels very dicey to me, knowing what we know about Kirov's condition."

"A military coup?"

"That's always possible, Mr. President," Sawkins said. "It could be Novikov—the police chap. Or Yuri Leonov. Yes, it could certainly be something like that. But these—" he tapped the print-outs—"don't indicate enough internal movement fully to support such a conclusion. I mean, the troops would be moving on Moscow, not Aral'sk, wouldn't they?"

"That's the way I would expect any such stroke to work," Lambert said. "And I'd also expect a great deal more military activity." He looked at Grant. "Is anything else coming through?"

"There was a more-to-come signal, sir."

"All right, Harry. Thank you. Get back to it and keep me informed. Where, exactly, are we now?"

"We have passed Žagarė. We should be across the Soviet Lithuanian border in five or ten minutes. Pskov Air Traffic Control informed us that we now have an escort." His face remained impassive. "MIGs, Mr. President. A 'guard of honor.' "

A ghost of a smile touched the President's face. "This isn't Vietnam, Colonel. They mean us no harm."

"Yes, Mr. President."

"Call me the moment the threeway is in operation." He paused, considered, and as an obvious afterthought added: "Harold Hood had better be on hand, as well. See to it, Harry."

"Yes, sir." Grant nodded to the First Lady, who was no longer smiling, and left the compartment.

He passed by Jane McNary without a glance. When he reached the forward compartment and the communications console, a sheaf of print-outs was accumulating in the rack. Each page was imprinted with the legend REPLY TO REQUEST FOR BACKGROUND INFORMATION. Each carried, too, a historical-political code designation and a heading that read: CRISIS CONFRONTATION LECTURES. CROSS INDEX: LEONOV, YURI I., DEFENSE MINISTER, MARSHAL OF THE SOVIET AIR FORCE CODE NAME: BOYAR.

As he reached for the sheets, Grant noted that Ballard had gone deadly pale.

46

"The Americans are over Novosokolniki, Comrade Marshal," the deputy Communications Officer reported. "They are being escorted by a squadron of fighters and their estimated time of arrival at Moscow is 0601 hours, Moscow time."

"Thank you, Captain," Leonov said quietly. His eyes covered the circuit of the deep shelter. The television screens on the walls showed that the regiment's missiles were now at full readiness. Two had been targeted as air bursts; the remainder were programmed to make a footprint one hundred twenty-five kilometers by thirty kilometers. The first impacts would be in the Turfan Depression; the remainder would strike in a southeasterly direction and saturate the Lop Nor area.

Leonov felt a certain regret that after so many years of preparation, he had been unable to devise a method of keeping himself informed about the state of readiness to retaliate in the Chinese People's Republic. He realized that relations between the USSR and China were such that the People's Liberation Army never completely stood down in the regions facing the Soviet Union. He knew, too, that the destruction of Adanin's Svoboda was a deliberate provocation and must certainly have been accompanied by military moves.

It was not essential, he thought, to be informed about the intentions of the Chinese. One could surmise certain things: that they would reinforce the Manchurian armies; that they would alert their meager missile defenses (the destruction of the weapon in the Turfan would come none too soon in that regard); and that they would bring their IRBMs to some low level of readiness. It would be a low level because they could never imagine that their provocations would result in so terrible, so well-prepared, a counterstroke.

He glanced at Sergei Oblensky working at his nearby command-and-control console. There had been a number of times when he had been uncertain of Oblensky's absolute loyalty and obedience. But the man seemed to be functioning efficiently and with dedication at his complex tasks of preparing for the launch.

One had to assume a certain sang-froid, Leonov thought, in these matters. It was one thing to lecture about the wisdom of pre-emptive action in a musty lecture hall at the Military Academy. It was something different to sit, as now, sealed into the deep earth and know that within a few moments one was about to bring to life one of those speculative and academic situations described in the lecture syllabus.

If he were a softer man, he thought, he might even feel a certain compassion for the foolish Americans, who were about to lend, by their presence, an appearance of legitimacy to an act that some would call "treason" and all would certainly call "aggression." But these are the realities, as he had long ago concluded, of military geotechnics. Stalemates could not be allowed to continue indefinitely, and he intended to see that the stalemate between the USSR and the Maoists was resolved in the Soviet's favor.

A communicator pinged and he lifted the handset. "Yes?"

The voice of Colonel Feodorovna in the administration building above came through. "We have a message from Foreign Secretary Krasin, Comrade Marshal. They will re-establish the television link and speak to you in three minutes."

"Very good, Comrade Feodorovna. Now you had better come below ground with us here."

There was a note of relief in her voice, Leonov noted. It was possible, of course, that Novikov might risk an attempt to break into the deep shelter. Given time, he might even succeed. But he would hardly do such a thing one hour before Krasin's precious Americans arrived in Moscow. *Krasin's* Americans? More mine than his, he thought. The entire implementation of the plan depended, as many a thoughtful student had discovered, on a random factor: in this case, the chance to involve the Americans (and the shadowy threat of their still-considerable power) in the service of the Soviet Union. The ulimate détente, he thought grimly.

"Has Zabotin returned to the base, Comrade Colonel?"

"No. I think they are detaining him."

"As one would expect from policemen like Novikov. All right, come down at once. I want you here when I speak to the Politburo."

General Oblensky cleared his throat.

"Yes, Oblensky?"

"We are ready to go into the prelaunch sequence, Comrade Minister." He paused.

Is he wondering, Leonov thought, whether or not I really intend to carry this thing through? Or does he imagine that at the end, when the moment comes, it will all turn out to be a threat, a gesture?

"Hold on the prelaunch. We must discuss matters with my colleagues in Moscow."

It seemed to Oblensky that Leonov was somehow removed from the reality of what was taking place all around him. Yet that was obviously not the case. None of this would be happening had it not been for the fertile brain of the creator of the Crisis Confrontation Lectures. Oblensky, the tension building in him, thought of those sunny days at Frunze: the heat, the birch trees whispering in the summer winds. We were all so much younger then, he thought. And braver—and so much more certain that we were always, brilliantly, intuitively *right*.

The television screen on Leonov's console came to life.

There was a scratchy brightness as the raster flashed across the cathode-ray tube. Then Novikov's thick face appeared. "Do you hear me well, Yuri Ivanovich?" he shouted.

"I hear you and see you perfectly. Is the Politburo gathered as I requested?"

"It is not for you to make demands," Novikov shouted angrily. "It is for you to hear the decisions of the leadership and obey."

"Is Krasin there?" Leonov asked calmly.

"I am here, Yuri Ivanovich." Krasin appeared beside Novikov at once. Beyond them Leonov could now see the bearish shapes of Marshal Lyudin and General Sheremetiev.

"Valentin Kirov is dead," Leonov said. It was not a question. Immediately he could hear the murmur of agitated discussion in the background. He recognized the voices of Suslov and Viktorov. It was not the entire Politburo, but it would do.

"What I say is a fact, is it not? Comrade Kirov died last night," he said relentlessly.

Krasin looked helplessly at Novikov and said, "Yes, it is so."

"And you have been named First Secretary."

"Yes."

"Very well," Leonov said. "Now listen to me carefully, Viktor Stepanovich. There is not time for long explanations."

Novikov made a move as if to object, but Krasin silenced him with a gesture. Good, thought Leonov. At least he has them all under temporary control. He said, "The Americans will land at Moscow at 0601 hours. You have exactly thirty minutes—that is, until 0631 hours—to escort them into the deep shelter at Krasnogorsk. You should be able to accomplish this in the time allotted." He was gratified to see mystification and a growing concern on the faces of the military men in the Kremlin command center. It would take a civilian like Krasin a moment more to grasp the implications of what he was being told. "At 0631 hours exactly, Moscow time, I shall resume the prelaunch count-down on the missiles of the Aral'sk Strategic Rocket Regiment. The target area is the Lop Nor–Turfan region of Sinkiang."

Krasin's face distorted with shock and disbelief. *"What are you saying, Yuri Ivanovich?"*

Leonov said evenly, "You have all assumed that what I had in mind was a military coup. We will not discuss that now. We will save it for a more appropriate time. When these matters are successfully concluded, we may then consider what is to be done about a proper successor to Comrade Kirov—"

Novikov let out a roar of fury, but he was swiftly shouldered aside by General Sheremetiev. "Comrade Marshal! You must give us more time to consider—to prepare—"

Krasin spoke sharply. "Sheremetiev, you forget yourself!" He turned back to the image on his television monitor. "Let me understand you, Yuri Ivanovich. You are going to attack the Chinese—with a single rocket regiment—while the Americans are *here*—" He glanced away at a wall chronometer. "In less than *one hour* from now?"

"I can certainly do this, as you may or may not know, Viktor Stepanovich," Leonov said. "Ask Sheremetiev or Lyudin. The Minister of Defense has always had that prerogative. We do not operate the way the Americans do."

Krasin turned to Lyudin and asked the question swiftly. The old soldier said, "Yes, Comrade First Secretary. What he says is true. He can do as he chooses with the Aral'sk Regiment."

"Kindly listen to me carefully," Leonov said. "We have no time to waste." His manner became pedantic, almost as though he were addressing one of his classes at Frunze. "I know that you have been arresting my men wherever you could uncover them. *This must cease.* Each of the commanders and diplomats trained by me has his special assignment to perform, and you would do well to let them all get on with them."

"This is insane," Novikov protested. "Why are we listening to this man?"

Leonov disregarded the KGB chief as though he had not spoken. "You, Viktor Stepanovich, have some sophistication in the matter of world opinion and how it affects the behavior of nations. To launch a strike against the Maoists under cover of a summit visit by an American President will imply a great many things to other nations. They will conclude that the Americans are in collusion with us. It will paralyze them. You know this is so. It bears no argument, Viktor Stepanovich."

Krasin's pale face showed strain and real fear, but he could not deny what Leonov was saying.

"Actually, the time limit is something more than one hour. The final countdown on the Aral'sk missiles will recommence at 0631 hours. I am prepared to hold for an additional hour to allow Marshal Lyudin, General Sheremetiev, and Admiral Viktorov to deploy our forces to support the initial strike. By 0730 hours the armed forces should be in position to deliver a crushing blow to the Maoists. It is even possible that they will be totally unable to employ their counterforce—"

"Possible—" Finance Minister Suslov's voice was scratchy with terror and disbelief. "Did you say *possible?*"

"In war," Leonov said calmly, "there is never absolute certainty. It is conceivable that they may be able to launch one or two weapons in retaliation. But the risk is insignificant."

Krasin said hoarsely, "You are talking about the death of perhaps a million of our citizens, Leonov."

"I am talking about the destruction of the Chinese threat, Comrade First Secretary. Forever."

"And what will the Americans do, Leonov?" Lyudin demanded. "Have you thought about that?"

"The Americans will go quickly and quietly to the shelter at Krasnogorsk. The United States military forces will do nothing. What *can* they do, Lyudin?"

The men in the Kremlin stood in stunned silence. Leonov spoke again. "I do not recommend any attempt to evacuate Moscow or the larger population centers, Comrades. Even on this accelerated schedule, it could betray our intentions to the enemy. And the effect would be negligible. In any case, I do not believe the Chinese will be capable of any retaliation if each of you performs your duty properly."

Krasin attempted to compose himself. "Comrade Marshal, what you suggest is monstrous. It is the act of a man who has abandoned both his sense and his duty to the Soviet state."

"Spare me the lectures, Viktor Stepanovich," Leonov said. "Accept this: what I say will be done *will* be done. Prepare the nation to take full advantage of my actions. You have always known—all of you—that it had to come to this eventually. Well, the moment is here. You may grasp it and live as Soviet citizens and patriots, or you may falter and die. The choice is yours." He glanced at the wall clocks, settling his gaze on the one labeled "Moscow," and said, "Time is short. You must begin to act now. I have nothing further to say."

The television monitor in the Kremlin went dark.

Immediately, the room erupted into argument and shouting.

Krasin called for order. When a semblance of silence had come, he said to Lyudin, "Can we reach him?"

"Attack the base, you mean?"

"Yes. Can it be done?"

"If the GRU forces he has in place fight, it would take us three days to penetrate the command bunker."

"Can his power sources be shut down?"

"The base was built to withstand near-misses by nuclear weapons, Comrade First Secretary. It is self-sufficient. Even the air supply is recirculated. In time, perhaps. But—" He shrugged his heavy shoulders and shook his head. "Who could have fore-seen this?"

Krasin said bitterly, "Someone should have."

Novikov said, "We have Zabotin."

"What good is he?" Lyudin demanded. "What can he tell us that Leonov has not?"

"We must make a decision, Comrades," Krasin said. "Shall we tell the Americans?"

Sheremetiev said, "We don't dare, Comrade First Secretary. We need them for insurance—if—" He broke off in bafflement.

Suslov protested, "We cannot make decisions in this way. We must have time to consider, to discuss—"

"There *is* no time, Comrade Minister," Lyudin said.

"There *is* no choice," Krasin said.

Sheremetiev said agitatedly, "I must give orders for the disposition of our forces, Comrades. So must Marshal Lyudin and Admiral Viktorov. To be caught unprepared would mean disaster."

Krasin looked at the circle of concerned faces. His eyes were bleak and suddenly rimmed with tears. The others had never seen such emotion on the face of the quiet diplomat. "Our name will be a stench in the nostrils of the world if we do this thing."

"Do we need a Stalin now to make our decision, Comrades? Do we have any option but to obey?" Sheremetiev demanded.

A telephone pinged, and Krasin lifted it to his ear. "Krasin."

After listening for a moment and replacing the instrument, he looked again at his colleagues before speaking. "The Americans. They are forty ninutes from Moscow. President Lambert wants an immediate conference."

"My God," Suslov said thickly. "Can he *know?*"

Lyudin shook his head. "Impossible."

"Whether or not he knows," Krasin said, "we can't refuse." He faced the others and said, "Make your dispositions, Comrades. For the moment that is all that can be done."

Comrade Dr. Soong looked about the bleak hospital ward in disbelief. The long, narrow temporary building was thin-walled, and the bitter cold of the high desert seemed to leak unhampered through the flimsy boards. The old doctor shivered in his quilted uniform. The scene that met his eyes reminded him of the western version of Hell in Dante. The ninth circle, the frozen pit of agony and despair.

The building was twenty meters long by six meters wide. It had originally contained forty beds, a number barely adequate to care for the ordinary run of injuries and illnesses encountered in the course of a building project the size of the Dragon.

But now two dozen more beds had been added, and there were more in the halls leading to the meeting rooms and administration buildings. It was like a nightmare, Soong thought. The cold air was heavy with the smell of rotting flesh and astringents. The fact was, quite simply, that the project was in no way equipped to take care of an accident on this scale. Nor was his medical team prepared to deal with the nature of the injuries that had been visited upon the technicians who had operated the giant laser against the Russian satellite.

Thirty technicians, a dozen junior scientists, twenty-two laborers, and eight of the cadre—including young Chou Tsing-wen, the Chairman of the Workers Council—lay in various stages of delirium and pain on the crowded cots. Most of them had suffered deep burns on nearly one hundred percent of their bodies. Soong was simply overwhelmed. He had no means of coping with this tragedy.

Li Chin had escaped the devastation because he had not been in the immediate vicinity of the giant laser. He was now busily at work explaining and correcting the source of the catastrophe.

The burns had come from high-energy light escaping the laser tube under the pressure of the millions of kilowatts poured into the system when the shot into space was made. Li had said something about plasmas and surging bloom and photon leakages, but none of that made sense to Dr. Soong. His reality was the cooked flesh of some sixty men—ten had already died and another dozen who would not last the day. The shot at the Russian satellite, the first full-power test of the Dragon, had been an undisguisable disaster. Dr. Soong was sick with pity and anger, exhausted from hours of work trying to combat this sudden onslaught of accidental pain and death.

He left the hospital and walked furiously across the frozen, marshy ground toward the buildings housing the laser. There was feverish activity in this part of the base. Soong had demanded that Li Chin, now totally in command, send to Peking for assistance, but the engineer had refused. Instead, he had set the remaining technicians to work building sandbag barriers and earthen walls around the laser tube.

Soong found Li directing the work. The man had gone mad, the doctor concluded. Instead of saving the men and women in the hospital, he thought only of his device—his Dragon.

"Five more have died," Soong said without preamble. "You *must* ask Peking for assistance."

"I have recalculated the thermal coefficient of the bloom," Li said. "The barriers will protect the crews now, I am certain of it."

The old doctor's dark eyes filmed with anger. "Surely you can't mean to fire this devil's device *again?"*

"The sand barriers will serve," Li said. His voice was edged with the hysteria of his monomania. The accident, Soong realized, had done something terrible to his judgment. "Dense metal barriers would be better, of course, but the sand will do—I am certain of it."

"Comrade Li, you can't repeat this. I cannot permit it. You must tell Peking." The doctor had difficulty controlling his own voice. He trembled with a deep, bitter outrage.

Li stared at him coldly. "It is not for you to permit or not permit, Dr. Soong. Chairman Chung has authorized a full test of the Dragon, and that is exactly what I intend doing."

Soong's mind seemed clotted with images of burned men and women. The horror of it seemed about to suffocate him. And here he stood in conversation with a madman, talking about still another "test."

"No," he said. "Not again."

Li's eyes focused on him. It was as if the engineer saw him clearly for the first time.

"What's this?" Li said.

"I said *no*. There will be no further testing."

"That is not for you to say, Comrade Doctor."

"I shall call Peking and report what has happened."

The engineer stared at him with a fixed expression. He turned and called one of the soldiers working on the sand barrier.

"Comrade, take the doctor back to the hospital. He is to remain there. You may use force, if necessary."

The burly peasant soldier, huge in his quilted uniform, his flat, dull face without animation, advanced on the frail medic. Dr. Soong's fury turned to an icy despair. Is this what we have done to our people, he thought, with our revolution? Didn't the man know what had happened to dozens like him thanks to Li Chin's great experiment?

He made one more despairing effort to reach the engineer's closed mind. "Comrade Li. I beg you to think rationally. The test was a terrible failure—"

Li's eyes brightened with anger. "The test was *not* a failure. The Russian satellite was destroyed just as my calculations predicted it would be."

"Come to the hospital and look at the results, Comrade." Soong heard the note of madness in his own voice. *"Come see what you have done!"*

Li spoke only to the soldier. "Take the doctor to the hospital, Comrade," he said. "If he attempts to leave again—shoot him." Then he turned away to study the terrible machine slowly disappearing behind the primitive wall of sandbags and rubble.

47

Both Harold Hood and DeWitt Sutton were attending a dinner party at the Portuguese Embassy on Kalorama Road when a military aide brought word that the Vice President was required in the Pentagon's communications room.

Hood, faintly ridiculous in ill-fitting dinner jacket and archaic starched shirt, and Sutton, resplendent in ruffles and maroon velvet, had been enjoying an after-dinner drink with the Portuguese Ambassador when Colonel Rockford arrived.

Between the Vice President and the California Senator a wary rapport had grown up since their sharing of Gerald Ransome's leaked information. For a day both men had been silently considering how best to derive political advantage from what Dalland and Ransome had brought them.

Colonel Rockford had delivered his message and retired to a reception room to wait for Hood. He was joined by Sutton. The Senator, gracing Rockford with a long-toothed smile, appeared from the ballroom.

A symphony, Rockford—an austere career officer—thought sourly. A symphony in dark red and old lace.

"What seems to be the trouble, Colonel?" Sutton asked lightly.

"I couldn't really say, Senator," the soldier replied. "I was instructed to fetch the Vice President, that's all."

"To the Pentagon? At this time of night?"

"Yes, sir."

"I find that rather strange, don't you, Colonel?"

Rockford, a thin-featured man with colorless grayish eyes and sandy hair, disliked the Senator from California, but he would be on the list for promotion to brigadier general soon—a list that must be approved by the Senate. "General Devore's orders, sir. That's all I know."

Hood came rather breathlessly into the room, followed by their host and Mikhail Baturin, the Soviet Ambassador. The resurgence of the Communists in Portugal had made close associates, if not friends, of the two envoys.

Sutton moved swiftly into what he perceived as an opening that might be to his advantage. He said, "If you don't mind, Mr. Vice President, I'd like to come along with you. I might be useful."

Hood very much doubted this, but he did not want to discuss the matter before Baturin and the Portuguese. He made a typically Hood-like disclaimer. "If you insist, Senator. But I don't really think you need to leave this splendid party to keep me company—"

The Portuguese Ambassador exchanged a look with Baturin and said, "Please, Senator. If you feel you must go, there is no need whatever to stay longer. Duty above all things, no?"

In the back seat of the Vice Presidential limousine, bundled against the wet Washington cold, Hood said to Sutton, "The President wants to talk to me personally, DeWitt. I'm not sure it's a good idea for you to sit in on this. You know how he is."

"I'll stay in the background, Mr. Vice President. But after our talk of yesterday, I think you'll agree it is a good idea to let the Senate have some knowledge of whatever Cleveland Lambert is planning now." He glanced at his watch. "Nine-thirty-five. Has he reached Moscow yet?"

"I don't think so."

"He's called an in-flight conference with you?"

"And with the Joint Chiefs."

Sutton's expression hardened into one of self-righteous conviction. "I might have guessed. It's as we feared, Harold. Something's gone wrong with our leader's glorious peace mission."

Hood glanced edgily at Colonel Rockford, riding in the front seat beside the driver. A soundproof glass partition separated the men in the back from the Colonel and driver, but Hood did not like direct criticisms of the President under these conditions.

"You are jumping to conclusions," he said.

"Justified conclusions, I think."

"I'd prefer not to make any such judgment just yet."

Sutton turned away to hide his expression of contempt. Presently he said, "I think I should warn you that I am going to call Gerald Ransome as a witness before the Overwatch Committee next week. We are having new hearings on unnecessary secrecy in government."

Hood's tone had an element of uncharacteristic skepticism in it. "When did you decide that?"

"I have been thinking of it ever since Allan Dalland and I had our meeting with you."

"A very poor idea, DeWitt."

"I disagree. With respect, Mr. Vice President."

"How can you possibly justify attacking an administration of your own party, Senator?"

The car was approaching the Arlington Memorial Bridge. Behind them, the brilliantly illuminated Capitol dome dominated the rainy night, ahead the lights of Arlington reflected in the still, dark waters of the Potomac.

"I thought we were substantially in agreement about this junket of the President's," Sutton said.

"We are, we are," Hood said. "But is it wise to take all this into the Senate for public hearings? Shouldn't we wait and see whether or not the peace initiative is successful?"

Sutton made a scornful sound. "The Russians and the Chinese have been rattling rockets at one another for thirty years, Harold. You don't *really* believe our fearless President thinks

349

they might actually go to war, do you? Not for a moment. No, this trip is a covert encouragement to internal dissension in the Soviet Union. It's an exercise in destabilization. An anti-Communist's dream. The Cold War revisited. And it is incredibly ill-advised and dangerous. I think the people have a right to know about it."

"I don't know, Senator. You don't really know what is taking place over there," Hood said.

But I will, thought Sutton triumphantly. I'll have McNary's account. "I know this much," he said. "Our President forces himself on a perfectly legitimate disarmament conference with the socialist countries and NATO, then uses it as a cover for a surreptitious flight to the USSR and the People's Republic that he wants to keep hidden from the American electorate. That's cause enough for concern, I think."

"You will do as you think best, I suppose," Hood said, looking out the window at the river they were now crossing. "I just wish you would be more temperate, Senator."

"I shall always be intemperate in the service of the People, Mr. Vice President," Sutton said. "That is why I came to Washington."

When had the trimmers like Sutton (and yes, God help me, he thought, like Harold Hood, too) become the standard-bearers of the people? He shuddered slightly and looked up at the great blind pile of stressed concrete that was the Pentagon. Somehow, for some reason that he could not rationalize, the building, the night, and the pious Senator at his elbow frightened him suddenly.

The practice hall, dark and empty, smelled of wax and dampness. The single bare bulb of the night light cast a dim and unfriendly illumination over the familiar surroundings.

Bronwen, weary and sleepless, looked at Madame Zelinskaya and said, "I shouldn't trouble you with my problems, Madame. But I am grateful. I truly am."

The old woman, slender and unlined in this uncertain light, touched Bronwen's wrist with her hand. "Where should you come but here to your friends for comfort and support, my dear?"

Bronwen stood at the tall window, looking down into the wet darkness of Hobhouse Close. "That story in the *Express,* Madame—it was not true. Colonel Grant wanted me safe, that is all."

"Of course it was not true. In the morning we will set it all straight."

Bronwen hugged herself against the chill in the cavernous room. She had been here, talking fitfully with Madame Zelinskaya, for hours. She was achingly tired, but she knew that she could not sleep. Her mind still tumbled with the events of the last days. Images of Dover and Alek mingled with other images, of Grant and their love-making in Rye. Was it truly love-making, she wondered, or had it been some sort of animal reaction, some plea for protection? She thought about his scarred body and the feel of him inside her. What had he thought, she wondered.

Madame Zelinskaya busied herself with a small electric kettle. The steam dispersed in the air like dreams.

"Madame, don't stay up because of me."

"I sleep very little at my age."

"One would never guess your age, Madame."

The old dancer preened herself. There was still a surfeit of vanity in her. She was proud of her strong and sinewy body. "Yes," she said, "we are almost of a size, you and I." She stood near Bronwen as though to measure herself against the younger woman.

At the far end of the hall a panel on the glass doors shattered. Through the remaining panes Bronwen caught just a glimpse of movement in the dark and then the shots came. She heard three before she felt a sting on her skull and fell, as though from a great height, and never knew when she struck the cold dancing floor.

. . .

Outside in the close, Chief Inspector Alfred Owen heard the gunfire and let fly a volley of furious curses. He signaled his men forward at the run toward the entrance to Zelinskaya's establishment.

The men of Squad Alpha had run halfway across the street when the American girl who called herself "Bridget" appeared on the stone steps. Owen cursed himself again for not realizing that the door to the place had been unlocked. He did not like to think about what they would find upstairs.

He shouted, *"Stop right there! Halt!"*

The girl had a moment to hesitate and then she raised her weapon and fired at Owen. Almost without conscious thought, he aimed and fired his heavy Magnum. There was a ragged volley from his men, and the girl collapsed against the door. He knew before climbing the stairs to look that she was dead.

As the print-out appeared in the computer's rack, Grant reached for the sheets. Ballard gripped his arm, and Grant turned to look at him in surprise. The Englishman's face was white, etched with deep lines of strain and tension.

"Before you look at that, Grant, let me say something to you."

Grant waited impatiently. Ballard's behavior was strange, tinged with a kind of desperation that seemed at variance with what Grant knew of the man.

Ballard drew Grant away from the computer, still holding his arm.

"For Chrissake," Grant said in exasperation, "get on with it. We don't have much time."

"We have even less time than you think."

"Say what you have to say, Ballard."

Ballard's eyes held an intensity that Grant had never seen in them before. The faintly facetious manner was quite gone.

"You were a prisoner of the Communists, Grant, so you must

feel something like what I feel about them." He squeezed Grant's arm again. "Something is about to happen, old man. Something big. It can make all the difference in the world to your country and mine—*if we just let it happen.*"

Grant disengaged himself and stepped back toward the computer. "We don't have time for political discussions, Ballard. Not now."

"Listen to me, Grant. *Listen* to me." A note of desperation rose in his voice. "I said something was going to take place, something that needs to take place. Don't interfere."

"I don't know what the hell you're talking about. Now let me do my goddamn job, will you?"

Ballard followed him back to the computer. He stood tensely as Grant took the Boyar print-out from the machine and skimmed it swiftly. Quite suddenly it was as though the words had leaped off the printed page at him. His throat felt dry. He stopped, went back, began again at the top of the page.

CRISIS CONFRONTATION LECTURES, he read. Defense Minister Marshal Leonov's famous course in military geotechnics. The intelligence evaluators at CIA headquarters had condensed the chapters of the syllabus, but the sense of each lecture problem was clearly outlined. His eyes moved down the page.

CASE WHITE. YOU ARE THE COMMANDER OF THE FORCES OF THE WESTERN MILITARY FRONTIER. YOU DISCOVER THAT A MAJOR ADVERSARY IN THE WEST HAS SECRETLY ARMED THE MILITARY FORCES OF A FORMER ENEMY STATE WITH NUCLEAR WEAPONS. WHAT RECOMMENDATIONS DO YOU MAKE TO THE POLITBURO? A standard exercise in any military academy, Grant thought, and went on.

CASE BLUE. YOU ARE COMMANDER OF THE SOVIET FLEET (ATLANTIC). YOU DISCOVER A EUROPEAN POWER HAS MINED THE WATERS OF THE DENMARK STRAIT. . . . Again, a required exercise in any academy: if they do this, do we do this? Or this?

CASE RED. YOU ARE MILITARY ADVISER TO THE POLITBURO.

353

YOU DISCOVER THAT IT IS POSSIBLE TO ENCOURAGE AND ARM A CARTEL OF MIDDLE EAST OIL-PRODUCING NATIONS. . . . Common Soviet military doctrine, nothing more.

CASE BLACK. A defection to the West by a socialist-bloc power. What did the student recommend? Grant could see that such an exercise would be of some value in teaching potential staff officers to plan for the improbable. Every military staff college had similar courses.

CASE YELLOW. Grant felt a great icy calm descending over him. Case Yellow. What Voronin had said to Bronwen was not a yellow case, but case meaning an example. God, Grant thought, how could we have been so bloody stupid? Voronin, who had been one of Marshal Yuri Leonov's many protégés, who had been subverted and promised asylum—by whom? Grant turned to stare at Ballard.

"You son of a bitch," he breathed. "You knew. *You knew all the time.*" There it was "Case Yellow," right in his hands. YOU ARE SUPREME COMMANDER OF THE ARMED FORCES. . . . Leonov *was* supreme commander. In the Soviet system, the Minister of Defense had absolute control over the military. YOU DISCOVER THAT ONE OF YOUR NUCLEAR-FORCE COMMANDERS HAS SUBVERTED THE FAIL-SAFE PRECAUTIONS . . . Which one would he choose? Or would he simply take command of the force himself? Yes, that would be the simplest way. Relatively easy for a marshal of the Soviet Air Force and a minister of Defense. That was what Voronin had to sell in return for asylum. The when and where of Leonov's real-life version of Case Yellow. . . . AND IS ABOUT TO LAUNCH A PRE-EMPTIVE STRIKE AGAINST AN ENEMY WITH LIMITED, BUT SUBSTANTIAL, RETALIATORY CAPABILITY. . . . Not the United States, then, or Western Europe. The Chinese, of course. Their damnable Turfan laser had supplied the last, full measure of intention. Grant's mind raced. When better than now, while an American President was in the Soviet Union. Such an act could only signal to the world that the Soviets and the Americans had come at last to the final, despicable détente. . . . YOU MAY JOIN THE STRIKE . . . OR YOU MAY DESTROY YOUR INSUBORDINATE COMMANDER. . . . RECOMMEND A COURSE OF ACTION. . . .

It was a nightmare. Grant held in his hands a one-paragraph commitment to nuclear war. He looked at Ballard. "And you knew all of this. From the beginning, you knew what was being planned." He wanted to kill the Englishman.

Ballard said, "Let it happen."

"What?"

"Think for a moment, Grant. For God's sake, think about it. Remember what they are like, the Communists. Think about the rot in your country and mine. About the gutless way the politicians behave. Let it happen. Let them kill one another. The Chinese will strike back. They'll have to. Your President will be safe. The Russians will protect him because *they* have to. So let it go, Grant. Don't try to stop it. It will be a cleansing thing. *Let them kill one another—*"

Grant caught Ballard by the coat and held him. "When does it happen, Ballard? Tell me."

"You can't stop it, you know."

"When?"

"In an hour or less. Not more."

"What's the target? Peking?"

"The Turfan and Lop Nor," Ballard said. *"Let them do it."*

Grant thrust Ballard back and he stumbled against the navigator's chair. The officer's face was white. Grant realized that he had heard everything that had been said.

"What's our position?" Grant snapped.

"We are entering the Moscow Air Traffic Control area. We're twenty minutes from touchdown."

"Don't land," Grant said.

"What?"

"Don't land," Grant shouted, and started out of the compartment.

Ballard blocked him. "Don't try to prevent this. It can't be done," he said.

"Armageddon? Is this what you signed up for?"

Grant reached for the latch to the weapons rack. Ballard tried to interfere, and the two men scuffled in the confined space. Then Major Barrow appeared and grasped Ballard in a bearlike embrace. *"What in Christ is going on here?"*

Grant took a pistol from the rack and pointed it at Ian Ballard. To Barrow he said, "Search him. Then stall around. Hold. *Do not land this airplane at Moscow.*" To Ballard, he gestured with the weapon and said, "Walk ahead of me."

The two men walked aft from the flight deck, leaving the craft's commander bewildered.

The communications officer's head appeared from his cubicle.

"Major Barrow?"

The pilot turned.

"That three-way the President wanted—we have it set up. The Kremlin and the Pentagon are waiting."

Conspiracy (kŏnspi·răsi) . . . A combination of persons for an evil or unlawful purpose; an agreement between two or more persons to do something criminal, illegal, or reprehensible (especially in relation to treason, sedition, or murder).

—The Oxford English Dictionary

PART FOUR

48

The faces of the men gathered in the National Command Center at the Pentagon mirrored various and conflicting concerns. The military people—Generals Devore, Steyning, Dahlberg, and Lazenby, and Admiral Muller—displayed a silent anxiety over what they considered a dangerous and exposed position in the never-ending power game with the Soviets. The politicians—Vice President Harold Hood and Senator DeWitt Sutton (still formally dressed and looking oddly out of place against working uniforms and the military-electronic hardware of the command center)—stood by with a wary regard for the political implications of this extraordinary conference with the distant President. And Professor Christopher Rosen, his face flushed and hair in disarray, seemed mainly to be occupied in devising some way to accept empiric proof of a theory he had, until an hour ago, contemptuously regarded as fantastic.

The men sat in one of the theaters ringing the central chamber of the command center. Two cameras faced them, remotely operated by the military technicians behind a soundproof glass wall. Between the cameras, a battery of six large television screens, three of which were dark, dominated what would have been, in a real theater, the stage. Three of the screens were active. One displayed the camera's view of the men in the theater. A second was coming to life with an interior view of the President's plane, now near Moscow. The third screen was tied into a landline link through East Germany and thence to an Intelsat communications satellite. It showed a room similar to the one in the Pentagon. Russian technicians moved about. As yet, Viktor Krasin had not appeared, nor had any members of his staff.

Sutton, excited in spite of himself by this immensely complex electronic conference, and aware that he had only Harold Hood's cachet to be present, watched the preparations eagerly. This, he was thinking, was one of the things it meant to be President. You sat in a plane over European Russia and decreed that there should be an instant international conference. Thousands of bureaucrats, soldiers, and technicians went into a frenzy of activity. Hundreds of thousands of kilometers of space were linked; thousands upon thousands of landlines were plugged in. Buttons got pushed, and computers clacked and whirred—and there it was. A three-way link between Pentagon, Kremlin, and Lambert's plane. He wondered if the People realized what godlike powers they bestowed on the man they chose to lead them every four years. *He* realized it, and the hunger was sharp and deep inside him.

Hood leaned forward to speak to Steyning. "Will we need translators?"

"Foreign Minister Krasin speaks fluent English, sir. Some of his people might not, but there will be simultaneous translations through these headsets if you need them." He showed the Vice President how to adjust the earphones on the set racked on the arm of his chair.

"Have you any idea what this is about, General?" Hood asked.

"No, sir. The President received the regular update on schedule. We got back orders to set this up."

Hood sat back unsatisfied. He felt stiff and uneasy and he could not have said why. This place and these people seemed to create an air of tension and growing crisis.

The President's concerned face appeared on the screen and he spoke without preamble from the operations compartment of the plane. "Before we cut into the Russian net on this end, gentlemen, I am going to say some things for the record. I want all of this conference taped. Understood, Clint?"

The Chairman of the JCS said, "Understood, Mr. President."

The President seemed to be studying the group in Washington. "I see we have Senator Sutton present," he said. "Was that your doing, Harold?"

"I saw no harm in it, Mr. President," Hood said.

Sutton spoke up quickly. "I don't wish to compromise any security, Mr. President. Is it your wish that I leave?" He accented the word "security" in a way that was all too familiar to the military men in the room. It was an article of faith among them that to discuss a confidential (let alone secret) matter before the Senator from California on Friday was to read of it in Jane McNary's column no later than Sunday, and possibly sooner.

"No. You stay, Senator," the President said, his voice cold and firm. "Since you and your friends bear responsibility for what we don't know and can't seem to find out, perhaps you can suggest some solutions to the problems you've spawned."

Sutton's face flushed with anger at the harshness of both the tone and the indictment. Admiral Muller glanced at General Devore expressively, but said nothing.

The President moved on swiftly. "Based on the material contained in my last update, I conclude that not only does the Chinese device in the Turfan work, despite Professor Rosen's assurances to the contrary, but they have used it to commit an act of war against the USSR."

Rosen stiffened, but remained silent.

The President asked, "Has the Secretary of Defense returned to Washington?"

"Not yet, Mr. President," Devore answered.

The President nodded. "We'll carry on without him, then. I shall question the Soviets about their intentions in view of the Chinese action. If they plan a reprisal, I shall tell them that I am aborting my mission and returning to England. Meanwhile, General Devore, I suggest that you return to Red One."

There was obvious acquiescence among the military men. Hood shifted uneasily in his seat. He wondered if the President knew that he had pressured Devore into downgrading the alert. The President's next words informed him.

"I would not be surprised if you were to report, General Devore, that pressure was brought on you to stand down to Yellow Three. We will discuss that later, together with what should be done to prevent such interference in purely military matters in the future." He glanced over his shoulder at someone just entering the compartment behind him. Hood was startled to see what he thought was someone holding a pistol and then the man—it looked like Colonel Grant—moved out of camera range. The President's compartment was suddenly crowded with people. The sound cut out, and the men in the Pentagon moved forward in their seats in an unconscious gesture of alarm.

The President's voice came through clearly as the sound link was restored. He sounded angry and disturbed. *"Put this damned thing on stand-by. Do it now!"*

The television picture changed to a scene in the forward compartment of Air Force One. Major Barrow, the pilot of the plane, spoke crisply. "The President wants this link kept open, Pentagon. Do you copy?"

A communications technician outside the theater said, "We copy, Olympus." His voice came clearly through the speakers.

Devore was on his feet. "Barrow, this is General Devore. What the hell is happening there?"

"All I can tell you, General, is that I have been ordered not to land at Moscow airport."

"The Russians won't let you land?"

"No, General. Colonel Grant gave the order. He's back there with the President now."

Hood, alarmed, said, "What's happening, General Devore? What is it?"

Devore ignored the Vice President and turned his attention to the screen showing the communications center in the Kremlin. The bearish figure of Marshal Lyudin, the Red Army Chief of Staff, filled the screen.

Lyudin said, in heavily accented English, "Lyudin here. Is the link complete? We can see you, Washington, but not the President."

"There is a momentary delay, Marshal," Devore said. "It will be set right in a minute or two."

The Russian conferred with someone behind him and then turned back to the camera eye. "It has just been reported to me that your President's aircraft is no longer on course for Moscow airport, General. Are you aware of any problem aboard the aircraft?"

"None that I know of, Marshal Lyudin," Devore said, maintaining an unfelt calm. He turned slightly to lean off camera and said in a swift, low voice to Steyning, "Find out what Nathan Hale is seeing." The Air Force Chief of Staff hurried from the room.

The Russian spoke again. "The President's aircraft is now turning to the southeast. It does not respond to our traffic controller's instructions. Is something wrong?" The old man, Devore thought, sounds frightened.

"We are having a small problem with communications, Marshal," he said. "It will soon be corrected." He signaled for the sound transmission to be broken.

Behind him, Sutton complained, "What's happening, General Devore? I don't understand any of this."

Devore picked up a telephone, waited a brief moment, then spoke. "Devore. Red One," he said.

Sutton, petulant, asked, "Is that *really* necessary?"

Lazenby, the Marine Corps Commandant, said harshly, "You can bet your ass it is, Senator."

Devore stared hard at the now blank screen of the link with Air Force One, willing it to come to life again. He knew Red One was useless. He resisted an impulse to turn and look at Vice President Hood, who would never order an attack on the USSR while the President was in Russia, no matter what the provocation. In all the confusion of this strange moment, one thing was certain: the United States was quite helpless to act. The men in the Pentagon could only wait.

Steyning hurried back into the room and signaled to Devore, who rose from his seat and joined him at the door. Steyning said in a low voice, "Nathan Hale is recording what looks like a general mobilization. The sons of bitches are preparing for a strike. The President is in a box, Clint."

Viktor Krasin looked at the wall clock and felt a chill. The time was 0621. In ten minutes, the final countdown would resume at Aral'sk. And the Americans were behind schedule, turning unaccountably southeast instead of entering the Moscow Air Traffic Control area. He felt sick with his own helplessness.

A light flashed on the table before him, and he picked up a telephone.

Sheremetiev, the Air Force Chief of Staff, said: "Comrade Krasin, the Americans are now south of Moscow. They are in heavy cloud; the fighter escort has lost visual contact with them."

"Is Novikov in the War Room?"

"He is here, Comrade Krasin."

Even under these circumstances, Krasin could not help but note how reluctant the military men were to address him as "First Secretary." Years of dominance had made them suspicious of civilians. He wondered if Yuri Leonov's conspiracy was not even more widespread than he had supposed. No, such thoughts invited disaster. If he started mistrusting all the soldiers now, there would be no way out.

"Let me speak to him."

Novikov's voice came through the receiver. "I am here, Comrade Krasin."

"Have you learned anything more from Zabotin?"

The KGB chief spoke harshly. "He is still being interrogated." Krasin knew what that meant. They would take Leonov's coconspirator and wring him dry. But it would come to nothing.

Leonov would not have sent him out of Aral'sk if he had information that could be used to stop the attack on China.

"Can you reach Leonov again?"

"We have tried to re-establish a link, Comrade Krasin, but he does not respond. I have ordered the KGB units in Aral'sk to move on the base. There has been resistance."

General Lyudin approached to say that his warning orders had gone out to the Far Eastern Army. "They have acknowledged. It will take them two hours to move the first units of armor into attack position."

Krasin felt a shivering revulsion at the calmness with which Lyudin and the others had accepted the conviction that Leonov had made war with the Maoists inevitable. Leonov, of course, would have counted on that, too.

"But the Americans, Lyudin—what is happening with them?"

The old Marshal frowned. "We have an open link with the Pentagon, Comrade Krasin. They claim there is some minor malfunction with the communications connection to the President's aircraft."

"Do you believe it?"

"No."

"Why have they changed course? Sheremetiev says they are already south of Moscow."

The old soldier's face was impassive. "I suggest that Sheremetiev order his fighters to guide the American aircraft back to Moscow. There is really very little time for delays."

Krasin's eyelids felt grainy with lack of sleep. We are all of us worn out, he thought. No one has slept. What sort of decisions did exhausted men make in moments like these? Had there ever *been* moments like these in the history of Russia?

"Keep trying to reach Leonov, Comrade Marshal. Tell him that the Americans are late. Make him understand."

"That won't be easy," Lyudin said heavily.

"I don't suppose it will be, Comrade Marshal. Just try to imagine what the Americans will do if anything happens to their President. Yuri Ivanovich must give us time to make him safe."

"When will you move to Krasnogorsk?"

"When Lambert is with me," Krasin said sharply. "Not before."

Back in his lounge, the President held the Boyar print-out in a hand that trembled slightly. He had to decide, and quickly, whether or not Grant's hypothesis was valid. If it was, something must be done immediately.

He looked up at the composed face of Ian Ballard. He stood in the compartment, Grant and an armed sergeant behind him. The two British officials sat staring at their countryman in complete disbelief. Lambert didn't blame them. Ballard's attitude was beyond understanding.

"Tell it to me again," Lambert said.

"It is all there, Mr. President. Leonov spelled it out for hundreds of prospective staff officers at Frunze," Ballard said calmly. "All it needed was this visit of yours. Having Valentin Kirov sick—maybe dead—was a bonus."

Sawkins interrupted in fury. "But *you*, Major Ballard. An *Englishman*. How could you be involved in something as despicable as this? It is unbelievable!"

Ballard gave the diplomat a cold smile. "The Communists and I have a long history, Mr. Sawkins. Colonel Grant might understand what I mean. I saw nothing treasonable, or even, as you put it, despicable, in helping the Russians and the Chinese cut one another's throat. That doesn't make me a traitor, sir. Some might say it makes me a patriot."

Matthews broke in, his voice thick with anger. "You are talking about nuclear war, you bloody idiot! Don't you have any idea of what that will mean? Even if the West is not directly involved—the side effects, the fallout. You are mad, Ballard!"

"Perhaps so, sir," Ballard said in that same calm voice. "It doesn't matter now. It is too late to prevent it. All we can do is land and take shelter."

Lambert turned away from Ballard. "Get this man out of here, Sergeant. See to it that he stays under guard."

When Ballard had gone, the President looked from Grant to the two Englishmen and across the compartment at his wife and Lyman, who had followed the discussion with a look of stunned horror on his face. "All right," he said. "We must assume that what we have is accurate information. The problem is whaᵗ is to be done? There is very little time. Paul?"

Lyman spread his hands. "I'm still having trouble grasping the idea, sir. Are we really to believe that the Russians are going to launch a strike against China using *us* as cover?"

"As hostages," Grant said.

The President turned to the Englishmen. "Gentlemen? Any thoughts?"

Matthews said, "Many, Mr. President. But they are all very bloody-minded ones. I particularly deplore the part Major Ballard has played in this."

"We haven't time to worry about that," Lambert said impatiently. "The point is, what do we do? Do we confront them?"

"That could be extremely dangerous, Mr. President," Sawkins said.

"The whole situation, Mr. Sawkins, is more than dangerous. We are flying over a volcano that will erupt, possibly in less than one hour." He picked up an intercom telephone. "Barrow?"

On the flight deck, Major Barrow, now at the controls himself, answered.

"How far are we from the nearest Soviet border, Major?"

"Against the present winds, sir, we could reach the Baltic coast in one hour—plus maybe ten minutes. Shall I inform Moscow Air Traffic Control that we are turning back?"

"Hold on that. I'll get back to you."

The President replaced the handset and said, "Barrow says it will take us more than an hour to reach the Baltic. That's cutting it pretty fine." His face was grim.

Grant spoke quietly. "Ask Barrow how long to the Chinese border. The Lop Nor–Turfan area "

A wire-taut stillness fell in the compartment. For what seemed minutes, no one spoke. Then the President said, "Let me understand you, Colonel. Are you suggesting we fly directly to China?"

"Is there another choice, sir?"

Lyman said, "Harry, for Chrissake. You said yourself that the Lop Nor testing facilities and that thing in the Turfan were the number-one targets."

"That's right," Grant said.

The President looked long and hard at Grant.

Grant nodded.

The President looked at the Englishmen. "Opinion?"

"I'm too damned frightened to have an opinion, sir," Sawkins said. "But I'm afraid Colonel Grant is right. It's the only possible way to stop this."

The President looked searchingly at his wife. Pale, she managed a semblance of an encouraging smile. "We didn't sign on for this, did we, Helena?"

"It's all right," she said. "Do what you must."

The President said to Grant. "What makes you think that Leonov won't go ahead with his strike anyway?"

"Leonov will, sir. He will have to be stopped."

Lyman protested. "Ballard said there was no way the Russians *could* stop him."

Grant's eyes were hard. "There is always a way, Paul."

The President said, "I think I know what you mean, Harry."

"Then it will be their problem, Mr. President."

"And ours."

"Yes," Grant agreed, "and ours."

___

Lambert managed a bleak smile. He turned to Lyman. "We are going to have to open all this up, Paul. Or at least we are going to have to convince the Russians that we will. Get that McNary woman. She's going to get a bigger story than she imagined."

He picked up the handset and called the flight deck.

"Major Barrow, notify Moscow that we are overflying them." He hesitated and then added in a calm voice: "Tell them that our destination is the Chinese military airfield at Lop Nor."

"Stop them!" Viktor Krasin, his nerves frayed almost to the breaking point could scarcely credit what General Sheremetiev had been saying.

The Soviet Air Force commander stared back at Krasin and said quietly, "How, Comrade Krasin?"

Krasin turned desperately to Lyudin, who stood before the large plotting board on the wall of the small room. "How did they find out about Leonov, Pavel Semyonovich? How is it possible?"

The old Marshal shrugged fatalistically. "I do not know," he said. He stood regarding the large-scale chart on the wall. Leonov had said he would begin the final countdown on the Aral'sk missiles at 0631. That time had just passed. Presumably the traitor had done as he said that he would. He had granted additional time for the Americans to be taken to Krasnogorsk, and for Soviet forces to assume attack status. That gained another half hour. But from then on, Yuri Leonov might at any time launch the attack.

Lyudin calculated swiftly. The transonic American aircraft was capable of a top speed of seven hundred knots. The Air Force meteorologists reported a jet stream of one hundred and ninety knots at the altitude the Americans were flying. Taken together, those factors would allow the President's aircraft to cross into Chinese air space in one and three quarter hours.

Whatever was going to be done to persuade the Americans to land and seek safety must be done within that time—provided Leonov's timetable permitted it. Once the President of the United States entered China, the staggering risks in Leonov's fantastic game soared beyond speculation. Lyudin did not like to imagine what the Americans might do if their President was murdered by Russian missiles.

A technician appeared from the War Room. "Comrade First Secretary, the link with the American aircraft is restored. You are wanted in the communications room."

Krasin looked starkly at Lyudin and Sheremetiev. "What am I to say to the President?"

"Convince him that he must return to Moscow."

Krasin heaved himself to his feet wearily. "Madness," he said, and left the room.

The Air Force man looked at Lyudin. "Can he do it? Will he hold together?"

Lyudin shook his head and followed Krasin. Sheremetiev sat in deep thought. What would he do in the worst case, he wondered, the very worst. His rocket forces could support Leonov's strike. But they would have to be divided, a percentage of them held back in case the Americans became involved. The thought of that made his blood congeal.

He picked up a telephone and gave the code for the air base at Tbilisi. It was there that his best and most disciplined bomber wing was stationed.

Jane McNary was torn between outrage and fright. First, Harry had plunged through the main cabin of the plane with that Englishman, Ballard, and—though it happened so quickly—she thought Harry had carried a pistol in his hand. Next, she had had to sit for what seemed a very long time while people rushed in and out of the President's quarters, their faces grim and, in some cases, obviously frightened.

Now came Harry again, his expression frozen and harsher

than she had ever seen it. He was angry about the *Express* story, she knew, but this was something else again. Something different. She had never known him to be so brusque.

"Get up, Jane."

"What in *hell* is happening, Harry?"

"Up, goddamn it. Move!" His eyes were those of a stranger.

As he took her arm and moved her quickly toward the President's operations compartment, he said, "The President wants you to hear what he says to the Russians. You are to sit, listen, and keep your mouth shut."

She could not allow Harry to deal with her this way. Despite her fright and uncertainty, she had her self-esteem to guard. She said, "Who do you think you're talking to, Grant?"

He paused and looked directly into her face. She was chilled by the bitterness she saw. "You don't have any idea how much trouble you've caused, McNary. You and Sutton and the others. I thought I could handle it. I can't. But that's personal. That's also the last personal thing I'll say to you. Now just sit and listen to what the President says."

"Why haven't we landed in Moscow by now?" she demanded.

Grant stared at her coldly. "We're going to China. If we're very lucky, we might even get there." He opened the door to the compartment.

The cabin was crowded with people and equipment. The President sat before a double television monitor. Paul Lyman and Helena Lambert sat with the two English diplomats near the window. Beyond the plexiglass, McNary could see that a faint dawnlight was suffusing the cloud through which they were flying.

The President said, "Please sit here behind me, Miss Mc-Nary."

Jane did as she was told. She felt tense with resentment and apprehension. From the expressions surrounding her she knew that something was seriously wrong. And what had Harry said? They were going to China? But that was all wrong. Lambert himself had told her they were on the way to Moscow—

She turned her attention to the television monitors and drew a sharp breath at what she saw. On the right-hand screen she could see Clinton Devore. With him were some of the other Joint Chiefs and, behind them, DeWitt Sutton and Harold Hood. On the left-hand screen a man in a Russian uniform was saying, "Comrade Krasin is here, Mr. President."

Krasin's familiar face took the place of the uniformed man. The men in Washington leaned forward. McNary realized that this was a three-way television link.

"Mr. President," Krasin began, "we have received word from our air controllers that you are overflying Moscow—"

The President interrupted him. McNary had never heard Cleveland Lambert so rude, or so obviously angry. "Comrade Krasin," he said, *"why have you failed to inform us about the implementation of Case Yellow?"*

Krasin's face looked frozen.

The President continued. "I have information that a member of your government is contemplating a strike against certain installations in the People's Republic of China under cover of my visit to your country." His voice was flinty. "This is an outrage against the usages of civilized diplomacy. I wish to make my protest known to First Secretary Kirov *in person."*

Krasin spoke in a weary, barely audible voice. "That is impossible, Mr. President. The First Secretary died late yesterday."

The tension in the compartment increased. McNary's thoughts raced. Kirov dead. And the Soviets had failed to notify the President in any way but to ask for that twenty-four-hour postponement of the visit. She wondered if Krasin was lying; Kirov could have died at least forty-eight hours ago. And what was Lambert accusing the Soviets of doing? Had she heard him correctly? A strike against "certain installations in the People's Republic of China"? She looked at the other television monitor to catch Senator Sutton's reaction. Did her "Cranmer" realize what was being said? The fool had given her bad information.

The destruction of the Soviet satellite and now this insane business confirmed it.

"Then it is to you that I address myself," the President said, still in that rock-hard tone. "I have been informed that Minister of Defense Leonov is somehow in a position to mount an attack by missile against the People's Republic. I find this incredible. What action have you taken to prevent this act of international murder, Krasin?"

A new figure appeared. A grizzled soldier was whispering angrily to Krasin. Krasin waved him away. "Marshal Lyudin wishes to protest your tone, Mr. President. For myself, I make no complaint. You have the right to be angry. Now I beg of you, sir, return to Moscow at once. This is a matter of your safety. We can come to terms later, when you and your party are no longer in danger."

"I refuse to assume, Krasin," the President said, "that you are actually inviting me to participate in this. Is it possible you are going to let this revolting crime take place?"

Krasin's voice was that of a man near to the breaking point. "Don't you understand, Mr. Lambert? *We cannot stop it.*" The desperate words seemed to hang in the air of the compartment.

From the group in Washington came the voice of General Devore. "Mr. President, may I make a comment?"

"Go ahead, General."

"I would like to ask for an explanation of what appears to be a general mobilization now taking place inside the Soviet Union."

The President raised the computer sheets so that Krasin might see them. "As projected by your Marshal Leonov, Case Yellow suggests that the pre-emptive strike will be supported by a full-scale attack. Speak plainly, Krasin. Is this your intention?"

"Mr. President Lambert," Krasin said, his English slipping under the strain of the moment. "Case Yellow is an exercise. A copybook exercise."

"Then I have your assurance that there will be no general attack," Lambert pursued.

Again Lyudin spoke to Krasin in whispered, agitated tones.

Krasin said, "We are conducting operations against Leonov. The matter will be resolved. Now, I insist that you order your pilot to turn back to Moscow. We are vitally concerned for your safety."

Lambert's tone remained cold. "No one could be more concerned than I, Comrade Krasin. My wife is with me, and many of my closest advisers." He spoke even more deliberately. "Behind me, sir, you may see a young lady. I believe you are familiar with her work. She is the correspondent Jane McNary. I want you to understand me very well. This entire discussion has been and will continue to be taped. Miss McNary will undoubtedly prepare a full report on it for her newspapers. I want you to consider very carefully what this means, sir. If war begins here, Comrade Krasin, there can never be a doubt as to who is responsible."

"Mr. President," Krasin said angrily, "I will not be blackmailed."

"I am delighted to hear that," the President said. "You will undoubtedly have found a way to prevent the commission of an act that would leave you open to such a charge. For myself, however, I intend to continue on my present course. My first call will be at Lop Nor." He stared coldly into the camera eye, willing Krasin to understand that he meant what he was saying. "If I or my people are harmed by *any* Soviet action in the course of this journey, the United States will consider it an act of war." He addressed himself directly to the men gathered in the Pentagon now. "And I expect that an appropriate response will be made."

"Mr. President—" Krasin protested.

"I think we had better end this discussion, Comrade Krasin," Lambert said. "I have no doubt that Chinese listening posts are searching for the electronic code that secures these transmissions. I should not like to guess what their reaction would be if they should succeed in finding it."

He nodded curtly to Krasin's image and signaled the flight deck to end the transmission to the Kremlin.

374

When the screen went dark, he slumped in his seat, his face suddenly slack. "My God," he murmured.

Behind him, McNary whispered in a shaky voice. "You *used* me, Mr. President."

"Yes," he said. "I did."

He looked at the stunned gathering in the Pentagon and said, "Poker, gentlemen. I hope I'm as good at it as Harry Truman was. If not, we're in deep trouble."

49

General Sergei Oblensky was having second thoughts. He had passed through a number of stages in his association with Marshal Leonov. At first, during the purely theoretical discussions that surrounded the delivery of the Confrontation Lectures at Frunze, he had been captured by the daring and brilliance of Leonov's concepts. As an ethnic Pole, Oblensky had been touched by the racism inherent in many of Leonov's theses. Yet he had been younger then (though not much younger than Leonov) and susceptible to the force with which Leonov had been able to put forward his ideas.

It had seemed self-evident to Oblensky that a war with China was both inevitable and desirable. No modern nation, he thought, could long tolerate nine hundred million fanatics on her doorstep. The fact that these fanatics had yellow faces made his conclusions all the more logical. It had hardly been necessary for Leonov to tell his students, as he invariably had, that civilization in the modern sense was the product of the white races' industry and culture. The Russian word *kulturny* had always figured largely in the Leonov lectures. When Leonov's patronage had brought Oblensky advancement in the Soviet Air Force, he had congratulated himself on the good fortune that had sent him to those sunlit lecture sessions at the Academy.

More recently, however—perhaps it was the growing conservatism of advancing age and rank—Oblensky had tended to think less of Leonov's plan than of his own chance to survive it. What was discussed at Frunze as theory had become a harsh and frightening reality in the command center of the Aral'sk Strategic

Rocket Regiment. Like many radicals and revolutionaries, Oblensky had assumed subconsciously that rhetoric would never actually be transformed into action.

Within the last two hours he had teetered atop the wall of personal commitment. He had experienced dread, exhilaration, apprehension, conviction, and all mixed with a strong element of wonder. The plans that he had lived with, in one form or another, for much of his military career were about to be implemented. Rhetoric—or what he had always rather suspected was rhetoric —was about to be translated into a fearful reality.

He had already placed himself outside the pale of normal Soviet loyalties. When Novikov had ordered him to arrest Marshal Leonov and he had first temporized and then refused, he had committed an act of, at best, insubordination and, at worst, treason. Now as he looked at the wall clock above the television monitors and computer displays in the blast-resistant sanctum of the Aral'sk Regiment, he was having second thoughts.

The Moscow clock stood at 0635 hours. The final countdown on the missiles had been under way for four minutes. When Yuri Ivanovich might choose to launch them at the Chinese was a matter of conjecture—of whim, if it came to that. He had promised the members of the Politburo that he would allow at least an hour to alert the rest of the armed forces so that they might support the strike against Turfan and Lop Nor. But there was no assurance that the Marshal would wait so long. The launch could take place at any time after 0645 hours, a mere ten minutes from now.

Leonov had sent another short and peremptory message out of the base only minutes ago. He had ordered Novikov to stop his attempts to penetrate the outer perimeter of the base with his KGB troops. His message had a kind of mad loftiness. "It is not fitting that Soviet soldiers should die fighting Soviet soldiers." It was delivered with a threat to launch the Aral'sk missiles "without further delay" if compliance was not immediate.

The KGB units aboveground had withdrawn swiftly, and so

the situation stood. There had been no word from the Kremlin on the arrival of the Americans, though by this time they should be on the ground and on the way to the special shelter at Krasnagorsk.

Inside the command post the atmosphere was strangely peaceful. The quiet, underscored by the occasional voices of the technicians as they confirmed readings or made reports, was not dissimilar to the stillness Oblensky remembered from visits made in his early youth to the ancient churches that still dotted the Soviet Union. Instead of the smell of wax and incense, the deeply buried shelter's air carried an odor of ozone. The twentieth century's own scent, Oblensky thought, looking about him. *Every civilization makes its own holy places, and this is one of ours.* The wry thought was unsettling—worthy of the Marshal himself.

Leonov had risen from his place before the command console and was slowly pacing the concrete room, stopping to exchange a word or two with a soldier here, a technician there. Like a metropolitan of this dark church, Oblensky thought, a metropolitan overseeing his congregation of perhaps two dozen human souls. He shivered inwardly, wondering at the religious images that dominated his thoughts. Why, he asked himself, did his fear take this peculiar form? He was a lifelong atheist, by conviction as much as by education. Yet he let his mind run along these disturbing paths. Was it because of the nearness of a kind of man-made, materialistic Hell that lay gestating in the warheads buried all about them in the Russian earth?

Like most Russians, Oblensky was a lover of poetry and now some lines from the Irishman Yeats came to him:

> . . . somewhere in sands of the desert
> A shape with lion body and the head of a man
> A gaze blank and pitiless as the sun,
> Is moving its slow thighs, while all about it
> Reel shadows of the indignant desert birds.
> The darkness drops again; but now I know

That twenty centuries of stony sleep
Were vexed to nightmare by a rocking cradle,
And what rough beast, its hour come round at last,
Slouches towards Bethlehem to be born?

Oblensky felt a coldness. In the heart. In the blood. What terrible, prophetic words. The beast was there; the hour come round. And we—he looked with growing fear at the slender figure of Marshal Yuri Leonov—he, and I, and all of us are to be the midwives.

DeWitt Sutton, his long face pale and uncertain, stood in a group apart from the military men. The gathering had broken into two factions, polarized by the events of the last minutes. Sutton stood with Christopher Rosen and Harold Hood in the passageway between the communications theater and the National Command Center, now teeming with feverish activity.

Sutton said, "I don't believe it. It's some sort of obscene trick. Lambert has gone too far."

Hood looked at the Senator in amazement. The Vice President was never above making political capital of whatever windfalls developed, but he knew that Lambert was incapable of the duplicity Sutton was suggesting.

Rosen, still smarting in the aftershock of having been proved so dramatically wrong in his evaluation of the new Chinese weapon, seemed to misunderstand what Sutton was saying. "It could be a trick, of course. The Svoboda could have had a malfunction. That's entirely possible—"

Hood ignored him. He turned to Sutton. "What are they doing?" he indicated the military men gathering in the Pit.

Sutton said, "They are putting the nation on a war footing, Mr. Vice President. I think you should take some action to stop it."

"The President himself ordered them back to Red One," Hood said.

Rosen asked, almost plaintively. "Why didn't we get any information? Where was the Central Intelligence Agency? They should have known what was happening."

Hood's voice took on an unfamiliar firmness. "The Senator can answer that better than I."

Sutton, aroused by the Vice President's implied attack, bridled. "That is an absurd thing to say, Harold," he snapped.

"You know to what I am referring, Senator," the Vice President said, his broad, high forehead shiny with sweat.

"I most certainly do not, Mr. Vice President."

"I feel I should tell you, Senator, that there is a recording in my files of the conversation we had with that young man on your staff. If there should be an investigation of this unfortunate business, it will have to be made available."

Sutton, about to protest, was forestalled by the appearance of Colonel Rockford. "The Joint Chiefs' respects, sir, and would you join them on the balcony?"

Sutton's mind was racing now. Harold Hood had turned out to be an untrustworthy ally. He should have known, he told himself bitterly, that the man would never stand firm. He never had when the going got rough. What was important to Sutton now was to get his own side of the controversy before the public, and in his own words. He did not dare wait for McNary to return with her version of this fantastic affair. He mentally reviewed the Washington reporters he had so assiduously cultivated over the years. One of them would have to do. He would state his case and let it be known that he had opposed the President's secret maneuvers between the Russians and the Chinese, had done all he could to prevent the situation that was now developing. He turned to leave, but Hood said pointedly, "Please remain here, Senator. Colonel Rockford will see to it that you and Professor Rosen are made comfortable."

Sutton could not contain his shock. "Are you *detaining* me, Mr. Vice President?"

"In my capacity as temporary commander in chief," Hood

said, "I think it best that no one leave here until the President's situation is resolved." He mopped his damp forehead with a handkerchief and hurried away.

"I don't understand, Senator," Rosen said.

Sutton turned on him in a fury, "What is there to understand, damn you? We're prisoners here until Harold Hood in his great wisdom decides otherwise." Rockford looked pained, but did not comment. Sutton turned away from Rosen and sat in one of the seats overlooking the floor of the Pit to stare unseeing at the activity there. As the United States prepared for possible war, Senator DeWitt Sutton concentrated on salvaging his political career.

50

"Mr. President," Major Barrow said, "we are trying to get through to Peking, but our transmissions are being jammed." The officer's face was lined with strain.

"The Russians?" Lambert asked.

"Yes, sir. They keep trying to break through on the Nathan Hale net, demanding that we return to Moscow and land."

The President turned to Grant. "How much time do you think we have, Colonel?"

"It's 0700 hours, local time, sir. Maybe another hour."

The President asked, "What will our position be at eight, Major?"

"We're riding a jet stream, Mr. President. Captain Stevenson estimates we will be over the Tien Shan Mountains at 0755, Moscow time."

"Out of Russian air space?"

Barrow nodded. "Over the northern Talimupendi region of Sinkiang, sir." He produced a chart and spread it before the President. "Here, sir." His finger touched the tiny dot that indicated the high-desert settlement of K'uerhlo. His fingertip moved east on the chart, and the President identified the symbol for a marsh and salt pan.

"That's it?"

"That's the Turfan Depression, yes, sir," Barrow said.

"I make it about one hundred and eighty miles from K'uerhlo. Is that right?"

"That's correct, sir."

The President looked steadily at Grant. "You're the weapons

expert, Harry. If we should be in the air that close to the Turfan and that Russian maniac actually does what he plans, what are our chances?"

Grant glanced across the compartment to where Helena Lambert sat quietly looking out the window at the half-lighted mist. He looked back at the President.

"The truth, Harry," Lambert said.

"Our chances would be nil, Mr. President. The Aral'sk Regiment—the Wing, as we would call it—has six SS-19 missiles. Each carries five warheads. A single air burst over the Turfan would probably knock us out of the air at under two hundred miles. The regiment can make a footprint two hundred kilometers long—that's about one hundred and twenty-five miles—if they use all thirty warheads. And the Soviets have always gone for large warheads, Mr. President. In the multimegaton range. You'll remember they would never agree to reduce the size of the weapons."

"My God," Lambert breathed, "you don't really understand what the word 'overkill' means until you realize someone really intends to use it."

"My guess would be," Grant went on grimly, "that Leonov would try to cover the entire western Talimupendi, the whole plateau. Lop Nor is about seventy miles south and a bit east of the Turfan. He can do it easily with one missile wing."

A communicator pinged, and Barrow lifted a telephone from the niche in the bulkhead. He listened in silence and then said shortly, "I'll be up right away." He replaced the handset and said to the President, "That was Captain Stevenson on the radar, sir. Our escort of MIGs is closing in. I think they are going to try to make us turn back."

The President glanced at his wife and back to the plane commander. "Under no circumstances, Major," he said quietly.

"Yes, Mr. President," the pilot said, and left the compartment.

"Harry," Lambert said, "you had better do what you can for

our passengers. They didn't bargain for this and they must be—concerned. I'll want another contact with Washington in five minutes. Right now Helena and I would like to be alone."

Grant looked at the gray face, deeply etched now with lines of worry and fatigue, and felt a surge of admiration for Lambert. In spite of all that was said of him, all that was always said of all Presidents, there must be an ennobling quality to the office. An ordinary man could not face the next hour or two with such grace otherwise. On his responsibility, and on his alone, the men and women on board this aircraft were being offered as hostages in a grim game of nuclear threat and counterthreat. It took a very special sort of man to run such risks. But Lambert, of all men, knew how high the stakes were, and he had found the courage to act, to seize the moment.

Grant turned to go, but the President stopped him. "That girl, Harry," he said quietly, "she was important to you?"

"Yes. She was important," Harry said as quietly.

"I hope she's all right."

The President rose and moved to sit by his wife.

Grant gently closed the door to the compartment behind him.

At five minutes after five in the morning, Secretary of State Margaret Kendrick was awakened in her room high on the top level of Labour House at Sissinghurst.

The day and night before had been spent in a round of meetings and discussions, primarily with representatives of the NATO allies, in an attempt to formulate a negotiating position agreeable to all. The talks had been frustrating. The French refused to relinquish any of their obsolete *force de frappe* nuclear capability, and this despite the opinions of several commissions of military experts who declared that the French strategic force was worse than worthless—that it would, in fact, only attract the attention of Soviet missileers in the event of a war.

The French Foreign Minister had withdrawn from the discussions in a temper "to confer with Paris."

The Netherlands' representative further disturbed the proceedings by stating that he was unable to make any solid commitments regarding the Royal Netherlands Army without consultations with, and the approval of, the National Soldiers' Union.

Kendrick had retired from the discussions at midnight, weary and preoccupied. Despite her well-deserved reputation for self-discipline, she found herself thinking about the President and his party en route to Moscow.

The press at Sissinghurst had already begun to question Cleveland Lambert's absence. Word was passed that he was engaged in a round of personal talks with the Prime Minister at Chequers, but that story was unlikely to satisfy the bloodhounds of the media for long.

It had been well after two when Kendrick had finally fallen asleep. Now, at a few minutes after five, she was awakened by an aide with word that there was a call for her from State in Washington.

To take the message it was necessary for her to descend to the next lower floor of Labour House, where the American communications team had set up her secure landlines and radio net.

She took the telephone from a technician and said, "Margaret Kendrick here."

For the next ten minutes she listened, breaking into the report from Washington only to ask a question or two. As she listened, the color drained slowly from her face. At last she asked, "Where are they now, then?"

The voice of the Undersecretary in Washington went on for several more minutes. Then Kendrick said, "Yes. Thank you. I understand. Keep me informed." She was amazed at how steady her own voice sounded when what she wanted to do was to cry out, to protest, even to deny what she was being told.

When the connection was broken she sat marshaling her thoughts. Her own reflection looked back at her from the blank television monitor facing her chair: an old woman sat there, behind the dark screen, an old woman with a crumpled face and uncombed gray hair, dressed in a flannel bathrobe. She wanted to ask that woman what she did here, in this improbable place, and why she wasn't at home in Maryland with her daughters and her grandchildren. She hugged the robe about her and shivered. The technician on duty asked her solicitously if she was cold, did she need a coat.

"Thank you, no," she said to the young man. She drew a deep breath and said, "Get me through to Chequers. I want to speak to the Prime Minister."

Of one thing she could be sure: Cleveland Lambert would want the British warned, though she wondered if any man now asleep in his bed or listening cozily to the sound of the rain falling out of the winter sky this night could be convinced with mere words that a holocaust might be only hours away.

Still, she must try. The British had been good friends to the United States. They deserved a warning.

As the call came through, Margaret Kendrick wondered why she had begun to think of friendship and peaceful winter nights in the past tense.

51

At five minutes after one o'clock in the afternoon, a watery
sunlight had broken through the gray skies over Peking. In T'ien
An Men Square, orderly throngs of bicyclists and pedestrians
hurried about their affairs. The wall posters, a new crop, asked
whether or not Wang Po-ling, the Minister of Agriculture, was
taking the capitalist road by encouraging production of food on
the minute private plots newly allotted to farmers in Kwangtung
Province. The posters were rather mild in tone and relatively free
of invective. This was in keeping with both Chairman Mao's
directive on "continuous revolution" and Chairman Chung's
most recent speech on the need for encouragement of public
servants.

The portrait of the deified Mao over the gate to the Forbidden City was in need of fresh paint. The portrait of Chairman
Chung was not. The youthful face beamed benevolently down on
the masses in the square.

In the communications center buried under the buildings that
had once housed the concubines of the Manchu emperors, Chairman Chung and the Minister of Defense, Marshal K'ang Pei, of
the People's Liberation Army, were alone except for the silent
technicians who tended the masses of American-made communications gear that filled the concrete-walled room.

K'ang, his peasant's face grim, said, "We have been intercepting a tremendous amount of radio and television traffic between
the American aircraft and Moscow, but we haven't been able to
break the frequency code yet—"

"Explain," the Chairman said.

"The transmissions are being shunted through the new American Nathan Hale satellite. The device carries an extremely sophisticated computer that changes the transmitting frequencies in random fashion every so many seconds. Unless the Americans working the satellite net command the computer to synchronize the receivers, it is very difficult to break the code. We are doing our best. We have received some useful information from the devices we have installed in our Washington Embassy, but not enough to decode what the Americans call 'the Olympus mode,' the Presidential codes."

"But you say they are calling us."

"That's the strange thing. Yes, they have been trying to open a link with us for the last ten minutes on another track of the Nathan Hale code system. I've delayed taking the call because they are almost surely up to something." K'ang checked the bank of world-time chronometers on the far wall of the cluttered room. "It is five minutes after seven in Moscow. They should have landed there thirty-five minutes ago. But they have not. We heard them tell Moscow Air Traffic Control that they were now on course for the Turfan–Lop Nor area."

Chung's face darkened. "I knew it. I knew it would come to something like this." He sat tensely. "Is there any proof that their President is actually on board that aircraft?"

"Only their word and the agreement they made with us."

"Their word," Chung said scornfully. "The world is littered with the remains of countries who trusted the Americans' *word.*"

"What are you suggesting, Comrade Chairman?"

"Exercise just a little imagination, Comrade Marshal. And then consider what our circumstances are at this moment. We have an unscheduled aircraft—purportedly carrying the President of the United States—about to cross our frontier *from the Soviet Union.* Without permission, without discussion. We are simply informed that they have changed their plans *and will land at Lop Nor or Turfan,* our most closely guarded military area. And please note that this happens only hours after we have success-fully tested Comrade Li Chin's laser device." The smooth young face seemed to grow visibly older, more suspicious. "What proof have we that this aircraft is even American?"

"We can open the radio-television link they want, Comrade Chairman."

"And what will that prove? If their communications technology is as sophisticated as you say it is, Lambert could speak to us from anywhere on earth and claim to be aboard that aircraft, couldn't he?"

"Yes."

"Have you re-established communications with Li at Turfan?"

"There is no trouble on this end, Comrade Chairman. But apparently there are some problems at Turfan. Li reported by telephone that the test caused some difficulties."

"What sort of difficulties?"

"Mostly in the power grid. He was rather sketchy and in a rush to get back to setting things right. But I gather that the power drain was so high that some equipment failed and some people were burned. But he says that the Dragon performed almost exactly as predicted and that he will be ready for a second test almost immediately."

"Are our communications secure?"

"I believe so, Comrade Chairman."

"Doesn't it strike you as odd that Li's test is no sooner a success than the so-called American airplane changes direction to Turfan–Lop Nor? Why there? Why the one area that contains both our nuclear-test facilities *and* the Dragon?"

"I understand, of course, Comrade Chairman. You are right to be suspicious. But shouldn't we first try to divert the Ameri-cans?"

The Chairman's eyes glittered in the brilliant overhead lights. "You said 'shouldn't we *first* try,' Comrade Marshal. Assuming that we do as you suggest, what is your next recommendation?"

K'ang shrugged his shoulders slightly. "The decision will have to be yours, of course, Comrade Chairman. But if you say so, we can prevent them from landing at Turfan."

The Chairman hesitated, his agitation growing. Before he could speak, an aide hurried into the room and placed a sheaf of papers before him. He read through them quickly, his lips tightening to a thin line. When he had finished, he shoved the papers across the table with his fingertips.

"From our embassy in Washington. They are reporting a great amount of unusual military activity. The Comrade Ambassador says it appears that the Americans are alerting their strategic forces."

The Marshal's perpetual frown deepened. He read the report and said, "There is a great deal of Russian activity along the frontier, as well. And we have reports from Shanghai Center that there are Russian submarines and aircraft carriers operating in the China Sea." He looked through the papers in his own briefcase and extracted a sheet marked with the chop of Naval Intelligence. "The missile ship *Kronshtadt* has turned on the submarine we have had following her in the Denmark Strait. There are two of the new Soviet carriers near Hainan Island and perhaps as many as three missile-firing submarines." He looked steadily at the Chairman and added, "We have no idea of where the American Tridents might be. They are too deep and too fast for us to track them. But an American carrier is operating in the Sea of Okhotsk, off Sakhalin Island. That could threaten us, as well as the Russians. It is simply impossible to read their intentions."

"Which brings us directly back to the aircraft heading for Turfan," the Chairman said. "How long before we will have it on radar?"

"Thirty minutes, perhaps less. The new installations in the Tien Shan Mountains can look into Russia almost as far as the Sea of Aral'sk." He hesitated before asking, "Am I to assume, Comrade Chairman, that you think the so-called American Presidential airplane might be a nuclear bomber?"

The Chairman's face was bleak. "It is a possibility, isn't it?"

"Yes. A possibility."

"How many times have the revisionists and the capitalists talked about 'nuclear castration'?"

"It couldn't be done now, Comrade Chairman. We have operational missiles."

"And we have the Dragon now. Mightn't that frighten them enough to risk such a move?"

"It is possible, Comrade Chairman."

The aide who had brought the report from Washington appeared again. He laid a single sheet of flimsy paper before the Minister of Defense.

K'ang's suspicion increased suddenly and he looked steadily at the Chairman, wondering just how deeply the younger man's courage really ran.

"The aircraft is over the northern Caspian, Comrade Chairman. Our listening posts have been monitoring the Soviet Air Force frequencies. Our untimely visitor has a fighter escort."

Chung Yee hesitated for only a moment. First they send spies, he thought bitterly, and now this. Perhaps the Dragon test had been too provocative, after all. But it was too late to regret it. "Alert our air defenses, Comrade Marshal," he said. "And then open the link the Americans want. Let us see if we can find a grain of truth in this bushel of lies and deceptions."

"Yuri Ivanovich." Krasin addressed the image on the television screen carefully. "The Americans have been delayed. I ask that you give us more time."

"Explain the delay, Viktor Stepanovich," Leonov said calmly.

The men sitting behind the new First Secretary in the Moscow command center murmured anxiously.

"The weather is very bad in Moscow. And there is some malfunction on board the aircraft," Krasin said.

"You are lying, Comrade," Leonov said in that same calm

voice. "The American airplane is now east of the Caspian Sea on course for Sinkiang. You have not shut off my sources of information, Viktor Stepanovich. I warn you to stop trying."

Krasin said desperately, "I have ordered them to return to Moscow, Yuri Ivanovich. But they have refused. I beg you to give us more time."

"Do they understand the position?"

"We have admitted nothing. But yes, I think they know what is happening. The President accused me of implementing Case Yellow."

The ghost of a smile touched the young Marshal's face. "Some one of them has been researching my career. I imagined that might happen."

"Time, Comrade. You must give us more time."

"It is a game we are playing now, Viktor Stepanovich," Leonov said. "Not chess, but the American game of poker. One seldom knows how far to carry a bluff, however. What is your opinion of Lambert? How are his nerves?"

"I don't know. But mine are nearly worn through, Yuri Ivanovich. Your plan will fail if you kill the Americans. The results would be catastrophic. We are all agreed on that here." Krasin's flesh seemed to have shrunk tight on the bones of his face. He looked like a living skull.

"You had better turn them back, then," Leonov said.

"We are trying," Krasin said thinly. "The fighters are attempting to turn them before they reach the border. But what if we fail?"

"Do not fail," Leonov said. He spoke briefly to someone offscreen and then turned back. "Have you done all that must be done to support my strike?"

General Sheremetiev stepped forward to join Krasin. "We have done all that is possible in so short a time, Comrade Marshal. But our deployments are not yet correct. The shift from American to Chinese targets needs more time."

Marshal Lyudin joined in, his large face ruddy and damp. "I

have corroborated your orders for Task Red Glory, and the land forces in the east are ready. But the western frontiers are being weakened. There is a great deal of confusion among the senior commanders. We need at least a day to sort it all out, Comrade Marshal."

"Don't play the fool with me, Lyudin," Leonov said. "There was nothing in the operational plans for Red Glory that would weaken the west. NATO will do nothing at all." He shifted his attention back to Krasin. "The countdown is continuing, Viktor Stepanovich. I advise you to get the Americans to safety."

"What if I cannot?" Krasin asked.

"Successful wars and political movements are not built of 'ifs,' " Leonov said coldly. "I have not come this far and taken such risks to retreat now. For years I warned all of you that the Maoist menace would have to be dealt with. Understand me clearly. It *will be* dealt with. It is now up to you to do your duty and convince our Americans that they must co-operate. It was unfortunate that they became suspicious, but they are *in* the Soviet Union and the strike will take place as scheduled. If they are killed or injured by any Chinese response, their death will serve the plan well enough. It increases the risk of American involvement, but that is a risk I am willing to take. So turn them or not, as you choose, Viktor Stepanovich. The operation goes on."

Krasin, his nerves frayed to near breaking, looked across the room at Novikov.

The KGB man nodded reluctantly and mouthed silently: "Tell him."

"Yuri Ivanovich," Krasin said, "the Americans were recorded by the Pentagon when I spoke with Lambert. They have the evidence of the tapes that you have acted independently. They can let the world know what is taking place here if they choose. And I was warned that if any harm came to them because of your actions, they would consider it an act of war by us against the United States."

"You are lying to me again, Viktor Stepanovich," Leonov said.

"I swear that is the truth. We have our own recordings of the exchange. We will play them for you," Krasin said pleadingly.

"Then they were bluffing you, Viktor Stepanovich. You are a fool to believe them."

"Listen to me," Krasin shouted. *"They were not bluffing. They will kill us if Lambert is harmed!"*

Leonov's voice had a steel edge. *"Then see to it that he does not cross the border into China. The attack will take place as planned."* He checked the time at the Aral'sk command center. *"I give you one hour. That is all,"* he said.

Leonov's image contracted to a point of light and vanished.

In the main cabin of Air Force One, Harry Grant stopped beside Jane McNary's seat. The woman's thin face was gray and strained as she met his eyes. Beside her lay a sheaf of notes, and Grant was struck by the notion that if Jane were ever on her way straight to the ninth circle of Hell, she would take the time to record the event for her column. He felt a flicker of admiration for her courage. It helped to soften the bitterness he felt toward her.

"How is he?" she asked. Grant understood that she meant the President.

"Hanging tough," Harry said. "You know him."

Paul Lyman and the two men from the Foreign Office hurried by on the way to the forward compartment, where Ian Ballard was being guarded by two of the Secret Service men.

McNary said, "This is a nightmare, Harry."

He managed a thin and mirthless smile. "When you write about it, you can tell the people what happens to covert missions."

"I still say this whole trip was a mistake," she said firmly.

"More so now than ever, I suppose?"

"I can hardly believe what's happening." She studied his face carefully. "Are they bluffing us? The Russians, I mean?"

"I don't think Leonov is bluffing, Jane."

"God."

"He might be a little bit crazy, but he's not the sort of man who would go this far and then back down." He took the Boyar print-outs from his pocket and handed them to her. "I thought you might want to look at these for background."

She took the computer sheets and held them in nerveless hands. "If you're right, I won't need any 'background,' will I?"

Grant stared at the lightening sky outside. The plane was flying through an increasingly broken cloud cover. When the weather system was behind them, they could expect some action from the MIG escort. The fighters would do their best to turn them back, but how far they would go and what chances they would take, Grant could only guess.

"I have to believe the Kremlin will stop it, Jane," he said.

"How?" she asked, unbelieving.

"There is really only one way, if Leonov won't back down."

Her eyes widened. "You mean bomb their own base?"

He nodded slowly.

"I thought missile bases were all—what do you call them?— *hardened* now. Christ, those euphemisms you damned people use."

By "you people" Grant knew that she meant "you soldiers." You monsters, you hired killers. Well, God knew she had a right to feel that way now.

"They are," he said.

"Then what hope is there?"

"One."

"You mean bomb the base with a nuclear weapon?"

"Yes," Grant said. "That would be the only way."

"You're as mad as they are."

He shrugged and started to move on toward the flight deck.

She stopped him. "Harry. Don't go yet." Her hand closed on his. Her touch was icy.

He said, "I'm sorry you pushed your way into this, McNary. I really am."

"For old times' sake."

"Yes. For old times."

"Christ, that was only a few days ago, Grant."

"A long time, as it's turned out," he said.

"That English bitch, right?"

"Cut it out, Jane. We don't need that kind of problem right now."

"Oh, shit, Harry, I'm terrified. Do you know that? I don't want to die."

Grant touched her coppery hair with the back of his free hand. "We won't die."

"I don't believe you," she said, "but keep telling me that."

"Leonov may be insane, but the rest of them aren't. We won't die, Jane."

"Is he insane?" she asked. "Because if he is, I think it's all going to happen."

"I shouldn't have said 'insane,'" Harry said carefully. "But he's a man who made a plan and worked on it a long time. He's what some people still like to call a 'charismatic leader.' You know about people like that. They are *committed*. They don't let themselves think about failing, about being balked. Pretty soon the consequences of the plan going wrong just don't exist for them. It's a kind of insanity, I suppose, but it isn't treatable. It just has to be stopped."

"My God, Harry, with atom bombs?"

"With whatever it takes." He inclined his head toward the President's compartment. "He understands that. That's why we are on the way to China."

"I don't understand why we didn't have some warning," she said bitterly.

Grant's eyes turned stony. "Ask your friend Sutton. Ask all the Suttons."

She looked at him expressionlessly. "And the McNarys. Is that what you're saying?"

"Yes."

She dropped his hand and put her clenched fists in her lap. "We'll never really understand one another, will we?"

He shook his head. That much was true. Despite her ceaseless attacks on America, he supposed that she loved her image of America as much as he did his. But he would never understand her way and she would never understand his. Yet they stood a fine chance of dying together, soldier and radical, their atoms intermingled in a nuclear cloud. There was a lesson of sorts there, he thought, if people were ever to understand the world they inhabited in these dark last years of the twentieth century.

Somehow, he felt, he owed it to her and to their situation to make one last effort to open some semblance of communication between them. They had been lovers, of a sort, not so long ago, and now they faced extinction together. "If I've been critical of you, Jane," he said, "it is because I can't accept your view that we—our country—is always automatically guilty if it can't be proved innocent. You wouldn't deal with an ordinary citizen that way. Why do you apply such standards to the United States?"

"Harry, you never could see and you never will see. For over two hundred years we've been posing as 'the best hope of mankind,' and what I wanted was for us to live up to what we claimed for ourselves."

"Perfection, Jane?" Grant asked gently. "Won't anything else do?"

"Every time we accept less we cheapen ourselves."

"You are unforgiving, Jane. You ask too much."

She shook her head and looked away. Intolerant, Grant thought, even here and now.

When she turned back to meet his eyes, what he saw there

was pure hatred. "It's people like you, Colonel, who have brought us to *this*."

"That's strange," Grant said. "I thought it was the idealists."

He left her there in the main cabin, her fists still knotted in her lap, her face lit by the cold dawn that was filtering through the plexiglass windows.

President Lambert, hunching forward toward the television screen, said, "The circumstances surrounding our change of flight plan are extremely sensitive, Chairman Chung. I ask that you accept my word for this and clear our aircraft to land at Turfan."

Chairman Chung Yee, an interpreter at his elbow, listened, then said, "I wish you to ask him why he has chosen Turfan."

The interpreter, a moon-faced woman dressed in a drab uniform, spoke in unaccented American English.

"It is the nearest Chinese base, and our fuel supply is limited," Lambert said, his expression masked. "There are other reasons that I will discuss with the Chairman privately."

"Do you ask that I come to Turfan to meet you?"

When the question was translated, Lambert hesitated. This was a risky point. When the true situation became known, if it ever did, he might be accused of attempting to lure the Head of State of the People's Republic of China into danger.

"I have to leave that to you, Chairman Chung," the President said. "It is imperative that we talk privately, but I suggest that you do not leave Peking until I have landed at Turfan."

"Turfan is a sensitive military area," Chung said.

Lambert read the man's suspicion in his expression, in his posture. "I realize that, Chairman Chung. But there are no military personnel with me except my aide and the crew of the aircraft."

"I would prefer that you fly directly to Peking. We will provide an escort."

Lambert controlled his impatience. "That is not possible, Chairman Chung. It must be Turfan."

The Chairman's black eyes stared hard at him across the miles. "That seems odd to me, Mr. President."

"It will be explained. You know my mission. My itinerary has been changed but my purpose remains the same. Peace."

There was a long and pregnant pause. The Chairman said, "We will consider."

"I must insist, sir. I cannot tell you how important I consider your permission."

Again a long pause. Lambert could almost see the suspicion surrounding the younger man. It was palpable, a heaviness in the atmosphere.

At last Chung Yee said, "Very well. You have permission to land at Turfan. But your Russian escort must turn back at the border. Our aircraft will escort you from there."

"I will do my best, Chairman," Lambert said.

"We will await your next transmission, Mr. President."

The screen went dark, and the President said to Lyman, "He's not sure I'm even *on* this plane, Paul."

"But we can land, sir."

Lambert's face showed the strain. "Now it is up to the Russians," he said.

In the command center at Aral'sk, Marshal Leonov regarded Viktor Krasin's image coldly. "You have not turned the Americans back. They are nearing Alma-Ata," he said.

Krasin said hoarsely, "They have received permission from Peking to land at Turfan. You must stop the countdown *now*."

"You have forty minutes to turn them back," Leonov said.

He became aware that General Oblensky, seated near him at the command console, was staring at him intently. He half turned to look at him. The man's face was gray. "What is the matter with you, Comrade General?"

Oblensky, who had been a witness to the televised conversations between Leonov and the men in the Kremlin, said, "What do we do if the Americans refuse to turn back, Comrade Marshal?"

"They will not refuse."

"But if they *do?*"

From the television monitor came Krasin's agonized voice. "They *have* refused, Yuri Ivanovich. Your plan has misfired. I beg of you to stop the countdown."

"Have Sheremetiev and Lyudin made their dispositions?"

"Listen to me, Yuri Ivanovich. *Listen to me!*"

"And Viktorov? Has he alerted the fleet?"

From the television monitor came a shout of mingled fear and frustration. *"Oblensky! Oblensky! Stop him!"*

Leonov reached for the power switch and shut off the monitor. He turned back to Oblensky. "Sergei—"

He found himself looking into the muzzle of an automatic pistol.

A stunned silence spread through the command center.

The muzzle of the pistol trembled.

Leonov's voice was clear and steady. "Put away the pistol, Sergei Vissarionovich," he said.

Oblensky said in a thin-edged voice, "Comrade Krasin is right, Comrade Marshal. The plan has miscarried. We can't go through with it."

"Put the pistol down," Leonov said again.

"I have been loyal, Comrade Marshal," Oblensky said unsteadily. "I have followed you faithfully. But if the Americans are killed, the imperialist forces will attack us. The risk is too great, Comrade Marshal."

Leonov looked around the command center. Every man and woman in the room had been picked by him, trained by him for this moment. Even Oblensky. Yet no one moved.

Colonel Louisa Feodorovna stood and walked slowly between the consoles and the instrument banks.

Oblensky said, "Tell him, Louisa. Make him understand that it is not possible now—"

The Colonel's face was sad, composed. She looked at Leonov and said, "The Comrade General is right, sir. The plan cannot be implemented now. We can all see that—"

She moved around the command console, speaking in her soft, rich voice. "We must make the best of the situation," she was saying. "We must now do whatever is necessary and best for the Soviet Motherland—"

There was sudden flat crash of sound. Oblensky leaped forward, as though he had been struck from behind by a giant fist. His eyes bulged, and his mouth opened to spill a torrent of brilliant blood. He pitched forward over the metal console. Leonov could see the spreading stain of red on the back of his uniform. Feodorovna's slender hand still held the heavy service revolver with which she had killed her immediate commander. She swayed slightly, her face white, but she did not give way.

Leonov stood and called to one of the nonplused security soldiers standing near the blast doors. "Sergeant. Come remove this offal."

He took the revolver from Feodorovna's hand and sat her down. In his heart were a savage joy and pride. It had all worked. For every faulty bit of human material that had come untempered, like Oblensky, there were a hundred others, steel-hardened and loyal, like Louisa Feodorovna.

He gripped her shoulder with an intensity that matched his fervor. "Thank you, Comrade General Feodorovna. You are commander here now." He lifted her chin and looked speculatively into her shocked eyes. "Are you all right?"

"Yes," she said faintly.

"Good." His eyes found the clock. "In twenty-nine minutes the launch sequence begins."

In the largest of the glass-walled rooms overlooking the National Command Center in Washington, a group of grim-faced men watched the computer predictions printing across the display screens.

General Steyning, a gold telephone in his hand, reported to General Devore. "NORAD needs twenty minutes more to come to full readiness. General Buckner says we'll have to use some Air Guard units to cover the Southwest." The bitterness in his voice was not lost on Harold Hood, who had presided over the Senate sessions that had cut by thirty percent the appropriations on which NORAD depended.

Devore asked, "What is the time to impact for an Aral'sk missile targeted on Turfan–Lop Nor?"

Admiral Muller said promptly, "Thirteen minutes."

"How the hell did you manage to have *that* at your fingertips, Jay?" General Lazenby exclaimed.

"I got a computer run on possible targets when we learned Aral'sk was retargeting," the Admiral answered.

"Chalk up one for the Navy," General Dahlberg murmured.

Devore looked across his monitors to the Vice President, uncomfortable in a steel-and-plastic chair near the guarded doors. "We have a serious problem, Mr. Vice President," he said. "We have come to Red One status, but anything more requires specific permission from the Congress."

Hood's large forehead gleamed wetly in the harsh overhead lights. He was sweating profusely in spite of the air conditioning. "Surely our activities will act as a deterrent on the Russians, General. Is it necessary to carry them any further?"

"I believe you heard the President tell Krasin that any attack launched by Marshal Leonov would be considered an act of war against the United States, sir."

"Surely the threat alone will be enough?"

"I don't feel free to make that supposition, Mr. Vice President," the chairman of the Joint Chiefs said.

"You can't actually believe that General Leonov"—in his agitation the Vice President got both Leonov's rank and the pronunciation of his name wrong—"actually intends to attack China?"

"I not only believe it, sir, I also believe it is going to happen momentarily," Devore said grimly.

A bell pinged, and Devore spun around to speak into a television line. "Devore."

A young Air Force officer appeared on his monitor. "SAC is airborne at 0546 Zulu," he said.

Steyning, the former fighter pilot, frowned. SAC now consisted of four B-2 bombers—all that Congress would authorize—and a fleet of thirty-five-year-old B-52s. Fewer than one hundred planes in all.

Devore punched a key, and another face appeared on the row of screens. It was an aged man in the uniform of an RAF Air Vice Marshal. "SAC is airborne, Thomas," Devore said.

"The Vulcan Force is scrambling now," the Englishman said. He spoke from an underground command center in southern England. "How serious is this, Clint?"

"The Soviets have gone a little bit crazy, I think," Devore answered. "Krasin says Leonov is going to use the Aral'sk Regiment to attack Turfan–Lop Nor. Our people are caught in the middle of it. I don't know how bad it will get."

Air Vice Marshal Sir Thomas Jerremy, one of the last Battle of Britain survivors remaining in the tiny RAF, touched his mustache in a characteristic gesture. "I see. The Defense Ministry people are in a bad flap here. No one seems quite sure what's happening."

"We will keep you informed. There's always a chance it won't involve you people," Devore said.

"That's very comforting, but I think I'll keep the V bombers up just the same. May one ask what the naval situation is? There is some interest at the Admiralty."

Muller moved into camera range and said, "The Admiralty is being Telexed a complete situation report, Thomas. But for your own information, there is a Chinese nuke playing tag with the *Kronshtadt* in the Denmark Strait. I suggest Coastal Command keep an eye on them. It looks like a little private side match, but one can't be certain."

"And where is the President now?"

"Nathan Hale puts him southwest of Alma-Ata."

"What are the Soviets doing about Leonov?"

"That's the question, Thomas. We just don't know."

A telephone pinged on the Navy console, and Muller picked it up and listened. He replaced the instrument and said to Devore, "The *Vishinsky* is withdrawing from the South China Sea, Clint. Apparently on orders from the Moscow command center. But the *Ho Chi Minh* has launched a combat air patrol and looks to be readying long-range aircraft."

Hood asked, "What does that mean, actually, Admiral?"

"It could mean that the captain of the ship has decided to support any action Leonov takes."

Muller's expression was noncommittal. It was not the way of high-ranking American officers to show their feelings to civilian members of the government, even those whose policies, in their view, weakened the armed forces. "Since our bases in the Philippines were closed, Mr. Vice President, our nearest carriers are based at Pearl Harbor and Midway."

Devore said, "Which brings us back to my earlier request for guidance, Mr. Vice President. We have done very nearly all that we can do under the Red One alert directives. We can't do more without congressional permission. You are, in effect, acting commander in chief, sir. What now?"

Hood blustered. He was a foolish man but not a fool. Not the least of his abilities was the capacity to recognize his own limitations. "You are the military commanders, gentlemen. What do you recommend?"

"I think we should go to full alert and to hell with Congress," Lazenby said harshly.

"That would be illegal, General," Devore said bleakly.

Dahlberg asked, "Could we reach enough key members of the House and Senate to authorize a full alert?"

"In two or three weeks," Lazenby said sarcastically.

Muller could not withhold one slightly barbed comment. "Senator Sutton is still down in the Pit. Perhaps we should ask his opinion."

Devore asserted his rank and overrode them. He looked directly at the Vice President. "Well, Mr. Vice President?"

Hood had no answer. The spate of laws controlling authority over the military had followed the conventional lesson of Vietnam and forgotten the atomic lesson of Hiroshima. Those laws were finally bearing their bitter fruit. Still immensely powerful, the United States was helpless to respond to the threat from Aral'sk.

"Then we wait," General Devore said. "That is all we can do."

52

At 0747 hours, Moscow time, General Sheremetiev received the computer predictions on the potential results of an American response to Leonov's attack. What he read in the print-outs destroyed his composure entirely.

The computer at command center predicted that an American counterforce attack had reached a probability of eighty-seven percent if Lambert's aircraft was destroyed by Russian action. The expected casualties in European Russia were estimated at between fifty and ninety megadeaths. Because of the placement of most of the Soviet strategic forces, few of the major Russian cities would suffer total devastation. But the destruction of property attendant on a counterforce strike would reach a value of sixteen billion rubles.

The second deck of the prediction concerned itself with the smaller amount of damage that would probably be inflicted by the Chinese nuclear IRBM force. These weapons, the computer predicted coldly, lacked the power needed for use as counterforce against hardened installations and would therefore most probably be used against major Russian population centers. The casualties expected from this sort of action exceeded the estimate of American-inflicted losses by one million. Taken together, the damage that must result from a combined American-Chinese attack would destroy the Soviet Union.

Sheremetiev, like Leonov, was an airman. And like many airmen, he tended to place a far greater value on automated decisions than on the sentimental, and therefore fallible, choices made by individuals. He had been the first of the Kremlin mili-

---

tary experts to accept the possibilities of the Defense Minister's action. Had the plan run as smoothly as Leonov believed it would, Sheremetiev would have been willing to support it with the full force of the strategic forces under his command. A truly pre-emptive strike against China, either with American approval or, at least, with American power immobilized, would have resulted in an acceptable casualty rate inside the USSR. Soon after Leonov's announcement, Sheremetiev had ordered a computer run using Leonov's parameters. Casualties of no more than fifty or sixty thousand had been predicted. To Sheremetiev, as to Leonov, this was an acceptable figure.

But Leonov's parameters had broken down. Someone on board President Lambert's aircraft had unraveled Case Yellow, and now the rules were very different.

Sheremetiev looked at the wall clocks. Earlier, before breaking contact again, Leonov had given them one hour to complete the preparations to support his action. That meant an actual launch time from Aral'sk of approximately 0815, Moscow time, less than one half hour from now.

Sheremetiev decided he could wait no longer. He turned to Marshal Lyudin and said, "I am sending in a bomber."

The old Marshal bridled, his heavy face red and angry. "There are twenty thousand people in Aral'sk, and another five on the collective farms on the Priara Plain."

Sheremetiev said, "There are two hundred and fifty million people in the Soviet Union."

Lyudin shook his head emphatically. *"You cannot do it."*

The two men, locked at angry cross-purposes, turned to Krasin.

Sheremetiev, holding in his hand the telephone that connected him with the air base at Tbilisi, said: "Comrade First Secretary—decide."

Across the room, a computer display changed. Admiral Viktorov said: "The Americans have SAC on full airborne alert and on course for their fail-safe points."

Sheremetiev, his clear blue eyes steady, said: "Comrade First Secretary, the flight time between Tbilisi and Aral'sk is twenty-five minutes for a supersonic aircraft. You must decide."

"No," Lyudin shouted. *"Do not do this."*

The younger officer, bred in a different time to different standards, looked at the wall clock. It stood now at 0750 hours. As he watched, the second hand completed another circuit and the clock moved to 0751 hours. "Comrade Krasin," he said, "the responsibility is yours. You must decide. Now."

At the radar station at Tekesi, seventy kilometers from the Soviet border, a Chinese technician of the People's Liberation Army watched the blips on his screen. He worked the measurement scales and noted speed, altitude, and direction. Then he picked up a telephone and spoke into the mouthpiece: "Target: one large aircraft with escort of fifteen. Course is one hundred ten degrees, altitude is nine thousand meters, descending. Apparent speed is sixteen hundred kilometers per hour."

For the last fifteen minutes the radar technicians on the high ridge of the Tien Shan range had been watching as the targets moved across their area to the south and east.

An officer stepped out of the darkened radar room into the glassed-in hut where weather observations were made. The light shining on the snowy slopes all around him made him squint. Clouds still covered much of the sky, but they were thin and high, so that the mountaintops seemed bathed in a silvery, shadowless light.

He glanced at a clock and noted the time in his logbook. It was 1155 hours. He picked up the landline telephone connecting him to the interceptor base at Shaquan, in the valley to the north across the mountain spur. "This is Tekesi," he said. "Your targets will cross the border in twenty-one minutes if they hold course and speed. We have a good return. We can control the intercept from here."

On the airfield, the radarman knew, the alert bells would be sounding now and the pilots would be running for their aircraft. Red Dawns, fighters developed from the old MIG designs that had been sent into China by the revisionists in the days before Chairman Mao uncovered the Kremlinites' treachery.

The officer said, "There are fifteen escorts. They are not to be permitted to cross our frontier."

He replaced the telephone, looked once more at the brilliant metallic sky, and returned to the dark cave of the radar room.

In the forward compartment of Air Force One, Harry Grant regarded Ian Ballard steadily and said, "What I don't understand is what you could have hoped to gain by it."

Ballard spoke calmly, almost with resignation. "You, of all people, should have the answer to that. You were a prisoner in Hanoi. You know what they are really like." He drew a deep breath and looked out the window at the gleaming metal of the wing, which sent spears of new light into the compartment. The sun was reflecting from a thin overcast of ice crystals high in the air over the mountains that showed white thirty thousand feet below.

"After all, Grant," Ballard said, "what exactly did I do that was so terrible? I knew, but I kept still, that's all. If sin there is, it's one of omission only."

"You let us all get involved, for one thing," Grant said. "I could kill you for that." He was thinking of Bronwen, and Ballard knew it.

"There is always a price," Ballard said.

"A price. Just like that. As though you were ordering a new suit or a pair of shoes." Grant's voice was edged with cold anger. "Don't you really know what you're talking about? Don't you have any realistic idea of what a nuclear war—*any* nuclear war—will mean? The 'price' you're so willing to pay is the death of millions of human beings. My God."

"Yes," Ballard said, but without any real regret. "Human life is cheap, Grant. It always has been. There are things that are more important. Look at your country. Look at mine. You can see the rot. You can smell it. There's only one way, and that's to let the Communists burn themselves out, like a cancer." He drew a deep breath and looked again at the brightness outside. "If I helped them murder each other, I'm well repaid for whatever I went through—for whatever I will go through."

Grant said, "I can see why you set Voronin up. But why did you have to use Bronwen Wells?"

"I didn't want to, but the opposition—the official opposition, that is—thought they were onto something with her. All that about the yellow case was too bloody near the mark to let it go. You worked it out, finally, but so might they have done if they'd got onto her. You mustn't worry now. She's out of it. Quite safe, I'm sure."

Grant turned to go. He rapped on the door for the Secret Service man to return.

Ballard, momentarily flippant, asked, "What will they do to me, old man? Have my countrymen dropped any hints?"

"I hope they shoot you, old man," Grant said.

"I suppose the question should be regarded as hypothetical," Ballard said. "We haven't turned back, have we?"

"No."

"Then we're all as good as dead right now." Ballard returned to his scrutiny of the world outside and far below.

Grant squeezed past the Secret Service men and along the passage into the flight deck. The navigator, Captain Stevenson, looked up and said, "We are eighteen minutes from the Chinese border, Colonel. Is that the time of decision?"

"I think so," Grant answered.

"Jesus, Colonel," Stevenson said, "I don't mind telling you I'm scared shitless."

"So am I, Captain. So is everyone on board."

The Air Force officer gnawed briefly on his lower lip as he turned his attention back to his chart. Grant moved forward into the pilot's section of the flight deck. Barrow had taken over the controls again. The second and third pilots and the flight engineer sat at their stations, faces pale, eyes hidden behind their dark flying glasses. They were strangers to Grant, and he had the momentary thought that it was a seeming anomaly that one should come to die in the company of strangers. Yet, when considered carefully, it became obvious that dying with strangers was the hallmark of life in these times. There was never a choice, when it came to that, and the nuclear footprint that Defense Minister Leonov planned to lay across the face of western China would volatilize thousands, perhaps hundreds of thousands, of strangers. How does it happen, Grant wondered, that we came upon this willingness to slaughter each other like vermin. But that was nothing new, nothing even remarkable. A few hundred miles from the mountains over which Air Force One was flying, Tamerlane, in his time, had built a mound of two million skulls. And all he had to work with was the sword, the spear, and the impaler's stake.

"Major Barrow," the second pilot, a young captain named Burgess, said agitatedly, "one of the fighters is moving in close."

Barrow turned and said to Grant, "The bastards have been flying across our track for ten minutes now, signaling for us to turn back."

Grant tapped Burgess on the shoulder and moved into the right-hand seat. The Russian fighter, a camouflaged MIG-37 swing-wing fighter, hung, seemingly motionless, a dozen meters from Air Force One's right wing tip. Grant could see the pilot's helmeted head, the gleam of light on his face shield.

Grant punched in the air-to-air frequency on the UHF radio and picked up the microphone. "This is Air Force One," he said. "Bear away. You are too close."

Over the speaker in the overhead came a stream of Russian that Grant could understand only imperfectly. The fighter came closer. Grant signaled with his hand for the smaller aircraft to move away. The Russian rocked the airplane from side to side to indicated that he understood the message, but he didn't move out. He hung there, dark against the silvery sky.

Barrows said, "Try Moscow ATC."

Grant tuned in the Air Traffic Control frequency. There was nothing on the air but a soft, hissing static. Moscow ATC had gone off the air. A dryness thickened in Grant's throat. The suspension of normal air-to-ground radio communications was part of any attack alert procedure.

"Nothing?" Barrow asked. Grant shook his head. He turned back to Stevenson. "Captain, are we still plugged into the Nathan Hale net?"

"Yes, Colonel."

"Olympus Base, this is Olympus. Do you copy?"

"We copy five by five Olympus. What is your situation?"

Stevenson leaned forward and handed Grant a slip of paper. He read it and said, "We are forty-two fifty-one north, seventy-nine fifty-nine east. Does Nathan Hale have us in sight?"

"Wait one, Olympus," the reply came. Then, "Yes, Nathan Hale is recording."

Whatever happened, Grant thought, there would be photographic evidence. He hoped that the Russians were monitoring the exchange. It was vital that they believe that the United States, the evidence incontrovertible, would react. Grant knew, though, as the President and the others did, that it would take their actual deaths to stir the hamstrung giant to action.

He referred once again to Stevenson's figures and said, "Olympus estimating the Chinese border in fourteen minutes."

"Roger, Olympus. We copy fourteen minutes."

Grant, not secured in the seat, was suddenly pitched toward one side as Barrow cranked the wheel over hard and shoved the nose down. The Russian fighter had folded his wings and spurted ahead, cutting sharply across Air Force One's flight path.

Barrow breathed, *"That crazy son of a bitch!"*

A second fighter raced in from the right and cut across their line of vision. Again Barrow took evasive action.

Grant removed himself from the copilot's chair and let young Burgess resume his seat. "They're getting desperate to turn us. Head for the deck, Barrow. They won't be so eager to take chances down low. I'm going back to talk to the President."

Barrow nodded and let the nose of the big Boeing drop. The airspeed began to build up immediately, and Grant caught a glimpse of the Russians circling wide for another pass across their track.

As he went through the main cabin, Sawkins stopped him. "What's happening, Colonel? Why are we crashing about so?"

"The Russian fighters are trying to make us turn back, Mr. Sawkins," Grant said. "I think you had better sit down and strap in tight."

Sawkins said, his narrow face flushing slightly, "How bloody unseemly of them."

Grant could not suppress a smile at the understated Britishism.

His smile vanished as the plane rocked and plunged again, forcing Sawkins to hold onto him for support. Grant looked across the cabin at McNary. She was strapped in tight, her eyes closed, lower lip caught between her teeth. Her hands on the arms of her seat looked like claws, all sinew and nail.

He regained his balance and reeled aft toward the President's compartment. Inside, Lambert and a Secret Service man were tightening Helena Lambert's seat belt. The First Lady's face was drained by terror, but she was insisting that Lambert and the Secret Service man look to their own safety.

"What the hell is happening, Harry?" Lambert demanded, falling into a seat before the television console.

Grant explained, and Lambert's eyes seemed to light up with fury. This, at least, was something he could respond to in ordinary terms of anger and outrage. He picked up the intercom-telephone and said, "Do we still have communications with Krasin?"

The television monitor came to life instantly. Krasin was not in view. Instead, there was an old man in a marshal of the Army's uniform at the console. Grant recognized Lyudin. He was immediately struck by the dazed look on the old soldier's face. He looked shocked, drained by a terrible despair. A man having watched a child die, or a beloved, might look like that.

The President said harshly, "Marshal, I demand that you order your fighters away from this aircraft immediately!"

Grant put out a hand. "Wait, sir—" He could not fathom, even in this hour of extremity, what had brought such a look to old Marshal Pavel Lyudin's face.

Lyudin said, "What? What is that—?" His English was suddenly broken, rusty. It was as though only a part of his mind was functioning and the rest was lost in that dark and awesome reverie.

"May I, Mr. President?" Grant asked.

"Go ahead," Lambert said. "What's happened there? What now, in God's name?"

"Marshal Lyudin," Grant said.

The old man's attention focused at last.

"The fighters. Please withdraw them. We are not returning to Moscow. It is dangerous to allow them to try to turn us."

The Marshal's voice was cracked. "Yes. Yes. It does not matter."

Grant said carefully, "Can you tell us what the latest developments are?"

Lyudin's image projected a surge of bleak, raw hatred. "I cannot. This net is no longer secure."

"I think I understand, sir," Grant said. He switched off the audio circuit. "They've sent someone to take care of Aral'sk, Mr. President. I think they have done it."

Lambert frowned. "Take care of it? How?"

"The only way they could, sir," Grant said quietly. He looked at his watch. It was still set to London time. He added the hours for the time zones they had crossed: 0758 hours. He looked again at the ravaged face of the old Russian. It was almost too much to bear, that lost and ruined face. He reached out and blacked out the monitor. That kind of grief should be a private thing.

Helena Lambert, perhaps more sensitive than her husband, seemed to understand best what was happening. "How many will die, Harry?" she asked softly.

"Too many, Mrs. Lambert," Grant said.

"Will it save us?"

Grant shrugged. There was simply no way of knowing, and this was not the time for comforting lies.

53

In the command center of Aral'sk a stillness had fallen, a quiet that was broken only by the voices of the pod commanders reporting their missiles' states of readiness.

Yuri Leonov glanced at the wall clocks. It was 0810 in Moscow, ten minutes after midnight on the East Coast of the United States. He tried to imagine the scene in the Pentagon command center at this moment. He was aware that the United States had by now probably reached the highest stage of readiness permitted by American law. Now they were balked, helpless.

The Chinese, however, were another matter. The Code Section had been working on the electronic keys to the Nathan Hale transmissions the Americans had been using to communicate with Moscow and Peking, but the messages still remained garbled. Each time the tapes were played and the keys recomputed, the messages became slightly clearer, but they were not yet intelligible.

His timid colleagues in the Kremlin had now managed to impair some of his communications. More and more circuitous routings were becoming necessary each time the Aral'sk technicians attempted to use the low-frequency net. Leonov had managed to send an order to the *Kronshtadt* in the Denmark Strait, an order concerning the Chinese nuclear submarine that had been dogging the missile ship and her escort.

The commanders of the Far Eastern Army were not responding to his messages, and he was forced to the conclusion that old Lyudin had contrived to prevent the last stages of Task Red Glory. That, he thought, was a serious mistake and would cost heavily in casualties when the inevitable Chinese response came.

Sheremetiev, though, would certainly by now have put the strategic units of the Air Force into the air and alerted the ICBM units all along the Arctic slope. Though not a bona-fide Leonovite, Sheremetiev was one of the new breed of Soviet soldiers: he believed in arithmetic.

He glanced across at Louisa Feodorovna. She was weary, but composed. As she reached across the console that had been Oblensky's, Leonov noted that she shied slightly from the drying, red-brown stains on the metal.

The voice of the launch controller came over the speakers.

"Code sequence commencing. Launch in five minutes."

Feodorovna asked, "Where are the Americans, Comrade Marshal?"

"It no longer matters," Leonov said quietly. It was true. He reviewed the events that had brought him to this place and this time. He realized that his satisfaction over the end to be achieved was less than his fulfillment in the means.

There are no ends, he thought. There are only means. He had the sensation of having experienced an epiphany. Had he always known this? he asked himself. As long ago as his tour at Frunze, had he somehow understood this truth?

He looked about him at his *means*. The room was peopled by men and women of his own creation. Their dedication and discipline were absolute, and they were his to direct. Where else in all the world were there men and women like these?

"Silo caps retracting," the launch controller announced.

Leonov sat in an aura of power. If this was being insane, he thought, then it was glorious. He looked again around the concrete room at the soldiers and technicians performing their complex tasks like well-trained machines.

He thought again, and still again: "Where are there men this disciplined?"

"Comrade Marshal." A voice from the intercom distracted him from what came near to being a silent ecstasy.

"Please activate monitor three, Comrade Marshal."

Leonov touched a switch, and the image of a radar screen appeared on his television tube. In the background he heard the Launch Control Officer say: "Ignition sequence beginning in pods one and two."

"Comrade Marshal!" The voice of the radarman was suddenly harsh with alarm. "We have a contact."

Leonov focused his attention on the image of the radar. The scan was coming from the large air-defense antenna on top of the exposed administration building aboveground. He could see the familiar fluorescent map of the region around the base: the town just outside the forty-kilometer scale, the irregular shoreline of the Aral'sk Sea beyond. The map was reborn with each sweep of the antenna.

"There is a bandit at eleven o'clock, Comrade Marshal," the radarman said over the speaker. "Range: seventy kilometers and closing."

"Ignition sequence beginning in pods three and four." The calm voice of the Launch Control Officer was in sharp contrast to the radarman's.

"Bandit range now sixty kilometers, Comrade Marshal."

Leonov watched the radar screen with growing concern. Around him, members of the launch crew, freed of their duties by the automatic sequence, drifted quietly toward the radar monitor.

Feodorovna said, her voice quiet, "Surface reports that all KGB troops have been withdrawn, Comrade Marshal."

"Ignition sequence in pods five and six. The regiment is fully committed," reported the Launch Control Officer.

On the radar screen the brilliant signal of a transponder blossomed.

Someone behind Leonov said, "It's one of our own aircraft."

Feodorovna said, "Surface reports that civilians have been evacuating Aral'sk since 0745, Comrade Marshal."

"Bandit range now fifty kilometers."

The command center crew were now gathered around Yuri

Leonov, the brilliant fluorescent green of the radar sweep giving them the look of men and women long dead. The automated missiles, counting down to launch time in ninety seconds, were forgotten. The blip on the radar screen held them fascinated.

A woman technician behind Leonov whispered, "It's a stand-off bomber."

Leonov turned on her savagely. "It is *not*. It is a surveillance aircraft."

"Range forty kilometers."

Leonov asked, "Where are the Americans now?"

Feodorovna answered, "They are crossing the frontier."

Someone said, almost plaintively, "They did not turn back," as though he could not believe the betrayal.

The blip on the radar screen changed. It split into two. The larger turned north. The smaller continued on course, accelerating fiercely.

"My God," a technician whispered.

Leonov felt a great coldness, which seemed to turn his limbs leaden. He had been thinking, only moments ago, of his disciplined followers and wondering where on earth there might be others so loyal. He realized with a great and growing despair that he was watching them: the crew of the Soviet Air Force bomber that had just fired their stand-off missile.

On the flight deck of Air Force One, the navigator said: "We are in Sinkiang. We have just crossed the border."

Grant, wedged between the pilots, craned to look up and out through the side window at the Russian fighters. They had followed over the border, still trying to turn Air Force One back, but the dangerous passes across the larger plane's flight path had stopped.

"Colonel Grant! More fighters at two o'clock!" Burgess was pointing off to the southwest. Grant could see the thin shapes of ten jets against the silvery overcast.

They closed with tremendous speed, veering to meet the

Russians. He saw the flash of high-rate cannon fire along the leading edge of the first Red Dawn interceptor. The Russians broke away and vanished behind Air Force One. Grant could not tell whether they were retreating back to the Soviet Union or only regrouping to take the Chinese attack.

"Get on the deck, Barrow," Grant said. "If they use heat-seeking missiles, we could catch one by mistake."

Air Force One plunged lower still between two spurs of the icy Tien Shan Mountains. The maneuver required a slight turn to the south, and now Grant could see that the Russian and Chinese fighters were locked in deadly combat above them. An aircraft vanished into a smear of oily flame and debris as he watched. He could not tell if it was a Red Dawn or a MIG. A trail of ruin spilled down into the Tien Shan Valley below.

Barrow held Air Force One down to a thousand feet above the falling terrain. The air was growing turbulent.

A fighter separated from the scramble above them and closed swiftly. Another followed it. Grant watched as they swung in a long circle and vanished behind Air Force One's high tail.

The sky went from silver to gold to orange. The high clouds turned color, reflecting a hot light that even tinged the snow under them with fire.

"My God, what was that?" Barrow said.

The sky color went swiftly from red to lavender in a riot of changing hues. It was beautiful and terrible.

Grant turned to Stevenson and asked quietly, "How far are we from Aral'sk, Captain?"

The navigator measured swiftly with his dividers stepping across the chart. "Just over six hundred fifty miles, Colonel."

The colors were fading now, slowly. Grant took a headset from a rack and held it to his ear. There was no sound on the radio but a strong hissing static.

He looked for the fighters, but they had gone. Air Force One seemed alone in the sky flying over the Tien Shan. Ahead, the terrain sloped lower, into the barren high desert of Sinkiang.

He tried to imagine what lay six hundred and more miles behind them. He could almost see it, a vision of Hell—a rising column of smoke, dust, and fire. Yes, there would still be fire, but it would be grimed with vaporized earth and metal and human flesh from the ground burst. And the column would still be boiling up into the stratosphere to spill over into the familiar, terrible, mushroom-shaped head. Across the cap the ice crystals would already be forming, sloughing away in the jet streams to spread sickness across China, down the curve of Asia into India, across to the islands of the Philippine Sea, and, carried by the trade winds, across the Pacific and around the world. It was a thing too terrible to contemplate, and yet it had prevented worse. Only that rationale allowed a hold on sanity.

He wondered where they had found the man—some disciplined, unimaginative airman. He hoped the man was unimaginative—or dead. Then he asked himself if he could have done it. It brought back his last conversation with McNary. When and if it came to such a choice, was he soldier enough to do what had to be done? McNary would ask, "Are you killer enough?" He thought the answer was yes. He hoped he would never have to know for certain.

Barrow had turned in his seat and was looking at Grant. "Was that what I think it was?"

Grant nodded.

"God," Barrow said shakily, "that took balls. To nuke their own base."

"There was never another choice," Grant said. "I'd better go talk to the President."

Chairman Chung Yee received the information that a nuclear explosion had taken place within the Soviet Union at 1415, Peking time. At 1416 he was on the telephone to the Dragon base at Turfan.

Engineer Li Chin, his face drawn and body enervated from the frantic night spent attempting to conceal the extent of the casualties caused by the testing of the great laser, listened to the Chairman's harried voice with mingled fury and despair.

"The Americans are due at Turfan no later than an hour from now, Comrade Li," the Chairman said. "You are to welcome them, do you understand? You are to show them every courtesy. Whatever they wish to see, show them." There was real fear in Chung Yee's voice, and it scraped across Li Chin's raddled nerves like a knife edge.

"Are you instructing me to show them the Dragon, Comrade Chairman?" Li Chin found this possibility intolerable, knowing as he did that to share the Dragon with the Americans was tantamount to abolishing any further development of his laser.

"That is exactly what I am telling you to do," Chung said. "As a servant of the People I do not owe you an explanation, but I will give you one, nevertheless. There has been a nuclear explosion inside the Soviet Union. Their Far Eastern Army is on full alert. Fighters have crossed our border at Tien Shan and there has been an air battle. The situation is critical." His tone became accusatory. "Shooting down the satellite was a mistake, Li. Did you know that there was a pilot in the machine?"

Li's gut griped with outrage at that. He bit back the retort that came to his lips. It was obvious that some sort of political crisis was suddenly brewing in the Forbidden City and Chung Yee was not going to accept any responsibility whatever for the disastrous test of the Dragon.

What would happen next, Li wondered. What would become of the Dragon when it was known that the unforeseen thermal bloom had decimated the operating crew? He felt his entire world tottering, and he fixed on the single object of his hatred: the Americans.

Somehow, Lambert had connived with the Russians to destroy the Dragon project. Li's racial prejudice flared, fed by fear and bitter disappointment. He remembered a thousand imagined slights and insults from his days at Cal Tech. The bigoted administrators, the meaty, insulting students. The hateful *whites*.

"Did you hear me, Comrade Li?"

When Li spoke, it was in a dead, guarded voice. "Are you dropping the Dragon project, Comrade Chairman?"

"It must be re-evaluated in view of what is taking place," Chung said. "It is too dangerous to continue now until we have consulted with the Americans."

The Americans, Li thought bitterly. They even reached into the heart of the People's Republic to torment and balk whoever rejected them.

Chung said, "There have been rumors that there were problems with the laser test. Is there any truth to them?"

"No," Li lied. His mind was teetering on the brink of a hazardous decision. He knew—yet did not wish to know—that he was too tired, too emotionally shattered, to make plans and take action. But with each hostile exchange with the Chairman his desperation grew. The whole fabric of his life seemed drawn and woven into this one project, this one absolute need to prove his genius.

"Further work on the Dragon is now forbidden," the Chairman said. "I am leaving Peking for Turfan within the hour. I will speak with you further when I arrive."

The walls seemed to close in on Li Chin. The moment the Chairman arrived and saw the casualties of the test, all would be over. There would never be a chance to continue, to develop the weapon that would give the People's Republic the immunity from threat he had dreamed of. Li Chin would be a cipher, a person of no worth, lost in the muck of some peasant collective.

The Chairman was saying, "The Russians have sunk one of our submarines in the Denmark Strait. This is almost certainly a reprisal for what was done to their Svoboda satellite. These provocations have gone far enough. It is time to stop and reconsider."

He is afraid, Li thought. That is the key to his behavior. He has lost his courage. He has lost face.

Like fragments of a puzzle falling together, the engineer's

doubts, fears, hates, and ambitions formed a sudden sharply defined pattern in his mind. The Chairman had heard rumors, whispers that had sapped his will and his faith in the Dragon project. What was needed was one final and conclusive proof that the laser *could* protect the revolution, the regime, and the nation. With that, all would be as it should be. It was so simple, Li thought.

Harold Hood's image on the monitor on Air Force One was distorted and streaked with interference from the radioactivity in the air. The Vice President, even in the imperfect transmission, looked stunned and badly shaken.

"Are you all right, Mr. President?" he asked.

Cleveland Lambert drew a deep breath and said, "All's well here, Harold. We are going on to Turfan–Lop Nor. We land there in forty minutes or so."

"The Russians are saying there was an accident at a nuclear power station at Aral'sk. Of course, Nathan Hale saw it all," Hood said. "There is no count of the casualties yet."

"It will be high, Harold," the President said.

"Will you speak with Viktor Krasin again?"

"Later," the President said. "This isn't the time."

Hood said, "General Devore wants to stay at Red One. Senator Sutton suggests—"

"You tell Sutton for me," Lambert said with jagged bitterness, "to stay the hell out of it. I am going to demand an investigation by the Senate, Harold. You tell that to Sutton, too."

"Yes, Mr. President," Hood said meekly. "In that regard I have a tape you may wish to listen to when you return to Washington."

Lambert made a weary gesture. "No more for now, Harold. I will speak to you again when we go on to Peking."

For a long while Lambert sat staring at the dark monitor. He was aware of the slight turbulence of the air through which they were flying now. Helena had retired to the private compartment to rest. The President drew a deep breath and said to Grant, "How much longer?"

"Less than half an hour, Mr. President," Grant said.

Lambert studied Grant's gaunt face. "A man doesn't know what to say at a time like this, Harry. It is too terrible to deal with. To do what they did."

"What they had to do, sir."

"We forced their hand, Harry."

"Yes. We have to live with that, sir."

"But what was the alternative?"

Grant made no effort to reply. No answer was needed. Both men knew too well what the alternative had been.

"At least old Valentin Kirov didn't live to see it," the President said.

"Can Viktor Krasin and the rest of the Politburo survive this?" Grant asked. "Can the regime survive it?"

"God knows," Lambert said.

Grant turned to look outside at the high desert over which Air Force One was flying. The snow of the mountain slopes had given way to an occasional patch of dirty white in a sea of brown, sere earth. Ridges of high rock, bleak as bones, showed through the naked earth.

"Can we land safely at Turfan?" the President asked.

"Facilities are sparse, but there's a ten-thousand-foot concrete runway, according to Nathan Hale."

The President leaned back and closed his eyes. Grant had never seen him looking so beaten, so weary. If this had been a victory, it was the sort Pyrrhus would not have envied.

He stood up and silently let himself out of the compartment.

Comrade Dr. Soong marched between two soldiers toward the low buildings housing the laser. The glaring brightness of the white sky hurt his eyes and he wondered if Li Chin was summoning him to use or to kill. The engineer, Soong was certain, was paranoid. There was no longer any doubt of it.

As the old doctor walked across the hard, frozen ground through a slope of rattling, sword-pointed reeds, he remembered the death of the Mongol spy the Russians had sent. He held no brief for spies and potential saboteurs, but the needless murder of the Mongol in a useless quest for information that the man very likely did not possess had been a clear indication of the way in which Li's mind was warping.

He reviewed his many protests about the terrible conditions under which the people at this base had had to work: the cold, the inadequate housing and medical facilities, the absolute malnutrition. All of that.

But the final proof had come with the laser test. Soong's own mind balked at accepting the callousness of Li's action. The hospital was still filled with burned, dying men and women. To a physician, his own life had little meaning if he was to be prevented from exercising his art in a time and place where it was desperately needed.

Soong, a small and frail figure in his bulky quilted clothing, marched with unsteady steps between the soldiers.

In the building housing the laser, where he had not been permitted since the satellite test, Soong could see only a maze of earthen walls surrounding the equipment. From somewhere in the next bay of buildings he could hear the familiar whine of the electric generators powered by the high-pressure steam from the nuclear plant across the marsh.

Li Chin, leaving a group of technicians working on an exposed bank of heavy copper bus bars, came to meet him. Soong noted Li's drawn face, the pulpy bags under his eyes and the wet look of the black eyes themselves. The man, he thought, was near to breaking under the self-imposed stress.

When he spoke, it was as though he were addressing an engineering student. "As you can see, Comrade Doctor, we have completed the earth barriers around the laser tube and its ancillary equipment. I have calculated the plasma flow that is likely to result from the thermal bloom and designed what amounts to a giant circuit card—" The words went on, Soong not understanding any of it and not at all certain that Li himself did.

He interrupted to say, "You have still not asked Peking for medical help, Comrade Li. The hospital is a shambles. I am told four more have died, though I have not been permitted to attend them. I beg you to send for qualified medical assistance—"

Li said, "That will come. The vital matter before us is the completion of the next test, which we are about to conduct."

Soong stared in amazement. "I cannot believe you are going to activate this—thing—again, Comrade Li."

"It is not necessary that you believe, Comrade Doctor," Li said testily. "I need you here to assist in case there are any incidental—minor—injuries to our key personnel." He indicated a revetted bank of instrument racks. "That will be your station. Please go there at once. The test is about to begin."

Soong was shocked to feel himself trembling with a barely controllable rage at the callous disregard for human life and suffering displayed by the engineer. I am old, he thought furiously, I do not belong in this new time.

From an overhead speaker came the voice of a technician somewhere outside the building. "Target acquired. Range is fifty kilometers, height is one thousand meters."

"What 'target' is he talking about?" Soong demanded.

"That need not concern you, Doctor," Li said. "Please go to your place."

"I protest this," Soong shouted. "You have no right to endanger more workers."

Li spoke to one of the soldiers. "Take him to his place until the test is complete." The soldier gripped Dr. Soong's frail arm and led him into the protected area. Li turned away and called the twenty or more technicians in the bay to attention. He gave a series of orders that Soong did not understand, and the whine of the generating equipment grew louder.

The voice from the speaker said, "All radars tracking well. Target range: forty-five kilometers; height: nine hundred eighty meters."

The whine of the generators rose to an almost hypersonic scream. It pained Soong's ears and set his teeth on edge.

He looked wildly about him. On the floor near the instrument racks lay an open toolbox. In it he could see a large insulated steel wrench. The soldier who was assigned to guard him was watching the technicians running for the cover of the earthen walls.

Li, using a hand-held speaker, was shouting instructions into the din. "Take cover! Take cover! The pulse will come in twenty seconds!"

The voice on the speaker said, "Target range: forty kilometers; height: nine hundred seventy meters."

Soong realized that the intended target was an aircraft, one that was apparently attempting to land on the runway north of the base.

"Pulse in ten seconds!" Li shouted.

Old Dr. Soong's patience and discipline snapped. His mind was filled with the horrible images of burned bodies lying everywhere in the hospital. He stooped, took the great wrench from the toolbox and ran toward Li. The soldier started, moved close behind him.

Soong shouted, raising the wrench. "Stop this! Stop this at once!" He stumbled forward, threatening the engineer as the soldier's fist tried to close on his bony shoulder and missed.

Soong fell forward, arms extended. The steel wrench in his hand struck the bus bars and there was a giant blue-white spark as more than one million volts leaped across the shorted gap.

Dr. Soong was cooked to smoking flesh in a tenth of a second. The current arced from Soong to Li Chin in a brilliant, burning flash, sending him spinning against an instrument bank, his heart exploded, his brain seared.

The current leaped to the framework of the building, seeking earth. The laser tube burst in a shower of flying, half-melted shards. The crew scattered in panic as the tar-papered roof of the bay burst into oily flame.

Despite the spectacular nature of the disaster, there were only two casualties: Li Chin and Dr. Soong. The soldier who tried to stop Soong escaped with only his padded uniform smoldering.

On the slope of the Depression a crew of peasant laborers stopped work to stare down at the burning bay. One of their number nodded wisely, saying, "See, the Dragon devours itself," as though he had always known that it would come to this.

54

Harry Grant stood on the edge of the vast, camouflaged ramp above the Turfan base, his single canvas suitcase in the jeep behind him. The wind was blowing and cold, laden with the icy breath of the Altai Mountains far to the north.

He watched the Royal Air Force crew working among the Chinese to refuel the De Havilland Nova that had been sent to collect the two Englishmen from the Foreign Office, and Ballard, and, at the President's request, Colonel Harry Grant. Some distance away, Air Force One stood parked with a Russian Tupolev next to it. The Tupolev was the newest SST, and the sight of it brought a bleak smile to Grant's lips. Even here, even now, the Soviets were afflicted with their near-fatal better-than-you syndrome. A number of smaller Chinese aircraft dotted the ramp. Over the last four days there had been a gathering, one that probably would have been impossible before Cleveland Lambert came to Turfan.

Over the ridge behind him, in the marsh at the bottom of the great Depression, the blackened ruins of the buildings housing the famous—or infamous, Grant thought—laser lay wet and tangled in the cold rain.

Lambert had insisted that the nuclear powers gather here. Without delay. It had been a stroke of his own political genius. "Do it now. Do it here, where we can all see a fraction of what it has cost—and have a vision of what it could cost the whole world," he had said.

The accommodations were bad, the climate terrible, and the atmosphere bleak. Perhaps that was what was needed. Act before what had happened was forgotten. Or twisted by propagandists to fit various philosophies—each called "truth." What better place was there than this high desert, Grant thought, which was what the whole earth might soon resemble if the powers were not curbed, did not curb themselves.

The Chinese soldier who had driven him to the airfield from the dismal barracks in which he had been housed cleared his throat. He could make nothing of sense out of this American devil who stood so thoughtfully in the rain gazing at nothing. What was there to see in this place but nothing?

Grant turned and climbed into the jeep. He pointed at the now-refueled De Havilland.

"I'm sending you back to Britain to report to Margaret and the Prime Minister," the President had said. "And I have made enquiries. There's a young lady just being released from the hospital you may want to see."

From Sawkins, who had received a report from London, they had learned of the events at Zelinskaya's. That grainy old woman, Grant thought. Thirty years a sleeper and killed by a female crazy who thought she was an Irish heroine. Christ, how little sense it all made.

And there had been that terrible thrust of anxiety and outrage on learning how near to being killed Bronwen had come. If Grant had doubted the depth of his feeling for the girl, the violence of his reaction to Sawkins's report resolved his uncertainties. While the world had fallen into disaster, he thought wryly, the Iron Colonel had fallen in love.

The soldier drove carefully across the vast ramp, as though he was afraid of distressing his strange charge. Will we ever learn about one another, Grant wondered. Will we ever even be able to sort all this out, all the death and terror of the last few days?

A strange thing was happening in Russia and all over the world. It seemed as though a kind of shocked hush had fallen, as though the world was quietly in mourning for the eleven thousand innocents who had died in Aral'sk and on the Priara Plain.

That at least made sense, he thought. More sense than the rivalries and power politics that had brought on those terrible deaths.

As he arrived beside the British airplane, a sedan rolled up from the gravel road into the Depression. Cleveland Lambert, wearing a Chinese quilted jacket and one of Barrow's Air Force flight caps, alighted. The RAF crew saluted. Grant could see Ballard watching from inside the airplane.

"Harry"—the President gripped both his shoulders—"try to tell them what it was like. Don't be easy on them."

"How are the Russians, sir?" Grant asked. He was curious to know how a man like Viktor Krasin handled the guilt of having made the choice to sacrifice so many civilian lives.

"They are hurting," the President said somberly. "I feel for them, Harry. There but for the grace of God."

Grant studied the President's deeply lined face. It seemed to him that Lambert had aged a dozen years in the last days. "Really, Mr. President? Would you have done it?"

"I'd have done it, Harry. Believe me, I would have done it."

Grant glanced at the plane and up at Ballard's pale face. The man was shocked, lost. He had been prepared for death, but not for survival on these terms. Ballard remained the enigma, his brilliance channeled to cunning, his hatred to patience. Madness. But who shared the malady, who the cause? "What about him, sir?" He's guilty of murder, at the very least, Grant thought bitterly. He had Voronin killed, and the Provos. He would have shopped Bronwen, too, if there had been a need. And, finally, he would gladly have loosed unspeakable devastation upon millions of human beings.

The President shrugged. "It's a British matter, Harry. I have an idea they'll save appearances, keep his bloody side of it quiet. What else can they do, actually?"

So we haven't grown totally moral after all, Grant thought.

"Be careful with McNary, sir," he said. "Being terrified doesn't purify a persona like Jane's."

The President nodded. "I'll take care. I always have with McNary and her friends."

"How long will she stay?"

"You didn't say good-by? She will stay until the other media people arrive, then she'll start yelling for transport home, I should imagine. Or to Peking," the President added wickedly. "She does love it so there."

"You've cut yourself a groove in the pages of history, Mr. President," Grant said, switching from the painful, pointless subject.

"Maybe, Harry, maybe for a little while. But the eye of history is nearsighted. And history is certainly fickle."

"And the eye of eternity?"

"Ah, well. Sufficient unto the day. Let eternity see to itself. It will, you know. Our job is to cope with the here and now."

It will never really end, Grant thought wearily.

The President said, "Good journey, Colonel. I'll see you in Washington."

Grant watched as President Lambert climbed back into the muddy sedan and drove away from the airfield. He lifted his almost empty suitcase and walked over to the boarding ladder of the RAF transport. His thoughts were depressing. How long, he wondered, would the shock and relief last? How long would it be before it was all to be done again? In a different way, perhaps, with different players, but with the same distrust and suspicion and at the same terrible, terrible cost.

The second pilot of the transport met him at the foot of the ladder. He was a fair-haired, apple-cheeked boy, it seemed to Grant. Too young to be piloting an aircraft across China and half of Russia, too young for the two and one half rings of a squadron leader on his battle dress. His open friendliness made Grant feel better.

"Welcome aboard, Colonel," the young man said pleasantly. "I bet you'll be glad to get back to London."

Grant was thinking of Bronwen as the aircraft took off and climbed into the overcast. Perhaps, he thought, the thing that made the world worth saving was that it was populated with people like Bronwen Wells: imperfect, terribly vulnerable, and uncertain—but capable of great courage and faith and love.

He was thinking about that when the airplane broke from the cloud deck and climbed into clear air, heading directly into the redness of the westering sun.

Appendix

_____

(Full text of transmission to Colonel Harry Grant on board Air Force One from the Soviet Intelligence Section of the CIA.)

Reference: Crisis Confrontation Lectures
Cross Index: Leonov, Yuri I., Defense Minister,
              Marshal of the Soviet Air Force
Code Name: Boyar 100001110010011100001101001

THE CRISIS CONFRONTATION SYLLABUS: The basis for a series of lectures and essay examinations in the special military geotechnics course conducted for selected officers of the Soviet Armed Forces at Frunze Military Academy by Colonel Y. I. Leonov (Air Force) during 1969, 70, 71.

Case White
You are commander of the forces of the Western Military Frontier. You discover that a major adversary in the West has secretly armed the military forces of a former enemy state with nuclear weapons. What recommendations do you make to the Politburo?

Case Blue
You are commander of the Soviet Fleet (Atlantic). You discover that a European power has mined the waters of the Denmark Strait and the Skagerrak with nuclear weapons that will

effectively blockade your surface and submarine units in the Baltic. The Soviet Air
Force has the capability of detonating these
weapons. What are your recommendations to the
Politburo?

Case Red
You are military adviser to the Politburo. You
discover that it is possible to encourage and
arm a cartel of Middle East oil-producing nations. If you can accomplish this without
interference from the West, within ten years
the Soviet Union will control the energy
sources upon which Western economies depend.
The chances of accomplishing this without
counteraction from the West are only slightly
in your favor. Recommend a course of action
and support it with economic and military
projections.

Case Black
A major socialist nation enters into negotiations with the most powerful imperialist nation. There is evidence that the imperialists
will attempt to develop the economy and military power of the socialist nation to a degree
that will threaten the USSR's position of
leadership in the socialist world. You are the
military member of the Politburo's Council of
Economic Advisers. Present your recommendations.

Case Yellow
You are supreme commander of the armed forces.
You discover that one of your nuclear-force
commanders has subverted the fail-safe precautions and is about to launch a pre-emptive
strike against an enemy with limited, but substantial, retaliatory capability. Limitations

of time reduce your choices to two: you may join the attack with sufficient power to neutralize the enemy's second strike or you may destroy your insubordinate commander with an internal strike. Recommend a course of action to the Politburo.

Case Green
You are military adviser to a major Middle Eastern power. It is the intention of this power to attack and destroy the single outpost of imperialism in this strategic area. You have previously recommended that the USSR arm the nation you are advising for political reasons. But the nation is, in your opinion, incapable of accomplishing its military objectives and faces certain defeat. Recommend a course of action to the Politburo.

Case Gray
Imperialist intervention in South Asia is successfully halted by a People's war. Progressive forces of the imperialist aggressor force a withdrawal from the region. As military member of the Politburo, recommend which nations of South Asia should be annexed to the Soviet bloc.

Case Gold
After a series of inconclusive engagements in the Middle East, the socialist and imperialist combatants are prevailed upon by a major Western nation to accept a demilitarized zone policed by foreign troops. The Soviet Union is given the opportunity to participate in the peace-keeping function. This will place Soviet and imperialist troops in direct confrontation. Does this reduce the number of options available to the USSR for progressive actions

throughout the world? If so, why? Recommend
either participation or rejection of the offer
and support your conclusions with Soviet military doctrine.

These are the eight basic scenarios that
formed the curriculum of Colonel Leonov's
military geotechnics seminars. The classes
were conducted for carefully screened officers
of field grade or equivalent in the Soviet
Army, Navy, and Air Force, and in the Committee for State Security (KGB) and Army Military
Intelligence (GRU).

It is worth noting that as early as 1969
Leonov was speculating on such matters as
American withdrawal from Southeast Asia, an
Arab oil embargo, and a policed, international
settlement of the Egypto-Israeli conflict. (No
mention is made in the syllabus of the United
Nations, supporting the conclusion that
Colonel, now Marshal, Leonov considers that
organization unreliable. It is believed that
Leonov's attitude toward the UN is based on
his known prejudice against the races of the
Third World, most specifically the People's
Republic of China.)

A high percentage of the officers who attended
the Leonov seminars at Frunze are now highly
placed within the Soviet armed forces and in-
ternal-security units. Others have been seconded to the diplomatic service as military,
naval, and air attachés.